THE HOUSE AT MIDNIGHT

Lucie Whitehouse

HarperCollins*PublishersLtd*

HALDIMAND COUNTY PUBLIC LIBRARY
JARVIS BRANCH
P.O. BOX 636, 2 MONSON STREET
JARVIS ON N0A 1J0

The House at Midnight
© 2008 by Lucie Whitehouse. All rights reserved.

Published by HarperCollins Publishers Ltd.

First Canadian edition

No part of this book may be used or reproduced in any manner whatso-ever without the prior written permission of the publisher, except in the case of brief quotations embodied in reviews.

HarperCollins books may be purchased for educational, business, or sales promotional use through our Special Markets Department.

HarperCollins Publishers Ltd
2 Bloor Street East, 20th Floor
Toronto, Ontario, Canada
M4W 1A8

www.harpercollins.ca

Library and Archives Canada Cataloguing in Publication

Whitehouse, Lucie
The house at midnight : a novel / Lucie Whitehouse.—1st Canadian ed.

ISBN 978-1-55468-163-1

1. Title.

PR6123.H58H69 2008   823'.92   C2007-907034-5

Printed and bound in the United States
HC 9 8 7 6 5 4 3 2 1

For my parents, with love

Danny / Martha

Lucas / Joanna

Greg / Rachel

Michael

Chapter One

Even now, I can remember the first time I saw the house as clearly as if there were a video of it playing in my head.

Danny, Martha and I had driven up from London together, the force of our collective will keeping my elderly 2CV from one of its increasingly frequent breakdowns. Cold night air had forced its way into the car round the loose windowpanes as I coaxed it along at speeds for which I could feel it reproaching me. I think we all had a feeling of adventure that evening, leaving the city as so many other people had been pouring into it, going against the tide.

Lucas's directions had been easy to follow until the last part. We came off the motorway and soon were lost in the maze of minor roads that laced across southern Oxfordshire. A part of me was glad; I wanted to be ready before seeing him but the miles had disappeared too quickly. The half-hour we spent shuttling along the same dark lanes again and again had given me time to think. Finally I pulled up at the side of the road in the village we had been circling.

Danny leant forward between the seats. 'This place is like the end of the world.'

He was right. Even for a village, Stoneborough was nothing. The cottages, five or six of them huddled together, had an empty air; only one was showing any light, the blue wash of television seeping through the net curtain in an upstairs window. There was a pond, its edges sharp with frozen reeds, and a village green that was little more than a patch of crisp white grass. No one had been across it since the dew fell.

'We can't go round again,' I said. 'We're going to have to ask.'

'Can't we call him?' said Martha.

'There's no reception.'

Across the road was a pub called the White Swan, a squat stone building whose roof covered it like an oversized hat. The upper windows looked out slyly from underneath. On the ground floor the curtains were drawn but a rim of yellow light was visible around them.

'It's like the place doesn't want to be found,' said Martha. She opened the passenger door and got out. With her usual long stride curtailed by the cocktail dress that clung tightly above her knees, she crossed the beam of the headlights and went in.

The radio was too loud now the car had stopped so I turned it off. Danny leant forward again. 'It had better not be much further. It's gone nine – I'm dying for a drink.' His breath carried an unmistakable whisky tang.

'You've been taking nips from that hip flask all the way. I've seen you in the rearview.' I twisted round to look at him. The light from the pub's carriage lamp cast the planes of his face into sharp relief. He looked elvish.

'It's New Year's Eve, Joanna.'

'Light me a cigarette, will you?' I asked. 'Mine are in the boot.' He rummaged around among the newspapers on the back seat and found the packet. The match flared and died. 'Thanks.'

'Your hands are shaking.'

'Are they?' I held one out flat and observed my fingers in the light from the dash. 'Maybe it's the thought of the big house. These things intimidate English teachers' daughters, you know.' I shrugged and wound down the window to blow out the smoke. It was a policy I had developed with Danny: to reveal my weakness rather than give him the pleasure of discovering it himself.

'That's one of the things I like about you. You're always so honest about your humble beginnings.' He sat back and started flicking through old text messages on his mobile.

'It'll be a thrill for me to be allowed above stairs.'

Martha came out of the pub, the heavy wooden door slamming shut behind her. 'That way, about a mile on. I think we must have gone past it at least three times. There's no sign on the road, apparently, just a track on the left that leads into a wood.' She pulled her red fake-fur jacket more tightly round her shoulders. 'It is so cold out here.'

'I thought New Yorkers were used to hard winters,' said Danny.

We drove on out of the village. Living in London, I had forgotten how dark it got in the country. Hedges flashed past, illuminated only by our headlights and falling back into blackness behind us. We saw several pairs of small eyes in the undergrowth. After we'd gone about a mile I slowed down and started to look for the driveway. We were coming into a wood. Huge trees made a skeletal tunnel over the road, their bare branches tangled and swaying eerily. I pulled slowly along the verge for a couple of minutes.

'There,' said Martha. 'That must be it.'

I turned and we started up an unmade track. I had expected to be able to see the house from the foot of the drive and squinted forward looking for lights but there was nothing, just an intricate mesh of leafless branches opening up in front of us and pulling tight as a net behind us as soon as we passed. I thought of those fairy-tale woods where the trees sprout at supernatural speeds to ensnare those foolish enough to enter but there were no signs of new growth here. Everything around us was dead or dormant, in the widow's

3

weeds of winter. We fell silent, as if the looming and falling away of the branches was weaving an enchantment around us. The car made heavy work of the road; we bumped and lurched over potholes for the best part of another mile before we veered left and found ourselves on a circular gravel drive.

I stopped the engine. There, in front of us, was the house. Stoneborough Manor, the Cotswold-stone pile – it really was the only word – recently inherited by Lucas, my best friend.

Three storeys high, it reared up out of the night as if it were facing the darkness down. There were seven windows on the first and second floors, all blankly reflecting the tiny sliver of moon, but light spilled out of every one on the ground floor on to the two small lawns in front of the house. An avenue of yews lined the long path to the door, which was sheltered by a portico on two smooth round columns. I felt a pang of anxiety. Lucas had described it to me pretty well, but even so the reality of it shocked me. How could it not change things between us?

We unloaded our bags from the boot and I locked the car, although who would break into it so far from civilisation was anyone's guess. I held Danny's arm as we made our way up the path; the flagstones were slippery with frost and the heels I'd just changed into didn't offer much in the way of grip. Martha rang the bell and we heard the echo of it reaching back into the house like a Chinese whisper. For a minute or two there was nothing and then the shape of a body appeared behind the stained-glass panels in the door. Suddenly there he was, lit from behind and grinning. I saw immediately that he had lost weight.

'Lucas, it's incredible,' I said, stepping forward. He put his arms around me and held me tightly. The collar of his dinner jacket was rough on my cheek.

'Hello,' he said, next to my ear.

He let me go and embraced Martha then clapped Danny on the arm.

'Mate. Come in. Did you find it all right?'

4

'Not without some effort,' said Danny. 'Fuck, it's fantastic. You kept this a secret. Why haven't I been here before?'

'Well, it was Patrick's. He did his entertaining in London. He was quite private here; it was a sort of family place.'

We left our bags by the door. We were standing in a central hall lit only by two large table lamps on a wooden chest. Their light pooled on to a black-and-white chequered floor. Around the edges of the room were a number of marble busts on pedestals; one of them, I saw, was wearing our college tie. Above us, the upper floors of the house spiralled away like the inside of a snail shell, getting darker and darker as they receded upwards. Our voices echoed coldly off the walls, rising away from us until they were swallowed by the body of the place. There was a strong scent of old-fashioned furniture polish.

'We'll have the champagne now everyone's here.' Lucas opened a door into an enormous drawing room. There was an immediate rise in the air temperature. The room was dominated by a white marble fireplace carved with an oak leaf-and-acorn design, and in the grate a fire was burning, sending up flames a foot high. Brocade curtains hung from ceiling to floor at the three windows, their sun-faded rubies and greens complementing the ivy-pattern border of the artfully threadbare carpet. Here, too, the light came only from lamps dotted around on low tables and from a pair of thick church candles on the mantelpiece. In front of the fire there were two grand chesterfields of burnished burgundy leather that looked as if they had been there since the house had been built. They were so much a part of the room I could imagine that they had grown there, sprung from seed in the carpet. Aboard these were Rachel and a man I didn't recognise. They stood up and Danny bounded over, caught Rachel in his arms and spun her around and around.

'Put me down,' she laughed. 'Put me down, Danny. You'll ruin my dress.'

He set her down on the carpet and stood back to scrutinise her. She was wearing a silver slip dress, crumpled like tin foil, deliberately torn at the shoulder and hem. 'Nice.' He nodded with approval and pouted at her.

She turned to the man and smiled at him. 'Greg, this is Danny – the inimitable – and Joanna and Martha.'

'Ah, the new boyfriend,' said Danny.

'God, you're rude.' She hit him lightly with the back of her hand. 'Not quite so new, either. It's been three months now.'

'Good to meet you.'

Greg held out a large hand and I shook it. His grip was strong and dry. Although I'd almost managed to get rid of the shyness that near crippled me as a teenager, there was still the odd person who could revive it. He was going to be one of them, obviously. Rachel's boyfriends were always good-looking; Greg had short brown hair and warm brown eyes fringed by long lashes. It was also plain that he was someone who had to encounter a razor more than once a day to stay clean-shaven; the shadow around his chin and a light tan gave him a vaguely dissolute aspect. It wasn't that, though. Although he looked only three or four years older than us, there was something indefinably adult about him. When I smiled at him, I found he was watching me as if he were taking my measure. I looked down again quickly, in case I was unwittingly giving something away.

'Where's Michael?' asked Martha. 'Isn't he supposed to be here?'

Lucas turned from the highly polished table where he was putting out champagne glasses. 'He's upstairs, getting a couple of hours' sleep. I don't think he got home last night.'

'Jesus, why do people do it to themselves?' Martha went over to look at the framed photographs on the mantelpiece. She picked one up and looked at it closely. 'What can possibly be so urgent between Christmas and New Year that he can't go home?'

'They've got some big deal on. Hostile takeover, from what I can gather. He looked knackered.'

6

To me, Lucas looked knackered himself. Apart from the weight loss, his skin was pale. His hair, though black and curly as ever, didn't have its normal blue lustre and was in need of a cut. The champagne bottle gave a hollow sob as he pulled out its cork. He handed out the glasses then folded himself down next to me on the chesterfield. Taking out a packet of cigarettes, he lit one, tilting his head to one side in his diffident way. I found the gesture strangely reassuring, a familiar thing in foreign surroundings. 'So, how're you doing?' he said. 'It's good to see you.'

'I've missed you,' I said.

He looked down at his knee, where his fingers were picking at a loose thread in the seam of his trousers. 'I should have called you.'

'For God's sake, Lucas, that doesn't matter. How are you?'

'OK, really.' He smiled sadly. 'It's just that I can't get over the idea he's not coming back. It doesn't seem right that someone like that could just be extinguished.' He drew hard on his cigarette and a column of ash fell on to his trousers. 'To have that much – I don't know – *life force*, and for there to be nothing left . . . So soon after Mum died, too. Three months – Jo, six months ago I had both of them. The two people I loved most in the world. And he chose it – that's what I'll never understand.'

All the careful words I'd prepared deserted me so I took his hand and squeezed it. He returned the pressure and then rubbed his thumb slowly against my fingers, as if it were he who was trying to reassure me.

'He liked you, you know.'

'I liked him. I've never met anyone like him,' I said truthfully. I had been shocked to hear about Patrick's suicide. He had been more like a father to Lucas than an uncle. I had met him on a number of occasions, mostly when we'd been at university and he'd taken Lucas and me out to lunch. Even now, the times that I'd spent in his company were especially bright beads among the memories of my university years. Patrick had overwhelmed me. Although he must have been in his late fifties even then, he gave the impression of great strength, both physical and mental. His black hair had been greying a little at the temples but still looked vivid. There was something Homeric about him, as if a measure of the old heroic blood had somehow survived down into a less noble age.

He'd also made me feel as if I had something to offer. One time at the Randolph Hotel, when I'd felt intimidated by the lunching grandees and the formality of the dining room, I'd been trying to describe to him a particularly brash girl in the year above whom Lucas and I both loathed. Although I couldn't remember what my words had been, I still thought about how he had reached across the table for my hand and said, 'You must write one day. You have a wonderful gift for metaphor.' From anyone else it would have sounded affected but from him, as successful as he was and with what I perceived as his hotline to the cultural hub of things, it was the best compliment I'd ever had. Although our relationship had never been close enough for me to tell him so, he became a sort of inspiration to me, someone who thought I was worth encouraging. In his presence, the world opened out, ready for conquering. And he, this man who could have done anything, had decided to take his own life.

'He hoped you were my girlfriend.'

I laughed to cover my surprise. The question of the relationship between us was an old one, although we had never spoken about it ourselves before.

The first time I had seen Lucas was in our tutor's room at Oxford in Freshers' Week. He was wearing a navy fisherman's jumper, jeans and Converse shoes and, despite his height, was being swallowed by the brown velvet sofa with the dodgy springs we soon learnt not to sit on. He didn't fight it or nervously try to sit further forward, just let himself disappear into it. I immediately put it down to a public-school self-assurance. There were plenty of examples walking the quads as if they were on their ancestral estates and propping up the college bar with the confidence of the long established. I found them excruciating. One part of me was intimidated, and envious that people of eighteen and nineteen could be so confident; the other part wondered how they could be so obtuse as never to experience a moment's self-doubt.

I soon realised that Lucas was not of that type. After our tutor had prescribed huge swathes of Homer for translation almost overnight, assumed a deep familiarity with authors of whom I had barely heard and alarmingly made a number of jokes in Latin, the five of us repaired to the junior common room for coffee and cigarettes. Lucas, who had hardly spoken in the hour before, turned out to have been to a very low-key private day school in London and lived with his mother, a writer for children, on the borders of West Hampstead. I had watched his long fingers as he rolled an expert cigarette and waited in vain for him to tell me more. He was reserved in a way I hadn't encountered before.

It was Danny who had always had the line in flashy confidence. He was one of those people who seemed to start university knowing everything and everyone already. When the rest of us had herded together for our virgin trip to the college bar, he had only been able to join us for one drink because he was going on to a party at Balliol.

'He was like this at school,' Lucas had said, shredding a beer mat.

'You went to school together?'

He nodded. 'Only for sixth form. And he didn't start until halfway through the second term – got kicked out of somewhere smarter. But he was centre of attention by lunchtime on his first day.'

'Sounds annoying.'

'No, actually he's all right. He's good fun.'

Over the next few weeks I learnt about the friendship

between Danny and Lucas. It had an unusual dynamic. If you'd have asked any of us whether we thought that loud, sociable Danny with his wardrobe of cutting-edge urban clothes would have got on so well with quiet, kind Lucas in his jumpers and jeans, we would have laughed. But it became clear that there was a strong symbiosis between them. Lucas appreciated Danny because he took it as read that any friend of his was part of the in-crowd and so Lucas was, right from the start. As I was Lucas's friend, all invitations also extended to me and that was how the two of us, who, left to our own devices, probably would have spent four years flying undetected by the social radar, came to know a lot of the set at Oxford who lived their lives on larger canvases.

My own relationship with Danny was complicated. I think if I hadn't been close to Lucas I would have been beneath his notice. As it was, he was obliged to acknowledge me. Sometimes he and I got on quite well. Other times I knew he saw me as an irritating third wheel in their friendship.

Because it wasn't one-way traffic. Lucas provided Danny with something that he didn't get elsewhere: simple, genuine friendship. At eighteen Danny's self-assurance had alienated those less confident but Lucas had seemed oblivious to it. He also gave him a sort of grounding: he was Danny's earth wire. From the sound of it, Danny had been out of his parents' control – such as it was – for years, but when things got a bit much and he needed perspective it was Lucas he sought out.

Sometimes at university Danny pushed himself too hard. Not academically; there was never any danger of that. Annoyingly, there never needed to be. He'd done English with Rachel and he had the greatest natural academic flair of us all. It was galling, especially when he was the only one to get a first. No, when Danny pushed himself too hard, it was a question of too much drink, too many drugs, too many nights without sleep. When that happened, he went to find Lucas and after being talked down he would go to ground in his room for a few days, swaddled in a dressing gown and piteously downing Lemsip as if the whole thing wasn't self-inflicted. Even in that, he managed to exude glamour.

Martha and I had talked in the past about how Danny was a little bit like one of the really hedonistic rock stars, a Steve Tyler or Anthony Kiedis. Being in his orbit, we did feel as if some of his star quality reflected on us but it wasn't just that. It was enough to know that there was someone out there doing the stuff we talked about. We didn't have to do the drugs because Danny did them; we could talk as if we knew all about it without actually risking it ourselves. Danny made us feel we were like him – rock 'n' roll – when in fact we were nothing of the sort. We liked this version of ourselves, and to some extent I think he liked us because we were the background against which he shone.

Ironically, the only person who could match him in excess was Lucas. He didn't do drugs but he drank more than anyone else I knew. Whenever Danny was in a drinking phase, he could rely on Lucas to be his brother in arms. Lucas was both a steady drinker and a binge drinker, able to keep up on even the most extreme bender. Most of the time at college he had been a fun person to drink with but occasionally, underneath the jolly social-drinking façade, I saw an edge of need that none of the rest of us had, even Danny. I had never mentioned it – it was something I didn't even like to think about – but now and again it had drawn the attention of those in authority. Once in particular I remember waiting outside in the corridor while our tutor had kept Lucas back for a minute. I hadn't deliberately listened but I couldn't avoid catching his final words. 'Just remember the old Greek wisdom, Lucas,' he'd said. 'Μηδὲν ἄγάν. *Nothing in excess.*'

In our first term there were several occasions when Lucas and I sat up in the library doing all-nighters when I hoped our growing friendship would shift sideways into something different. We had a surprising amount in common for people from very different backgrounds. We hated sports, especially the team varieties, and loved indie music, which we listened to all the time. We became close quickly. We worked together on essays, sharing notes and breaks in the pub and cooking supper together a couple of times a week to avoid eating in the college dining-hall. There were even a few days in the middle of that term when I began to wonder if my feelings for him were reciprocated.

One night, though, I had been out with Martha, with whom I had also become friends, and decided on my drunken return to college that it would be a good idea to go and see Lucas for a nightcap. Lucas was out but his roommate, an historian from Liverpool, had been in and had a bottle of wine open. He poured me a glass and I talked to him while I waited. Lucas had been over to St John's to see a schoolfriend and didn't get back until gone two, by which time I had been drunk enough to be kissing the historian when he opened the door.

After that, things had subtly changed. There was no longer any doubt. As far as Lucas was concerned, I was his friend and that was as far as it went. Martha tried to cheer me up by saying that he clearly liked me and that I'd dented his confidence, but I couldn't believe that. I was bitterly dis-appointed and furious with myself about the historian, whose name I now struggled even to remember. I went home for Christmas feeling wretched. I'm not sure how much my family enjoyed having me back that holiday.

Gradually, though, I got used to the idea and soon became aware that lots of people envied me my closeness to Lucas, platonic as it was. Men liked him and so did women. He was good-looking in a moderate way but it was his kindness and lack of interest in fighting for a place in the university pecking order that made him different.

'I'm going to go and wake Michael up,' said Martha. 'He'll miss everything otherwise.'

'OK,' said Lucas, looking away from me. 'He's in the

second room along on the left on the first floor. By the painting of the woman with the enormous hat. Great picture – you'll see it properly tomorrow.'

I was looking forward to seeing Michael. He'd been so busy at work that I hadn't seen him at all before Christmas. I missed his dry sense of humour.

'Do you have plans for the weekend, Lucas?' asked Greg. His voice was deep.

'Nothing specific. I thought we'd just relax, have a few drinks, you know. I'll show you the rest of the house tomorrow and then I thought I'd cook dinner.'

'Lucas is a great cook,' Rachel explained to Greg. 'The best of any of us, by far.'

'Oh, come on,' he said. 'Anyway, about the house. I don't want to set the agenda here. I didn't earn this place: it's mine purely by good luck – or bad. I don't want it to be a big thing; I'd rather we thought of it as belonging to all of us.' He threw the butt of his cigarette into the fire and stood up to pour some more drinks.

I got up, too, and went over to the other chesterfield. I knelt behind it to speak to Rachel, resting my forearms along its studded back. 'You've had your hair cut,' I said. It was short, not more than an inch all over, with a small fringe that stopped precipitately above her high forehead.

'Thank you. It's quite "fashion"; you don't think I look like Joan of Arc?'

I laughed. 'Not at all – far too beautiful.'

'That's bollocks.' Rachel's directness still had the power to surprise me. It had taken me almost a year after we met to realise that she didn't mean to be rude.

The door opened and Martha reappeared with Michael. Even after a nap, he looked exhausted. It was amazing that he could do the hours he did. The only thing I could think was that after several years his body had become accustomed to it and no longer expected reasonable amounts of rest. He had developed a useful type of narcolepsy that allowed him to fall asleep at any point when he wasn't required to be doing something else, no matter how uncomfortable his position at the time. I gave him a hug.

Danny went out to his bag in the hall and returned with a bottle. 'Why did the Mexican push his wife off a cliff?' he asked the room at large.

'Tequila, tequila, tequila.'

'I think Patrick had some shot glasses.' Lucas opened the sideboard and peered in towards the back of the shelf. With a chink, he produced seven tiny glasses. 'I'll go and find some lemon.'

Martha perched on the back of the sofa next to me. She was excited; I could tell from the twinkling in her grey eyes. Her long brown hair was tied up in a sleek arrangement that made her look older and more sophisticated than usual. I felt a rush of affection for her. 'I might have known Danny'd do this,' she said. 'Things are going to get messy now.'

'You know how much I hate tequila.'

Lucas brought salt and a couple of lemons. He took out a penknife and cut one of them into eighths while Michael filled the glasses. I felt my usual literal gut reaction at the prospect as I held my left hand sideways and let him tip salt into the dent that appeared at the base of my thumb.

'The anatomical snuff box,' he said.

'Let's not get medical about this, Michael.' Danny held out his hand.

'He may have to,' I said.

'Everyone ready? OK, go.'

We pressed our tongues to the salt, knocked back the tequila and clamped our mouths over the lemon pieces. I struggled against the impulse to gag. 'Why do we put ourselves through it?'

'Because it's party juice, brings out the South American in you,' said Danny, grinning. It was difficult not to get caught up in his enthusiasm. He had always been a fire-starter, the one of us who could kick off a three-day party by opening a bottle and putting the radio on. Martha looked as if she were about to do the military two-step across the carpet. Tequila seemed to hit her immediately. Her eyes were glistening.

'What time is it?' asked Lucas.

'Eleven.'

'Shall we have some music?' He crouched in front of a powerful-looking stereo, selected a CD from the pile and slid it into the machine.

Danny grinned as he heard the first bars of Shirley Bassey's 'History Repeating'. 'Good choice, man.' The song wrapped its rich, rough sound around us so completely it seemed to be oozing out of the walls. We all danced, even Lucas who usually appointed himself DJ to avoid having to. Danny stood in front of the fire, gyrating his hips so provocatively I felt indecent for seeing it. His jeans, which he always wore at holster-level, looked about to slide off him entirely.

After a few songs, I started to cough. Clearly we had raised old dust. Greg, dancing next to me, touched my arm. 'Are you all right? You're asthmatic.' It wasn't a question and I wondered how he knew.

'Inhaler's in my coat,' I said. 'I'll get it.' My chest was getting tighter. Near my diaphragm, my lungs felt inert; my breath was shallow and ineffectual.

It was colder in the hall again. Quiet, too. Although I knew the music was loud, the drawing-room door was so solid that I could only just hear it. I groped quickly in my coat pocket for the inhaler. People are confused about asthma: they think that you can't breathe in. In fact, what you can't do is breathe out. It's like being buried alive; there's nowhere for the dead air to go.

After a couple of shots of Ventolin, I began to relax. I coughed to clear my chest and the sound echoed through the house. I looked up, seeing the balconied floors tiered above me, unlit. All the doors leading off the hall were closed. There

15

was a passageway opposite, leading darkly away to the back of the house.

I had the sudden sense that there were eyes on me. 'Lucas?' I said, more to puncture the silence than expecting an answer. I knew I was the only person in the house who wasn't in the drawing room. My skin prickled. The sound of my voice played in my ear. I took a breath and forced myself to stand still for a minute and look into the unlit corners away from the lamps and up above my head to the landings. I half expected to see someone there, leaning over the banisters watching me. There was nothing. And yet there was. It seemed to me that there was something lurking, something that was not benevolent. With a sudden swell, the darkness seemed to gather around me. A rushing started in my ears, as if the walls themselves were whispering. I couldn't stand it any longer. I yanked the drawing-room door open and threw myself back into the blaze of light and sound.

'All right?' Lucas was standing just inside.

'Just wheezing a bit. I've had some Ventolin.' I smiled. My fear felt irrational and ridiculous now.

'Good.' He handed me my glass. 'We've finished the champagne I brought up. I'll go and get some more so we're ready for midnight. Back in a minute.'

I sat down on the edge of the fireguard, glad to have the heat on my back. The chill was still on my skin. Michael came to sit next to me and we watched the dancing, Danny with Martha, Greg with Rachel. Rachel stood on tiptoe to whisper something in Greg's ear; he laughed and bent his head to kiss her.

'Have you met him before?' I asked Michael quietly.

'Once, a few weeks ago. He's away a lot with work. He's phenomenally bright.'

Lucas came back with a tray of fresh glasses and two more bottles tucked under his arm. 'Three minutes to go.'

I decided my lungs were working well enough to manage a

16

cigarette. One of the things I appreciated about my real friends, all of whom were around me, was that they never tried to make me give up, despite my asthma. They knew I knew I should and that was enough.

New Year's Eve was my least favourite night of the year. I didn't like the weight of expectation it carried, both in the sense that everyone felt obliged to have a good time, as if what they did would set a pattern for the coming year, and with the idea that this year would be different, as if on the turn of midnight we could cast off our old weak-willed selves and become new, better people. I especially disliked resolutions. You can take too many long, hard looks at yourself.

'Turn on the radio, Martha,' said Lucas, tearing the foil from one of the bottles. We were just in time: Big Ben had already started tolling. The sound of it made me shiver, as it always did. Another year gone.

'Happy New Year!' The cork flew out and Lucas poured the champagne, streams of bubbles running down the sides of the glasses. He handed me one and kissed me on the cheek, close enough to my mouth almost to touch my lips.

I returned his look as he pulled away. 'Happy New Year.'

'Happier, anyway,' he said. 'Cheers.'

Out of the corner of my eye, I saw Danny turn to cut another lemon. I touched Lucas's sleeve. 'Let's go outside for a cigarette. He's doing more tequilas.'

We took our drinks and slipped out. Lucas snapped on the light in the passageway, which I could now see led to the kitchen. The chequered floor of the hall gave way to large flagstones and roughly whitewashed stone walls. I felt safe with him close to me. Of course there had been no one else in the house. I had imagined it in the panic of my asthma.

We took a turn just before the kitchen and came to a door that was heavily bolted. Lucas pulled back the locks and we stepped outside. At first I couldn't see anything but then objects began to draw themselves out of the night, edging themselves round with indigo and assuming form. We were at the side of the house on a sort of high terrace about fifteen feet above a garden, which stretched away from us over a great expanse of lawn to a rim of black trees. It was bitingly cold, even though we had taken coats from the stand. I looked at Lucas and made out chin, nose and glittering eyes. He handed me a cigarette and lit it, a small explosion of light. Above us, the stars were needle-sharp.

'There's Orion's Belt and the Plough. Can you see?' I pointed.

'I'm hopeless at constellations. People show me but I can never see them for myself.'

'I used to be like that. Until that time we went to Greece – do you remember? – and someone showed me Orion's Belt and now I can always find it.'

We sat down on the balustrade that ran around the edge of the terrace and I swung my legs out over the drop. A sole milky cloud moved off the moon. Below us the lawn sparkled with frost.

'This is an incredible place. I can't believe it's yours.'

'I never imagined that Patrick would leave it to me. No, that's a stupid thing to say: who else would he leave it to?' He ran a hand through his hair. 'I didn't expect him to die, anyway, and somehow I thought the house would go when he did. It was so much a part of him.' The tip of his cigarette glowed orange. 'I got pretty much the lot. The flat in Hampstead is sold already and I've found an agent to sell the gallery and the stock for me. I couldn't do anything with it. I don't know the first thing about art and people bought from Patrick because of his reputation. I mean, who'd buy art from me?'

I shivered and moved closer to him for warmth. Without thinking, I slipped my arm through his. I had done it on a hundred other occasions but tonight it didn't feel comfortable and uncomplicated. In the past he wouldn't have thought anything of it but now Lucas turned to look at me and our eyes met for a moment. I looked down quickly in case he thought I was –

18

what? Flirting? I was embarrassed that he might think that and yet part of me wanted him to. Something was shifting, I could feel it. Why had he told me that Patrick had hoped I was his girlfriend? And that kiss earlier. I wondered whether he would lean in and kiss me now but he didn't and the moment passed. We sat in silence, the garden below us completely still. Now that my eyes were accustomed, I could see it quite distinctly, the formal bed below us planted with pampas grass and leafless rose bushes, the lawn and the evergreen laurels that bordered it where it met the wall at the back of the house.

'You could do anything here,' I said after a while. 'There's absolutely no one to hear you.'

'I'm serious about what I said earlier. I really do want you – and the others – to think of it as your place. It's no fun being king of the castle if you're on your own.'

I put my arms around him and squeezed. 'You're brilliant.'

After a little while, I grew more used to the cold and we stayed outside for some time, smoking more cigarettes and feeling the silence of the country night around us. Finally, though, Lucas stood up. 'Let's go in. I'm freezing my balls off out here,' he said, taking my hand as I swung my legs back over the balustrade.

Inside, Michael was asleep on one of the chesterfields. Greg and Rachel had gone to bed. The fire was burning down and the tequila was gone, the bottle on its side next to a pile of eviscerated lemon pieces. Martha was crouched at the stereo with a pile of CDs on either side of her. 'Can't decide what to play,' she said. Danny was sitting cross-legged in front of the dying fire rolling a spliff, the tip of his tongue sticking out between his teeth.

'Do you want another drink?' said Lucas, holding a champagne bottle up to the light.

I shook my head.

'Yeah, it's time for bed. I'll show you your room. I've just got to make sure everything's safe down here and set the burglar alarm. God, imagine if this place was broken into.'

19

Chapter Two

It was late morning when I woke and my room was suffused by a blank light, as if it had snowed during the night. I pulled out the heavy cotton sheets and went over to the window. It was cold out of bed. There wasn't any snow but the garden was white with frost. I stood for a while looking out at the long expanse of lawn, thinking how good it was to be able to stand there in a T-shirt without anyone to see. The house Martha and I shared in London was overlooked by the back of the terrace behind us and we had to keep the curtains drawn until we were dressed. There wasn't another house visible from here.

I had been so tired and drunk the night before that I hadn't paid much attention to the room. Given the size of the house it seemed comparatively small, although it was bigger than any I'd ever had. Being on the top floor, it must have been servants' quarters in the past. It was still simply decorated. The bed had a wrought-iron frame and at the foot of it there was a stout mahogany chest. There was a small fireplace, too, with an arrangement of dried flowers in the hearth and two crystal candlesticks on the mantelpiece. The walls, unevenly plastered and painted a milky white, were bare apart from a large oil painting over the bed. I knelt up on the pillows for a closer look. It was a classical scene, nymphs bathing in a river, their long blonde hair floating around them in the dark water. On the bank, entranced by his own reflection in the water, lay Narcissus. I wondered if it had always been there or whether Lucas had put it in my room, knowing I would like it.

My dress was in a silken pool on the rug; I picked it up and shook it out by the straps. It would have to be dry-cleaned before it was worn again but I put it on a hanger on the back of the door anyway. I changed into a navy jumper and jeans and put my boots on. Then I packed away my tights and shoes from the night before and made the bed, tucking the sheets in until they covered the mattress like fondant icing. As I pulled the door closed behind me, I checked that everything was tidy as if it were a hotel and not a friend's place at all.

It seemed that I was first up: everything was silent. I stood at the banister and saw the house in daylight for the first time. I had the feeling of someone left in a vast museum after hours, half alarmed, half excited by being alone with things that other people saw only under supervision. Below me was the whorl of staircases and landings and the chequered hall floor. Looking up, I saw that the roof was domed, something I hadn't noticed from outside in the dark. At the base of it there was a complete circle of windows and the white winter light poured through them.

Above my head was one of the most spectacular paintings I had ever seen. The inside of the dome was a painted bowl of almost unbelievable richness, myriad shades of blue and gold and pomegranate-pink and red, intricate and at the same time epic. It was like a secular version of a Renaissance church fresco. It depicted a convocation of the gods, a council or a drinking party. I thought of the scene at the beginning of the *Iliad* where the gods are lounging on Olympus, drinking and squabbling about whose favourite is going to be allowed to win the war while the human warriors are spilling their blood on the plains of Troy below.

At the centre of the tableau a figure I took to be Zeus lay

21

on a golden couch. He was an exercise in controlled male strength, muscular shoulders and arms at odds with the relaxed pose, a head of shining black hair. He wore a white robe bordered in purple, a Midas-worthy amount of gold jewellery around his neck and wrists. There were rings set with huge gems on his fingers. One of his arms dropped idly over the arm of the couch towards a woman with hair the colour of dark chocolate, which wound down her back and over the white folds of her dress. She was on her knees, her spine a smooth curve as she bent to kiss Zeus' hand. The dress was slipping off her shoulder to reveal the round of one brown breast. At the other end of the couch, also kneeling, was another woman, also dark-haired and identically clothed, although her dress sat demurely on her shoulders. This goddess held Zeus' feet in her hands, her long white fingers closing gently around his toes. It wasn't immediately clear which of the goddesses the two women were. The one kissing Zeus' hand was obviously more sexual. The other was ethereal, her expression contemplative, even a little sad, as she looked away from the group into the sky that surrounded them. Perhaps the first was Aphrodite, the second Hera. Zeus looked straight down out of the picture, as if he were trying to establish eye-contact. His gaze was dark and unreadable. There was no anger in it but also no pleasure, no joy at finding himself king of the world.

Around the main group were arranged a number of other figures. There was an easily identifiable Ganymede with an ornate drinking bowl, his muscles taut under golden skin as he proffered it. A couple of other gods stood a little way back, leaning together conspiratorially. Again, I had no idea who they might be. Near the neat white feet of the goddess I thought might be Hera two children played, round and rosy like putti. Vines grew around the scene, curling up the legs of the couch, the bright-green leaves here and there revealing clusters of fat ripe grapes.

Abruptly the light withdrew and the painting faded. What sun there had been was gone. I gave the ceiling a last look then turned and made my way downstairs. Years of feet had worn away the centre of the pale strip of green carpet that ran down the landings like a stream. All the doors I passed were closed but I didn't think about what was behind them. My attention was on the art: the walls were bristling with paintings of extraordinary quality. On the main wall of the first-floor landing there was a huge Jackson Pollock. I had never seen one in the flesh before. I had to stop myself reaching out to touch the storm of red and black paint. A little further down at a platform in the stairs there was one of Julian Schnabel's famous plate portraits. I understood now why all the walls were white. The entire house was a display case for a world-class art collection.

We had breakfast in the kitchen, a large room with a black-and-white floor like the hall's and French windows that opened on to a walled garden at the back of the house. A long oak table stood in front of the glass and I looked out as we ate. The garden was still ice-bound. A fine film of glittering frost covered the paths and the leafless espalier trees trained up against the far wall. Most of the raised beds were empty, although there was a small herb garden and also a cluster of gooseberry bushes and raspberry canes. A robin pecked at the thin layer of ice on a puddle about five feet away until Martha dropped a knife. The noise reached him through the glass and he looked up and saw us for the first time, before taking off in alarm.

'You don't see that very often now,' said Greg, pointing at the ceiling.

I looked up. It was studded with black hooks. 'For hanging meat?'

'Like something out of an S & M parlour,' said Danny.

'Imagine having dead animals hanging in your kitchen.'

Martha grimaced and reached for the coffee pot. She poured me another cup, then filled her own.

'People had to be tougher then,' said Lucas. 'Nowadays everyone seems to pretend death doesn't happen.' There was a fraught silence, punctured only when Danny took a loud crunch into a slice of toast. Lucas smiled. 'This is a morbid conversation for the first day of a new year.'

'Sorry,' said Michael, appearing at the doorway. 'Completely overslept, obviously. Don't know what's wrong with me.'

'You work too hard, that's what's wrong,' said Martha. 'Anyway, we saved you some.' She got up and took his cooked breakfast out of the oven, where it had been keeping warm.

'Thank you, you're a sweetheart.' He gave her a kiss on the cheek.

After we'd washed up and tidied the drawing room, the others went out in the car to get cigarettes and the papers. Danny went off for a long bath and I asked Lucas to show me the house.

We started in Patrick's study, the only room on the top floor that was neither a bedroom nor a bathroom. 'He liked the atmosphere in here and the view,' said Lucas. I followed him over to the window and saw more or less the same as I had from my own, two doors down. The room itself was remarkably plain. It was painted white, of course, but there was a simple beige carpet under our feet instead of the Turkish rugs and rich fabrics of the rooms downstairs and even my bedroom. The curtains were plain green and there was no art on the walls. Two leather armchairs were the only furniture, apart from sun-bleached cushions on the window seats and a bureau.

I picked up the photograph that stood on top of it. It showed Patrick at what I guessed was his gallery, looking very seventies in a velvet jacket, sideburns and longish black curly hair remarkably like Lucas's. He was with Thomas Parrish, one of his most famous artists, and a feline woman in a Bianca Jagger-style trouser suit. He looked slimmer but otherwise very like the Patrick I had known. He was in the middle of the shot, his arms around the shoulders of the other two. It was the classic pose of people celebrating their success. Patrick and Parrish were grinning; I suspected they'd had a few drinks. The woman's smile was less open and although she was looking straight into the camera there was something guarded about her expression.

Lucas riffled the edge of a stack of paper with his thumb. 'As you can see, I haven't pulled myself together enough to sort through his stuff yet.' The desktop was like a still life in itself. There were piles of glossy catalogues, letters, invitations, postcards advertising exhibitions. A glass ashtray full of paperclips had found the one paperless patch. I took a step back. It felt like an invasion of privacy to be in the room, let alone looking over the paperwork. It was as if Patrick had only just walked away.

That feeling stayed with me as we did the tour. It seemed as though Patrick were one room ahead of us, slipping away just as we opened each new door. I've never been in a house that so strongly bore the imprint of its owner. All houses give clues to the people who live in them, in the decoration and the things left lying around, the photographs, the books, the tennis rackets, but this was something beyond that. It was as if Patrick's spirit, his energy, his fierce intelligence, the sheer scale of him, was manifested in this building.

Lucas hesitated in front of one door, his fingers on the handle. I looked at him questioningly. 'My parents' old room,' he said and opened it.

We went in and stood just inside. It looked much like any of the other bedrooms on this floor, several of which he had shown me. There was a large double bed covered by an embroidered throw with a wildflower pattern, a small table on either side. The large sash window gave on to the lawns by the front door and the drive beyond that. There was a low Victorian chair by the window and a tall chest of drawers. But if the appearance of the room was unremarkable, its atmosphere was different to that of the rest of the house. It had no energy. Instead the room had a mausoleum air; it was a sad place, closed off from life. I wondered if Lucas had crept away here sometimes, to try to imagine that his parents were still here, waking up in the bed or dressing for dinner. Only two things suggested who its occupants had been. There was no evidence of Lucas's father but on the top of the chest of drawers there was a brush and hand-mirror set and on the table to the right of the bed there was a silver-framed photograph of a smiling gap-toothed Lucas aged about seven. I didn't want to pry by looking closer, especially when he was radiating tension beside me. Now I noticed that the throw on the photograph side was slightly rumpled, as if someone had lain down there to be closer to the person to whom the bed had belonged, to catch the trace of her old perfume on the pillows.

'I just wanted to show you,' he said. 'I don't want this room used. I'll tell the others.'

It was the perfect opportunity for me to talk to him about his mother and Patrick but again, tongue-tied, I let the moment slip away.

On the second landing we stopped and looked at the ceiling. There was no sun to illuminate it now and it looked more remote somehow, although just as beautiful. A door opened behind us and Danny appeared, damp from the bath and naked apart from a small towel tucked neatly around his hips. His body was slim but with just the right amount of gym-worked muscle. I looked away, embarrassed.

'Who's who, then?' he said. 'I don't do gods.'

'What do you think?' Lucas asked me. 'I've never been able to work it out. Obviously the guy in the middle is Zeus but I

26

don't know about the women. Hera, do you reckon? But then who's the other one?'

I looked again for details that would help me interpret it but there were none of the usual symbols, the bows and arrows or winged feet or apples. 'There aren't many clues, are there? When was it painted?'

'It's modern, actually. Mid-eighties. I was eleven or twelve when it was finished. I remember being shown the whole of it for the first time.'

'Who's the artist?'

'I can never think of his name. I'm pretty sure he was American. There'll be paperwork; I'll find out for you.' As he moved away, I caught the scent of him, the expensive cologne that he once told me he started wearing because it reminded him of Patrick, and a hint of cigarette smoke.

'Lucas, the art here . . .'

'I'm almost frightened by it,' he said. 'The responsibility.'

There was a cracking sound above our heads and we looked up. One of the windows around the base of the dome must have been open because a bird had got in and was now thrashing around in the dish of the ceiling, unable to understand how it couldn't fly through into the false heaven beyond the painted figures. We watched as it grew increasingly panicked.

'What can we do?' I said.

'I'm not sure there is anything.' Lucas craned up. 'It's too high to reach, even if we had a net or something. We'll just have to hope it finds its way back out or comes further down.'

'I'll get dressed,' said Danny, going into his room.

We watched the bird for about a minute, its distress more and more obvious. Suddenly, with a great beating of wings, it swooped and for a moment I thought it had spied the open window. But instead of finding its way out, it threw itself against the glass. There was a dull thud, as if it had hit the windscreen of a car travelling at speed, and then it fell past us and landed below on one of the white flagstones. Lucas and I ran down to it.

It was clear at once that it was dead. It had fallen on its back, its legs bent up and its wings slightly splayed behind it. Its neck was twisted and it looked at us with one open bloodied eye. It was a robin. I pressed the back of my index finger against the red of its breast and felt the warmth of its tiny body. I looked round for Lucas and saw that he was some steps behind me. He was transfixed by the bird. He looked as though he was about to be sick.

'Are you OK?' I asked.

'Will you clear it up?' he asked, looking at me at last. 'There's a dustpan and brush and cleaning stuff in the cupboard next to the kitchen. I'm going upstairs for a moment.' He ran up the stairs past me and I heard his feet on the landings until he reached his room on the top floor. The door closed firmly behind him.

Danny passed Lucas on his way down and reached the hall as I returned with the dustpan and some old newspaper. 'What was all that about? Where's he gone?'

I indicated the bird, the blood around its eye quickly starting to congeal. 'I think it freaked him out.'

'Not like him to be squeamish.'

We parcelled the broken body up in the newspaper and cleaned the floor where it had fallen. Danny wanted just to put the packet in the dustbin but I couldn't. I took the door that Lucas and I had used the previous evening and went outside. The air was so cold I could taste it. I made my way gingerly down the icy steps at the side of the terrace, making sure each foot was firmly planted before moving the other. There was no handrail. When I reached ground-level, I crouched down and used the back of the little brush to dig a hole in the flowerbed that bordered the lawn. I laid the bird and its newspaper shroud gently inside and pushed the earth back over it. 'I'm sorry,' I said, although I wasn't sure why. As I stood to go back into the house, I saw Lucas watching from the window on the top floor. I raised a hand and he lifted his in response.

Lucas stayed in his room for almost an hour and so I gave up on looking round the house and sat in front of the fire with the others and read the paper. Danny lay across Martha, his head in her lap. 'You're getting it in my eyes,' he said, batting at the bottom of the review section she was trying to read.

'I'm not an armchair,' she said.

'True,' he said, wriggling down further.

Michael was using the phone in the hall to ring work. Clearly his boss was aggravated by his absence from the office: I could hear the defensive tone in the polite words that reached us through the open door. I wondered what it was like to have a job that meant being almost permanently available. Despite Michael's assertion that it was nightmarish, I thought it must be exciting sometimes to work at that level.

'I don't know why he puts up with it,' said Danny, shifting slightly.

'We can't all be like you,' said Martha. 'Some of us have to make an effort.'

Danny laughed, pleased with the answer. He was the first to acknowledge that he had no work ethic at all. His quicksilver brain allowed him to do the bare minimum required of him and at the last minute. Sailing so close to the wind seemed to inspire him. At university Rachel had told us that after the sketchiest readings of texts he would come up with insights that completely annihilated the opinions of the rest of their tutorial group, who had toiled over the books for days. We suspected the same was true of his job. He never seemed to be at the office. Lucas would often get calls from him in the middle of the day from parks and cafés by the river

29

or record shops. And yet he had been promoted way above his contemporaries at the ad agency. The quicksilver approach was ideal. Advertising didn't need someone who laboured; it needed someone who, having stared out of the window for most of the meeting, would casually deliver the definitive slogan, the one that the public would adopt into current parlance as naturally as if it was a figure of speech handed down from their parents. He had done it twice and on two of the agency's biggest and highest-profile campaigns, once for a vodka that was now the most ordered brand in the country and once for a new soft drink being launched in the UK by a major American manufacturer. His position as the agency's youngest VP was assured, as was a salary I couldn't imagine seeing before I was fifty, if ever.

We made sandwiches and ate them by the fire. Lucas was still subdued but brushed me away, saying he was fine. At a little past three o'clock, he stood up decisively. 'Come on,' he said. 'I want to show you all the garden before it gets any darker.'

'What are these other doors?' asked Michael, as we went down the corridor.

'That's a smaller sitting room, more like a den; this one goes into the pantry, but there's another door to it that runs off the kitchen. That' – he pointed to the last room before we got to the outside door – 'is the flower lobby.'

'Flower lobby?' asked Greg.

'For arranging the flowers for the house.'

In the thickening afternoon light the garden was eerie. The ice hadn't really loosened its grip during the day but I had the sense nonetheless that the garden was bracing itself once more against the coming night. There was silence.

'It's beautiful, isn't it,' said Lucas, looking out across it.

We picked our way down the stone steps and set off across the lawn, the compounded frost on the grass crunching under our feet. Our breath puffed out, feathered and vanished. I shoved my hands in my pockets; even with gloves on, they were quickly cold. After three or four minutes we reached the edge of the lawn and the beginning of the wood. The afternoon was more advanced under the trees. In the gloom I could make out a tangle of undergrowth and fallen branches. It was an old, natural wood; there were different types of trees and no pattern in the way they were planted. Now and again the breeze rushed the bare branches and sent them clattering above us like an ironic round of applause. I pulled my coat around me.

'Cold, Jo?' asked Lucas.

'No, it just looks a bit spooky.'

'More like something out of a fairy tale, you mean. Hansel and fucking Gretel. You could get lost in there and never be seen again. Come on, let's go.' Danny started to walk away.

'The wood is one of my favourite things here,' Lucas said. 'If you walk in a bit, there's a river. It's not that wide but it's great for swimming in the summer, really deep. You can even dive. It's probably frozen now, though.'

'Come on, man,' said Danny again. 'Let's go.'

We followed the edge of the wood around the perimeter of the lawn until we reached the back of the house. Behind it was the walled garden I'd seen from the kitchen window and beyond that an apple orchard. Lucas took us through the kitchen garden and past two old-fashioned wooden-framed greenhouses. There was the low hum of a generator. I looked through the glass to see vines with elephantine trunks and glossy green leaves. 'There'll be grapes later on. He looked after them himself, wouldn't let anyone touch them.'

The path took us to the gravel drive at the front. Lucas looked at his watch. 'It's a quarter to four now. I'm going to go and start cooking so why don't you walk down to the pub in the village? We'll have a drink in the library before dinner.'

'Lucas, you can't stay up here and cook on your own while we're at the pub. Do you want me to help?' Michael asked.

31

'No, you go; I like cooking on my own. Be careful on your way back up – it'll be very dark. You'll be fine, though: Jo can navigate by the stars.' He touched me lightly on the arm. 'See you later.' He walked up the path and disappeared through the front door.

The White Swan had the forlorn look of a place that had had its Christmas decorations up too long. There was something of the ageing showgirl about the tree in the corner: a good proportion of its needles had dropped and the wink of its lights suggested a desperate eleventh-hour invitation. Along the beams blue and purple tinsel sagged between drawing-pins. A young guy in a baseball cap and empty-looking jeans was feeding the slot machine, his left leg jiggling with the skittering of lights across the display. The publican, a tired-looking middle-aged man, made our drinks and pushed a fistful of packets of crisps across the bar. 'You from the Manor?' he asked and gave an upwards half-nod when we confirmed it. 'Poor bugger.' It wasn't a conversation either side seemed inclined to continue so we thanked him and took our drinks to the table in the corner. I guessed that what went on at the Manor was the subject of much village speculation. At the mention of the place, the fair-haired man hunched over the paper at a small table in the inglenook looked up at once and scrutinised us. I looked back at him. His eyes were a burnt-out paraffin blue. He met my gaze and quickly returned his attention to the paper.

'You'd think Lucas would be a bit happier about suddenly having all this money, wouldn't you?' said Danny, throwing his cigarettes on to the table.

'Would you? He had to lose someone he loved to get it,' said Rachel.

'That was ages ago.'

'What do you mean?' I was horrified. 'It was October, and Patrick and Lucas were so close. Patrick was like a father to him, you know that.'

32

Danny shrugged.

'Are Lucas's parents still alive?' asked Greg.

'No,' Rachel said. 'His father died years ago, when Lucas was nine or ten.' She looked at me, a question in her eyes. I nodded. 'Greg, only Lucas's close friends know this but it's probably best if you do, too. His father killed someone.'

He frowned. 'What do you mean?'

'He was an alcoholic,' I said. 'The day he died he was drink-driving. He hit someone, then crashed the car.'

'Lucas won't ever talk about it. His mother died last year, in the summer. She had cancer,' I said.

'Jesus. The poor man,' said Greg.

'He won't talk about his mother either,' Danny went on. 'They were really tight,' he explained. 'I mean, she was nice and everything, as much as you saw of her, but she was quite distant. It was like she and Lucas lived in a fantasy world together. It was only really Patrick they allowed near them. Bit weird.'

It was true that Lucas's relationship with his mother had been intense but I knew that it was quite common for children, especially boys, to try to fill the place of a missing parent and become a surrogate adult. It was also true that he had never talked much about Claire. Part of the reason, I suspected, was because he was very protective of her but sometimes in the past, when I had tried to bring up the subject and he deflected my questions, it occurred to me that perhaps by not talking about her he was almost selfishly keeping her to himself, making sure that no one else could know her or own her as he did. He was proud of her and her books – there was another full collection of them in the drawing room at the house, the titles large in their angular gothic script – and his own ambition to write was inspired by her. But she had been very reserved and at times I wondered whether Lucas might not have been more confident and easy-going if he'd had a mother with a lighter heart.

33

'Lucas is just quite private,' I said, feeling the need to defend him. 'His mother and Patrick were his world.'

'I think that's a bit reductive,' said Danny. 'What about us? I've been friends with him for years.'

'Was his mother successful?' Greg asked. 'As a writer?'

'Depends what you mean by successful,' I said, watching as he curled his hands around his pint glass, his hand able almost to span it. 'She had a following but most of her fans were adults. The books are actually very sad. There's always a missing parent – normally a missing father. And they're really dark. She didn't make much money, though, which is why having all this is a bit of a shock for Lucas.'

'Who did he spend Christmas with?' asked Michael.

'An old friend of Patrick's, somewhere near here, I think,' I said.

Danny ran his hand through his indie-singer hair and surreptitiously checked himself out in the smoked-glass mirror above my head. Wherever he woke up, he liked to give the impression that he'd just fallen out of bed in a studio in Hoxton. One of the things that had always fascinated me about his appearance was the dark shadowing around his eyes, like thick and expertly applied kohl. It made his eyes especially startling. 'Well, however you look at it, it's an amazing old place,' he said.

'Do you think it'll change him?' Martha asked.

'No,' he said emphatically.

'I hope not,' I said. 'Anyway, you know Lucas. If there's anything he believes in, it's achieving things for yourself.'

'Why bother? He probably never needs to work again.'

'It's called integrity, Danny.' Rachel laid a reassuring hand on his. I held my breath but he flashed her a smile. None of the rest of us, except Lucas of course, could have got away with a comment like that.

I lit a cigarette and took a long drag. I'd spoken to Lucas about work the evening before and he assured me that he had no intention of giving up his job. 'No,' he said. 'I've invested too much. Two years at law school, two more as a trainee and three since then. It would be stupid to leave before I really get anywhere. Anyway, I've got a point to prove.' He grinned. 'Patrick said I wouldn't do it because it was too boring but I told him I wanted a normal job. Now I have to show him.'

I didn't question his need still to do that. Although I knew I should try to talk to him about Patrick, and that maybe he was waiting for me to ask, I was finding it difficult to bring up the subject in any but the most glancing of ways. I didn't have the equipment to do it. His bereavement moved him away from me. Not in the sense that he had become with-drawn, although he had a little. It was more that, with my family complete, I felt I didn't have the right to try to empathise. In fact, I felt guilty for being unscathed.

Chapter Three

'I couldn't remember whether you liked olives or not.' Lucas handed me up a Martini, its surface tilting dangerously in the wide-rimmed glass. A single glossy olive was threaded on to a cocktail stick balanced across it.

'I'm learning to.' I put it in my mouth and pulled it off the stick with my lips. I felt suddenly self-conscious as I realised he was watching me.

I was sitting on the top step of the library ladder, high enough to give me a perspective on the room. One of the things I liked about Lucas was the trouble he took to make sure other people enjoyed themselves. He had been keen on drama at university and I sometimes thought that that creativity, firmly bottled in his professional life, was now channelled into his hospitality. When we had come down-stairs after changing for dinner, the library door was open for the first time. A rosy light fell a few paces out into the hall and Nina Simone's 'Sinnerman' was playing. Lucas, wearing a black corduroy jacket that gave him an air of the Left Bank and with a cigarette tucked into the corner of his mouth, had been mixing the drinks.

Even by the standards of the rest of the house, the library was an imposing room. Two walls were lined entirely with bookshelves that reached to the ceiling and were policed by ladders that moved across them on runners. At the near end of the room there was a large circular desk with two green glass reading lamps on it and at the other, in front of windows now masked by heavy tapestry curtains, there were leather armchairs in which Greg and Michael were sitting. Martha perched on the arm of Michael's chair, her arm along the back of it behind his head. Danny and Rachel were looking at the picture on the opposite wall, a nude of some proportions.

'New shoes?'

'What? Oh these.' I looked down at my feet, hooked over a lower step. My shoes were black ponyskin with two small diamanté buckles at the front. I was wearing them with fine-mesh fishnet tights. 'Yes.'

'I like them.' Lucas reached out his hand and with the pad of his index finger stroked the arch of my left foot where the leather was cut away.

I am sure my surprise showed on my face.

He drained his glass and balanced it carefully on the edge of the shelf. 'I'm going to get the starter ready. Can you get everyone to come through to the dining room in about five minutes?'

I stayed on the ladder and finished my drink. I was flushed and I could still feel his touch on my skin. There had been a time when there had been nothing I wanted more than for him to touch me in a way that suggested he found me attractive. Now it seemed possible that he might but so much had changed.

If he was trying to make me think differently about him, why now, after all this time, I wondered. There was so much more at stake. At university we could have tried it out and, if it hadn't worked, allowed a few weeks, a term, and gone back to being friends. Now we had history. We were at an age where former relationships were layered up on us like coats of old paint: if you chipped a surface you could see the unflattering shades that had gone before. Our ten years, more, of friendship had endured all that. It was worth a huge amount to me, too much to put in jeopardy unless I thought there was a chance that it might be right. And although none of us at the house were settled or even heading that way – except Rachel and Greg, maybe – other friends were getting married, buying houses, having children. It was not a time to get things wrong.

And what if I had misread him? A decade of being friends meant we touched each other without thinking now. It hadn't been like that in the beginning; neither of us were naturally tactile people and, as we did get to know each other better, the question of attraction meant we were wary of physical contact, at least until the night he found me with his roommate. For about six months after that we skirted each other hyper-solicitously and then slowly eased into our current familiarity. Perhaps he was now so relaxed with me that it didn't occur to him that I might interpret his stroking my foot as flirtatious.

Then again, if Lucas was showing me his heart and I didn't respond, I might never be given another opportunity. Although at eighteen, through the screen of my own self-consciousness, I'd thought he must have realised he was attractive, I knew now that wasn't true. He had never been confident with women.

'What are you brooding about up there?' said Martha. 'Come and join the party.'

'Actually, I think supper will be ready now,' I said, climbing down. 'Shall we go in?'

After the library, the hall was chill on my bare arms but there was another fire in the dining room. The flames cast a flickering glow on a mahogany table that stretched almost the length of the room and whose surface was so highly polished that there seemed to be two of everything on it, glasses, cutlery and the three silver candlesticks that marked the centre like masts on a schooner. The air was filled with the warm scent of burning wood and roasting meat. Against the back wall there was an antique sideboard with a tray of liqueurs and Benares-ware bowls of oranges and nuts.

Lucas put his head round the door next to it, which led from the kitchen. 'Danny, why don't you take that end of the table, Rachel and Greg on either side of you, Michael and Martha in the middle, then Jo and I?'

There was asparagus soup to start, then a huge joint of glistening beef that Lucas carved into slices so fine they were almost translucent. There were bowls full of roast potatoes, green beans, calabrese, parsnips, carrots. Horseradish circulated in a tiny silver cauldron with a blue-glass inside.

'You've outdone yourself, mate,' said Danny, spooning another couple of potatoes on to his plate.

There were five or six bottles of wine on the table and, though I was drinking quickly, my glass never seemed to get emptier. All the time we were eating I was aware of Lucas next to me as if I could feel the heat of his body. Down the table Michael was telling one of his ludicrous anecdotes involving colleagues of his and bonding visits to City strip clubs. Martha and I still found it amazing that he got taken along on these jollies but he was obviously popular on the teams he worked with and was dragged along for the fun, regardless of the fact that he wasn't at all interested in the dancers. Rachel was laughing, her head tipped right back, displaying her long neck and bringing her small breasts higher in her dress, a fact that hadn't escaped Danny, who was leaning in dangerously, ostensibly to hear better.

'It's going to be very hard to go home after this,' I said to Lucas.

'Come back at the weekend,' he said, topping up my glass again. I looked at his hand as it held the bottle, twisting it to avoid spilling any. He had very deft hands; he could shuffle a pack of cards like no one else I knew. They were lovely to look at, too, with long straight fingers and rounded nails. Artist's hands, Martha said.

'Jo,' he said. 'Come and have a cigarette with me.' He pushed back his chair and dropped his stiff cotton napkin on to the seat.

'Where are you two going?' asked Rachel, looking up.

'Outside for a cigarette.'

'Can't we smoke in here?'

'Of course you can.'

We went out on to the terrace, just as we had the evening before. I was glad to have the coat that Lucas had taken from the stand in the hall for me, despite the smell of dust on it. I wasn't sure, it might have been accidental, but I think that as he had helped me put it on his fingers had very lightly stroked the nape of my neck. The skin there still tingled. Again, the cold and silence outside made everything hyperreal, the stretch of lawn and the trees beyond all washed in pallid moonlight. We sat down on the balustrade and I swung my legs over, careful not to snag my tights.

'Cigarette?' He lit two and passed me one of them. The cold had sobered me up a bit and I was surprised when he suddenly took my spare hand. I felt the pressure of our fingers against each other. 'You're freezing,' he said and slipped my hand inside his jacket, holding it against his chest. Very faintly, I could feel his heartbeat. I looked up at him. He was watching me intently, as if he were trying to read my face.

Then he kissed me. He rested his lips very gently on mine, nearly motionless, testing to see if I would pull away. Almost imperceptibly, he moved up so that my top lip was between his. Little by little, he increased the pressure and then we were kissing properly. I had imagined it so many times I could hardly believe it was happening. He moved his leg back over the balustrade so that he was astride it and pulled me closer to him, his lips hardly leaving mine for a second, his hands pressing against the small of my back. I dropped my cigarette behind me and put my arms around him, feeling the furrows of his cord jacket under my hands.

He pulled away and took both my hands in his, holding them in the triangle of space between his knees and my thigh. We looked at each other sombrely, then smiled.

'I've wanted to do that for a very long time,' he said, making my stomach jump.

He pulled me back to him and we kissed again. Now the surprise was fading, I had a hunger for him. I wanted to fill up my senses with him, taste him, hoover up the smell of him, run my hands all over him.

We stayed outside as long as we reasonably could. When we got back in, the others had made coffee. Rachel pulled out the chair next to her for me. 'So?' she said, *sotto voce*.

'What?'

'You and Lucas. Spill the beans. Or at least tell me whether he made the first move.'

I couldn't help it; even though I wanted to keep it between Lucas and myself, I smiled and gave the game away. 'Yes, he did,' I said quietly.

'At last. I had almost given up hope of it ever happening.' She put a cup on a saucer for me and filled it from the pot. 'He's talked to me about you for years.'

I looked at her in astonishment. 'Why did you never say anything?'

'Not my secret to tell.'

It was very late by the time the others went to bed. Greg and Rachel were first, then Michael and Martha, who collared Danny and took him upstairs, picking up an open bottle of red and pressing it into his hand by way of persuasion. Lucas took a decanter from the sideboard and we went back to the library.

The fire had almost gone out but he coaxed it back to life with bellows and another round of kindling and small coals. I sat down on the rug and took the half-inch of whisky he handed me, twisting the cut-glass tumbler so that it glinted

41

with the light of the new flames. The first sip burned my throat.

Lucas sat down next to me. 'Did you notice the others watching us?' he asked. 'When we got back in, I thought I was going to die laughing. I've never seen such poor attempts to act normally.'

'Rachel was on to us,' I said.

'They all were. They were monitoring us so closely I was beginning to feel like the subject of an MI5 investigation.' He kissed me and pulled away again with a big smile.

I had another sip of the whisky and kept it in my mouth, breathing over it to feel how it burned. I liked the glow it left when I finally swallowed. Kissing Lucas felt a bit like smoking on my sixteenth birthday: I knew I could now but the glamour of having not been able to still lingered.

'Are you happy?' he asked. 'Is this all right with you?'

'You look worried,' I said.

'I don't want to get it wrong. It's too important.'

I rubbed my cheek against his, my nose in his hair. He smelled of cooking. 'You won't,' I said. 'You can't.'

The bumps and laughter upstairs stopped as the others went to sleep and the night took over. Little by little the house closed in around us. Lucas had turned off the lamps so the only light we had came from the fire and the two candles on the mantelpiece.

'I've hated every single one of your boyfriends. None of them seemed to realise what they had. And I wanted to hit them when they hurt you.'

'Why didn't you say something earlier?'

'I know you, remember. You're very single-minded. I thought that if you wanted me there's no way I wouldn't know about it. Like the Mounties . . .'

'I always get my man,' I finished. 'That's rubbish. You only get the things you're not afraid to go after.'

'Maybe it's the house,' he said.

42

'Yes, now you're a man of property I'm prepared to consider you,' I said.

'That's not what I mean.' He pulled away from me, picked up the poker and started stabbing at the embers. 'Being here makes me think you should go for what you want, stop wasting time.'

'*Carpe diem*,' I said. 'But why now?' I laughed at my bit of drunken wit but then saw the look on his face.

'Life's short, Jo. No one seems to realise. We act like we've got all the time in the world.'

He lit a cigarette without offering me one and looked straight ahead into the fire. 'I've never told you about my father,' he said suddenly.

Immediately the rushing sensation I'd experienced the previous evening started up again in my ears. 'How do you mean?'

'I've never told anyone the truth about it and I still don't want people to know. It feels important that you do now, though.'

I said nothing and waited for him to go on. There was dread in my stomach suddenly, its cold weight like a stone.

He turned and looked at me. His face was grave. 'My father wasn't killed, Jo.'

'What?' Now I was confused. 'How do you mean?'

'I always told you that he died in the accident that day but he didn't – or not how you think.'

'I don't understand.'

'He committed suicide, too. Both my dad and my uncle.' He put his hand over his face, covering his eyes. 'I mean, fuck.'

'Lucas . . .'

'Oh, some of the original story is true. It's true that he was pissed and that he was driving back from the pub in the village and he ran a man over, or hit him, I don't know. The one sure thing is that Dad vanished. He abandoned the car

43

and disappeared. We never heard from him again. He left his wallet with all his cards and his bank accounts were never touched. Patrick tried for years to find out what happened. After the police failed to come up with anything, he tried private detectives and looking himself but he never found a trace. Dad must have been so frightened and ashamed of what he'd done that he took himself off somewhere and committed suicide. Maybe he just walked into the sea.'

'Lucas . . .'

'Mum kept looking for him. She wouldn't give up. After two or three years Patrick told her that she should stop and that she was hurting herself by refusing to believe he was dead, in the face of all the evidence. He thought it would be best to have him declared dead so she could at least get some closure on it but she wouldn't do it, just in case. In the end he said the one thing that could convince her.'

'What?'

'That Dad had to be dead because if he'd been alive he would have come back to her. She knew that was true. Even if he had had to lie low for a while, he would have found his way back to her.'

My eyes were full of tears. 'Why haven't you ever told me this?'

'Because it was easier not to. Because I was ashamed. I mean, if you're killed in an accident, even if you cause it, it's out of your control, isn't it? But if you kill yourself, it's worse for your family. He abandoned us by choice. We still loved him but he chose to leave us.' He looked up and I saw that his eyes were wet, too. 'I always used to wonder whether, if I'd been different, he might have thought I was worth staying for.'

'Oh Lucas, don't think that. It's not true.'

'I find it so hard that everyone wrote him off as an alcoholic waste of space. I still loved him. He was still my dad. And now Patrick's done it, too.'

I held him silently, feeling him tremble through the layers of shirt and jacket. Over his shoulder I looked out into the darkness that had settled over the room like mustard gas. I had been completely uprooted by the evening: first the seismic shift in our relationship and now this new revelation. I tried my old trick, attempting to anchor myself in the real world by concentrating on the solidity of material things but the room seemed unwilling to help me. The furniture wouldn't pull itself out of the darkness. It stayed back, identifiable only here and there where the gleam of the fire and the candles landed on it. I hadn't imagined it. There was something here, in the house, something unhappy. I felt a sudden need to protect Lucas from it and what it might do to him. And us. On the one hand, the house had finally brought us together. But on the other, it was the cradle for this terrible secret. I could only hope that it didn't have the power to destroy what it had so recently created. Although this had taken me by surprise, I wanted us to have a chance.

Chapter Four

My office was on the first floor of a purpose-built sixties block on a side street in Putney, about ten minutes' walk from the river. I smiled at the girl at the desk as I crossed the entrance hall to the stairs. I didn't recognise her but that was nothing new: the receptionists for our building were temps on the whole, mostly Australians and Kiwis who did two or three weeks and moved on, either to another job or another city. I wondered sometimes what it would be like to drop everything to go travelling but I knew I never would. The office was on a street of small local shops but now and again in my lunch hour I walked down to Putney Bridge and looked east over the muddy water racing under me to the City. Even as a child I had wanted to work on Fleet Street, in the days when the printing presses shook the ground itself in the afternoons. By the time I was old enough to work in newspapers, their offices had moved further east to Wapping and Canary Wharf but I hadn't yet given up on the idea.

If the receptionists were temporary, upstairs it was a different story. The editorial staff of the *Putney Gazette* was long service personified and even with my three years there I was the new girl. The editor, Stephen Thomas, joined shortly after I did, which meant, unhappily, that he regarded me as part of the recalcitrant old guard.

The paint on the wall up the stairs was scuffed, which I

hadn't noticed before. In fact, the whole place needed painting. I pushed open the door to the office. Somehow I expected it to have changed in the ten days I'd been away over Christmas, shifted on its axis in the same way as other aspects of my life had, but it was all exactly as it had been, even down to its smell, the aroma of gently ageing newsprint.

I stayed at the *Gazette* because I was determined to wrest some career benefit from my time there. After university I hadn't been able to afford to do the year's post-grad journalism certificate so I'd got a job on a magazine for people in the travel industry. The staff there were nice but after a couple of years I'd woken up to the fact that I was still doing the listings pages and not a lot else. I started looking around and finally got my junior reporter's job at the *Gazette*. Having managed it, it now seemed stupid to leave without at least having a decent selection of cuttings to show a new employer. My mother, who applauded tenacity even in situations where most right-thinking people would cut their losses, agreed that staying was the thing to do. Over Christmas, however, my father had poured me a sherry and asked whether I'd seen any jobs worth applying for. He would never say as much but it had been enough to tell me he was disappointed I wasn't making more progress.

I sat down at my tiny Formica desk and switched on the computer. Jane was standing on a wobbling chair taking down the cards from local businesses and advertisers and tossing them into the bin.

'Good Christmas?' I asked.

'Very nice,' she said. 'We had my mother over and then we spent New Year in Reading at Terry's sister's.'

I told her I'd spent the holiday in the New Forest with my parents. It was largely the truth. In the office the memory of my New Year at Stoneborough became surreal. That house, the art, the grounds, getting together with Lucas – it seemed like a fantasy even to me; it would sound ridiculous spoken

47

about here among the cheap office furniture and the pervasive second-best atmosphere of the place.

I often felt that I was living my life in a lift stuck between floors. On the one hand there was the world of the office and also of my family that, although well-read and liberal, was cash-limited by my parents' teaching careers. On the other were some of my friends with their money and the sophistication that had been second nature to them by eighteen. The savoir faire that Danny had had at university eluded me even now. Initially, fresh from Hampshire and feeling green, I put it down to his having grown up in London but I had isolated other sources from which the sophisticates had drawn their self-assurance. The most obvious was money, of course. Lucas had never been like some of the others and I attributed part of that to his not having grown up rich, with the associated expectation of how the world should treat you.

I opened Outlook. Apart from spam, there were no new emails in my inbox; the most recent were to do with family arrangements and meeting friends for drinks before the holidays. It already seemed a long time in the past. I was disappointed not to have a message from Lucas confirming dinner that evening but told myself firmly that he must be very busy.

After the meeting to discuss the week's paper, I started writing up the most recent wedding reports, the sort of undemanding job I could do when I was thinking about something else. Since Lucas had told me about Patrick and his father, I had been turning the information over in my mind as if it were a Rubik's Cube. It wasn't hard to understand why his father committed suicide: after all, he'd killed a man. Patrick, however, was a mystery. Lucas had said little beyond what he'd first told me. I had lots of questions but it hadn't seemed right to ask them.

I thought about Patrick's memorial service in November. It had been a wet day in London, the sky sodden, the grey of the clouds a perfect match for the drab concrete of the buildings and the wet streets. A gusting wind had made carousels of litter and snatched at the hats of the women who gathered on the steps outside St Thomas's in Mayfair, five minutes' walk from the gallery on Cork Street where, four weeks earlier, the man whose life they had come to remember had been working. The church had been full, to the point where latecomers had no choice but to stand at the back. I wondered how many of them had been real friends. The newspapers had been running the story all week: the charismatic kingmaker of the art world brought low. The archives had yielded enough material to whip the mid-market tabloids into a moralising frenzy, Patrick's suicide painted as the only fitting end for a life such as his. I'd read the pieces every day, furious for Lucas that something that affected him so deeply could be offered up for the entertainment and self-satisfied judgement of those who had never even met Patrick. So what if he had been extravagant? He'd made a lot of money at an age where he'd wanted to enjoy it. What if his group had always been surrounded by women? And perhaps one of his artists had been a heroin addict; surely that couldn't have been unique in the art world?

We had all taken the day off work to support Lucas. Rachel and Michael were sombre but Martha was angry and I had to tell her to keep cool about the paparazzi standing on the pavement on the opposite side of the road, their cameras hungry for the famous faces they knew would come. 'Blood-sucking bastards,' she said. 'He's dead. Isn't that enough?'

I hovered near Lucas as he welcomed people and thanked them for coming. Among the impeccably dressed and wealthy, there were several prominent figures. I saw a very well-known Labour MP and a former BBC foreign correspondent, as well as Louis Finch, the hot black actor everyone was talking about. There were also a number of elegant women who looked familiar but who I couldn't name. Ill at ease in the formal clothes required by the occasion were a number of bohemian-looking types who I took to be artists, either Patrick's own or friends of his. There was also the cleaning lady from his London house whom I had met when I went to meet Lucas there once. She gave him a hug.

Danny was great that day, I had to admit. He was restrained but efficient, handing out orders of service and showing people to their seats, even if the level of his involvement did cause some confusion. 'I'm so sorry for your loss,' I overheard one of the glamorous middle-aged women say to him. 'I know how close you were.'

'Thank you,' Danny had said seriously before catching my look over her shoulder and hurriedly moving away.

Inside, a dim underwater light had filtered through the stained-glass windows but did little to illuminate the dark wooden pews and many unlit recesses. It smelt richly of dust and the Establishment; I could imagine Patrick undercutting the formality of it all with a levelling remark. Lucas gave a tribute and my heart had ached for him as he stood at the lectern in front of all of those people, holding it together for them when it was he who was most in pain, now left completely alone in the world by his family. I had tried not to notice the tremor in the paper on which he had written his notes.

I hadn't known much about Patrick's previous life apart from the few facts that had made their way into the newspapers; he seemed like someone who had been born just as he was. It had almost been a surprise to find that there had been a process involved in becoming that version of him. From Lucas's tribute I learnt that Patrick had grown up in Northamptonshire, one of two sons of a local businessman, and had been educated at grammar school and then Cambridge, where he read English. Shortly after university he met Simon Harcourt, who had started work on his *Elysium* series of oil paintings. Patrick offered to represent him and when Harcourt became a success, other artists began to approach him.

Lucas described Patrick as the first of a new breed of art dealer, an entrepreneur who had set up his gallery by his mid-twenties, championing off-beat unknowns and making them stars. One of his protégés, as I had known, was Thomas Parrish, a major British player of the seventies and eighties, whose work hung in Tate Modern.

'Come on, wake up. You've got to stop daydreaming, Joanna,' said Stephen, as he dropped a batch of local-council documents on my desk. 'About the pedestrianisation of South Street. Not particularly exciting but all part of serving an apprenticeship, eh?'

I had to go, I thought, picking up the papers. This had to be the year I left the *Gazette*. My apprenticeship had become an elephant's pregnancy.

The place Lucas had chosen was in Soho. There was a small reception area at street-level but the restaurant itself was at the bottom of a long flight of stairs. It had clearly been a cellar of some sort originally; the room consisted of small alcoves serviced by a central hub from which the waiting staff operated. The murmur of voices and some gentle oriental music were the only things I could hear. It was a classic seduction venue and the thought both horrified and thrilled me.

I was shown over to an alcove in the corner. Lucas was waiting for me, his dark head bent over the wine list. He had come straight from work and was wearing a suit, a look that I liked on him, although it impressed me less on other men. Lucas looked as if he had just come out of a successful meeting. Danny, on the other hand, who wore anything else with panache, always looked like a young offender before a court appearance if he wore a suit. Lucas stood as he saw me, smiled and gave me an ambiguous kiss close to my mouth. I made to sit on the couch opposite but he moved along and indicated that I should sit next to him. I lowered myself down carefully.

We made small talk in a way that I couldn't remember us ever having done before. Scrutinising the handwritten menu self-consciously, I felt a twinge as I realised the prices weren't included on it, then made a decision just to enjoy it and eat toast for the rest of the month if necessary.

'What do you think of it?' he asked, as our waiter silently retreated, having taken the order that Lucas, as the knowledgeable one, had given him.

'The restaurant? Wonderful – it's like having supper in a shrine.'

He picked up his napkin and pulled it out of its ring of woven reed. 'I came here with Danny once, a few years ago.'

'Danny?'

'You know what he's like. It was when I was at law school and really strapped. He'd just got that massive pay rise, do you remember, a couple of months after the vodka campaign? He used to take me to all sorts of crazily expensive places.'

'He's such a show-off,' I said. I had my own views on why Danny was so lavish towards Lucas. He'd once even taken him to Barcelona for a week. While I didn't doubt that he meant to be generous, I also suspected that he used his money as another way to promote his role as the senior partner in their relationship. I knew I did something similar with my younger brothers, albeit on a much smaller scale. While it was lovely to be able to treat them occasionally, it also made me feel good that I was in a position to do so.

'He's just over-generous. Now he won't have to be generous with me any more. But I'm glad he brought me here. Otherwise I wouldn't have known about it and I've had this fantasy since about coming here with a woman I was in love with.'

'So are you a regular?' I said, hoping that the jokiness of my tone would mask the seriousness of the question. It was a risk but I had to be sure.

'No.' If I hadn't known better, I would have described the expression that ran across his face as disappointed. 'This is the first time.'

'Flatterer,' I said, in my relief.

'That's not flattery.' He fixed me with one of his candid looks. I stared at him, unable to break eye contact. I was beginning to feel as if I were being fitted for new contacts, an optician dropping different lenses in front of my eyes every two seconds. Whenever I was getting used to the situation, Lucas upped the stakes. I wasn't sure how it worked, getting together with someone whom you'd been close to for a long time. Could you say straight away that you were in love?

'Jo.' He took my hand. 'I know this is all happening very quickly and I don't expect you to tell me that you love me but do you think you could fall in love with me?'

I looked at his large honest eyes and saw the entreaty in them. I thought of his kindness and his warmth and how much I had wanted him. 'Yes,' I said. 'I do.' A huge smile lit up his face.

The waiter brought over the first of our dishes, tiny spring rolls and dumplings like purses tied up with chives. I took a spoonful of the sweet chilli sauce.

'Can I ask you something?' I said.

'What is it?'

'Do you promise not to be insulted?'

'Within reason.'

'Is all this because . . .'

'Patrick's dead and I'm grieving?'

'Yes.'

'I wondered whether you would think that. I thought about it myself. I've tested myself – that sounds ridiculous, doesn't it? – to see if I think about this more when I feel really low. And I don't.' He took a sip of wine. 'I did think about you when it was bad and it helped. But I felt better just knowing you were around. I know some people might think

53

that a romantic thing is a stronger tie than friendship but I don't, not with you. You're my best friend.'

'Why didn't you ring me?'

'I needed to do it on my own. Everyone's grief is different, I think. Mine felt private.'

I nodded that I understood. It was consistent. Lucas would talk about the things that bothered him until they reached crisis point and then he would disappear. At college, towards the end, worried that he hadn't worked hard enough for finals and was going to let his mother and Patrick down, he vanished for four days without telling anyone, even me, where he was going. I hadn't been too concerned, knowing there would be a simple explanation, as in the end there was: he had booked into a guest house in Torquay to calm down and read Vergil's *Georgics*.

'Your cheeks are rosy,' said Lucas, reaching over and pressing the back of his finger on my face. I felt the blush deepen in response.

'It's the wine.'

'Not the company?' He smiled.

'Are you like this with all your girlfriends?' Once I had started the word rolling, there was no reclaiming it. It fell off my tongue like a stone. I had gone too far, too fast in my destabilised, confused frame of mind.

He didn't blink. 'No, just you.'

We left without having any green tea. Lucas wouldn't let me go Dutch on the bill; after a discussion, he let me put my card with his in the silk folder and then, after the waiter had gone off to swipe them, he handed mine back to me. 'You can get the cab if you feel so strongly about it,' he said.

Upstairs on the pavement, he took my face between his hands and kissed me. I didn't care that the street was still busy and people were walking past us: I wanted all those strangers to see. In the taxi, I pressed into his side, enjoying the feel of his arm around me. The idea of going to bed with

54

Lucas was unreal, in the way that something imagined over and over again can become. But I wanted to, I knew that. The rain had just stopped. Everything was slick and noirish and the wheels of the taxi fizzed in the water on the road as we wove quickly through Soho and into Bloomsbury. We pulled up outside Lucas's building and I paid the driver.

'I'll make some coffee,' he said, walking ahead of me to turn on the table lamp in the sitting room then doubling back to the kitchen. 'Put some music on.'

I skimmed along the rows of his CD collection, noticing the recent purchases. There were new records by a couple of bands he'd told me about, but now wasn't the time. I chose the Cowboy Junkies' *The Trinity Session*, which we'd listened to together over and over again.

Lucas's flat had been expensively furnished about thirty years previously and as a result reminded me of a beautiful woman for whom the impact of ageing was made bearable by good underlying bone structure. The leather on the arms of the sofa was worn through almost to the horsehair underneath but it was still the burnished brown of autumn leaves. He'd had the flat since we graduated and it had acquired a feel of home that my flats never did. Like Patrick, he had books everywhere, on shelves, in piles on the floor, open face-down on the armchair and by the phone, hardbacks, paperbacks, books I'd lent him, books he'd bought or borrowed from the library. Unlike Patrick, he only read fiction. We had a theory that serious non-fiction was something one grew into.

The walls were covered with old movie posters, originals that he bought and framed. Outside the bathroom door, the closest he could get it to the shower without steam damage, was a genuine *Psycho*, the most expensive of the collection.

Lucas brought the coffee and settled next to me on the lumpy sofa. He stretched out his arm and I slid along so that I was inside it. I heard the clock from the church two streets away gently chime midnight and thought to myself that I knew the room as though it were a person in its own right, from the draught under the door to the way the radiators ticked as they cooled. I slid down and lay along the sofa, putting my head on his lap. He stroked my hair, smoothing it back from my forehead. We listened to the album all the way through. I'm not sure but I suspected that as we listened Lucas was doing the same as me, remembering all the other times we'd heard it. When it ended, he bent down and kissed me. 'I'll get you a cab,' he said.

I hope I managed to control my face sufficiently to mask the storm of emotion that broke out in me. Even though a small part of me breathed a sigh of relief that the nerve-wracking event wasn't going to happen now, I still felt cheated, as if the promised end of the evening had been suddenly snatched away.

The next few minutes were a blur. He made the telephone call, helped me on with my coat and held my hand as we walked downstairs. Now I was anxious. Though Lucas didn't set great store by his own powers of attraction, I knew several pretty girls who would love to go out with him. Perhaps he'd had second thoughts about me. Perhaps now, when it started to become a reality, he didn't actually find me sexually attractive. Misery swept over me.

We were on the pavement before the cab arrived. I stamped my feet both to warm them and to create a distraction. Lucas was looking at me. Maybe he had been waiting for me to make the first move, to show that I wanted him. After all, he was the one who had kissed me first at Stoneborough. Perhaps he needed me to show him that I wanted him, too. Again I wondered about the protocol for getting together with your closest friend. Did all the years of friendship that went before cancel out the point of delaying sleeping together? After all, we hardly needed to get to know each other, did we? I pulled him close to me and kissed him but it was too late: the cab pulled up beside us. Lucas opened the door for me and kissed me again, another proper, passionate kiss. He stood and waved until we turned the corner.

The driver was listening to some pop music with lyrics in what sounded like Greek. He had a crude glass evil eye hanging from the rearview mirror on a piece of cord and I watched it swing as we made our way quickly back to West London. He didn't try to engage me in conversation, for which I was grateful.

Perhaps I was out of practice. After all, it had been almost a year since I had slept with anyone, my previous boyfriend, Rob. We'd met at a barbecue at Rachel's house. He was one of her sister's friends and we'd started talking and got on like a house on fire. Lucas had left early, I now remembered, though I hadn't thought anything of it at the time. Rob taught media studies and at first we'd had a lot to talk about, including music and films. After about six months, though, the conversation began to run dry. One evening when I was putting on my make-up before going out to supper with him, I realised that I was rehearsing things to talk about. I decided to give it a week or two to see if it improved but the same evening he told me that he had fallen in love with his flatmate, Sarah. Even though I'd known it wasn't right, I had been surprisingly shaken. I'd done what I always did, retreated into the group and waited for the pain to go away.

Lucas wouldn't hurt me, I knew. He would do everything in his power to make sure he didn't, even if things didn't work out between us. I told myself that that must have been why he hadn't asked me to stay. He didn't want to rush me or create pressure. It was typical of him. And it was a big step. There couldn't be any going back once we had been to bed together. But the impulsive side of me was disappointed that he had been able to do it. That side wished that he had dragged me to his room the moment we set foot in the flat. However much I tried to rationalise it, I couldn't dispel the feeling that if he'd really wanted me he would never have sent me home.

Chapter Five

When I woke at Stoneborough that Saturday, Lucas had moulded himself against me so that my body fitted inside the curve of his larger one as neatly as a layer in an onion. It was early. I could tell from the slow pattern of his breath on my shoulder that he was still sleeping and I shifted gently so that I could lie more comfortably without waking him. He murmured something uninterpretable and settled again.

It had been just five of us the previous evening, as Greg and Rachel had had to stay in London for dinner with one of Greg's new clients. We'd had supper in the kitchen and then taken our drinks through and sat around the fire in the drawing room. It was still early when Lucas and I made an exit.

'Be gentle with him, Joanna.' Danny hadn't been able to resist. Although I knew it was stupid, I flushed with embarrassment and couldn't think of a response.

'Please, Danny,' said Lucas. He squeezed my hand as he pulled the drawing-room door shut. 'Just ignore him.' I waited nervously in the hall while he set the burglar alarm, shifting my weight from foot to foot.

His room was next to mine on the top floor. He hadn't shown it to me when we did the grand tour. It was plain, done in white with white sheets on the bed, but taking up almost the whole of the wall opposite the bed was a painting that I recognised.

'Lucas, isn't that . . . ?'

'Not now.'

His hands moved over me surprisingly. At Stoneborough things were different, as if his personality changed subtly when he stepped over the threshold. I felt as if I were with someone bolder. There was no question about what was going to happen. His hands slipped into the back pockets of my jeans and held me hard against him as we kissed. After a while he pulled away and pushed me gently back on to the bed. My heart soared with relief at his obvious desire. He did want me and the knowledge turned me on, too. When we had taken off all of each other's clothes I took a second or two to look at him. His nakedness made the parts of his body I was familiar with from days at the beach and in the park look different. I could see the weight loss around his chest and stomach and it moved me, as if I could read his sadness on his body. He looked vulnerable.

I had fantasised – I was embarrassed to admit it even to myself – of how it would be with Lucas, whom at times I had allowed myself to think of as a soul mate. I had imagined all the closeness of our emotional relationship would transfer to the physical and there would be none of the awkwardness or fumbling around that reminded one of what a strange thing it was to have sex with someone. Instead it would be seamless, both of us knowing exactly what the other liked, and there would be none of the usual self-consciousness at being naked and utterly revealed to someone else. In fact, there had been a very awkward moment when Lucas had had to stop to find a condom and the pause had broken the spell. I caught his eye as he was putting it on. We looked at each other as if we were suddenly realising what we were doing and questioning whether we should. I winked at him then, to make him smile and dispel the tension. Things got a bit better after that and the second time had been an improvement again. I was sure it would be different as we got used to the idea.

I lay awake now for a while watching the morning brighten the window, enjoying the warmth of the bed and of his body behind me. After ten minutes or so, he stirred and I wriggled round so that we were facing one another. He opened his eyes and smiled at me. 'Morning,' he said, pushing a strand of hair out of my eyes. 'It's true then.'

'What is?'

'That you should never touch your idols. If I'd known you looked like this without make-up . . .'

'Bugger off.' I kicked him under the quilt.

He laughed and rolled over so that he was on top of me. He held my arms back above my head and kissed me; I worried for a moment about not having cleaned my teeth. 'I like waking up with you,' he said, pulling back. 'I'll make some coffee. Don't go anywhere.' He put on jeans and a jumper and padded out of the room. I watched his broad back disappear round the door.

I waited until the sound of his footsteps faded away then got out of bed and went to look more closely at the painting over the mantelpiece. It was a Goldstein, a piece that I had seen exhibited at Patrick's gallery some years before. Lucas, Danny and I travelled together from Oxford to London on the bus to go to the opening. Even though I had picked up a bit of self-confidence at university I remembered feeling gauche that night. We got the tube to Bond Street station and walked down. It was October and chill. The shop windows exhibited models wearing outfits of untouchable sophistication. Lucas was walking fast, excited about the paintings. He knew Goldstein from meeting him at Patrick's and had heard that the show was particularly good.

Cork Street was dominated by galleries. The majority of the ground-floor windows were plate glass, each embossed with the name of the artist currently on show there. There was traditional English and Islamic art, posters from Japan, some striking modern sculpture that loomed stonily behind the

60

darkened window of the gallery next to Patrick's. Light spilled out from the Heathfield on to the pavement. The place was full of metropolitan people, well-dressed men and women in elegant middle age, younger people, some of them artists, I guessed, in ensembles so outlandish they were walking installations in themselves. One woman was wearing a hat with a long green feather that trailed behind her, reaching almost to the floor. She had a quick, sharp way of turning her head and the feather flicked sinuously with her, like a whip. I was acutely conscious of my cheap black trousers and plain jumper.

Lucas had opened the door for me and ushered me inside. Patrick was near the back talking to a short man in an expensively cut suit, stooping gently to catch what he was saying. He saw Lucas almost immediately, excused himself and came over to swamp him in a bear hug. Lucas was over six foot but Patrick dwarfed him. He shook Danny by the hand and kissed me on the cheek.

'Good to see you again, Jo,' he said. 'Have a glass of wine and take a look around. It's extraordinary work, even by Goldstein's own standards. I'll be interested to hear what you think of it.' His naturalness put me at my ease at once.

That evening was like visiting a foreign country and I drank it all in, the paintings, the people, the gallery itself. It was a large white space, very bare. Even the doors looked like part of the walls, without detail and painted white to cause minimum distraction from the exhibits. Goldstein lurked in a corner, smoking incessantly, eyes inscrutable under enormous black brows. Patrick came over to talk to me later in the evening and explained in an undertone that he hated shows and only attended his openings under duress. Lucas told me that, in fact, even though he was American, Goldstein only came to his openings at Patrick's; he never turned up for his New York shows.

I remembered another conversation from that night. I had been standing a little apart, near the wall at the back, to allow

Lucas to speak to Patrick on his own. They were about fifteen feet away. Annoyingly, Danny hadn't seemed to realise why I'd moved; he had been carelessly chatting up a confident girl with a club-cut black fringe but as soon as he saw Patrick talking to Lucas he excused himself from her and joined them.

The room was hot and busy and I felt as if I had perhaps had one glass of champagne too many. I was about to seek out a chair when I heard a woman behind me ask her neighbour in a low voice, 'Isn't that Lucas Heathfield?'

'Yes. Not quite as beautiful as his father was, is he?' came the response, prompting me to a fierce protective surge.

'No, but I always preferred Patrick of the Heathfield brothers. Oh, I know Justin was the golden boy and beautiful in that very ephemeral way but the famous Patrick magnetism . . . I don't know many people who could have resisted if he'd turned his beam on them. And being the less handsome of the two didn't seem to cause him any problems when it came to women. God, do you remember?'

'But none of it mattered when he met her, though. Do you remember that? As soon as she came on the scene that was it for anyone else. Eclipsed was the word . . . Oh, there you are, darling. Did you buy it?'

The woman's husband had returned. I turned round and made to cross the room, eager to see who had been talking last. She was, I guessed, in her fifties but still very pretty. Her well-cut blonde hair and slight air of mischief gave her a look of Honor Blackman and she was wearing a cream pussy-bow shirt and dark suede trousers. I wondered if she had ever had a fling with Patrick. I wouldn't have blamed her. I wondered who they had been talking about, this woman who had eclipsed everyone else. I knew Patrick had had affairs with some very glamorous women. Lucas told me that he had seen the actress Marie St Jacques for a while, which impressed my father when I told him.

The paintings on show had been extraordinary. Huge

62

oblongs of colour, they dominated the place. They were landscapes in oils and the texture of the paint was like nothing else I'd seen. Modern in style, they showed seas and fields and woods under siege from weather. The one that now hung on Lucas's wall had been my favourite. It showed a wood in a storm but its focus was tight on the trees. The artist was right up against them, so that the bark on the individual trunks was visible. The thickness of the paint, almost a centimetre in places, gave an impression of the force of the storm. The picture looked wet with rain and it was as if the physicality of the artist had transferred to the canvas and showed in the way the branches bent tight against the wind. The palette was dark, a hundred shades of muted green and grey and brown.

I heard Lucas's footsteps on the landing and quickly got back into bed. He put two mugs of coffee on the bedside table and slid in next to me.

'I loved that painting,' I said.

'Patrick bought it for me.'

'Bought it for you?' I was shocked. I didn't know how much Goldsteins cost but I knew that he was extremely expensive.

Lucas looked at me. 'You know Mum wouldn't ever let him give us any money, even when we were really broke? He used to buy me things instead and then present it as a fait accompli.' He sipped his coffee. 'This was something else though. Most of his gifts were practical and usually I knew what he was planning. I didn't know about this until I came up here one weekend and then he made me promise never to tell her about it.'

'Why wouldn't she let him give her any money?'

'She was very proud. You should understand that. You'll never even let me buy you a cup of tea without a fight. You'll have to get used to it now, though.'

I pulled a face meant to convey indignation and

independence and he laughed, put his cup back on the table and pulled me down with him into the bed.

Later that morning Lucas took Danny, Martha and me round to the back of the house where there was a group of outbuildings around a small second driveway. A fringe of leafless beech trees filled the gaps in the skyline and had dropped a crust of seed cases that crunched underfoot. The earth under the gravel was frozen hard. The largest of the buildings was a barn with wooden double doors that reached almost up to its roof, but there were two lower buildings, one of which was open on one side and had old orchard ladders hanging horizontally on its wall. Parked under its cover was Patrick's car, a navy Jaguar XJS. Danny gave a low whistle and circled it, running his hand down the long sleek bonnet and peering through the driver's door at the dash.

'His car. Jesus, mate, why are you still driving the Renault 5?' he said.

'It doesn't feel right. Not yet.'

'It's yours now, isn't it?'

'I'm not ready.'

'Can I look inside?'

Lucas hesitated and then passed him the keys. 'Be careful, won't you?'

Danny opened the door and lowered himself into the leather driver's seat. Lucas moved to say something but stopped himself. Danny traced his fingers along the mahogany dashboard, examining the various knobs and dials. Suddenly the engine started and the white reversing lights came on. A gentle cloud appeared at the end of the exhaust pipe, as if the car was taking its first breaths of the January air.

'Danny, don't,' said Lucas over the hum of the engine.

'Just a quick one.' He turned to look over his shoulder and reversed the car out of the shed at speed. Martha and I hurried out of the way as he turned through a tight circle in the little yard.

'Danny,' shouted Lucas. 'You haven't passed your test.' He ran to block the way. I heard Martha gasp. We both thought that his legs would be broken. Somehow Danny stopped the car. Lucas angrily indicated to him to open the window. 'For God's sake, can't you listen to me? I said not yet.'

'All right, all right. I'll put it back.' Danny pressed the button and disappeared behind the glass again. He drove the car gently back into the shed. 'She was in safe hands. I don't know what you were worried about,' he said, getting out and throwing Lucas the keys. He stalked off back to the house.

'Was I being unreasonable?' Lucas asked me, after he locked the Jaguar up again. 'I just don't feel right using some of Patrick's things yet. The house is OK: I used to come and stay anyway. But driving his car . . .' He took his cigarettes from his pocket and lit one. He looked a little shaken. 'It's a question of respect, you know?'

I raised it with Danny later that afternoon, when I found myself temporarily alone with him in the drawing room. I chose my words carefully; there had been occasions in the past when I had suspected him of wilfully misconstruing me.

'Danny,' I said, pretending to flick through the newspaper, 'Lucas is quite sensitive about Patrick's things, you know.'

'Really?' His face showed polite concern but his voice was sarcasm distilled.

'I mean, the car . . .'

He laughed. 'Aren't you sweet? You've only been going out five minutes but already you're trying to protect him – and from me, of all people. Don't worry, Joanna, I'll always think about what's best for Lucas.'

'I didn't mean . . .'

He flung his paper down on the seat behind him. His eyes were glittering with anger. 'He's my best friend too, don't forget. I'm just as important to him as you are. If you do anything to hurt him, I'll make sure you hurt, too – and far worse.'

I was stunned. The threat – if I wasn't dreaming – was genuine.

'And in fact,' he said, 'shouldn't I be the one protecting him from you at the moment? It's a bit of a coincidence, isn't it, that you've been friends for years and then, hours after you see his new country house for the first time, you think it might be a good idea to try going out with him after all.'

'You can't think that.' I was horrified. 'You know I'm not like that.'

He looked at me with something not dissimilar to hatred. The shock must have shown on my face because suddenly he laughed and the bitterness in his expression was gone, the shift so quick that I might almost have imagined it. 'Of course not. I'm teasing you, Joanna – don't take everything so seriously.'

'Well, I have news,' said Michael, pushing his supper plate away and reaching for his cigarettes. He lit one and exhaled, looking up to make sure he had all our attention. 'I told my parents.'

'You mean, you came out to them?' Martha reached over and clutched his hand where it lay on the tabletop.

'Shit,' said Danny.

'How? What did you say?' I asked.

Michael had been leading his double life as long as I had known him. He was out to all of us, our other friends and everyone at work but he hadn't been able to tell his parents. Things were especially hard for him because he was an only child and his mother was keen for him to settle down and have children. She was a sweetly old-fashioned woman who longed to have another woman to chat to in the kitchen on family Sundays. Michael adored her and knew how deeply the truth of his sexuality would hurt her.

'John dumped me,' he said.

'What?' said Lucas. 'When?'

'The week after Christmas.'

'You didn't tell us. Last week, New Year's Eve . . .' I said.

'I thought we might sort it out.' He ran a hand over his soft blond hair. I noticed for the first time that it was beginning to recede.

'Oh Michael,' said Martha. 'Did he say why?'

'He said I wasn't committed. He said he couldn't be with me if there were bits of my life that I shut him out of. I met his parents and they were great. They made me feel welcome in their house, not like I was some hideous little homosexual. I really liked him. I thought maybe . . .' He shrugged.

'So when I was round at my parents', I lost my temper. I was helping Mum clear the table and I thought what a fantastic marriage they have. Nothing flashy, not high passion or drama, just respect and love and a sort of comfort. It's like an anchor. Their life is real, in a way that mine isn't. It made me really angry. I know that they want all that for me but I can't have it. Not their way, at least.'

'What happened?' asked Lucas.

'I just said it. It kind of burst out of me. "Mum and Dad, I am going to tell you something that you are going to hate. I'm gay." I've thought about how I was going to say it – if I was ever going to say it – for so many years. It was like an out-of-body experience or something. I could hear my voice saying the words.'

'Shit,' said Danny again. His face was free of any sign of the violent anger of earlier that afternoon. Instead he was watching Michael with a curious interest. I averted my eyes; his outburst had unnerved me to such an extent that I was finding it difficult to look at him longer than absolutely necessary.

'Yeah.' Michael flicked the ash from his cigarette into the ashtray. 'I swear Dad kind of faded. I'm not joking – he went grey. He dabbed his mouth with his napkin in this really prissy way then folded it up and put it on the table. Then he walked out.'

'Walked out?' I said.

'Of the house. He didn't come back while I was there.'

'What did your mother say?' asked Martha.

'She wouldn't stop crying. I sat with her for hours. She was like a dormouse or something, perched on the edge of the sofa with big red eyes, hunched over her handkerchief.' He ground out his cigarette. 'I put my arm round her at one point and she flinched. Can you imagine that?'

'Think what it would be like if I came out to my mother,' said Martha, trying to lighten his mood. 'She'd probably weep for joy. I don't think she's ever really forgiven herself for being straight.'

Michael smiled weakly. 'Swap you.'

'So what are you going to do?' said Lucas.

'To be honest, I don't know. I don't even want to speak to them at the moment. I'm having one of those weird times when you feel more mature than your parents. You know, when you can almost see their generation becoming obsolete?'

'My parents were obsolete many moons ago,' said Danny. 'Superseded by newer, shinier, more fashionable models.' He topped up Michael's glass and emptied the rest of the bottle into his own. 'Have a drink and try to take your mind off it. You were brave. You'll patch things up again in the long term.'

'I hope so. I'm not sure.'

I watched our images copying us in the glass of the French windows. The garden had been swallowed whole by the darkness and made a mirror backing. Greg and Rachel had arrived just after lunch and now Rachel dragged her chair over so that she was next to Michael. She was listening carefully to him, occasionally asking a question. Danny was standing behind Michael, his hand on his shoulder, conducting a loud conversation with Martha at the other end of the table. Greg was opening another bottle. I was impressed by how quickly he had become one of the group. I caught Lucas's eye in the glass and he winked at me.

*　　*　　*

We built up the fire and opened the bottle of port that Greg had brought up with him from London that afternoon. We pulled the two chesterfields forward so that they formed a V-shaped draught-break between us and the rest of the room. Danny sprawled on the rug like a cat. His T-shirt had ridden up, revealing three inches or so of flesh where his hips joined his jeans, and a faint fuzz of hair was visible tapering down from his navel and disappearing under the waistband. He was playing with the tiny wheel on the side of his new toy. As far as I knew, he'd never expressed the faintest interest in deep-sea diving but that hadn't stopped him spending a couple of thousand pounds on the state-of-the-art watch as a late Christmas present to himself. He'd explained to us earlier how it was waterproof to some depth totally irrelevant to a man who never got much wetter than in the bath.

I watched the fire as it blazed, even though the heat and the intense brightness dried out my eyes. Once again, it seemed to me that the house had closed in around the small area that we had staked out. I could feel it beyond the chesterfields and above us, huge and silent. It was Martha who started us on telling ghost stories. Whether she felt the same as I did about the house I wasn't sure but I couldn't imagine a better place for it.

The problem was that, when you've known people for a long time, you know all their stories. The first time I'd heard Martha's, about a couple who go camping in a wood in Maine, we ourselves had been camping. I'd been scared to death then but now, having heard it at least twice since, I wasn't frightened by it. I'm sure, too, that the reaction of the others to my story, about a widow haunted and then murdered by her dead husband, was exaggerated, both to reassure me that I'd done a decent enough job of telling it and also to convince themselves that they'd been spooked by it.

'My God, Jo, that is gruesome,' said Rachel, shivering as she always did.

'I've got one,' said Greg.

We settled down again, excited by the prospect of a new story. Lucas poured more port into my glass and his. Greg was opposite us on the other sofa. Rachel sat on the floor between his legs, her head tipped sideways so that her cheek rested on his thigh. They looked good together, the femininity of her face emphasised by the sheer heft of him. He waited until Lucas had put the bottle down and Danny had found a new position on the rug. When we were all still, he began. His voice was low and confidential.

'About three miles out of the village where my parents live in Worcestershire,' he said, 'there's an old house everyone says is haunted. It's a big place, Tudor, built in grey stone with leaded windows. No matter what time of day it is, it always seems dark. Even at night I've never seen any lights on there. It's surrounded by fields that are never cultivated but there's a stream running through them and sometimes a low mist rises up from it and hangs over them like a sort of shroud. No one ever stays there long. It seems to come on the market every six months and it's always advertised by estate agents in London, never locally. No one local would ever have bought it.'

I watched him as he spoke. He was absorbed in his tale, watching us as we watched him but distant at the same time, as if he were seeing the house in his mind's eye and describing it to us from the image. I'd thought of him as a scientist. It hadn't occurred to me that he would tell a good story, too.

'When I was a child and I used to ask my mother about it, she told me that there was no such thing as a haunted house. Even so, she always took the long way round to avoid that road when we were driving home at night.'

He looked round at us again, confident of our attention. 'The story went that there was a murder there in the seventeenth century. A local girl working in the kitchen had fallen in love with the man of the house and he with

70

her. They started an affair and, unsurprisingly, she got pregnant. The man panicked. He wasn't wealthy himself, most of the money was his wife's, and he knew if the truth got out, he would be destitute.

'To make matters worse, his wife had just announced that, after years of being unable to conceive, she herself was pregnant. The kitchen maid was desperate. She knew that her father would throw her out if he knew she was going to have a child out of wedlock. In the end, she confided in another of the kitchen maids. Their mistress sensed that something was wrong in the house and put this other girl under pressure until she had no choice but to reveal what was going on.

'When he was confronted, the man denied all knowledge of it and claimed the girl was mad. A story began to circulate, put about by the family no doubt, that she was a witch.'

'What happened?' said Martha, leaning forward.

'They put her through a trial, which found her guilty of witchcraft, of course, and then suffocated her to death in the village. They put her under a board and loaded it up with stones until she suffocated. She died and so did her unborn baby.'

'My God,' I said, unable to stop myself.

Greg trained his gaze on me, watching me until my odd shyness of him came to the fore and I had to look away. 'But she hadn't finished with him,' he said. 'Soon people started to say that, late at night, you could hear breathing in the house, sometimes just quietly, but then loud and jagged breaths, like someone gasping for their last lungfuls of air. The woman was tormented. She swore that something came to her at night and whispered about her child. That there would be a curse on any first son born in the house. When the woman went into labour, she did give birth to a son and lived in fear that he wouldn't survive. But he thrived and she told herself that she had imagined it all, that there was no curse and it

71

was just a trick that her mind had played on her in the later stages of her pregnancy.'

A log slipped in the fireplace, sending up a spray of sparks. I jumped.

'So?' prompted Martha again.

'One day, when the child was three years old, his father went away on business to London for a month. In the three years, he had convinced himself that the kitchen maid had in fact been evil and he had come to blame her for bewitching him. He had also fallen deeply in love with his son and had made him the centre of everything, his reason for being. He carried a curl of his hair in a locket around his neck. Coming home after this month away, he couldn't wait to take his horse to the stable but rode it into the yard. But his son was playing there and ran to see him. He was kicked in the head by his father's horse and killed outright.'

We were silent. Greg waited for a second or two to let us grasp the horror of it.

'The firstborn son of that house never reaches the age of five. It happened again, in the next generation,' he said. 'And again. It happened in the thirties, too. There are church records to prove it. Lots of people who buy the house don't have young children, of course, but it's the breathing that gets them. No one ever stays there long.'

I pulled Lucas's arms tighter around me, grateful for the solidity of him and the closeness of the others. Danny turned on to his front and reached for his rolling tin. There was something so nonchalant about him that I found him reassuring. Things like haunted houses couldn't exist in a world where men wore silver trainers and hipster jeans, surely. And yet, feeling the weight of Stoneborough around us, I entertained the possibility.

Chapter Six

Martha pressed her nose against the glass of the kitchen door, looking at the terracotta pot she had planted with daffodil bulbs to brighten up the patch of concrete behind the house. As yet growth was slow, limited to four sharp green javelins that the compost had stuck forth in response to the weather's martial approach. She sat back down at the table and filled in the answer to a clue in the crossword we had been stuck on. 'It's the change of scene,' she said. 'Always gives you a new perspective. If you do the washing-up you're bound to get another one.'

'Nice try,' I said.

'The next place we live, we're getting a dishwasher. I won't move anywhere that doesn't have one.' She flicked back through the paper to see what was on television. 'Do you think you'll move in with Lucas?'

'What?'

'Things are going well, aren't they?'

'It's a bit early, isn't it?' I said.

'You've known each other for years, you've secretly wanted each other for years, he's your best male friend. There has to be a good chance that you'll end up together.'

'I don't know.'

'Come on, Jo.' She reached forward and grabbed my knees. 'Tell me about it. You're like a bloody clam.'

I loved it when Martha said bloody. It sounded totally

different in an American accent, as if she were playing an English part in a film, badly. 'He told me he loved me,' I said.

'That's great, isn't it?' She looked delighted for me and I was touched.

'Well, yes.'

'So what's the problem?'

'I don't think I fall in love that quickly.'

'Is that all it is?' She looked concerned.

'Yes,' I said. 'Yes. You know me. Things just take me longer, that's all.' I smiled to reassure her.

The pace at which things were moving wasn't my only concern, though. I couldn't stop thinking about Danny. The memory of my conversation with him was so surreal I'd wondered whether I might have dreamed it. It seemed to have come out of nowhere, a dragon's tongue of rage. I asked myself whether I was to blame: had it been wrong of me to try to talk to him about Lucas? Had I embarrassed him by pointing out his insensitivity? Perhaps, but even so, his reaction was incommensurate with the hurt I could have inflicted, surely?

'My God, Lucas said he loved you. That's great! I'm all up for falling in love but I never meet anyone I like.'

'You will,' I said, feeling more comfortable as the spotlight moved away.

She shrugged. 'The only men I meet are the wife-beaters who come to the shelter to find their families.' To some extent, I could see her point. Her feminist politics had put her in a world where she was surrounded almost exclusively by women. She worked as a fundraiser for a women's refuge in Hammersmith and her commitment to it left her little time for anything else, beyond her friendship with the members of our group. I admired her dedication, though.

I laughed. 'Come on, it's not that bad. It'll happen. Let's go and watch the news. The washing-up can wait until tomorrow.'

On Wednesday I had to go into the West End to do some

74

research for an article so I arranged to meet Lucas after he finished work. I was running late by the time I reached Piccadilly. At a quarter to seven the place was still busy with tourists and people making their way home, streaming down the steps into the tube as I fought my way up and clotting on the pavement by the bus stops. I wove along as fast as I could, hating that odd winter feeling of being too hot in my coat but cold in my feet and hands. I could feel my nose starting to run. One of the late-night hotdog-stands was already in situ and the smell of frying onions reminded me of how hungry I was.

In Waterstone's I couldn't immediately see Lucas and I wondered if he'd gone to look for me in another part of the shop. Then I caught sight of him further back, partially hidden by some freestanding shelves. He was wearing his long black woollen coat and had stuffed his scarlet scarf loosely into a pocket so that about a foot of it trailed rakishly out. He'd been to the barber's, I noticed, and his hair was cut tightly against his neck. I walked up behind him quietly and put my arms round his waist.

'Hello,' he said, turning round and kissing me. He handed me a book. 'Look, this is out in paperback now.' It was *Under Jupiter's Eye*, a novel written by a guy who had been three or four years ahead of us at university. We had gone along together to see him read from it when the hardback first appeared about six months previously.

We browsed for a while and then I found an empty chair and settled down to start the collection of John Cheever short stories I'd bought. I'd meant to get it out of the library but there was something so appealing about the chunky virgin paperback that I'd given in to temptation. Lucas could take hours in a bookshop but I didn't mind at all. It was one of the things we had in common and besides, watching him move between the tables reading the backs of the books was like observing an animal in its natural habitat. This was Lucas's world, much more than a corporate law firm. I had always known he wanted to write, but having a father like his had left its mark. He was proud of the fact that he was managing what Justin hadn't: working hard at something, achieving success through application, even when it bored him, even now, when there was no financial necessity for him to do it.

Twenty minutes or so later I looked up and saw him making his way to the till. I packed away my book and went over. 'Shall we walk back?' he said, sliding his purchases into the bag he had slung across his body. 'I feel like it tonight.'

We crossed Piccadilly, less busy now, and walked up Sackville Street. At the top, I felt a pressure on my hand. Lucas pulled me with him and we took a left towards Cork Street and stood outside the gallery. It was empty. The Heathfield name had been removed from across the front and there was nothing at all on display, not even a single picture on an easel to keep up appearances. There was a discreet card in the bottom left-hand corner of the window giving a telephone number and email address for enquiries. Lucas stood still, looking through the glass. Only his chest moved, inflating and deflating, pushing out regular clouds into the night air. About five doors down there was a burst of noise as a door swung open then shut again. Someone was having a private view, like the one we'd been to in the empty building in front of us. Lucas paid no attention. I squeezed his hand, not knowing what to say but wanting to remind him that he wasn't there on his own.

He turned to me, as if coming round. 'Let's go,' he said. 'I'm sorry. I just wanted to see what it looked like.'

We walked a little way up the road without talking. 'Do you want to stop for a drink?' I asked, hoping it might lift his sudden melancholy.

'Let's keep going.'

I waited a minute or so before speaking again. 'Lucas, have you had any more thoughts about why. . . ?'

'You know I haven't. I told you, didn't I? He was successful, he wasn't ill, he had friends, he had me. I don't know. I don't want to talk about it, OK?'

We walked on again. He had dropped my hand and despite my nudging it against his hopefully while we waited to cross Regent Street, he didn't try to hold it again.

'Did he have a girlfriend?'

He stopped in the middle of the pavement, causing loud annoyance from the man walking behind who stumbled in the effort to avoid him. 'What is the matter with you? I said I don't want to talk about it. Why does no one listen to me?'

I felt as if someone had reached in and given my stomach a hard squeeze. The thought that I had upset him hurt me more than the sharpness of his tone. I was ashamed of myself and embarrassed. I lowered my head and carried on walking, a little further apart from him. I took my bag off my shoulder and carried it in my arms, held tight against my chest. We crossed Soho in silence.

We walked without talking for about a quarter of an hour and I began to wonder how long he could keep it up. He was striding up Charing Cross Road and I struggled to keep pace in my work heels. I considered going home. Obviously he didn't want me around now. I imagined what it would be like, going back alone on the tube and having to explain to Martha why I was home when she wasn't expecting to see me until the following day. I began to feel very low.

As we rounded the corner into Lucas's road he stopped again and turned to face me. His face looked sad and serious in the halogen glow of the street lighting. 'I'm sorry. I didn't mean to be unkind. I'm still raw.' His eyes were bright, with a suggestion of tears in them.

I nodded. 'I'm sorry, too. I shouldn't have asked. It's none of my business.' I wanted to comfort him but something held me back.

'I want you to be involved in my life. Everything. Just give me time on Patrick, OK?' He blinked quickly and gestured towards the pub. 'Shall we? I feel like I need a drink now.'

Chapter Seven

After lunch at Stoneborough the following Saturday Danny suggested a game of table tennis. The table was in the single-storey part of the house that formed the second side of the walled garden, at a right-angle to the kitchen. It was a long room with a dark stone floor and a window with a wide still that ran along most of the inside wall. It smelt differently from the rest of the house, musty and unused. Lucas opened a cupboard and got out bats and a ball.

'OK, championship,' said Danny, cracking his knuckles and examining the bats to find the best one.

'Give us a chance to warm up at least,' said Martha. She passed me a bat and started gently patting the ball across the net. It was years since I'd played and it took a while to work out how hard I needed to hit it. The hollow plastic bounce of ball on table echoed off the floor and the low ceiling.

Danny played Michael first and had him running from one side of the table to the other. The ball danced back and forth, mocking him. He put his hand up. 'Take pity on me. I haven't seen the inside of a gym in months.'

'No mercy.' Danny tossed the ball in the air and served it directly at his body.

'Twenty-one–nine to Danny,' said Lucas.

Michael came to sit next to us on the windowsill and pulled his jumper off. 'The man's vicious,' he said.

'There's some beers in the fridge, mate,' Lucas told him. 'There's seven of us, so someone will have to play twice. Danny, you again and Rachel.'

'Here,' said Martha, handing her a bat. 'Do it for the girls.'

Rachel looked like she was taking it seriously. She stretched her arms behind her head and squared up to Danny. 'Come on then,' she said.

He smiled slowly and slammed the ball at her. To my surprise, she returned it with interest, directing it at the very furthest edge of the table. Danny got it back, just, but left himself wide open and she tapped it lightly over the net, killing it. Greg, Martha and I cheered. I found I really wanted him to lose.

Danny geared up and took the next two points but Rachel came back again with another demon shot. As Danny stooped to pick up the ball from the floor, I saw Greg wink encouragement at her.

'Way to go, girl,' said Martha, as Rachel took the set.

'Not everything has to be a battle between the sexes, Martha,' said Danny, taking a bottle of beer from Michael.

'Not everything has to be a fight to the death, Danny,' she replied.

I was up against Lucas but it was a foregone conclusion. I sat back down on the windowsill and pressed my feet against the radiator underneath. The stone floor amplified the coldness of the room. Michael put his jumper back on.

Even though his arms seemed to span the table, Greg couldn't get the better of Danny, who punched the ball back at him with venom. He threw his bat down in triumph. 'You and me for the final, Lucas. I hope you're ready to bleed.'

'It's a game, Danny,' said Michael.

'Look,' said Rachel. 'It's snowing.' I turned to the window. The air was saturated with tiny particles that fell too slowly to be rain. As we watched, they grew, becoming soft flakes like duck down. The sky was suddenly filled with grey

Haldimand County Public Library
JARVIS BRANCH

feathers that turned white as they reached the ground, muting the strong winter brown of the earth in the vegetable beds. Even as we watched, the first layer began to settle.

'Do you think we'll get snowed in?' asked Martha.

'It's happened before,' said Lucas.

'Come on, then.' Danny got a coin out of his pocket. 'Heads or tails?'

I had forgotten how competitive Lucas could be. He had assumed an attitude of expressionless determination. Danny, too, had stopped playing to the crowd. It was clearly important to him in some way to beat Lucas. I'd never seen that in him before; was it new or had I just never noticed? Michael kept score. As they reached nineteen and twenty, there were no two clear points between them. They played on, reaching twenty-three–twenty-four, Lucas now serving. He flicked his fingers up, releasing the ball into the air like a handful of magician's dust, then tapped it lightly over the net. There was a deceptive amount of spin on it and Danny was visibly annoyed not to get his return quite where he intended. Lucas reached and sliced it back, catching it so hard that it bounced three feet. Somehow Danny got his bat on it but didn't have control and sent it long off the end of the table.

'Good game,' said Lucas, putting his bat down.

Danny came round and clapped a hand on his shoulder. He was wearing the ironic smile of the just beaten but there was nothing gracious about it. 'I'll get you next time, mate.'

I wandered off to the library to find something new to read. The snow was falling steadily and I planned to sit in one of the leather armchairs and watch it cover the long expanse of lawn down to the wood. Away from the table tennis, a strange silence had settled over the house, as if the snow had muffled sounds inside as well as out. It was the sort of silence that veiled an expectancy, like in the moment, lying in bed alone in the house, when you hear a sound and lie rigid waiting for the footfall of the intruder on the bottom of the stairs. The thought of being snowed in at Stoneborough gave me a flash of pure panic for reasons that I couldn't explain. I stood in front of the fire and looked into the spotted antique mirror over the mantelpiece. The familiarity of my reflection was reassuring. But then I realised I had started to look behind me and I swung round to face the room, as if I expected something to be there. I laughed out loud at myself to pierce the buzzing in my ears. I was determined not to be intimidated by the atmosphere of the place and run off to be in the safe company of the others. I had to learn to spend time alone here. This was my boyfriend's house.

On the nearest ledge there was a stack of old orange-spined paperbacks and I shuffled through them until I came to *The Rockpool* by Cyril Connolly. Patrick had had great taste: I'd never come across a collection of books before in which almost everything interested me. I took the book over to the window and sat in the armchair, angling it so that I could see as much of the room as possible.

It took a few minutes to calm my nerviness but I was just beginning to settle down when out of the corner of my eye I saw the door open. My heart bumped. Lucas's curly black head appeared and I breathed out. I could see in the mirror that he thought I hadn't noticed him so I carried on reading, pretending not to know he was there. He approached my chair from behind and put a hand on my shoulder. Even though I knew it was coming, I jumped.

He laughed and sat down on the floor in front of me. 'You OK?' he said. 'You disappeared.'

'Fine. Just wanted to be quiet for a while and watch the snow.' I looked at his face, the eyes locked on mine and sparkling, the freckles on his cheekbones. I ran my hand through his hair and watched it spring back as my fingers passed over it. I wanted to ask him about the house and whether he was aware of the atmosphere, too. It might make me feel less irrational if someone else felt it in the same way but I knew that, if he thought I was probing him about Patrick again, I risked another situation like the last one. I couldn't do it. Not knowing was the price of keeping things on an even keel, at least for now. Wednesday evening had given us a scare. We had seen how easily this tentative new thing between us could unravel. We had spent most of the morning making love and dozing, the winter light falling through the window on to the bed. I knew I was hoping that we were stitching each other more tightly into our personal tapestries, tight enough, with luck, never to come unpicked.

'I was going through the cupboard in Patrick's study the other day,' he said, getting up again. 'I found some cine films.'

'Did you? What's on them?'

'I don't know. I tried watching them but I couldn't get the projector machine to work. Greg looked at it for me this morning and he reckons he's fixed it. We're going to go up now and watch one, if you'd like to see. Maybe one of Patrick's artists made them.'

The cardboard box was on the desk. Whoever had packed up the films had clearly been conscious of keeping them secure: there were multi-layered belts of masking tape around the box in several places. It looked as if Lucas had tried to unpeel them and then given up and taken his penknife to it instead. Inside, the tapes were packed in two rows. Each cassette was numbered and next to its proper neighbours.

The projector was set up on a table in the middle of the room, its eye on the blank white wall in front of it. Greg fitted the first cassette into the machine and snapped on the power while Rachel and Martha drew the curtains. An oblong of light, rounded at the corners, appeared on the wall. Once he was sure the tape was running smoothly, Greg turned off the main light and went to sit next to Rachel on the window seat.

I had taken the desk chair and Lucas came to sit on the floor in front of me, leaning his head back against my legs.

Suddenly the wall was animated. I felt Lucas tense.

In front of us was Patrick, alive again.

He was young – our age, late-twenties, perhaps thirty. He was slimmer than when I'd known him and it made him seem even taller. He looked about seven foot. He was in blue jeans and a navy polo-neck, his hair black-brown and curling over the neck of his jumper. His face was broad and open, radiating that peculiar energy I'd never encountered in anyone else. He pulled a big grin and bowed, flourishing like a court jester at the Manor behind him.

'Welcome to the house of fun,' said Danny.

Now Patrick stepped to the side of the picture and the camera focused on the house, delivering it to the screen in considered sections. Clearly the cameraman – or woman – had an artist's eye: this was not an amateur home video. It panned up from ground-level, the stone path to the front door, the lines of yew trees on either side. Fewer of the flagstones were cracked, I noticed, and the front door was painted green. Otherwise the house looked the same. In the flowerbed that ran round the bottom of the front wall crowds of daffodils were jostling, the centre rings of their flowers like egg yolks against paler outer layers.

Patrick was back in the picture now, springing up the front path. He darted in and out of the yews, hiding behind one and then running out from behind the next, like one of those scenes in films where people chase each other in and out of hotel rooms all the way up a corridor. He paused, laughing, at the front door and produced a key from his pocket. He put it in the lock and made a show of trying to turn it. The door yawned open in front of him and a group of people stood ready inside, laughing at how funny they were. Normally I would have found such staginess irritating but Patrick somehow made it charming, his great height adding an unintentional comic note.

83

The camera stopped first on a dark-haired woman. There was something familiar about her, although I didn't think I'd met her before.

'That's my mother,' said Lucas without moving. I looked again and then I saw it, but even so the woman in front of me was more like the sister or perhaps cousin of the one I'd met several times. Claire had had a more developed case of Lucas's reserve. My mental image was of her emerging to greet us from her silent, ordered study on the first floor of her house in West Hampstead. Her hair had been cut in a disciplined long bob, the front of it run through with silver seams that Lucas had, without success, urged her to dye. She had had an assessing gaze and looked at one a second or two longer than felt comfortable, as if wanting to make sure she'd got you right.

By contrast, this woman on camera looked alive and open, with none of the wariness of that Claire. She looked like someone who was happy and unrestrained. But I supposed when the film had been shot she hadn't lost her husband and brought Lucas up on her own. I wanted to communicate to the woman on the wall what a good job she would do and to say thank you, both things I would never have dared even to think in the presence of her later avatar.

'Is your dad here?' asked Martha.

'I didn't see him, no.'

The cameraman moved on across the group, introducing others, mostly men. Even if we hadn't known the relative ages of Patrick and Lucas's mother, it would have been easy to date the film to the seventies. These people wore their trousers tight at the top and flared from the knee, and a small, fair woman had her hair tied back from her face with a Pucci-printed headscarf folded into a wide band. It was clear, too, that this was an artistic set. Apart from Patrick, the men looked dishevelled in a faintly self-conscious way. Two or three of them had beards and one had a particularly extrovert moustache.

'Imagine having to show your kids pictures like that.' Danny laughed.

'He didn't have kids. That's Peter Hampton, the sculptor. He was one of Patrick's best friends. He died of Aids in New York five or six years ago.'

'Sorry.'

'Don't worry about it. You weren't to know.'

The camera moved on. The soft tint of the film was like amber, preserving everything in perfect high-lit detail. It stopped again on another woman. Although she was with the others, she was marked out. Her skin shone and her hair, which she wore long and down, gleamed a rich chestnut colour. She was wearing a polo-neck like Patrick's but black, and her tiny hips were gloved in a pair of tight trousers that widened below the knee. The camera rested on the planes of her face for a moment and she smiled at us knowingly down the years, confident that the challenge of her beauty would remain unmet.

'Who is that?' asked Danny, his voice low as a wolf whistle.

'That's Elizabeth Orr. She's a family friend. She and Patrick used to go out, years ago.' Immediately I thought of the conversation I'd overheard at the gallery. The woman who'd eclipsed all the others.

On the wall, she laughed and showed a mouthful of sharp white teeth. Her hair fell forward to cover one eye and made her face a stunning chiaroscuro. I realised I'd seen her somewhere else. Where was it? The photograph behind us now, on top of the bureau. She was the woman in the white trouser suit.

'Why the hell did he let her go?' said Danny. 'She's incredible.' I looked at his face, his profile illuminated by the light from the wall. He still hadn't taken his eyes away.

Lucas shrugged. 'I don't know. Not the kind of thing people tell children, is it? I think she's really missing him now – she talks about him a lot at the moment.'

'You're in touch with her?'

'Yeah. She lives just outside the village.'

'What did she do?' asked Danny. 'She must have been an actress.'

'She was a model first. She was pretty famous in the seventies. She used to sit for Thomas Parrish – that's how she met Patrick.'

'Are artist's models usually famous?' I asked. 'I don't know any, not modern ones. Apart from that big guy who used to sit for Lucian Freud.'

'Leigh Bowery,' he said. 'Well, she modelled for Parrish first and then she did photographic work, fashion stuff. I don't think she was tall enough for the catwalk but she did magazines and advertising, even a couple of films. She was one of the in-crowd, from what Patrick told me. Always in the gossip columns, that sort of thing.'

'Is she still beautiful?' asked Danny.

'I think she is, yes.'

He laughed. 'When can I meet her?'

The snow put us all in that heightened mood that unusual weather conditions elicit, a sort of excited siege mentality. After supper, there was drinking and dancing like we'd had on New Year's Eve. Michael, who was always better by Saturday when he'd had a good night's sleep, was dancing more flamboyantly than I'd ever seen him before. Perhaps no longer having to hide his sexuality from his parents made even his life away from them easier to live. He looked freer. Rachel and Greg were dancing with him to Stevie Wonder's 'Superstition', laughing and trying to match his moves. The chesterfields had been pushed out of the way and Danny was astride the back of one of them, flicking through the travel case of CDs, dispensing advice to Lucas and Martha, who were mixing complicated cocktails from a book of recipes. Lucas had been quiet for an hour or two after we'd watched the film and I was reminded again of how recent his losses were, even though he was determined not to bring everyone else down by talking about his grief.

I danced and drank Harvey Wallbangers, which he made for me and I discovered I liked. A little later on, as the alcohol began to kick in for real and things became less frenetic, I left the others beached in various positions around the drawing room and went outside. The snow had stopped falling and now lay as deep and clean as a freshly laundered duvet across the terrace and the garden beyond. Even though I had taken Lucas's big coat from the stand, the contrast between the temperature in the house and the night air came as a shock. My breath formed clouds as I crunched across the terrace to the balustrade and where I used the side of my arm to clear a space to sit, the cold against the bare skin of my wrist was so sharp it felt acidic.

I kicked my heels against the wall underneath me, feeling them swing out involuntarily as they bounced off the stone. The night was perfectly silent apart from the sound of it. There was no noise from the party inside and even the owl who had been mourning in the wood the first times I had been out here had packed up for the night. I felt completely alone, as if the world had freeze-framed and I was the only moving thing in it. I was suffused with a feeling of total freedom.

Suddenly I heard the sound of a door being closed, then voices, two, and stifled laughing. They were at the front of the house, whoever they were. 'Ssssh,' I heard, then more muffled laughter. A minute or two passed and I sat absolutely still. There was the creak of footsteps compacting snow. Around the corner and into the virgin landscape wove two figures, pulling together and apart, stopping to kiss each other and laugh with hilarious complicity. There were no lights from the house behind to give me away and I lowered my cigarette so that its burning tip was hidden. They walked along the path that ran fifteen feet below me, unaware that they were being watched, making a racket as only people who are trying to be quiet can. As the path reached the end of the side of the house they veered off across the lawn, still with their arms around each other. Only when they were far enough out from the house to give me some perspective in the patchy moonlight did I establish who I was looking at. It was Danny and Michael, leaving a double set of prints in the snow.

It was Martha's idea that she and I walk down together into the village for the papers the next morning. We borrowed boots from the row underneath the coat hooks in the passage and set off from the front door, slamming it hard behind us and making its stained-glass panel rattle. The sky was wide and opaque, a mirror for the snow underneath it, which was still unmarked apart from the tiny first-position prints of birds and the larger marks left by two pairs of trainers.

'Looks like people have been out already,' said Martha. 'I thought we were first up.'

'Hmm,' I said. 'Maybe they're from last night.'

I'd been thinking overnight about whether I should tell anyone what I'd seen. About twenty minutes after I'd gone inside the previous evening Danny and Michael had returned as well, five minutes apart, and then hardly talked to each other for the rest of the evening. They were clearly not prepared to go public yet. I found myself watching them minutely but they were very good. Their hardly talking was pitched at precisely such a level that no one would have noticed it. I remembered that Michael had got really drunk at Rachel's birthday a couple of years previously and confessed to me that he had a crush on Danny; perhaps it was reciprocated now.

'I didn't know anyone was in the garden.'

We were just rounding the corner of the drive on to the

stretch to the village, out of sight of the house. The avenue was bridal. The snow had given the branches a look of white lace and everything in front of our boots was pure and untouched. It seemed a shame to mark it with our footprints.

Martha looked at me. 'I said, I didn't know anyone was in the garden.'

No, I decided, Michael would tell us when he was ready. 'I don't know that they were,' I said. 'Perhaps Greg and Rachel got up earlier for a walk in the snow and then went back to bed.'

The moment had passed; I couldn't now backtrack and tell her. And yet I wanted to talk around it, to talk to her about Danny and my unease about him. And now there was the question of how he would treat Michael. He was famous for his tequila-slammer flings: one shot and it was over. He was also famous for being wickedly unkind about his conquests.

'Marth,' I said, 'do people think I've started seeing Lucas because of all this?'

She looked genuinely surprised. 'The house? No. Why do you think that?'

'Just something someone said to me.'

'Who?'

I hesitated. 'Danny. After the thing with the car. I tried to talk to him about it but he turned it round and said that he should be protecting Lucas from me, given that I obviously considered him worth a pop now that he had all this money.'

Martha laughed. 'Oh Jo, he must have been joking. He wouldn't think that.'

'I don't know. Sometimes he's really odd about me.'

'Sometimes you're really odd about him. You're really hard on him.' An edge had come into her voice.

I was annoyed. I didn't like to think of myself as a harsh judge of people and I couldn't see what reason she had to defend Danny, especially against me. 'I'm not hard on him. You know what he's like.'

'Come on. Just give him the benefit of the doubt for once.'

I said nothing and we walked on in silence for a hundred yards or so. Martha's response had irritated me and in a peevish way I was glad I hadn't told her about Michael and Danny. But I still hadn't decided whether or not I should tell Lucas. On the one hand it didn't seem right that I should know and not tell him, especially as we were going out, but on the other it wasn't, as Rachel had said the night I got together with Lucas, my secret to tell. After all, Danny and Lucas had been close before Lucas and I ever met; was it right that he should hear Danny's news from me?

We were coming on to the road into the village. Cars had been along it since the snow fell but only two or three and the individual tyre marks were still distinguishable from one another where the treads had printed out their icy pattern. The hedgerows were white and pillowy. If I were Lucas, would I want to know? Probably. But it still didn't feel right for me to tell him.

Chapter Eight

The bar, when Lucas and I found it, was off-puttingly
fashionable. Round the corner from Danny's office in War-
dour Street, it was below pavement-level and reached by
rusty metal steps that looked as if they might lead down to a
gangsters' hang-out or late-night poker den. My shoes made
an attention-seeking clung-clung-clung as I descended. A
bouncer with a shaved head and an earpiece pushed the
heavy fire door open, giving us a quick once-over. Inside, a
strip of mirror about two feet wide ran around every wall at
face-level; it was disconcerting not to be able to look away
from one's reflection. The air was stifling. Even early on a
Wednesday it was busy and we had to thread our way
between tightly packed groups to look for Danny and
Martha. We found them lolling on a sort of low black
bed in the far corner.

'Lucas, thank God.' Danny raised himself on his elbows a
little to acknowledge our arrival. 'Are you going to the bar?'
His eyes looked particularly blue against their kohl rims
today.

'Hold on a moment.' I took off my coat, conscious of my
suburban-hack get-up: knee-length skirt, pale shirt and plain
jacket. Martha, by contrast, looked great in her best Seven
jeans and the black polka-dot jacket that tied with a ribbon
at the side.

'What do you want?' asked Lucas.

'Scotch.'

I went with him to help carry the drinks. When we returned, Danny was leaning in towards Martha, as if whispering a confidence. I wondered if he were telling her about Michael and was glad again that I hadn't.

'So, what's going on? Why the school-night cool fest?' Lucas lowered himself gingerly on to the edge of the mattress.

Danny turned to him and raised an eyebrow. 'I've been sacked.'

'What?' That was the last thing I'd been expecting to hear. 'Why?'

'I got caught doing coke in the lavs with a client.'

'You idiot, Danny.' Lucas shook his head slowly.

'What's the big deal? Everyone's doing it.'

'Well, if that's true, why have they fired you?'

'Because I got caught. There's a big difference between doing it and being seen to do it. I was just unlucky. It's a while since they've made an example of anyone. If they do this now and again, it reminds everyone else to keep their heads below the parapet.' He flexed his arm distractedly and watched the muscle bunch in it.

'So, what are you going to do?'

'Don't know. I'm screwed.'

'Surely you can get another job, especially with your reputation,' Martha said.

'Maybe, but I'm going to have to lie low for a while. The whole thing'll blow over in a couple of months but until then I don't stand a chance.'

'But you've got savings, haven't you?' asked Lucas. 'You're covered?'

Danny laughed without humour. 'I haven't got anything, mate. Except debts.'

I was amazed. 'Debts? How?'

He turned to me with the sort of patient face that let it be known he was about to explain something I couldn't possibly understand. 'Jo, sweetheart, when you operate at a certain level, people have expectations of you. I've had to look right, for example. I couldn't dress off the high street.' He cast a disparaging glance over my outfit. 'Advertising is about image.' He turned to Lucas. 'It's mostly credit cards.'

'Jesus. How much?'

'Twenty, twenty-five. But that's not the pressing issue, as it happens. I was going to say something the other day. Mate, I've got to move out of my flat.'

Suddenly I could see what was going to happen. Danny knew that Lucas's flatmate had just bought his own place and moved out. A bolt of anxiety ran through me. I didn't want Danny at Lucas's. I knew that he would take him out every night and tell him that he shouldn't feel constrained by having a girlfriend. A jealous flower unfolded little petals in my gut.

'Why do you have to move?' asked Martha.

He pulled a face. 'Well, you know Stacie, my flatmate? She and I . . . yeah, it's a bit of a mess. Don't know what I was thinking.'

'You can have our sofa while you get yourself sorted,' I tried.

'No,' said Lucas, and I saw it was inevitable. 'I've got a spare room at the moment. It's ridiculous for you to sleep on a sofa while I've got a bed going.'

Danny was doing a convincing job of looking like the thought had never occurred to him. 'Are you sure? Just till I get myself sorted out?'

'Well, let's see. If it works out, you could stay. We've never shared before. It'll save me looking for another housemate and it'll be fun. Go on, it's perfect. And I'll just carry on with the rent; you can start paying your half when you get a new job. You've helped me out in the past.'

'Lucas, really, that's beyond the call of duty but if you're sure . . . ?'

Danny moved the next day. He had nothing else to do so he packed his stuff and got a cab across town. I worked late and then had supper with Martha so it was ten o'clock by the time I rang Lucas to see how they were getting on.

'It's going to be good. I can't think why we haven't done this before,' he said.

I didn't remind him that he'd once told me he thought Danny would be exhausting to live with. 'He goes out all the time and he'd make me go, too. His lifestyle is too erratic. I'm a lawyer, Jo – we can't do erratic.' If Danny with a job was erratic, I dreaded to think what he would be like untethered by employment. And then there was the question of money. Although Lucas was now in a position to help Danny out financially in the short term, I hoped that Danny wouldn't take advantage of him. I had to try to trust him not to.

Lucas didn't call me the following evening and, when he didn't ring until gone eleven on Saturday night, I was angry. We hadn't made any plans to go up to the country and I had expected to do something with him during the day. I'd called him regularly but got voicemail every time. All day I had been pacing up and down and constructing ludicrous scenarios in my mind. When I finally heard from him, he was drunk and calling from a phone box. I could hear a car engine idling in the background and Danny opening and closing the door to the booth, stage-whispering to Lucas to hurry up, he was getting cold.

'Jo? It's Lucas.'

'I know.' I picked up a biro from the telephone table and began to bite the top.

'Are you angry with me?'

I tapped the pen against my teeth. 'Should I be?'

'I'm really sorry, I'm drunk.'

'Why do you have to apologise to me for that? I'm not your bloody mother.' I felt an immediate flash of embarrassment as I realised what I'd said. 'Why are you in a call box anyway? Where's your mobile? I've been trying to get you all day.'

'I left it in a taxi last night. We went to a party in Clapham.'

'Whose party?'

'I don't know. A girl – a friend of Danny's.'

The end of the pen splintered in my mouth. I grimaced and picked the tiny shards of plastic from my tongue. I heard the door of the phone box open again. In the background Danny said impatiently, 'Come on, mate. He's got the meter running. You can speak to your bird later.'

'Jo, I've got to go.'

'So I hear.'

'Listen, will you come to dinner at the flat on Monday? Danny's going out and I'll cook something for us.' A softer note entered his voice and he was whispering so that Danny, presumably still agitating on the pavement outside, couldn't hear. Annoyingly, I felt my anger begin to dissipate. Bugger Lucas and his charm, I thought.

'What time?' I asked.

I took the tube to Lucas's after work. The underground was muggy and permeated with the smell of wet wool but outside again the rain had a hard edge. By the time I got to Lucas's building my chest was tight and I rested a minute in the dimly lit lobby to take some Ventolin and let my lungs recover.

When I reached the flat, the door was ajar. I stepped inside and pushed it gently closed. The hall light wasn't on but a warm glow fell from the kitchen doorway on to the carpet outside. I could hear voices, Lucas's low and serious and Danny's joky. 'Oh lighten up,' I caught.

I walked into the kitchen and put my bottle of wine on the counter, still wrapped in its twist of cheap tissue paper. 'Jo, I didn't hear you come in.' Lucas turned in surprise and pulled me into a tight hug. 'God, you're so cold,' he said. 'Let me feel your hands.' He took them in his own and rubbed our four hands together to warm my two. He kissed me gently on the lips but I pulled away quickly, conscious of Danny behind him, leaning against the sink.

'Don't worry, Jo,' he said with an amused look. 'I'm going out any second.'

I tried not to let my annoyance register. 'Doing anything interesting?'

'No, just meeting an old friend.' He finished his cigarette and half-heartedly stubbed it out on a side plate behind him. 'Right, see you later.' He winked at me.

When the front door slammed, I put out the cigarette, which was burning into the filter and giving off a chemical aroma that mingled badly with the delicious scents from the oven.

'Why don't you go and sit down?' said Lucas. 'Dinner's almost ready.'

The food was really good, even by his standards. I was touched that he'd made so much effort, especially after a day at work.

'Danny was in a good mood,' I fished.

'Hmm,' he said, non-commitally.

'He seeing anyone at the moment?' Had Danny told him about Michael but asked him not to tell me, I wondered. If so, I reckoned I would see it in Lucas's face.

He put down his knife and fork and looked at me. 'Jo, do you think I've got it in me to write? As a career, I mean? Like my mother?'

'Why do you ask?' I said.

'Well, you know. I'm not enjoying law and I've got enough money now not to have to do it. Realistically, am I going to stick it out for the next thirty years?' He took a large gulp of wine and I watched his Adam's apple plunge.

'But you're brilliant at it, partner by thirty-two, all that . . .'

'That doesn't mean anything.' He ran his hands through his hair, pulling the black curls flat against his skull.

'Has something happened?'

'I'm just thinking about it, that's all. You only have one life. You might not even get a long one – look at my family.' He fixed me with a stare, challenging me. 'Patrick did what he wanted to do. He didn't do a job that he hated for years on end. He wanted to work with art so he did, even though my grandparents pressured him to have a profession.'

'It's a privilege of money,' I said, returning his hard look. 'You have more freedom to do what you want because you know that, if you screw up, you can afford to stay alive while you find something else.'

'But if you do have money, why not use it to follow your dream?'

I shrugged. I couldn't think why the conversation was annoying me so much. 'I don't know. It seems like a good idea.'

Lucas looked pleased with that. He stood up and cleared the starter plates. 'No, stay where you are.'

I leant back in my chair and reached into my bag for cigarettes. I lit one and sat with my elbow on the table, listening to the musical clatter of crockery and looking out of the window down into the street. The noise of the traffic was muffled by the time it reached the third floor. A car pulled up on the double yellow lines underneath and a man jumped out and ran across the road to the all-night chemist opposite, his scarf whipping behind him.

Lucas returned, bringing an Italian chicken casserole, polenta and a green salad. His mood seemed to have lightened and he chatted about a book he was reading. 'I want you to know that, whatever happens, I think you're the best,' he said, reaching across and putting his hand over mine.

97

I got up from my seat and went to stand behind him. I put my arms around his neck and bent down so that we were ear to ear. He smelt of herbs and very faintly of sweat.

'Nothing's going to happen,' I said. 'I love you.'

As soon as the words were out of my mouth I couldn't believe I'd said them. I hadn't planned to tell him that at all. I wasn't sure it was true. I had thought about it on Friday night and Saturday, waiting for him to ring me. I had tried it the other way round. If I didn't love him, I had wondered, why was I so bothered by his not calling?

His face was shining and he pulled me round to kiss him. When we moved apart, he looked at me seriously. 'I've always loved you. Please don't forget that.'

He returned to the kitchen. The fridge door opened and closed and more plates were taken from the cupboard. 'Do you want coffee?' he called out. I heard the front door slam. Now the sound of voices came from the kitchen, kept low. Danny. He was back early. I went through, carrying my glass.

'Danny. I didn't expect to see you home so soon.' I leant against the counter and smiled at him questioningly. 'I thought you were meeting someone.'

'I was. He had to go back to the office. We just had a couple of quiet pints.' He looked around him at the dirty plates and pans. 'But it looks like you've finished dinner now, so I haven't spoiled your evening too much.' Lucas was unwrapping cheese and putting it on a board. 'Cheese, great. Shall I open another bottle of wine?' Danny went to the fridge and took out my bottle of Frascati.

I tried to catch Lucas's eye but he was looking down, carefully peeling the wax paper from around a wedge of ripe Brie. Touching his arm, I waited for a response, some sign of annoyance at Danny's behaviour. He flashed me a forced smile and turned away again.

'Well, you might as well come and have some of this with

98

us, Danny. You'll have to find another chair.' Lucas picked up the board and carried it through to the table.

With a theatrical gesture, Danny pulled the cork from the bottle and poured it. 'Cheers,' he said, bringing his chair up to the table. 'Now, who's for some cheese?'

We drank the white wine and Danny opened another. He was steering the conversation into areas where I couldn't contribute: old schoolfriends of theirs, people they'd seen the previous evening. I was tuning in and out, irritated by his efforts to exclude me but also just not bothered to compete with him for Lucas's attention. Perhaps it was because he was an only child that he had never learned to share.

Lucas stood and got down the decanter that Patrick had given him for his twenty-first birthday. He poured out three large measures of Scotch. 'Jo, there's something we need to talk to you about.' He handed me a glass.

The collective put me on my guard immediately. I poured myself some water.

Danny raised his eyebrows at Lucas, prompting him. Lucas cleared his throat and made a show of rolling down his sleeves and fastening the cuffs. 'Danny and I are moving to Stoneborough.' His eyes were looking anywhere but at me.

'What?' I took an angry swig of whisky, which burned my throat. 'What do you mean, moving to Stoneborough?' I tried hard not to cough.

'We're going to live at the house full time, not just at weekends.'

'Why?' But I knew the answer: it was what Danny wanted.

'Well, it's like this.' Danny leant back and lit a cigarette. He put out the match with a deft flick of his wrist. 'Lucas wants to write and I'm going to try working on some short films. It's what we both should be doing, not slogging in offices. Lucas doesn't want to be a lawyer, Jo, he wants to be a writer.'

99

'I know that.' Did he think he was the only person who understood Lucas at all? I could feel my anger as a physical sensation. I knew I was flushed. I wanted to get up and storm about the room but doing that would show Danny just how furious I was. 'It's no reason to move to the bloody country.'

'It's much cheaper, Jo.' Lucas looked at me imploringly. Please accept this, his eyes asked me. 'At the moment, I'm paying rent on this place. The house is already mine.'

'You were just telling me money wasn't an issue. And you intend to do what all day? Write books and make short films? Really?'

'Yes. Exactly that.' Lucas drained his glass and poured himself another large measure. 'If it doesn't work out, we'll reconsider.'

'What about your job?'

'I've resigned.'

'Well, thanks for telling me. There I was earlier, while you talked about what you wanted to do with your life as if it were theoretical and now you present me with this as a fait accompli. Thanks a lot.' The cough finally got the better of me and the force of it shook my body and brought tears to my eyes. Lucas got up and came to stand beside me, holding out my water glass and slapping my back.

'And another thing,' I said, as soon as I could. 'When will I see you, if you're not here? It'll change everything.' I wiped a strand of hair off my hot face. Danny was watching me with a detached interest, as if I were an ant and he a boy with a magnifying glass on a sunny day.

'At weekends, when you come up to the house.'

'And that's it?'

'I'll come down here sometimes, too. To visit you.'

'This is crap and you know it.'

'Danny, do you think you could make yourself scarce for a bit so that I can talk to Jo? There's stuff that we need to discuss on our own,' he said.

Danny took his wine glass and the bottle and went to his room, banging the door behind him. Lucas picked up our whiskies and led me to the battered leather armchair. He sat down and pulled me on to his lap. Maybe it was the sight of my legs crossed over his or the way that he stroked my hair, I don't know, but I started to cry. I was furious with myself, swiping the tears away with the back of my hand.

'I'm not crying because I'm upset about you moving away,' I said. 'It's because I'm drunk and tired and angry.'

Lucas turned my head to face him. He burst out laughing. 'Oh, Jo,' he said eventually. 'You're so funny.'

I sniffed disgustingly. 'What the hell's so funny about me crying?'

'You look lovely. And you've got nothing to worry about. Like I said, I love you and that won't change, whether I live here or at Stoneborough.' Ill-advisedly, he kissed me. 'Trust me: I just want to write my novel and I don't have the time now.'

'It's not you I don't trust,' I said.

'I can look after myself.'

'Three days it's taken him to persuade you to quit your job, give up your flat and move to the middle of nowhere.'

'I've been thinking about it for longer than that.'

'Lucas, what's he going to do for money?'

'I've got loads of money and he's got none, Jo. Think about it from my point of view. He's been taking me out, buying me drinks, meals, for years. I've always felt like the impecunious younger brother – it'll be good to redress the balance a bit.'

'But it's different.'

'How?' He lowered his voice. 'He's in a really tight spot. He's got no job and massive debts. It's nearer thirty than twenty thousand. Who else is going to help him? He can't go to his family – his father's probably in a worse position than he is.'

101

'What about his mother? She's got money.'

He shook his head. 'He'd never ask her. Jo, he wouldn't tell you but Danny loathes the way his father taps his mother for cash. He thinks it's pathetic, with the way he treats her. He just wouldn't do it – it'd make him no better than he is.' He sighed. 'Look, I just want to help him.'

I could see that he'd made up his mind. 'You know, I feel like I've been set up – that's what makes me so angry. I thought I was coming over for dinner and Danny was going out so you and I could have an evening together.' I fished in my bag for a tissue and blew my nose. 'Did you have this planned all along, to sweeten me up with the great food and a few glasses of wine before he arrived back at some pre-arranged time?' Another wave of fury broke over me and I kicked my heel hard against the base of the armchair. 'I feel really stupid, Lucas.'

'It wasn't a set-up. I was going to tell you. I was working up to it. When Danny came home early it forced the issue.'

'I just hope you know what you're getting yourself into.'

My anger with him began to drain away. I had to admit Danny had been clever. He had identified Lucas's weak spot, his worry that he wasn't living up to Patrick's example and that he was playing the game without taking risks, and put pressure on it until he got what he wanted: the freedom that came with Lucas's money. I could imagine him next door, raising a silent toast to his new life, and I wanted to break his door down and inflict real physical pain on him.

'So you'll miss me, will you, when I'm in the country?' Lucas always knew when I'd argued enough. He stroked my hair, following the shape of my head. It had a strange lulling effect on me.

'You know I will. We're just getting started.'

'There is an alternative.'

My heart lifted. 'Is there?'

'You could come and live with us, too.'

For a moment, I thought I'd misheard. And then it dawned on me that I hadn't. I jumped off his knee as if he had suddenly caught fire. 'You want me to come and live with you in Stoneborough?'

He had the start of a smile. 'What do you think?'

'I think you don't know me at all.'

'What?'

'You're asking me to give up my job – my career – to come and live in the middle of nowhere.' I reached for my cigarettes, my hands shaking with rage.

'But you don't like your job.'

'Only because I'm not doing well enough at it yet. That doesn't mean I'm going to quit. I love journalism. It's what I've wanted to do my whole life. You know that. You know how important it is to me.'

'You could freelance.'

'Who for? I don't have the experience or the contacts. If I could do that, I'd be doing it now. Don't you understand? This is the beginning, the groundwork. I'm just not at a point where I could do that and even if I was I wouldn't want to.' I started to cry again. 'How can you not get it? After all this time? I thought you were the one person who would understand.'

'I just want to look after you.' His face was pained.

'But I don't want to be looked after. I'm not ready for that. Maybe I never will be. I need to do things.'

To my horror, he looked as if he were on the verge of tears himself. The whole situation was awful.

'Please don't cry,' I said, trying to lighten things up. 'That's my job.' I sat back down on his knee and put my arm round his shoulder. I buried my face in the side of his neck and felt my tears soak into the collar of his shirt.

'I need you to love me,' he said, holding me tightly. 'Do you?'

I said yes, because I had to and because I was afraid to look too deeply into the alternative. What I did know was that one of the things I had taken for granted about Lucas and me, that we understood each other in a way that no one else understood us, was no longer true. It was like suddenly losing faith in the floor you're walking on.

Much later, in bed, he reached for me, sliding an arm over my waist and resting his fingers lightly on my stomach. I couldn't respond. He felt lessened. That he wanted to write I could respect but I found it hard that he could so easily let go of his determination to be different from his father, to live on money that he had earned, a principle we had talked about for years. It was more important to me even than I had realised. I knew I had worried from the start that Lucas's new wealth would affect the relationship between us. I had needed him to be especially grounded to prove to me that it didn't matter, to counterbalance its weight. I lay still and pretended to be asleep.

The following morning I made an excuse about having to be at work early and slipped out of the flat quickly. I went to the greasy spoon around the corner and sat at a small table with a coffee while I tried to assimilate my new feelings. The caffeine didn't help me come to any conclusions other than what I already knew: that our relationship would never be the same again. I had only one new thought, a childish one of which I was immediately ashamed: Lucas had chosen Danny over me.

Chapter Nine

The new tradition had it that when the car went through the cutting in the Chiltern Hills, where the chalk walls rise off the road like the parting of the Red Sea, the front-seat passenger would retune the radio. As Oxfordshire opened up in front of us, we lost reception of the London station. That night Rachel was with us. Her car was in for a service and Greg was working late. He had arranged to come up with Lucas and Danny, who were already bringing the first load of their stuff. Michael wouldn't be coming at all; he had phoned that morning to say that he had a deal going through and was going to be in the office all weekend. It was the Friday-night request show on the Oxfordshire station and the caller asked for something by REM.

The DJ put on 'Losing My Religion'. I spent my customary two seconds wondering why they always chose that song when REM had so many other good ones, then fell under its melancholy spell.

'That's me in the spotlight, losing my religion . . .' Martha tapped out the rhythm on the knee of her jeans. She began to sing and Rachel and I joined in. We turned off the M40 and into the countryside on the song's beautiful dying notes. There was a second's pause out of respect for it before the DJ took the next caller.

This part of the journey, like a labyrinth the first times I had driven it, was becoming familiar. The car threaded its way through the lanes to Stoneborough as if it were on automatic pilot. To our right, ten miles north, the lights of Oxford burnt the bellies of the clouds orange but where we were, everything outside the beam of the headlights was a rich soot. Only here and there did a cluster of lights shine out across the fields. I turned the radio off as we came into the village. The houses lining the road were silent and even though it was just nine o'clock, so few lights showed I was afraid we would wake everyone up as we passed by in our bubble of noise.

Since we would be the first to arrive, Lucas had given me the keys. The Manor, when we pulled up outside, looked sullen. Its unlit windows glowered in the gleam from the cuticle of moon, resentful of having been ignored for so long. The stone mass of it was bulked up against the wood behind like a dog with raised hackles and I had a premonition of the unease I was coming to associate with the place. Now, though, the feeling was tinged with a resentment of my own: the house was taking Lucas from me.

'Spooky old joint in the dark, isn't it?' said Martha, from the back seat.

'Yeah, but amazing,' said Rachel. 'I can hardly believe it, even now. How many people get the chance to spend time somewhere like this? It's like something out of a film.'

The key turned with a clunk and the front door swung open. I ran my hand along the wall until I found the switch. The alarm was loud and discordant and it was a relief when it accepted the code Lucas had given me and fell silent. We dumped our bags and went around putting lights on, our footsteps echoing up through the house. There was a strong scent of polish. Patrick had had a cleaning lady who lived in the village and Lucas had arranged to keep her on. Though we did our washing-up at the weekends and tidied up any real mess, the dusting, hoovering and changing the beds was left to her. She came in the week and left the house ready for our arrival on Fridays. I was glad she didn't come while we were there: I found it embarrassing to have someone cleaning up after me. My mother had never had a domestic help and the idea that someone else should do my housework made me uncomfortable. Even at university, when the scout came to empty the bin and wash the handbasin in my room, I had always tried to be out.

Returning to the hall now, I stood still for a moment and raised my eyes to the ceiling, the focal point of that enormous space. Tonight there seemed an obliquity in the expression of the dark man on the chaise longue, as if he were concealing something in the rich folds of his clothing. There was urgency now, too, in the way that the Ganymede character held out his wine bowl, the muscles straining under his golden skin with the effort of proffering it. Every time I looked at the painting I noticed something different. It was as if the characters in it lived and breathed whenever my back was turned and never quite managed to find their original positions when I looked at them again.

'I'm going to light the fire,' Martha called out. I followed her voice into the drawing room, where she was kneeling on the rug. She used the kindling from the fire basket and made balls of old newspaper to stuff around it. When the flames began to catch, she put on small pieces of coal, which soon established a heart. I went around the room switching the table lamps on and dragging the heavy curtains closed.

Martha stood back and brushed off her hands. 'I could do with a glass of wine now.' There was none in the drawing room or library and none in the fridge. 'We're going to have to go down to the cellar,' she said.

The three of us stood outside the white door that led off the kitchen. I reached up and took the key off the hook. The door opened inwards and we saw the grey stone steps falling away into the darkness. Nothing would have persuaded me down them. I thought of the house's atmosphere pooling down there, collecting in the deepest part. The idea made me feel suffocated, as if I were already breathing claggy, poisoned air. I fought an instinct to slam the door shut.

'Look,' said Rachel. 'Why don't you go down and choose some – you know more about it than I do – and I'll turn the oven on for the pizzas.'

'I can't believe you're scared of the cellar,' I said.

'I'm just no good at choosing wine.'

'This isn't an off-licence. Every bottle down there is good.'

'I don't see you hurrying.'

'I'll go,' said Martha, starting down the steps. At the bottom she turned left and disappeared from sight. Rachel and I unpacked the salad and turned on the oven so that we could heat the pizzas as soon as the others arrived. After two or three minutes we heard footsteps again and Martha reappeared with a couple of dusty bottles. She put them on the table and scrabbled through the drawer for the corkscrew. 'It's amazing down there,' she said. 'It's just rack after rack after rack. These two are quite modest compared with some I could have chosen. It must be worth a fortune.'

'Perhaps I'll get Lucas to show me one day,' I said, locking the door firmly.

Things felt better when we were sitting in front of the fire with a glass of wine. I asked Rachel about her shop, a boutique in Richmond from which she sold exquisite accessories. I was fascinated by it and went there often, even though I couldn't afford to buy anything.

'Things are good.' She straightened the tassels on the hearth rug, running her nails through them to untangle the threads. '*Vogue* did a piece on one of our handbag designers in the latest issue and we got a plug. It's brought a lot of people in.'

Martha poked at the fire, trying to coax more heat from it. 'I still can't get over this place,' she said. 'Open fires – I love them.'

108

'How do you feel about Lucas moving up here, Jo?' asked Rachel.

I shifted position to ease the pins and needles in my calves. 'I'm worried about it. Not so much Lucas but Danny. They won't work up here. He'll just sponge off Lucas and distract him when he's writing, if he lets him write at all. You know Danny – he's hardly motivated.'

'Not to work anyway,' she said.

'And now he's lost his job, that's the only real structure in his life gone.'

'There's nothing you can do about it, Jo,' said Martha, tucking a strand of hair behind her ear and drawing her legs up under her. 'You'll have to sit it out. If you ask me, Lucas feels guilty about having all this money, and sharing the wealth makes him feel better.'

'Look at these weekends,' said Rachel. 'He won't let any of us give him a penny.' It was true: we had tried to pay our way but Lucas wouldn't have it.

Through the curtains we saw headlights pan across the front of the house and there was an exuberant blast on the horn. We went out to meet them, leaving the front door open to light the path. I felt apprehensive about seeing Lucas. I hadn't seen him since the morning after our argument. I stood awkwardly on the gravel, waiting for him to open the door.

'Sorry we're late. Took ages to load up the car,' he said, getting out and giving me a formal-feeling hug, as if he were aware of new boundaries that would have to be negotiated before the old status quo could be resumed.

'Give me the keys, mate. Let's get some of this unpacked.' Danny opened up the boot, which threatened to spill its load of bags and boxes on to the drive. 'Here you are, Jo. One for you.' He held out a cardboard box. It was large and heavy. As he looked at me, making sure I had it, I saw the unmistakable light of triumph in his eyes. And he knew

109

I'd seen it. A little smile, perceptible only to me, played around his mouth.

He withdrew his hands from the underneath of the box very slowly, his eyes never leaving my face. I turned away, disgusted both with him and with myself, for giving myself away.

It wasn't spring yet but there were signs that the end of winter was coming. In the flowerbeds around the base of the house and in the grass verges of the drive, the snowdrops had gone and now crocuses had pushed their way through the hard earth. The rain and intense cold of the week was gone by Sunday and a flat blue sky stretched over the house, the sun behind infusing it with a blank light like a cloudless summer day's. There was something dishonest about it. With the wind and cold during the week one knew where one was, but that sky promised a warmth it didn't deliver.

Martha found me in my room on Sunday morning, brushing my hair. I shared Lucas's bed along the landing and now only used my original room for dressing and storing clothes. I looked up from the mirror as she came in.

'Danny's driving me mad,' I said, waving the brush. 'He's been swanning about all weekend, talking about what they're going to do up here when it's just the two of them.'

'Don't show him you're angry, for God's sake. It'll make things worse.' She sat down on the end of the bed and bounced a little. 'It's harmless anyway – he's just enjoying winding you up.'

'Easier said than done. And I don't think it is harmless.'

'Jo.' She stopped bouncing and looked at me seriously. 'You've got to let this go. You can't let Danny come between you and Lucas. Lucas is just helping Danny out for a while and it's really kind of him. Let him do it.'

'I don't know, Marth . . .' I decided to tell her what Lucas

110

had said about my leaving my job. That, too, had been playing on my mind. 'It is Danny but it isn't just that . . .'

There was a knock at the door and Lucas came in, fresh from the shower. He was rubbing his head with a towel and his hair stood up from his head in black spikes. He had another towel tied round his waist and I watched Martha take in the lines of his body, looking at his image in the mirror. I caught her eye in the glass and she smiled and looked away. The line of dark hairs that ran down from his navel and under the towel curled damply. He bent slightly to kiss me behind the ear. 'You were up early again.'

'So, gorgeous, what's the plan?' said Martha, as he joined her on the end of the bed.

'I'd just come to talk to you about that. Danny's been going on about Elizabeth, you know, Patrick's old girlfriend, the one we saw in the film. I've invited her for lunch; it seemed like the best way to shut him up.'

Had anyone else been responsible for her invitation to lunch, I would have been enthusiastic. I was intrigued as much as Danny clearly was. I wanted to see what she was like now, this beauty who had captivated Patrick. But Danny's involvement tarnished it for me. When Lucas turned away I looked at Martha and rolled my eyes. She pulled a mock-exasperated face but I knew that at least some of her exasperation with me was real.

Given what we knew, Elizabeth had to be fifty at least. It was hard to credit. I wouldn't have been surprised if someone told me she was thirty-eight or thirty-nine. She held herself with the sort of still power I imagined a life of posing must imbue. She was a temple goddess come to life, her skin almost unlined and her feline eyes subtly accentuated with dark shadow. She was wearing a black cashmere top and fine wool trousers that dropped in a long line to the floor, but I still had a mental image of the sharp white trouser suit she

111

was wearing in the photograph. Her shiny chestnut hair, even now showing only a whisper of grey, was tied in a loose knot at the nape of her neck.

Lucas stepped forward to greet her properly, kissing her respectfully on each cheek. 'Darling,' she said, holding his elbows tightly.

'Elizabeth, this is my girlfriend, Joanna.' Lucas took my hand and pulled me towards him a little.

'Good to meet you,' she said in a crisp home-counties accent that took me by surprise. I had been expecting something exotic or at least a mid-Atlantic drawl. She scanned me quickly up and down. Lucas introduced the others and she nodded and murmured. Greg held out his hand and she shook it, displaying long manicured fingers and a silver ring set with a large sea-green stone. She looked at him appraisingly and held the handshake a second longer.

'Shall we have a drink before lunch?' said Lucas. He ushered us into the drawing room and seated Elizabeth on the chesterfield. She crossed her legs, pressed her ankles together, and waited beautifully for her drink. I heard the ice crack as Lucas poured the gin.

'You haven't changed anything?' she asked, looking around.

We'd done a reasonable job of cleaning up after the night before. In a fit of zeal I'd even polished the furniture and the scent of beeswax vied with that of smoke from the new fire that was now crackling merrily.

'It reminds me of him, keeping it the same.'

'He had wonderful taste, didn't he?' She sighed. 'I miss him so much.'

Lucas smiled sadly and handed her the glass. 'Elizabeth, will you excuse me for a few minutes? I'm going to go and finish getting lunch ready.' He was doing a good job of staying calm. She had been forty minutes late and he had been pacing in the kitchen when she arrived, worried that the

112

food would be ruined. He had had to turn the oven off and was keeping everything warm as best he could.

'Of course, darling. Is there anything I can do?' The question was asked with an intonation that let it be known that the answer would be no.

'Not at all. I'll call you through in just a minute.' He pulled the door shut behind him. As he did so I indicated an offer of help but he shook his head.

We sat in silence for a second or two. Elizabeth reached into her bag and produced a cigarette case. Danny jumped up from the other sofa to offer her a light.

'Thank you,' she said, smiling up at him from under lowered eyelashes and exhaling. 'Tell me, how are you enjoying the house?'

'It's wonderful, so peaceful after a week in London,' said Martha.

'We always thought it was paradise. We used to pile into the cars and come up at the first opportunity. The first summer we spent here was one of the best of my life.' Somehow I couldn't picture Elizabeth piling into anything: I saw her instead in Patrick's Jaguar, sunglasses on and a headscarf streaming behind her as they zipped through the lanes with the roof down. I wondered if that summer was the one they got together.

'I can't wait till summer.' Rachel looked out over the lawn from her position on the window-seat. 'We'll be able to sunbathe without being spied on.'

'I envy you all,' said Elizabeth. 'So young. You have it all still in front of you.'

'You're not trying to tell us you're old?' Danny looked genuinely horrified.

She laughed him off with a modest expression that left me in no doubt she expected the compliment as her due.

Lucas called down the hall that lunch was ready. Greg stood and offered Elizabeth his arm. She took it and he walked her gently through to the dining room as if she herself were a work of art.

'Look at them all,' Rachel said in a low voice, walking behind with Martha and me. 'Do they realise she's old enough to be their mother?'

'Darling, I was just saying how much this reminds me of the time I spent here with your parents and Patrick and all our friends. It's like someone's rewound the tape – you could be us.' She declined with a wave the spoon of potatoes that Martha proffered. Danny refilled her glass and was rewarded with a cattish smile.

'We're not half as glamorous, I'm afraid,' Lucas replied, carving the lamb. He had prepared a huge roast, unable as usual to keep to the modest lunch he said he'd had in mind.

'Nonsense. And you're a much better cook than Patrick ever was. Your poor mother was left to handle that side of things in our day,' she said. That I believed: I couldn't imagine the woman in front of me ever stooping to vegetable preparation.

There was silence as we ate, punctuated occasionally by a remark about how cold the weather had been or a compliment to Lucas on the food. I was hungry all of a sudden and helped myself to another slice of meat.

'Take my advice and make sure you marry him, Jo,' said Elizabeth. 'Men who can cook are a rare breed. You have to grab one while the going's good.'

'Thanks for the tip,' I replied. 'But I haven't tested his ironing skills yet.'

'You wish.' Lucas looked sceptical.

As lunch went on, I watched the sun withdraw from the garden. The shadow that, when we started eating, had lain only on that part of it which was in the lee of the house spread like spilled ink across the lawn and drive. Greg opened more wine but I switched to water, conscious that

I had to drive back to London in a couple of hours. Lucas produced a treacle sponge pudding and Elizabeth looked visibly shocked that people could countenance eating such a thing. In my amusement I asked for a large slice. Danny was watching her intently, as if comparing the present version with the one he'd seen in the film.

'Do you have any children, Elizabeth?' asked Martha.

She turned and smiled serenely, as if giving an interview for television. 'A daughter. Diana. She's travelling in Africa. In fact, she's in South Africa at the moment, staying with Jonathan. You remember him, Lucas, the photographer?' He shook his head blankly. 'Another one of our friends from that time.'

'Where in South Africa is she?' asked Greg. 'I was in Johannesburg just before Christmas.'

'Really? How interesting.' She refocused her attention on him, her eyes wide. 'Were you on holiday or working there?'

'Working. I was setting up a computer system.'

'God, Greg,' said Rachel, laughing. 'Why do you insist on making your job sound so dull? He designed a system for an international diamond-mining firm,' she explained. 'It was a really prestigious contract.'

That interested me. I knew, of course, that he worked in computers but hadn't realised at what sort of level. Rachel pulled her chair closer to Greg's and stroked his hair. He let her for a few seconds then gently inclined his head away, obviously annoyed by her comment.

Elizabeth stirred her coffee languorously, the spoon chiming against the edge of the cup. 'Diana's in Cape Town. She isn't working, just seeing the country. God knows what she'll do when she gets back.'

'I haven't seen Diana for years,' said Lucas. 'Not since she was eight.'

Elizabeth smiled. 'Is that right? Eight? What a good memory you have.'

'It was a memorable day.'

'She has always been something of a force, I suppose.'

'No. I mean, it was the day my father had his accident.'

There was a moment's shocked silence from the others but I'd known that detail; Lucas had told me earlier in the day. Then Elizabeth reached for his hand over the table and gave his fingers a tight squeeze. The green stone flashed.

'I'd like to see her again.'

'You will. She'll be back in the summer. She'd love to see you, I'm sure.'

Lucas smiled. 'Actually, I expect that you and I will be seeing a bit more of each other in the meantime anyway. I meant to tell you.'

She looked at him questioningly.

'Well, I'm going to be here full time. I'm going to do the same as Diana and use some of Patrick's money to take time off. Danny and I are going to move up from London and live at the house for a few months. To "pursue our creative projects".'

'Creative projects?'

'I've always meant to write a novel . . .'

'Oh Lucas, how brilliant.' She clapped her hands together. 'You must both come to dinner with me.' She raised her glass to them. 'Oh well done, you. Patrick would be so proud.'

'Actually,' said Danny, 'if you don't think it's too much of an imposition, Elizabeth, I'd love to talk to you about your career sometime. Lucas tells me that you worked in film, as well as modelling. Film's my area – I'd be fascinated to hear about your experiences. Perhaps I could take you out to lunch?'

She gleamed then like newly polished silver. 'Of course. It would be an absolute pleasure.'

Chapter Ten

Danny opened the door when Martha and I arrived the following Friday evening. 'Martha, darling,' he said, throwing his arms around her as if he hadn't seen her for weeks. I stood awkwardly, waiting for him to unhand her. 'Give me your coat. Just leave your stuff there and come through.' He took her bag and put it at the foot of the stairs. I dropped mine beside it. We went into the drawing room and I wandered absently around, looking for signs, I think, that Danny's influence was making itself felt on the house. I stopped by the stereo and scanned the pile of CDs there. Sure enough, there was a healthy amount of dance by outfits of whom I'd never heard.

'Take a seat,' he said, waving a hand at the chesterfields and positioning himself in front of the mantelpiece. Martha sat down but I stayed standing.

'Where's Lucas?' I asked.

'In the library. I'm not sure he heard your car.'

'I'll go and say hello.' I walked over to the table and picked up the bottle of gin. 'Mind if I make myself a drink?' I was trying to keep my voice neutral.

'Help yourself. *Mi casa es su casa* and all that.' He smiled an impervious smile. For a second I thought about asking him how things were going with Michael. Danny loved to have secrets from people, even though he never kept anyone else's. Knowing how much Michael liked to talk things over with Rachel, Martha and me, I expected he was dying to tell us but Danny was clearly pressuring him not to. For Michael's sake, I kept my mouth shut and went to find Lucas.

The door was open and I stood just inside watching him for a moment. He was sitting at the large round table, his back to me, a fan of A4 spread out in front of him. With one hand he wound a small circle of hair round and round an index finger, with the other he was writing intensely. The green-glass reading lamp was the only light in the room and it framed him in its orbit. I didn't want to shock him so I called his name gently. He turned in his chair and smiled.

'You're hard at work already,' I said, going over.

He pulled me on to his lap so that I could look at the papers with him. Some were covered in his jaunty script, others had been mapped by an elaborate spider diagram whose legs reached over several sheets. In bubbles along its etiolated form there were names and places and the occasional phrase. 'Did you doubt me?' he said.

'Is it set in Athens?' I asked, seeing the name of a hotel in the Plaka district where we had once stayed for a night.

'Partly.' He took the glass from my hand and had a sip.

'What's it about?'

'I'm not telling you. You'll have to wait and see.'

Danny had bought the DVD of *True Romance* and after supper everyone settled down to watch it. I hadn't noticed before that there wasn't a television in the house. Now he had set up the one from Lucas's flat on a low table and connected it to his PlayStation. I'd seen the film before and wasn't a fan: Patricia Arquette's monotone grated on my nerves. I hovered about at the back of the room until Lucas told me I was distracting everyone and could I please sit down. I went back to the kitchen. It was the room where I felt the house's underlying atmosphere least, perhaps because, with its electrical appliances and the constant low-level hum of the fridge, it felt the most in touch with the twenty-first century, despite the butcher's block and ceiling hooks. I picked up the *Guardian* and began to flick through it before noticing a cloud of moths, like tiny angels, coming out of the dark to throw themselves against the glass of the French windows.

There were footsteps in the corridor behind me and I turned, expecting Lucas. It was Michael. He stood behind me and watched the moths for a moment. 'So stupid,' he said.

Surprised at the sharp comment, I turned to look at him again and saw there were tears in his eyes. I was taken aback. I'd never seen him cry before. 'What is it?' I touched his arm.

He moved into the body of the room, out of view from the corridor. 'I've been so fucking stupid,' he said, taking a juddering breath. He pulled out a chair and sat down at the table. He was still in his work clothes, although he'd removed his tie and undone the top button of his shirt. His heavy wool suit, a couple of shades off black, gave him the incongruous appearance of someone airlifted off Wall Street into an English country kitchen. The material of his jacket strained between his shoulder blades as he put his head in his hands. 'I'm sorry. I'm drunk. Ignore me.'

I pulled out the chair next to him. 'What's happened?'

'Danny and I . . .' he said. 'Have you got a cigarette?'

I lit two and handed him one, which he drew on with real need. I'd never thought of him as a smoker until then. 'Danny and I have been seeing each other. He dumped me on Wednesday.' His hand shook as he raised the cigarette to his mouth for another drag. I remembered the night that I sat out on the terrace, how happy his suppressed laughing had sounded.

'Oh Michael.'

'You don't seem very surprised.'

'I saw you together once, out on the lawn that night it snowed.'

He looked up. 'Did you? Shit. It was supposed to be a secret. Who else knows?'

'No one.'

'You haven't told Lucas?' He was surprised.

'No.'

He started to cry again, tears running down his face and dropping on to his shirt, making irregular semi-translucent circles on the material. 'That was the night it started. I knew it was a mistake even then. I'm so fucking weak. Everyone knows what he's like.'

'Don't be hard on yourself. He's worked on that magnetism for years.' It occurred to me suddenly that Danny was glamorous in the true, old-fashioned sense: he could be glamour one, put one under a spell.

'I tried not to get too involved. I've always fancied him. I thought it was just a sex thing and that I would be satisfied with that . . .' He swiped his hands under his eyes and tried to compose himself. 'I nearly didn't come up tonight. I knew it was going to be difficult. But then I thought about what it would be like to stay in London when everyone else was here. And I couldn't bear not to see him.' He looked at me as if asking me to tell him how stupid he was. 'Do you think he gets off on hurting people?' he said. 'It's like it was calculated: he waited until he knew I was hooked and then ended it – full stop, no warning.'

'He's enjoying letting me know that he's got Lucas to himself,' I said. 'I can't challenge him for his attention when I'm not here.'

'Do you think he wants Lucas?' Michael looked at me sharply. 'Is that why he wants him out here?'

'No, no, not at all.' I shook my head, realising too late that I'd opened up another avenue for his thoughts to go worrying down. 'It's the money and the fact that he can do nothing all day. That he can piss me off is just a happy by-product. Honestly.'

'If Danny wants him no one stands a chance.'

'Lucas is straight. He's my boyfriend.' As I said the words I wondered, what if Danny did want Lucas sexually? I discredited the idea quickly; it didn't feel true. Of course, even if he did, it would never happen. But also I knew Danny's attitude to his sexual partners, how dismissive he was of them, without any exception that I could remember. In the past I had wondered if somewhere deep in Danny there was buried a kernel of bitter self-hatred. It was the only reason I could think of for his immediate distancing of himself from anyone who got involved with him on a level beyond the platonic and superficial, as if, by liking him enough to sleep with him, people rendered themselves contemptible in his eyes for their poor judgement. I didn't think that he would ever jeopardise his relationship with Lucas by trying to seduce him. Their friendship was too important to him; he needed it.

But then I had another realisation: the idea of it wasn't making me jealous. Even the thought of Lucas with another woman that I conjured up now as a test didn't give me a twinge. In the past, I'd been painfully jealous when people had flirted with my boyfriends and over time I'd learnt to be more moderate but I wasn't the master of my emotions to this extent. My discomfort at the realisation must have shown on my face.

'Sorry, Jo, I don't mean that.' He smiled at me apologetically and sniffed loudly. 'Do I look like I've been crying?' he asked.

'A bit.'

'I'm going to go to bed. If anyone asks where I've gone, tell them I was exhausted, will you?' He stood up, then turned and grabbed my arm. 'Do you promise you won't tell anyone? Please. Especially now.'

'Of course.'

He let go of me and moved away.

'Michael,' I said. 'Try not to let him under your skin.'

'Too late.' He smiled briefly and was gone.

I was getting used to Stoneborough's night-time rhythms, the creaking as the central heating clicked off and the house cooled and contracted. A relay of clanking pipes started up at eleven and was set off again every time someone flushed a loo or turned a tap on, the tuneful rattling fading slowly afterwards into the distance.

On Saturday I lay awake long after Lucas. The house had settled for the night and it was hours since the pipes had finished their percussion accompaniment to the teeth-cleaning on the floor below. I really couldn't sleep. Lucas's body seemed to be radiating a supernatural amount of heat. I felt stifled and kicked my side of the blanket off, achieving a moment of easier breathing. It must have been three o'clock, maybe half past. He rolled over and reached for me. In his dream the argument we'd had last thing had clearly been forgotten.

When we'd come upstairs, I'd stood in front of the mirror and begun to take off my make-up. I'd seen him walking up behind me and thought he was going to put his arms around me, as he often did. I hadn't expected him to reach round in front of me for the buttons of my jeans. I'd jumped away from him as if he'd been a pervert on the tube.

He'd looked hurt and embarrassed. 'What's wrong?' he said. 'Why don't you want me to touch you any more?'

'What do you mean?' I was immediately on the defensive, horrified that he'd noticed what I could hardly bear to admit to myself.

'You've gone cold on me.'

'No, I haven't.'

'You've spent as little time as possible in bed with me in the past couple of weeks. At night you're too tired to have sex, in

122

the morning you're up and dressed before I've even opened my eyes.'

'I . . .' I wondered if I could ever explain the confusion of my feelings. He was waiting for me to say something. 'I've got a lot on at work.'

'I know you're angry about the move up here.' He sat down on the bed and pulled off his trainers, tossing them into the corner of the room. 'I'm just hoping that you'll snap out of it. It's not about you. It's not a rejection. It's about doing something that's important to me.'

Feeling selfish, I sat down next to him and put my arm around his shoulder. 'I know.'

He leaned in and kissed me gently. It felt good, non-threatening, and I kissed him back. But the bottle of wine or more that he'd had made him too fast. Immediately he pushed me backwards on to the bed and clambered on top of me. I just couldn't. I shoved my way out from under him and ran to the bathroom where I sat on the edge of the bath wondering what I was going to do. It felt right to sit in the dark so I left the lights off. There was a big moon outside the window and it shed a milky glow on the tiles. After ten minutes or so I returned. Lucas's back was towards me, a large cold shape under the quilt. I tried to talk to him but he pretended to be asleep. I'd considered going to my room along the corridor but that would have been inflammatory. I didn't want to make the situation worse before I was sure I couldn't get things right between us again. So I got into bed and waited in vain for sleep to come. After a while, Lucas's breathing had slowed and I was left alone in the darkness. Outside a fox was barking, and the bleak clawing noise was more like the cry of a bird than an animal. It was the emptiest sound imaginable.

On nights when she couldn't sleep, my mother made cups of tea and sat at the kitchen table reading. She was an experienced insomniac, although no one had ever known

123

why. I decided to try her method now. I eased out of bed, picked up my book and put on Lucas's big jumper over my T-shirt. The familiar scent of it was a comfort. I worried that the old brass door handle would rattle and wake him up but it was obligingly quiet.

The centre of the house was saturated with a ghostly blue light that spilled through the ring of windows under the dome and poured down to the hall below. The landings hung back, cloaked in gloom. I followed the helix of the staircase, past all the hundreds of thousands of pounds' worth of art, robbed of its power in the darkness. When I reached the ground floor, the flagstones were icy on the soles of my feet. There was a low light on in the library. Someone else was awake. There was a cough. Danny, staying up late smoking. Although he was the last person I wanted to speak to, any company was better than none at that hour. The door was open so I stuck my head round it.

On the hearth rug a couple were having sex. With the shock of it, it was a second or two before I realised who they were. Greg's body pinned Rachel against the carpet. Her slim pale arms were flung either side of her head. The noise came again and I realised that it wasn't a cough but a sound low in Rachel's throat as Greg moved over her. He put his finger against her lips to keep her quiet and she took it into her mouth and sucked it. I should have gone at once but I couldn't move. Greg's skin, tanned by the fading light of the fire, looked dark against hers. His body was long and muscled but he wasn't lean like Danny or Lucas. He looked heavy, immutable, as he held himself above her, a brute fact between her legs. He moved his hand and covered the whole of her breast with it, capturing her nipple between his fingers. I was transfixed. At last I managed to take a step backwards out of the room. The floorboard underneath me creaked with my weight. I froze. But Rachel's eyes stayed closed and Greg didn't stop or look up. I drew back as far as I could without

124

moving my feet and waited a second to be sure. Just as I turned away, Greg raised his head and smiled at me.

I ran across the hall and up the stairs, not caring now about the noise I was making. I had the horrible thought that all those Cubist faces were jeering at me from their frames as I raced past them on the first-floor landing. *Voyeur*, I heard them call, *Pervert*.

And then it happened. Just as I was rounding the corner to take the last small flight of stairs to the top floor, something moved in the shadows. My stomach lurched. A figure stepped out in front of me. I made an involuntary sound, more a gasp than a scream.

'Be quiet,' he hissed, drawing back into the darkness.

'Danny.' I took a ragged breath.

His whisper was serpentine. 'Did it turn you on?'

The floor tilted beneath my feet and I put out a hand to steady myself.

'Greg and Rachel. That is what you've just been watching, isn't it?'

Shame flooded through me.

'Did they look good? Come on, you can admit it. They're sexy together. You probably needed reminding what that looks like.'

'Why are you doing this?' I kept my voice low.

'I'm just looking out for Lucas. We talk, Joanna. And I see the way things are between you. Do you really think you stand a chance?' He laughed very gently and the sound of it hung around him like smoke. 'You and Lucas will never work out.'

'That's not true.'

'Oh, it is. Maybe you used to have a chance, when Lucas was slumming it, trying to do it the hard way, but he always had this coming.' He waved his hand around him in the half-light. 'You can't compete, Joanna. He's in another world now and you can't follow him.'

125

'Danny, this is horrible, please . . . '

'You're insignificant. He clings to you because of his misguided ideas, but it's over. Don't you wonder,' he went on, and I saw his teeth glint as he moved just for a moment into the moonlight, 'don't you wonder why you and Lucas aren't the ones downstairs fucking in front of the fire? It's because you're not good enough for him. Take my word for it.'

'I won't let you intimidate me.'

He laughed softly. 'What are you going to do? Tell him? Are you going to explain what you were doing wandering round the house in the dead of night, peeking through cracks in doors? Or would you like me to tell him?' He stepped back into the darkness and a second later I heard his bedroom door gently close.

When I reached Lucas's room I slammed the door shut, tore off the jumper and threw myself into bed, forgetting to be careful not to wake him. I could feel the heat of my cheek burning against the pillow. The blood was pushing through my brain so fast my temples were aching.

Lucas stirred. 'Everything OK?' he mumbled.

'Can't sleep,' I answered, turning on to my back and tangling the sheet still further.

'I'm sorry we argued,' he said.

'Me too.'

He propped himself halfway up and put a slightly sour kiss on my cheek. 'Friends again?' he said.

'Of course. Go back to sleep.'

I lay awake for the rest of the night. My heart was galloping and nothing I could do would return it to a normal rhythm. I tried lying motionless and controlling my breathing but still it continued its mad syncopation. My mind, too, was tearing across a new and twisted landscape, images of the scene in front of the fire tangling with visions of Danny stepping out of the night like a haunting. The thought of him brought a fresh coat of sweat. There was no ambivalence in our relationship any more: his animosity towards me had broken cover. I knew, though, that there was no way I could tell Lucas what had happened; I couldn't run the risk of him confronting Danny and Danny telling him that I had been watching Greg.

And on top of that, despite every attempt to distract myself, I couldn't get the image of Greg and Rachel out of my head. It looked like sex as it should be – powerful, adult, real. I also knew that I had never had sex like it. It wasn't about affection and warmth and messing around for fun but about men and women and want. I wondered whether all these years I'd got it wrong and shied away from precisely what I found most erotic, scared of what would happen if I let myself go. In the scene in front of the fire I had been looking at domination and surrender and I wanted to know what it felt like. Martha would be horrified if she knew I was thinking about sex like this, but in the remaining hours of that night I didn't care. I asked myself whether I had been so bound up in my politics and beliefs about relationships that I'd argued up a wall between myself and the stuff that really existed out there in the adult sexual world. I also wondered if this was why I had so often gone out with men with whom I'd been friends first. Perhaps in doing that I'd filed their teeth down, rendered them anodyne. There was no doubt that I had not been watching Greg and Rachel. I had been watching Greg. I wanted to be Rachel and to know what it was like to be overpowered by him. To lose myself to him.

I looked at Lucas sleeping next to me, his hair ruffed up on the pillow like the breast feathers of a baby owl, and felt immediate guilt. I loved him, I knew that, but I wondered whether it could ever be in that ecstatic, self-abandoning way in which I had seen Rachel respond to Greg. To my shame, it was exciting and made sleep even more of an impossibility.

127

For a mad moment I thought of waking Lucas but knew I could never forgive myself for the dishonesty – the faithless-ness – of it.

And then there was the question of the morning, getting ever closer as the dawn seeped across the ceiling like a stain in a tablecloth. In just a few hours I would have to sit and eat breakfast with a man who knew that I had watched him make love to his girlfriend. A man who had raised his head and smiled at me, knowing I had been there all along.

Chapter Eleven

In typical contrary fashion, I finally managed to sleep just as everyone else was getting up. Lucas left me in bed and I stayed there for another hour and a half, drifting in and out of a dreamless exhaustion. In the end I could put it off no longer, got dressed and went downstairs.

The smell of bacon drew me to the kitchen. From the corridor I could hear the sound of it crackling under the grill and the sawing of a loaf of bread. As I rounded the corner I saw that it was Greg and Rachel who were cooking. I had to stop myself running from the room.

'Morning, Jo,' Rachel said, with a normality of tone that told me that she hadn't seen me last night and Greg hadn't said anything to her.

Greg looked up from the tin of tomatoes he was opening. He was standing behind her and could have pulled any number of expressions. His face was completely straight. 'Morning.' He emptied the tomatoes into a saucepan.

I muttered something about finding Lucas and back-tracked out of the room, retracing my steps along the passage to the hall. Under that ceiling I could feel the rushing in my ears again, the pounding of blood too fast. It seemed to be resolving into a sort of beat now, like quiet tribal drums, full of menace. The floor was rising up to meet me, the walls crowding in. I had only fainted a couple of times in my life but here was the candyfloss feeling at the top of my head, the chequering at the edges of my vision. Instinct told me to kneel down before I fell, but even in that state I had another, stronger instinct: I didn't want to be alone under that painting. I looked up and saw Zeus looking down at me with judgement in his eyes. He knew. Panic whipped through me. I staggered the last few steps to the drawing room and half sat, half fell on to the nearest chesterfield.

Martha and Michael were reading the *Sunday Times* in companionable silence on the other sofa, she with the news review section, he with travel. They were sitting at either end, facing one another, their socked feet intertwined.

'You OK, Jo?' asked Michael. 'You look pale.' He lowered the paper and looked at me over the top of his glasses.

'Oh, I'm fine. Just tired.' I rested my head on the edge of the sofa and waited for the buzzing to pass. Today I wasn't sure if it was my nervousness at seeing Greg, fury with Danny or the house itself that was causing it. Martha was still looking at me, concerned. 'Honestly,' I said, 'I'm OK.' As soon as I could, I picked up the main section of the paper and took it over to the window-seat. It was cold away from the fire and I could see that the garden was full of a low-lying mist.

Rachel called to tell us breakfast was ready. I got up, feeling steadier on my feet, but Lucas came in and held me back. He waited until the others had gone then sat down on the arm of the sofa and pulled me in front of him. 'Jo, about last night . . .'

My mind raced. What was he going to say? Had Danny spoken to him? 'I'm sorry,' I said quickly, the first words to come into my head. I realised that it was an apology, however feeble, for a crime he knew nothing about.

'No, I am. I didn't think enough about what it would mean for us, my moving out here so soon. If I had, I might have left it longer, until we were more established.'

'Lucas, I don't . . .' Relief was coursing through me.

'Ssh.' He wouldn't let me speak. 'What I want to say is that I'm sorry. Also I love you and I'm committed to making it work between us.'

Trapped. The word flashed into my mind and out again almost before I had a chance to register it. I was shocked; I'd never thought that was a reaction I could have to the idea of being with him, especially as my instinct was to fight tooth and nail to prove Danny wrong about us. I made my eyes meet his. His pupils were dilating, as if to take more of me in. I could see myself in them, the big round head, the body disappearing underneath it like a seal's. I hated that person. I wanted things to be pure again, to be starting out on something with him that wasn't compromised. I didn't want to have seen Greg last night or to have the new feeling – whatever it was – about him. Lucas's face was balanced, full of expectation but not sure of what. He was preparing to hear that it was over between us but hoping that he'd said enough for it not to happen. I made a decision. I would not give up yet. I would stand my ground against Danny. He wouldn't have Lucas to himself to use and manipulate, not while I had any influence. And besides, there was too much that was good to let it go easily. I couldn't throw away all those years of loving Lucas before I knew I had really tried to make it work. I gave him a tentative smile. 'Let's try it,' I said.

The look of relief and happiness on his face told me I'd made the right decision. And made me feel like a bitch.

Over breakfast I began to think that maybe Greg hadn't seen me after all. He gave me no reason to think that anything out of the ordinary had happened. I was acutely conscious of him, aware of the way his hands moved as he served the bacon and sausages on to plates, watching the shape of his shoulders and back when he turned to cut more bread. Of course I'd known before that he was attractive but that morning it was like seeing him in an extra dimension. I was terrified that he would catch me staring at him but at the same time I couldn't look away.

I was also aware of Danny, whose usual morning malaise had today been replaced with an uncharacteristic energy. Presumably he thought victory was imminent. Well, he would learn otherwise.

I reached for a slice of toast, realising too late that the butter was on the other side of the table, between Lucas and Greg. 'Lucas,' I said, 'could I have the butter, please?'

Greg reached for it and held it out to me. I hesitated, nervous of catching his eye and seeing either accusation or, perhaps even worse, what I had read as the amusement in his smile of the night before. Again, though, there was nothing. Maybe I was off the hook. Maybe he had just happened to raise his head at that moment, his expression one of pleasure, nothing to do with me at all. I blushed nonetheless and as the blood rose from my neck to my face Danny looked at me and raised the corner of an eyebrow. A thought occurred to me: did he see my reaction? I felt suddenly as exposed as if I had been lying naked across the table. If Danny discovered that, he would make my life unlivable.

'Lions match today,' said Lucas.

'We're going to miss it, I'm afraid,' said Rachel, applying jam to her toast. 'I've got this designer who's over from New York and the only time we could meet was this afternoon.'

'Bad luck, mate,' said Danny, clapping a hand on Greg's shoulder.

Greg shrugged. 'Perils of having a successful girlfriend.'

Martha looked as if she'd had a bright idea. 'Why doesn't Greg come back with us? He can watch the match here and then get a lift with Jo later on. If you don't have any other plans? That wouldn't be a problem at all, would it, Jo?'

I looked up, feeling the flush intensify. I caught his eye.

Surely this time? But again there was nothing to suggest he knew me as the horrible voyeur I was.

'If you're sure you don't mind?' he said. 'I'd really like to see the match.'

'No,' I heard myself say. 'Of course.'

'And you'll want to see the match, won't you, Jo?' said Danny. 'You'll want to watch?'

I loved the bathroom that Lucas and I shared at Stoneborough. It was tiny compared to the other rooms, even to most of the other bathrooms. A huge cast-iron radiator belched out heat at all hours of night and day and the tropical feel was enhanced by a six-foot yucca plant and a collection of shells and sea urchins on the glass shelf over the sink. The bath was on the outside wall and the sash window was set low enough for me to lie there and look out across the garden. I ran a full tub and lowered myself gently in, acclimatising my skin and watching the water lap at the overflow hole. As it settled, there was total peace. The others were downstairs watching the match but I couldn't bear the idea of being in the same room as Danny any longer than necessary. My nerves were completely frayed. After breakfast, I'd washed up and then we'd waved Rachel off. As she'd rounded the corner in the drive, out of sight of the house, she'd given a pip on her horn. I'd jumped visibly. 'Jo,' Lucas had said with concern, 'try to relax.'

I picked up my copy of *Bleak House* and attempted to find where I had left off. After five or so minutes, my eyes on the same half-page, I gave up and tossed the book over the side. Something else was bothering me. Had Lucas really talked to Danny about our relationship, as he had claimed last night? I hated the thought that he would do that, discuss something so personal and expose me. But I could imagine it. He wouldn't have started the conversation; instead Danny would have invited his confidences, presented himself as a

133

concerned friend, all the time storing the information glee-fully, hungry for ammunition. Lucas wouldn't have sus-pected him at all, would have seen only someone trying to help. I found the idea intensely painful. Danny's presence made me want to fight him but when I was by myself the seeds of doubt he planted began to germinate.

The bathroom was full of steam; I had run the water a little too hot even for me. Outside, the mist of earlier that morning had slunk away and an intense rain was falling. The dark trees at the end of the lawn looked as if they had been brushed up into the sky. I slipped down deeper into the water, feeling the embrace of it around my shoulders.

My sleepless night and all its emotions caught up with me. My eyes closed and I let the water take the weight of my limbs. I tried to imagine the stress running down from my shoulders and leaving my body at the fingertips, draining away into the bath. To some extent it worked and I began to feel calmer. It looked like Greg hadn't seen me after all and Lucas still wanted to make a go of things. Don't fall asleep in the bath, I thought, as drowsiness pulled me harder towards it.

I came round conscious that something was different. I opened my eyes and saw why: Greg was sitting on the edge of the tub. 'Christ.' I pulled myself into a foetal position.

'That's not fair,' he said. 'How come you get to see me naked but I'm not allowed to see you?'

I was totally exposed, without so much as a sponge for cover. He loomed above me, fully clothed. My skin glowed up through the water, the hyperreal deathly pale of Millais's *Ophelia*. I looked at my legs, their image distorted as it reached the surface. I wanted to look better than this: white and rounded like an albino whale. My mind presented me with Rachel's long, lean image. For a moment neither of us said anything. The water that I had disturbed by my sudden movement slapped at the edges of the tub and the cold tap dripped into the waves.

'Is this some sort of revenge attack?' I said. 'I'm really sorry about last night – beyond sorry. I couldn't sleep and came down to make some tea. When I heard a noise in the library, I thought someone else was up . . .'

'I know. I just came to say I didn't mind.' He reached down into the water and traced his fingertip over my left nipple. I felt it stiffen treacherously under his touch. The cuff of his shirt was wet, the damp turning the pale-blue material a vivid turquoise. He smiled at me and walked away, shutting the door behind him.

I stayed in the bath until the water was almost cold. The tap was still dripping, but now the surface was flat and rings spread out across it, cause and effect. I focused on the way that the meniscus clung around my body where it rose from the water and the fine hairs that stood up on my arms as I got cold. I couldn't quite believe what had just happened. And again my response had been to feel sexually enlivened in a way I'd never experienced before. My skin was humming, my nipple the centre of a little quake. There was a bang on the door and I jumped, sending the water splashing again.

'Are you still in the bath?' Lucas's voice. 'The match has finished – you've been in there for hours. I've brought you some tea.'

'I won't be a minute.'

'Come to my room, I'll help you get dry.'

I pulled out the plug and watched the water twist away, the plumbing swallowing it rapaciously. I knew what I was about to do was wrong but to have refused Lucas then would have set us right back again and I couldn't let it happen. I would show Danny just how wrong he was about us. When the bath was empty I got out, shivering, and wrapped myself in the nursery comfort of a towel straight from the radiator. My feet left damp prints on the carpet as I walked slowly along the corridor.

I made love to Lucas that afternoon with a reel of images

of Greg in my mind: in front of the fire smiling down at Rachel, leaning forward to touch me as I lay in the bath. My body was as dishonest as my mind. It responded at the slightest touch and I was ready at once. The look of pleasure on Lucas's face was almost unbearable.

We left Stoneborough just after seven. The rain had stopped but there was still thick cloud cover and the stars were completely hidden. A great night for wreckers. I leaned against the side of the car while Michael and Martha clambered into the back seat. It had been decided that Greg needed the extra legroom afforded by the footwell on the passenger side. Lucas came round to say goodbye. It must have been obvious to everyone that we'd spent much of the afternoon having sex; although I was trying to hide it, he had an easy, slightly knackered smile and was kissing me more obviously in front of the others than I could remember him having done before. Now he pushed the hair away from my ear and leaned in, pressing me against the car with the full weight of his body, his pelvis hard against mine. 'Thank you for giving us another chance,' he said.

Greg came down the path, carrying his rucksack. I caught his eye over Lucas's shoulder. He quickly looked away as if embarrassed to have impinged on our privacy and ducked round to the back of the car to put his bag in the boot.

Danny was striding up and down on the gravel like a husband who has suffered his in-laws all weekend and now can't wait for them finally to clear off. As soon as I knew Greg wouldn't see, I pulled Lucas towards me again and kissed him hard, taking him a little by surprise. It had the desired effect: Danny spun on his heel and stalked back into the house, determined not to give me the satisfaction of an audience.

Michael was quiet in the car as we tacked across country back to the main road. In the rearview mirror, I saw him lean his head on the window, a deliberately expressionless look on his face. Martha tried to engage him and he answered her in short polite sentences that offered no leads to further conversation. I could guess at how he must be feeling as we drove away, leaving Danny in his new fiefdom.

It was clear to me that Martha really liked Greg. She leant forward between the seats, asking him questions as we drove. Their conversation gave me the opportunity to shoot an occasional sideways glance at him. His voice was warm and low in the semi-darkness, his face lit now and again by the angling beams of the headlights of the cars on the road behind us. His physical proximity was disturbing; I had to keep dragging my concentration back to the driving. I felt as though the thoughts about him that had been running through my brain all afternoon had somehow escaped my head and were at large, liable at any moment to make themselves known to him. They were so intense and vivid to me that I couldn't believe others wouldn't be aware of them. I was conscious of every minor movement of his body, the shape of his thighs in his jeans, just on the periphery of my vision. If I had shifted my hand just a few inches I could have touched him.

We reached the outskirts of London and crawled past Gipsy Corner and the Hanger Lane underpass, inching up to the rear lights of the car in front. As we approached the Shepherd's Bush roundabout, Michael came out of his reverie and asked to be dropped in Notting Hill Gate. I stopped in a side road and got out to pull my seat forward. He retrieved his burgundy-leather weekend bag from the boot and kissed my cheek. 'Thanks, Jo,' he said quietly. 'Sorry for being such a misery.'

'You're not.' I hugged him. 'You could never be. Are you going to be OK?'

He nodded. 'I'm going to go and see a friend of mine. Talk to someone removed from it all.'

137

I hugged him again and watched him go round the corner. Even if I hadn't known how he was feeling, his posture would have told me he was very down. I hesitated for a second or two, then got back into the car and did up my seatbelt. I felt another flash of pure hatred for Danny, for bulldozing into other people's lives as if they didn't have feelings, not giving a toss about anything as long as his own needs were satisfied.

'Are you hungry?' Martha was saying. 'Jo and I were thinking of getting some fish and chips to eat back at ours.'

He turned and looked at me again. Martha's question hadn't brought me out in the panic I would have expected. Instead, looking at his face in the glow of the streetlight, I found I was willing him to say yes.

'I'd love to – thank you – but I'd better not. I've got a couple of hours' work to do tonight. Actually, I'll hop out here.'

'Where do you live?' I asked.

'Shepherd's Bush, walking distance.'

'I'll drop you there,' I said.

'God, don't worry. It's very kind of you to have brought me this far.'

'I'd like to,' I heard myself say, and we looked at each other in surprise.

'Thanks,' he said.

Chapter Twelve

I managed to keep the situation on an even keel for a month. The afternoon I'd spent in bed with Lucas helped; it seemed to have reassured him that I still wanted him and he relaxed, which made things easier. I think it also helped that I didn't speak to him about Danny or the move to Stoneborough again. It was pointless, anyway: nothing I could say could convince him that Danny was anything other than a good friend – albeit a feckless one – and carping on about it only made me look bad. Also, if Danny suspected I was talking about him, he might retaliate and I didn't trust him not to tell Lucas about my watching Greg and Rachel or to concoct some even worse lie about me. Lucas interpreted my new silence on the subject as my coming to terms with the situation and was grateful to me for it, so I accepted that as the best of a bad lot.

The other thing was that he appeared to be getting on well with his writing. When we spoke on the telephone in the evenings, he told me the number of pages he'd done and often asked my opinion on a description or image that he was considering. I had to admit it looked as if I'd been wrong to think that he wouldn't get anything done at the house. There were only two or three occasions when he sounded a bit drunk when we spoke or the music had been too loud in the background or Danny had kept interrupting and made it difficult for us to talk.

Nonetheless, weekends at Stoneborough had become the opposite of what they had promised to be at the beginning of the year. Instead of a place to spend relaxing time out of town, the house had become the ground for a fraught carnival of watching. I was constantly on my guard. I knew that Danny was watching me, waiting for me to slip; I knew, too, that he derived continued satisfaction from my embarrassment at having seen Greg and Rachel. Several times it happened that I glanced up to find Greg looking at me: our eyes would lock and I would find myself in a paralysis of shame until the further weight of Danny's amused stare compelled me to look away. I was aware, too, of Michael's eyes following Danny, although he did his best to conceal the hunger in them.

There were also the films, which Lucas and Danny were watching avidly. It was obvious why Lucas was so interested in them: they gave him access to Patrick and his mother. Why Danny should be fascinated wasn't as clear to me, although I suspected that Elizabeth's appearance in them was a significant factor.

By the second week in March, winter was loosing its grip. Outside the French windows, the kitchen garden was coming alive. The earth was still heavy with rain but new leaves leavened it, in the rhubarb patch and on the gooseberries and the raspberry canes. The new foliage on the espalier trees on the back wall was as bright as freshly made glass. On Saturday afternoon I sat at the table drinking a pot of coffee and reading the paper. To my relief, Danny had announced earlier in the day that he was taking Elizabeth for lunch in Oxford and Lucas had given him a lift down to her cottage. We'd eaten lunch ourselves and then Lucas and the others had embarked on another of the epic table-tennis championships that were becoming a part of the weekend routine. They'd been playing for well over an hour. At intervals I could hear a shout or cheers of encouragement from down the hall. For the most part, the final round was an increasingly aggressive stand-off between Lucas and Danny but Greg had improved dramatically since the first time we'd played and now reached the finals himself from time to time.

I was thinking about work. I'd just turned in what I hoped would be my first front-page story, a piece about a local councillor who I'd discovered was awarding contracts for borough events to his wife's catering business. It would be good for my cuttings file. I was still resolved to leave the *Gazette* this year. More than anything, I wanted a job on a national, or the *Evening Standard*. It had to be possible, even if I started as the very lowliest of researchers or junior reporters for the gossip column. For the first time I was beginning to feel as though the lack of progress I'd made with my career during my twenties had a bearing on other issues. For years Martha and I had worried that we would never want children and I still didn't know if I did. But if it happened, I needed to make sure I had a career at a stage that I could return to; I knew that wasn't the case as things stood. I also felt I would have work to do on Lucas if marrying him was even to be a possibility. Although I was trying to explain it to myself as the mistake of someone searching for a quick answer to a tricky situation, his suggestion that I move to Stoneborough still rang a note of alarm.

There were footsteps in the corridor and Lucas appeared. 'Greg whipped my arse,' he said, sitting down.

'Coffee?'

'No thanks.' He waved the pot away. 'Can I show you something?'

'Of course. What is it?'

'Upstairs. One of the cines.'

'What's this one?'

He frowned. 'It's one with my mother.'

141

The picture projected on to the wall of the room is a picture of the room itself: Patrick's study. It is the same room but different. For one thing, there's no furniture: the huge roll-top desk is absent, as are the two armchairs in front of the windows and even the long window cushion. There are no curtains nor is there any art on the walls. Instead, as it pans round, the camera takes in a couple of canvases leaning against the far wall, their blank backs presented to the room. Further along, a large wooden easel has been folded up and laid on its side. The rich yellow light falling through the long sash windows puts the time somewhere in the late afternoon. The floorboards are covered with heavy white sheets that wrinkle here and there and with the play of light and shadow give the impression of a sea ruffled by a light breeze. On the window-seat sit a large tin of paint, a roller and a tray filled with white emulsion.

The camera flicks back across the room. Standing on either side of the fireplace with their elbows resting on the mantel-piece are Patrick and Lucas's mother. They are smiling at each other, big smiles of the sort that follow laughing. At first they are unaware they are being filmed: they haven't heard the cameraman enter the room, his footsteps on the boards deadened by the sheets. Lucas's mother is wearing old dungarees and one of the straps has come undone so that the front of the trousers hangs down on one side. A patterned headscarf holds her hair back from her face but a lock of it has escaped and fallen across her cheek. Patrick takes a step forward and tucks it back into place. She leans in and kisses him softly on the lips. In doing so, she notices the camera and smiles again, shyly this time. It is obvious that she doesn't enjoy being filmed: all her ease of movement of the previous six or seven seconds is gone. She puts her hands into the pocket of her trousers and goes over to the window, out of the shot. By contrast, Patrick faces the camera with a grin and waves his hands at the walls before bending down and sweeping the sheets up into his arms, revealing the dark-stained boards. Da-da, you can imagine him saying, it's finished.

'Well?' Lucas snapped on the light.

I hesitated. 'It looks like they were making it a painting room, with the easel and the canvases and all that white – some kind of studio. Did your mother paint?'

'I certainly never saw her. But I didn't know that she and Patrick had a thing either, which is the real issue here.' Lucas's face was hard. He switched off the projector and yanked the curtains open.

'How do you mean?' I said, stalling.

'Well, it's obvious, isn't it? They're clearly together. Would you kiss your brother-in-law like that?'

It was true: the film had captured an exchange between lovers, a casually intimate moment. 'Was he her brother-in-law? When this was taken?'

'Who the fuck knows,' he said. 'I just hope it was before I was born.'

'It must have been. Your mother wouldn't have had an affair, especially with Patrick.'

'How can you know that?' he said, his face suddenly right up in mine. 'How can you know?'

I wasn't sure what to say. He was staring as if he were trying to drag something out of me. 'Lucas, please . . .'

The door opened. Danny, back from town. 'Ah, there you are. I wondered where you were both hiding.' He saw the look on Lucas's face. 'Oh no. Have you been watching that cine again?'

'I wanted Jo to see it.'

'You're obsessing over it. You'll drive yourself mad.' He went over to the projector and took out the reel. He replaced it carefully in the box and put the lid on.

'I'm not obsessing, Danny. I just want to know the truth.

143

Surely that's understandable?' Lucas slumped backwards into the other armchair.

'Why don't you ask Elizabeth?' I said. 'She'd be able to tell you what happened. She was there.'

'I think that's an excellent idea. It'll stop you stewing once and for all. I'll ring her later and ask her for supper in the week,' said Danny.

'I can ring her myself.'

Danny noticed his tone. 'What? I was only trying to be helpful.'

'I don't need help. Anyway, how come you're so buddy-buddy with Elizabeth all of a sudden?'

'Lucas, she worked with some really interesting people, as you already know. I'm just trying to learn. Anyway, she's good fun. I like her. That's all right, isn't it?'

Chapter Thirteen

Elizabeth leant forward and rested her chin in her hand. Her slim gold watch slid down her arm a little. 'You've found the cine films? God, how incredible – I had no idea they were here.' She tossed her head, showing her clean jaw and smooth neck.

Friday lunch had been the only time she was free as she was going to Edinburgh for a week on Saturday morning. I'd thought I should be there when Lucas asked her about his mother so I'd taken the day off work. I wished I could claim that my motivation was just to support him; in fact, that impulse was diluted by a less commendable one which would not let Danny be the only one either to hear what Elizabeth said or to comfort Lucas if need be. It felt strange to be sitting in the kitchen at the house, just the four of us, while the others were in their offices in London.

'They were in the cupboard in his study,' said Danny, reaching across the table to refill her glass. 'There's a whole box of them.'

'Dear Patrick. He never could throw anything out.'

'Why would he throw them out?' asked Lucas.

'Oh, I don't know.' She turned her head slightly to blow away the smoke from her cigarette. 'I suppose they must have been special to him in a funny sort of way, a record of that summer here.'

'So what was the idea behind them? Who took them?'

Danny, sitting opposite her, leant forward in his seat and put his elbow on the table, mirroring her posture.

'Richard Appleton, the painter. Do you know his work?'

I hadn't heard of him but Lucas nodded.

'The Richard Appleton?' said Danny, surprising me. 'I saw some of his pictures when I was in New York last year.'

She nodded. 'He was much bigger over there. I think he was the one person who wasn't made here by his connection with Patrick. Anyway, he was always experimenting with new things. In a way, that was his problem. He was talented but he never stuck at anything, never really committed himself. He developed a big thing about the cine camera that summer and then just abandoned it. Not that it was work as such. He used to drive us mad, pointing it at things all the time. God alone knows how many sunsets he recorded. Have you found one of those yet?'

'One or two.' Lucas smiled. 'I'm more interested in the ones with my mother in, though, Elizabeth. How many of those did he take?'

Almost imperceptibly, her face clouded, then cleared. 'Oh, hardly any at all. It was mostly nature he was into.'

'Really? I've seen quite a few with her in already.'

Elizabeth was stroking the shiny petals of one of the blood-coloured tulips that Lucas had cut for the lunch table. Standing naked at the window that morning, I had been startled to see a man wheeling a barrow across the lawn and had ducked down below the sill before he could see me. I'd forgotten about the gardener, having never seen him at weekends. Tulips don't plant themselves, of course, though.

'Elizabeth, were my mother and Patrick ever together?'

'God, darling, it was so long ago.' She turned the vase round and subjected another of the flowers to her scrutiny.

'It can't be a hard thing to remember.'

She looked up, struck by the uncharacteristic irritation in his tone. 'Well, yes, I suppose they were.'

Lucas sat back under the weight of his confirmed suspicion. 'Was it serious?'

'Serious? No, not at all, not at all.' She laughed lightly and tossed her head again. Today her hair was in a neat chignon but I wondered if the gesture was a hangover from the days when she swung it back over her shoulder, as I had seen her do on the cines. 'Patrick met Claire first and they were together for a while but then she met your father and that was that.' She smiled and put her hand over his. 'They were so lovely together, Lucas.'

'Didn't Patrick mind?'

'Mind? Oh, not really. I don't think he and Claire were very involved. He was a little upset initially but that was bruised pride. And you know what he was like – he had such a generous spirit. He saw that Claire and Justin made each other happy and bowed out gracefully. And anyway, he and I got together then and that was a whole different ball game.' She smiled. 'It worked out for the best. For all of us.'

'I'd hate it if a sister or even a friend stole a boyfriend from me. I'm not sure I'd just accept it,' I said.

'Your generation can be so bourgeois at times.'

'But it was definitely before my parents were married?' Lucas said.

'Absolutely, darling.'

'I think Lucas has been worrying that he's the wrong brother's son,' said Danny.

'For God's sake, Danny,' he said.

'Oh Lucas, you poor thing. No, your parents were very much in love. There's no way your mother would even have considered anyone else after she and your father got together.'

'Did my mother paint?'

'Paint?'

'On a bit of film we've just watched, she and Patrick were decorating his study. It looked as if they were making it into a studio of some sort.'

'Oh, it wasn't for your mother. The study was painted for Patrick.'

'He painted? I didn't know that.'

'Well, he stopped by the time you were old enough to be aware of it, I suppose. But yes, he liked to paint then.'

'Was he any good?'

'He wasn't bad, for an amateur. But of course he was surrounded by all his artists so I think he felt a bit outclassed. It was fun, though, he enjoyed it.'

'Why did he stop?'

'I think he just got too busy, darling. His commitments at the gallery were huge, as you know.' She drained her glass. 'Danny, would you mind . . .' He was on hand with the bottle even before she'd finished.

'Is that one empty?' said Lucas. 'I'll go and get another.' He stood up from the table and took down the key for the cellar door.

'I'm in the process of getting a camera myself,' said Danny, as Lucas's footsteps faded.

'Are you? How interesting.'

I wondered for about two seconds where he was going to get the money for it. From the same place he got it for the new trainers he was wearing, I realised, and the lunch he'd bought for Elizabeth the previous weekend. 'I rather like the cines,' I said. 'They definitely add a historical flavour, like sepia photos.'

Danny rolled his eyes. 'You're such a Luddite, Joanna. This is just for fun,' he said to Elizabeth. 'Quite separate from the project I was telling you about.' That was news, too: he hadn't mentioned anything remotely like work to the rest of us.

She nodded, watching his face all the time. I had to hand it to her: she certainly knew how to make a man feel he had her full attention.

'Elizabeth, can I ask you something?' I kept my voice low, in case Lucas was within hearing.

She turned back to me, the smile she had given Danny now fading.

'The tapes. Is there anything on them that could hurt Lucas?'

'It's always painful to think about the past, don't you think?' she said. 'To realise that the older generation were people themselves before they were your parents.'

'You're next, Martha.' Danny, lying on his back in his usual place in front of the fire, reached over his head and handed her the joint. He opened his mouth and let the thick smoke rise out of it, as if he wasn't breathing at all but surrendering himself to the laws of physics, letting it move out of him by osmosis. Martha had a quick toke and then passed it to me. It was a highly professional rolling job. Normally I didn't but this evening I felt I needed it. The wine wasn't doing the trick, despite the fact that we'd been drinking since lunchtime. I couldn't seem to tip myself over into happy drunkenness but was stuck in an unpleasant limbo where I just felt tired and woolly-headed. Elizabeth had gone shortly after four o'clock but Lucas, Danny and I had carried on without a break. The others had some serious catching up to do when they finally arrived.

I took a drag, closing my eyes on the in-breath. When I opened them again Greg was watching me; I quickly looked away. The hit from the dope was almost instantaneous, a sudden heaviness in my arms and head, slight accompanying nausea. Other people always seemed to have a better time with it than I did.

'Hurry up,' said Lucas. 'You're wasting it. Smoke it or pass it on.'

'Mate, we've got plenty,' said Danny.

'Roll another one then.'

'You do it.' Danny picked the bag of weed from his stomach and threw it across to him.

'No, you do it. I paid for it.' Lucas tossed it back. Reluctantly Danny pulled himself upright and reached for his rolling-board, a hardback edition of *Bonfire of the Vanities*.

More to annoy Lucas than because I really wanted it, I took another drag, then passed the last inch to Martha next to me. Lucas had been wired since lunch and, as far as I could see, the weed was doing little to relax him. He had had a lot to drink and there was an edge to him tonight that I didn't like. Danny passed him the new joint, which he took without a word. He lit it, waited for the twist of paper at the end to burn away and took a huge lungful, closing his eyes and leaning back against the studded arm of the chesterfield. He smoked almost half of it before he opened his eyes again and gave it to Rachel.

'I'm fine, actually,' she said, taking it but passing it to Greg straightaway.

'Loosen up for once, Rachel, can't you?' Lucas said. She looked at me and raised her eyebrows. He saw the bemused look I gave her in response.

'What?' he said to me, becoming more alert.

'Nothing.'

'If you've got something to say, say it.'

I hesitated, trying to find the best way to put it. 'I just think you should relax a bit. Now you know there wasn't anything going on between your mother and Patrick after she and your father were married.'

'You know what? Why don't you mind your own business for a change?' He sat up.

'No, I don't mean . . .'

'Tell me what you know about difficult families, why don't you? You haven't got a clue. Everything's been easy for you, even though you play the outsider card when it suits you. I don't know why you feel qualified to comment on my situation, with your happily married parents and your

150

brothers and your family home.' He pronounced the last two words with bitter disdain. 'Why don't you just fuck off? Go on, fuck off.'

In the silence that followed no one said anything. I stood up, feeling a spin from the dope, and walked out of the room. In the hall, the strange beating in my ears started up but I was beyond caring. I wanted to be away from Lucas. I wanted to be outside the house and its unbreathable atmosphere. I fumbled at the bolts on the outside door with shaking hands, annoying myself with the delay. As soon as the door opened and I hit fresh air, I felt better. I took hard breaths in, wishing I had my inhaler. My lungs were tight with tension. I couldn't believe he'd spoken to me like that. Maybe he needed to be angry, to burn off some of the fear he must have had about what Elizabeth would tell him. I didn't mind that. But what he had said about my family shocked me. It sounded like something he had been festering over for some time, nursing resentment.

All of a sudden I realised that I was battling insuperable odds. It wasn't going to work out between us. There was too much in the way, too many differences. I couldn't have a relationship in which I was made to feel bad about having a happy family background or to worry that I would have to sacrifice my career.

We had stepped over the boundary, only to find that what lay beyond wasn't the great relationship we'd imagined. In my heart, I knew, I had suspected it from the start but I had ignored my instinct, hoping to prove it – and then Danny – wrong. The chemistry, that indefinable thing that makes great sex and cements a new relationship, wasn't there. We were struggling, even so early on, and the effort of the struggle was taking its toll. I wished I could think straight. The beating in my ears had stopped but was replaced by the beginnings of a hangover, a low drone in the temples.

There was little cloud cover and the night air was chilly.

The moon, though, was bright and cast the garden in a strange penumbrous light. I sat down at the place on the balustrade where Lucas and I had sat together on other evenings, blinked and felt the first tears tip down my cheeks. I gave in to them. I cried with self-pity for the break-up that was now imminent and with pity for Lucas because I knew it would hurt him badly. I cried for our friendship. I also cried for my parents, who suddenly I wanted very much. I had not seen them since Christmas and I couldn't now think why I had let so much time pass. I was surrounded by the Manor's garden and the huge elegant house itself and felt out of my depth. I wanted the comfort of my parents' little house and my old bedroom.

Behind me the flower-lobby door opened and closed.

Without turning round, I tried to work out which member of the party had been dispatched to make sure I was all right or whether it was Lucas, come either to apologise or to elaborate on my failings. The footsteps were male. I surreptitiously wiped the tears off my face and made an effort to blink back those still in my eyes. It was unlikely that I would be able to hide the fact that I'd been crying but I could perhaps disguise how much. The footsteps came closer.

'Jo.' To my surprise, the voice was Greg's.

I looked up at him. He registered my tears even in the darkness and sat down next to me, keeping his legs on the terrace side so that we were almost back to back. I stayed where I was, facing out from the house, my legs swinging over the drop.

'I'm sorry he spoke to you like that.'

'I shouldn't have said anything to him. I should have just let him drink and smoke himself to sleep. He'd have woken up in a better mood tomorrow.'

'If it's any comfort, Martha's just given him a pasting.'

'It's not like him. You know that, don't you?' I said.

'Of course. He's a good bloke.'

'Yes,' I said. Poor Lucas. He was right: I couldn't imagine what it was like to be him, to find myself at the end of my twenties without a single member of family, no parents, no siblings. Even divorce was alien to me, something which as a child I'd regarded as a faintly glamorous thing that other people's parents did. The tears started to fall again but at least they did so silently. I appreciated that Greg had faced away so that he couldn't see, giving me support but privacy at the same time. It was easier to talk this way, as if to an unseen and unseeing confessor.

'Are you going to be all right?' he asked.

'I think Lucas and I are going to split up. Although I know tonight wasn't really about him being angry with me. Please don't tell anyone this.' I put my hand on his arm and he shook his head. 'If I'm honest with myself, I know it's not right and it hasn't ever really been. I just wanted it to be. So much. Lucas has been my best friend for years, since right at the beginning of university. But it doesn't translate. I'm trying to force something that isn't there. I'm worried that if I talk to him about it he'll hate me, too. He's paranoid about people leaving him – his father, his mother and Patrick. How can I leave him? I'm the closest thing he's got to family.'

'But you're not going anywhere. Not really. You still want to be around, to be friends. It might take a while to find a way to do it but if you both want it – and Lucas won't want to lose you even if you do split up – you'll work it out.' He continued to look away from me, talking as if he were addressing someone else on the terrace. He moved his feet and I heard the grit between his shoes and the flagstones.

'I'm useless at relationships,' I said.

'That's not true. You've got loads of friends and you and Lucas are a far better couple than a lot I know, even if it doesn't work out. You have fun, you're supportive of each other . . .'

'It doesn't feel like that tonight.'

At last he turned round. 'Please don't cry, Jo.' He put his hand on my cheek and turned my face towards him. He looked at me without saying anything. Though I knew my eyes were swollen and my face puffy, I felt suddenly un-selfconscious. With his thumb, he brushed away the tears from each cheek in turn, still not breaking eye contact. The gesture felt protective.

He leant in and kissed me, his lips firm and warm on mine. When I didn't immediately move away, he kissed me again and this time I responded. I couldn't quite believe it. Even as it was happening, I was shocked by it. A picture of Rachel flashed into my head. We pulled apart.

'My God, I'm sorry,' he said. 'I didn't mean to do that.'

Despite everything, I registered a feeling of sharp disap-pointment.

'No, no, I didn't mean that,' he said quickly. 'Of course I wanted to kiss you. But not like this. Not when we're with other people, not when you're upset. I don't want to take advantage of you.' He turned away from me and started to address the darkness again. 'I really like you, Jo. I think you're funny and kind and – well, I just like you. Since that weekend when you saw Rachel and me, I've found it quite difficult to be around you, especially when I see you and Lucas together. And I don't have any right. Apart from anything else, you two have all this history. You've done so much together. All of you have, of course, but particularly you and him. How could I compete with that?'

'I don't think the history is helping us much at the moment,' I said, trying to leaven things.

'Maybe not. But there's also the fact that I'm going out with one of your best friends. I care about her, I really do. For a while, I thought I was falling in love with her but I realise now that it isn't going to work. There's not enough common ground. I don't share her thing about fashion.' He sighed. 'I actually find it quite frustrating, even though she's great at it.

154

And I need to sort it out because she wants to get married and have children and I'm wasting her time. But – and this is so callous – if Rachel and I split up, my line to you is lost. I've no other way of seeing you.'

'What a mess,' I said. 'What a complete bloody mess.' None of us had ever tangled with one of the others' partners before, not even fleetingly and not even when we were much younger, when relationships were less serious. I saw now just how important that had been to us as a group rule, unspoken as it was.

'Have I made a fool of myself?' he said.

I didn't have to think about it. 'No.' I shook my head. 'You know, it's this place, the house. Ever since we started coming here, everything's gone outside normal bounds. Lucas and I getting together after however many years, Danny and . . .' I stopped myself just in time. 'Maybe it's because we feel like we're on a bigger stage here. But sometimes I feel as if there's something in the house that's kind of egging us on towards catastrophe. Does that sound ridiculous?'

He took my hand and began rubbing up and down my fingers with the pad of his thumb. 'No, but I think the first seems more likely – that something about the scale of the place makes people act up – I'm thinking of Danny in particular, of course.'

I smiled and we looked at each other again. This time it was me who put my hand around the back of his head, where the soft skin of his neck met the line of his close-cut hair. I pulled him towards me and kissed him. Our mouths became the hot focus of everything. All the desire I had felt in the library and the bath was there, undiminished. But also there was my growing sense of his all-round rightness and how much I liked him. I wanted to get lost in the kiss, absorb him and be absorbed by him. With as little break as possible, he shifted position, swinging one leg over the drop, and in that second I realised that this exact spot was where I had first kissed Lucas. I pulled back.

155

'Greg . . .'

'We should go inside. We need to sort things out. Not tonight, though. Just kiss me once more and we'll go in.'

He pulled me towards him again, twisting his hands in my hair.

I think we both became aware at the same time that we were no longer on our own. We broke apart to find a figure standing just outside the flower-lobby door. Rachel.

'Tell me this isn't what it looks like,' she said, her voice carrying over the flagstones in the stillness of the night.

Greg closed his eyes and lowered his head. 'Shit,' he said, just audibly. He looked up at her again. 'Rachel, I'm sorry.'

She came closer, as if approaching an animal she knew could hurt her very badly and yet by which she was nonetheless fascinated. 'Sorry?'

'This is the first time,' he said.

'I can't believe this is happening,' she said. Even in the half-light her face was a screen for the emotions flashing across it in quick succession: genuine disbelief, bewilderment, anger. 'Tell me I'm asleep and this is a nightmare.'

Greg swung his leg back over the balustrade and stood. He made to walk towards her. She took a corresponding couple of steps back. 'Rachel.'

She made a dry sound that was somewhere between a choke and an ironic laugh. 'Is this where you tell me you can explain?'

'Please don't. It's a mess but please let me talk to you.'

'I don't want to talk to you, now or ever again. You've ruined it. I thought we had something really good. How wrong can you be? A friend of mine, too. Jo, you fucking selfish cow.' She turned and ran back into the house, slamming the door behind her. Greg and I looked at each other in horror.

'I'll go after her,' he said.

'Shit. Shit. Lucas.'

*   *   *

I expected the house to be mayhem when we got inside but it was strangely quiet. As when I'd left it, the only light came from the two table lamps on the chest in the hall and the bright strip under the drawing-room door. I thought of the eye of a storm, the deadly stillness, the inevitability. I imagined a tornado sitting over the house, the first half of the damage already done, the second coming any minute. It filled me with a sickening dread; at that moment I wished I had walked in to find it all breaking over my head rather than suffer the anticipation. I took a deep breath and opened the door, indicating to Greg to stay back so the others didn't see us together, just in case there was any chance, however remote, that the situation was salvageable. Inside, Michael, Martha and Danny were in the same positions they'd been in when I'd walked out. It was like a flashback. Although it was less than half an hour ago, that scene already belonged to a different era.

'Jo, are you OK?' said Martha, looking up with concern. 'I was going to come find you but Greg said he would go.'

'It's fine, it's fine,' I said, having almost forgotten that, as far as she knew, the major event had been Lucas swearing at me. I felt about as unworthy of anyone's sympathy as it was possible to be. 'Where's Rachel? Where's Lucas?'

'Don't know about Rachel but Lucas is throwing up,' she said.

'Calling God on the great white telephone,' said Danny without opening his eyes.

'He completely overdid it,' Martha said. 'Well, you saw him. He was on a total mission even before he screamed at you.'

'I'll go and talk to him. Where is he?'

'In the downstairs loo but he won't want to talk. I tried,' said Michael.

I closed the door behind me and faced Greg. 'Do you think she's with him?'

Upstairs there was the sound of a door closing and quick footsteps. Rachel appeared at the top of the steps, holding her weekend bag. I felt, more than heard, the first opening pulses of the house's secret rhythm. There was something sly in it now, knowing, taunting. I shook my head to rid myself of it but it only gathered pace, as if trying to match the beat of my heart. I looked up, wanting to see the picture on the ceiling. It was hidden in the darkness, too high to be touched by the light from the lamps, but I had the sense that the people up there were craning down to see what drama the house was cradling now. I could almost hear the creak of the couch as Zeus leaned forward, waiting. I said a silent prayer. Please don't let it come out like this. Please let me tell Lucas myself, decently.

'Haven't you had enough of sneaking around?' said Rachel, descending towards us. Guilt made it impossible for me to look at her.

'Where are you going?' said Greg.

'Home.'

'Have you called a cab?'

'My car's here. I'll drive. I just want to go. Leave me alone.' She struggled as he tried to take her bag.

'Rachel, however much you despise me at the moment, I'm not going to let you drive tonight. You've been drinking.'

'The time where you had any influence on my decisions has gone.' Her composure deserted her at last and she burst into tears. 'You idiot,' she said, 'I really loved you.' My heart filled with pity for her and then, a fraction of a second later, with shame that I, supposedly her friend, was the cause of her misery. She shook her bag out of his grip and turned to me, hostile again. 'I just can't believe you've done this. Bad enough what you've done to me but I can't believe you'd cheat on Lucas. How could you? After everything else that he's been through.' Her words caused me a visceral pain that sliced up through my stomach like a cutlass. 'I hope you can

158

live with yourself, Joanna, because I don't think I could. It's taken me ten years to realise what you are but I know now. I just want to forget I ever knew you.' She spun away as if the sight of me was repulsive.

The drawing-room door opened and Martha came out. 'What's going on?' she said. 'I heard shouting.'

'Nothing,' I said automatically.

Rachel snorted. 'Why don't you tell her, Joanna? Tell Martha what a lovely friend you are.'

'What's she talking about, Jo?' Martha looked at me and the thought that she was about to discover what I'd done made me want to cry. Guilt was roiling in my stomach. I could feel it burning my cheeks, too, and I couldn't get my eyes to meet hers for more than a second. The pulsing in my ears put in a couple of extra beats as if in a merry little flourish.

'We're all drunk and overtired,' said Greg. 'Why don't we call it a day?'

There were footsteps from the direction of the cloakroom and Lucas appeared in the mouth of the corridor. Even in the dim glow of the table lamps I could see that he was as pale as wax. He was unsteady on his feet and braced himself against the wall. 'What's happening?' he said. 'Why are you all out here?'

'Something's going on,' said Martha.

I stood there, looking at Lucas. My anger with him for his hurtful remarks was forgotten; all I could think of was the pain that I was going to inflict on him, surely inevitable now. I couldn't understand how the evening had suddenly turned my life on its head, how I could go from trying so hard to make a go of things with him to kissing Greg outside and now this, the revelation in front of everyone of what I'd done. I was trapped – no way backwards and no way forwards without pain, for me and people I cared about. There was no undoing it. I was going to leave Lucas just as surely as his

159

mother and father and Patrick had done but having hurt him first.

Michael and Danny had come to the drawing-room door now, drawn like Martha by the raised voices. Everyone's attention was on me.

'If you won't tell them, then I will.' Rachel turned to him. The air seemed to shimmer with the potential energy of the chaos she was about to unleash. 'Lucas, just now I went to see if Greg had found Jo and if she was OK. I found them out on the terrace – and they were kissing.'

Lucas looked at me. His face showed no change of expression apart from a slight widening of the eyes.

'Lucas . . .' I said.

'Is it true?' He looked only quizzical. I didn't think I could bear it, watching him absorb the news.

'No. Yes . . . I don't know. It's not like you think. It's . . .'

'Oh come on, Joanna,' Danny piped up from the doorway. 'It's been obvious for weeks that there's something going on between you two. Every time you're in a room together you're either staring at each other like zombies or pretending the other one doesn't exist.'

I turned to look at him in disbelief. He knew that nothing had ever happened. He had been watching me minutely for weeks, letting me feel the pressure of his surveillance. If anything had happened, he would have known almost before I did. In his eyes now, there was a light like glee. It was the moment he had been waiting for, when I was exposed as the cheat and the liar and he revealed as Lucas's one true friend. My hatred for him burned with a new intensity. I wanted so much to ask about his secret involvement, to see how he liked his affairs broadcast in public, but I could see Michael's stricken face behind him. And completely inappropriately my heart had leapt at the thought that Greg had been watching me, too.

'So, while we've been here, you and he have been meeting

in London? You've been sleeping together?' The pain was there in Lucas's voice now, as unmistakable as a knife wound.

'No.' My voice was loud and it echoed up through the house. 'No, Lucas. Tonight was the only time. We only kissed. It wasn't meant to happen.'

'It wasn't meant to happen? You mean you wanted it to.'

'No, of course not. I . . .'

'Look,' said Greg. 'This isn't doing anyone any good. We need to talk about this properly, not like this.' His voice, somehow, was calm and the composure of it seemed to incense Lucas.

'How dare you? How fucking dare you tell me what to do in my house?' He was moving now. He stepped out of the shadows at the end of the corridor and crossed the floor towards Greg. He looked wild. He had clearly been sick repeatedly and the hair along his brow was damp. His eyes were moving fast, flicking between Greg and me as if trying to catch us in some secret communication. He was glowing with anger, a pale rage that altered the air around him.

'Lucas, that's not what I mean. I just think it would be better if we talk about this privately.'

Lucas stepped forward and swung at him with his full might. His fist made contact with Greg's cheekbone and Greg spun round with the unexpected weight of it, putting his hand to his face. Rachel gave a sharp cry. Lucas stood, trembling with anger and with disbelief at what he had done, his fist still clenched in front of him.

Greg was feeling his jaw. There was blood in his mouth, making a red film over his teeth. He swallowed it away. The lack of retaliation seemed to inflame Lucas still further and he swung again. This time Greg turned and so the blow glanced across his ear. Nonetheless, it was enough to make him wince with pain.

'Come on then, you bastard. Come on – hit me.'

'Lucas, stop it.' Danny crossed the hall and grabbed his arm. 'This isn't the way.'

Lucas turned on Danny and I thought for a moment he was going to hit him as well but instead he started to cry. 'He's taking Jo, Danny,' he said. 'He's sleeping with Jo.' He put his head in his hands and sobbed, his shoulders shaking with the force of it. I saw that he was still very drunk.

'I'm not,' I said. 'We haven't. You've got this all wrong. Danny's twisting it. It was just a kiss. It's never happened before.'

'Rachel saw you, Joanna. That's not my evidence.' Danny stepped forward and pulled Lucas towards him, putting his arms around him and holding him. Over his shoulder he looked at me. His expression was unambiguous; he might as well have said it aloud: he's mine now.

'Lucas,' said Greg, swallowing again. He wiped his mouth with the back of his hand. 'This wasn't supposed to happen. And I promise you that tonight was the first time.'

'Fuck off. Just fuck off.' Lucas's words were muffled on Danny's shoulder.

At that moment I caught Martha's eye. She was staring at me with sheer disbelief, as if unable to understand what was happening.

Greg moved first. 'Rachel . . .'

'I'm not going anywhere with you.'

'Please. I need to talk to you.' I watched the resistance in her face melt and saw again how much he had meant to her. She let him guide her upstairs to their room. He walked slowly behind her, his hand feeling tenderly around his jaw. I waited for him to turn and glance at me as he climbed the stairs, for confirmation of some sort, but he didn't look back.

Danny took Lucas and led him into the drawing room, closing the door behind them. Martha looked at me in disgust, turned on her heel and walked away. 'Come on, Michael,' she said, her voice icy.

'Martha,' I tried but she ignored me. Michael shot me an ambivalent look and followed her down the corridor to the kitchen.

As quickly as everyone had gathered they were gone. Suddenly I was left alone in the hall and the atmosphere of the place rushed in, all focused on me. I felt as if I were the object of the exclusive scrutiny of a thousand pairs of invisible eyes. My head went light and the place started to shut in around me, the floor moving up in all directions and the walls moving in, coming to brick me up. My chest constricted further and then came the crash of blood in my ears, my heartbeat or the house's, I wasn't sure, just that it was getting louder and louder. My legs felt dissociated from the rest of my body and I didn't know whether I would have any mastery over them but I knew I had to move from that place.

The first few steps felt like dragging through thick mud, as if there were resistance to my going. The pounding in my head grew louder still. I reached the stairs and started to climb. The landings seemed to go on for an eternity and I stumbled on the steps as I went. All I wanted was to put a door between me and that terrible pulsing energy, whatever it was.

When I reached my room, I slammed the door shut and braced myself against it, as if there were something outside pushing to get in. I waited until the feeling had passed and the pounding had retreated a little. There was a spare inhaler on the bedside table and I took hit after hit on it until my hands were shaking from the overdose. Then I pulled my suitcase out of the bottom of the wardrobe and started packing. There was no method to it, just speed. I grabbed at things indiscriminately, snatching handfuls of the underwear I had started keeping in the chest of drawers, throwing my hair-dryer and shoes into the bottom of the case.

There were heavy footsteps along the landing outside and

the door cranked open. My stomach turned over. It was Lucas. We looked at each other as if across a great stretch of unfamiliar terrain. His eyes moved off me and took in my suitcase on the bed and the tangle of tights and T-shirts beside it. 'What can I do?' he said. For a stupid moment I thought he meant with the packing. His face was raw. With the strain first of being sick and then crying, his eyelids were puffed and pink, his eyes shot through with blood. The discoloration was made more striking by the graveyard pallor of the rest of his skin.

He closed the door behind him. 'It's my fault,' he said. 'I screwed it up.'

'Please, Lucas. Don't.' I turned away, unable to look at him.

'I didn't do enough things right. Tell me what I should have done differently. Tell me. I should have stayed in London, shouldn't I? Jo, if I could go back now . . . I'll try,' he said suddenly. 'I'll get another flat in London; we'll just come back here at weekends. That would change things, wouldn't it?'

I didn't say anything.

'What if I asked for my job back? I know you don't approve of me living on Patrick's money. What if I told Danny to move out?' He came round to the end of the bed, forcing himself into my line of sight. 'Tell me what I can do. Please. For God's sake.'

'Nothing.' Saying the word was so difficult. It felt like cutting a mooring line, setting myself adrift from him, or him from me, and from everything we'd shared, all those years of the best friendship I'd ever had. I felt as though I were floating, my head a whirl of sorrow and regret and the desire to be free.

His eyes filled with tears again. 'Nothing?'

I shook my head as gently as I could.

'Jo, I'm begging you. I'm telling you I'll do whatever you

164

want me to do as long as you'll stay with me,' he said, his voice getting louder.

I wanted so much to be able to give him an answer, the one simple thing he could change so that everything would come right again. But I couldn't. 'That's not what I loved you for,' I said. 'I loved the old Lucas, the self-determining, independent Lucas. I needed you to be you, not changing.'

'I can do that. I can. Jo, listen to me. I can go back.' He moved now so that he was in front of me and took me by the shoulders. He was gripping me hard; even through my jumper the pressure of his fingers was hurting my collar bone. The air around him was rancid, undercut with the smell of vomit. Careful not to anger him further, I stepped away until he was forced to let go of me.

He started to cry again. 'I love you,' he said but the words that once would have made my heart swell now filled me with despair. And, although I could barely admit it, I was frightened. I'd never seen him hit anyone before tonight. Alcohol and shock had vanquished the usual moderate Lucas. 'I love you,' he wept. 'And I need you to stay with me. I need you.'

'I can't.'

'You're one of the only people I have left. You can't leave me. Don't you understand? Don't you see that?'

I forced the lid down on the case and dragged the zip round, catching a pair of tights that had come free. I tore them out of the zip and shoved them back inside. There were possessions of mine scattered all over the house but I couldn't stop for them now. 'I've got to go,' I said, moving back.

'You can't.' Suddenly Lucas dropped to his knees. A low crooning sound came from his throat. He snatched at my trouser leg and when I looked down at him I saw that his reddened eyes were full of a terrible anger. 'If you go now, you can never come back,' he said.

I said nothing and pulled away. I didn't recognise this

165

possessive, frightening man. Grabbing my suitcase from the bed, I turned to open the door and, as I did so, he stood and grabbed at my jumper. 'You bitch. You won't even give me a chance.' His face was crazy with grief.

'Lucas, please, let me go.' I was in tears but they were tears of desperation and fear. I could feel them running down my cheeks and into my mouth. Every fibre of me was straining to go. The key to my car was in my pocket and my hand felt for it, checking it was there.

'I can't,' he said. 'I can't let you. I can't let you leave me.'

He lunged for me, grabbing at my bag, my shoulders, shaking me, hurting me. His hand caught a clump of my hair and pulled it so hard I thought it would be torn from my scalp. Even though he was thin, his body was strong. I don't know what would have happened if Danny hadn't appeared in the doorway and pulled him off me. In Danny's arms again, Lucas stopped fighting and let me go.

I remember the journey home to London only as a series of snapshots, a sequence of disordered images that deliver themselves to my brain now with the quality of hallucinations. I know I was still drunk and to this day I don't understand how I didn't have an accident. I cried all the way back down the motorway but it wasn't the sort of crying that I had been used to in the past. This was new, a weeping that hurt me and stretched my mouth into a great silent circle of misery from which no noise would come. When I left Stoneborough it was still dark but the horizon was lightening to the east, the intimations of dawn a virulent orange seeping up the sky. By the time I reached London I was driving through the pallid pink-and-blue light of the first hour of a new day. At traffic lights I looked straight ahead for fear that one of the few other drivers on the road at that hour would see my ravaged face.

Chapter Fourteen

Martha cut her weekend short and came back that night. I was sitting upstairs in one of the armchairs, clutching a cushion to my chest. When I heard the front door, my heart bumped. I had been dreading her return. I was staring at *Dalziel and Pascoe* on television. I couldn't concentrate enough to follow the plot but Dalziel's big, doleful face seemed to express all the sorrow and uncertainty in the world. The reverberation of the door slamming shuddered through the house. I heard her bags being thrown down and she came up the stairs two at a time.

She stood in the doorway like a Fury. 'How could you?' she shouted. 'How could you do that? To Lucas? To Rachel?' Even her hair seemed angry. Long as it was, it stood away from her head as if it was electrified. She held her hands out in front of her, the fingers stiff with tension, as if imploring me to give her an explanation that would go some way to helping her understand how I could behave like this.

'I didn't set out to do it, Marth. It just happened,' I said limply.

'Bullshit.' Her right hand cut through the air like a blade on the second consonant. 'Even if he had come after you in the biggest way possible, you could always have said no. You could always have said no, Joanna, but you didn't. And now you've dicked over two of your oldest friends. I just cannot

167

believe you did that.' She sat down on the arm of the sofa as if I had pulled all the stuffing out of her.

'I'm sorry,' I said, feeling the inadequacy of the word.

'That doesn't really cover it.' She shook her head. 'Of all people, I thought you'd get it. Anyway, it's not me you should be apologising to.'

'How can I do it? How can I ever tell them how sorry I am?'

'I'm not sure you can.'

'Please help me, Martha,' I said. 'I feel so bad.'

'You should have thought of that before. And I can't help you right now. Don't ask me to.' She stood up to go, as if she had exposed herself to my presence for as long as she could without becoming contaminated by it. 'Because all this makes me ask questions. Like, if you can do this to Lucas and Rachel, what's to say you couldn't do it to me, next time I meet someone I really like? I don't know whether I even trust you any more.'

That night was the closest I have ever come to harming myself. I don't mean anything as dramatic as trying to kill myself; I don't think I am courageous enough for that, or ever could be, even in a situation that merited it. Ending one's own life seems to involve a grandeur of scale, somehow, however despicable or cowardly the reasons for wanting to. No, that night I thought about inflicting pain on myself. In the empty kitchen the knives in the drawer shone with a dangerous glamour and I wanted to know if self-harming worked, if the infliction of doses of pain to the outside of the body could lessen the anguish on the inside, however momentarily.

I could not erase from my mind the memory of the pain I had seen in Lucas's face. My room felt like a stifling prison, the air rank with thoughts of what I had done. Every avenue I pursued to try to excuse what had happened offered me a dead end. I tried telling myself that it was just a kiss, nothing more, that the whole thing had been blown out of proportion, but I knew it wasn't true. The kiss was the culmination of weeks of watching Greg and wanting him, wanting to know what it was like to be with him, to sleep with him. To cheat on Lucas. I wept silently for fear that Martha would hear and judge me undeserving of any tears for myself. The hands on my alarm clock moved later and later into the night but it was pointless even trying to sleep.

In the end I left the house and walked. It was hours past midnight and London showed me its nocturnal face, turning familiar streets into a chilly alien landscape. The shops were battened against the night, the grilles locked down over the front of the newsagent's and the shop across the road that handled money transfers and the transport of packages to Poland and Eastern Europe. The streetlamps lit dirty canyons between rundown houses, grubby net curtains like restless spirits at the windows on the ground-floor flats of the council blocks up the Dawes Road. Every sound, every rush of litter along the gutter or rustle in the scrubby growth in the tiny front gardens was magnified and yet I walked on.

I saw almost no one. Those I did passed me in cars or on the occasional bus, looking out with dull eyes from the safe yellow light. I reached Putney Bridge and stood at the parapet facing upstream, watching the black water underneath. The Thames. Here the river moved quickly along the final miles of its journey, anxious for the sea, but it had come from Oxfordshire, its meander slower there, as though it were reluctant to leave those pleasanter banks behind. I'm not sure how long I stood there: twenty minutes, maybe half an hour. When the cold of the wind began to bite, I turned home.

At the foot of the bridge where Fulham High Street starts in its architectural mishmash of church and office block and the concrete monstrosity of the Travelodge, I felt someone watching me. It was a man by the gates to the park, partially hidden by the stone pillar, coat drawn tight around him as if he were concealing some dangerous or precious object inside it. He was too far from the stop to be waiting for the night bus. I avoided his eyes, and he mine, until I passed him and I felt his gaze dart on to my face like the flicking of a tongue. I walked on, waiting for him to follow me, to catch at my coat, but there were no quickening footsteps, no shadow running to overlap mine on the pavement. When I got home I stood in the kitchen again and felt my pulse as it slowed. It had been a stupid thing to do but I had needed it. It was a trial: I had offered myself up to whatever fate might befall a woman walking alone in a big city in the small hours of the morning. I had dared whatever was out there to come and take me if I deserved it.

I was an exile in my own home. I could not face Martha and, if I had, I doubt she would have spoken to me. We negotiated the communal areas of the house like a sort of no man's land; I would not come out of my room until I was sure that she was in hers or was in the bathroom with the door locked. Any sound of unexpected movement was enough to send me scuttling back in fear.

On Sunday afternoon I heard her go out. I waited for five minutes in case she'd forgotten something and had to come back for it, as she often did, and then I rang my parents. Since Christmas I had spent so much time with Lucas and at Stoneborough that I had neglected them. Our conversations had been getting shorter and shorter and I felt as if I hadn't talked properly to my mother since I was at home for the holiday. I was desperate to speak to her now, to tell her that Lucas and I had split up and to hear a sympathetic voice.

The phone rang for a long time. The cold of the night before was gone, its legacy one of those tricksy spring days that seem to presage summer with a persuasive heat at midday but turn bitter later on. I guessed my parents would be outside making the most of the sun, Mum gardening and Dad reading the paper at the table on the patio, hoping not to be roped in to any manual labour. Eventually, just as I was about to give up, my mother answered. 'Jo, lovely to hear from you. Let me just take my gloves off. I've been pruning.' Even her voice was a balm, making me feel less alone in seconds. 'There we are. How are you? Are you in the country with Lucas?'

'Mum, we've broken up.'

'Oh no, what happened?' She was genuinely upset.

I said as little as I could. I told her that I had begun to have doubts about him, that they had come to a head and we had split up. I couldn't tell her about Greg. She was a fierce believer in proper conduct and would find it an unacceptable blurring of lines.

'That must have been quite a shock for him,' she said, when I finished my account. 'I wondered whether he thought you might get married. After all, you've been close for an awfully long time.'

Her response surprised me. 'You're supposed to be on my side.'

'Yes, of course, darling, but poor Lucas. It's a shame. He was a kind soul, I always had the impression. Thoughtful, even at university. Is there any chance . . . ?'

'No. None.'

'Oh.'

I had been too abrupt. 'Mum, it's not just that. There were things against us.'

'Like what?'

I couldn't tell her about the strange atmosphere at the house – it would sound ridiculous. 'Well, Danny. He wouldn't accept that Lucas and I were together. I think he's trying to force me out of Lucas's life so that he can have him to himself.'

My mother laughed. 'Jo, don't be so melodramatic. I'm sure that's not true; why on earth would Danny want to do that? He's got his own life to live. But look, darling' – her voice turned serious again – 'don't do anything rash as far as Lucas is concerned. He's a good man. I really did think . . .'

I felt a flash of temper. 'Is Dad there?' I asked, rather than risk shouting at her. I knew myself well enough to know that when I was overwrought I couldn't always keep my cool, even with innocent parties.

She handed the phone straight over. My father had clearly been standing next to her. 'So you've split up with Lucas,' he said. 'What happened? Couldn't you make it work?'

I wanted his support and affection so badly then and his immediate assumption that it had been due to my lack of effort cut me. 'Sometimes things just don't work out, Dad.'

'Relationships are complicated,' he said. 'But I would have thought you and Lucas had enough there to make a go of it.'

'Look, I feel bad about it – can't you tell? Please don't make me feel worse.' I tried not to get angry. I couldn't understand why neither of them seemed willing to give me a sympathetic ear. I had been relying on them as my last source of potential comfort.

'I'm just trying to understand, that's all. I'm your father. I'm supposed to take an interest in your life.' There was a hint of anger in his voice now.

'It's not all my fault.'

'So tell me what happened. I'm just trying to help, Joanna.'

'I don't need help. We're not going to get back together, OK? Just leave it, Dad.' I couldn't tell them that Lucas had attacked me, although part of me wanted to, just to shock them into seeing my side. It felt like too gross a betrayal, though. Telling them would only make me feel that I had let him down in yet another way.

'Well, you're obviously upset and finding it difficult to be polite either to your mother or me so I'm going to hang up and we'll speak again when you're in a better mood.'

'Dad, please listen . . .'

'Goodbye, Jo.' There was the fumbling sound of him replacing the handset and then I was left with nothing.

Those were some of the loneliest days I had ever spent. Just the absence of my best friends would have been enough to make them so but in addition I felt that there was a monumental new wall between us, one that I had built and now could never scale. I was on one side of it, the Elysian fields of our former friendship on the other. Even if Lucas and Rachel were not happy now, they weren't barred from being happy again, as I now was, proven unworthy of those closest to me. The future yawned open in front of me, empty.

Without Lucas and Martha, my warp and weft, I saw how thin the rest of my life was. I would have given anything to go back. Now when I reflected on how things had been between Lucas and me, I couldn't see what had been so wrong. I wondered why I hadn't been able to handle Danny. I should have laughed it off, not given him the satisfaction. I had allowed him to work on the few insignificant grains of doubt I had – surely normal at the beginning of any relationship, let alone one that had started like ours – until he had undermined everything we could have had. How could I have been so stupid?

The only familiar structure left to me was work and there was no respite there, either. Although I tried to disguise it with make-up, which soon wore off, it must have been apparent to everyone in the office that I was having a bad time. No one even asked if I was OK. To get through it, I measured out each day into sections, morning, lunchtime and afternoon, and I punctuated each with as many cigarette breaks as I could get away with, and as many trips to the loo and rounds of coffee as possible, anything to avoid sitting at my desk with my thoughts and the inbox empty of any communication from the others.

I ate junk food on my way home – chips, noodles, sandwiches from the twenty-four-hour store – to avoid risking a confrontation with Martha in the kitchen. Up in my room, I cried and ploughed my way through still more cigarettes and a stack of American crime novels, my usual comfort reading, each plot disappearing from my head as soon as I'd finished it, all becoming part of some great churning morass of bodies and damaged detectives and wasted lives.

And Greg didn't contact me.

I don't know what I had expected. When I tried to remember how I thought it might have worked out, I drew a blank. With each day that passed the idea of us getting together seemed more and more outlandish, something I had constructed out of drunken wishful thinking and a crazily overgrown teenage fantasy. How could someone like him choose me over Rachel? Why would anyone choose me over Rachel? I was being punished now for my hubris in ever entertaining the thought. What had happened on the terrace that evening had been nothing but an illusion, an insidious *trompe l'oeil* which, when examined, resolved into two dimensions and left me with a sense only of having been cheated. When I thought about it, nothing after we returned inside showed he meant anything he said at all. He hadn't even looked back as he'd gone up the stairs. I despised myself for being such a fool.

I did consider calling him but I couldn't risk further humiliation. I had his number on the old group emails I read over and over again but if he didn't want me then I would not pursue him. Nonetheless, there were long periods in the office when my mind wandered completely away from whatever tedious piece I was supposed to be working on and instead fabricated reasons for calling him: I was worried about Rachel; I wanted to apologise for the chaos I had caused. But I knew these ideas for what they were: phantom roads that, if followed, led to nowhere but further unhappiness.

As the week passed and the next one began, I knew for certain that I had made a terrible mistake. I came to see that all that had happened at Stoneborough Manor was the result of the strange heightened atmosphere of the place. I cursed the house for wrecking what I had with Lucas and deluding me into thinking that Greg might ever be interested in me. Back in the real world, everything that had happened at the house evaporated like rainwater from a shallow puddle.

Chapter Fifteen

In the empty days after Lucas and I broke up, I was a ghost. I traced the familiar patterns at work and at home but could no longer connect. Physically I was out in the world but all my energy was channelled inwards, for the slow absorption of the guilt and grief and loneliness. It was a strange sort of haunting, where I, the one who had gone, grieved for those who were still living, and they were oblivious to the fact I had ever existed. There was a sheet of plate glass between us, transparent but impassable.

The first weekend was the worst time. On the Saturday I had lain in bed until noon, the day aching open in front of me. There was no need even for me to sneak around. The house was empty: Martha had gone to Stoneborough.

I had heard her on the telephone discussing the arrangements. It was like listening to a lover making a date with someone else. Instead of our usual ride up together on a Friday evening, my car the capsule that transported us between the real world and the private world of the house, she and Michael were taking the train and Lucas was going to pick them up at the station. The fact of it had shocked me. I think that in some way I'd thought that weekends at the house would stop without me. That they continued emphasised just how disposable I had been.

*　　*　　*

It wasn't until the following Wednesday that there was a change in the situation. I was at my desk, slowly getting through another afternoon, when a message from Greg arrived in my inbox. The shock of it made my heart thump. I hesitated before opening it, my hand poised over the mouse. Email was the perfect way to keep me at a distance, to apologise but let me know very politely that it had been a mistake. I had been making progress in the past couple of days; that morning had been the first since it all happened that I hadn't had to disguise the fact that I had been crying before getting into work. I was reluctant to have my wounds reopened. I stood up and walked around for a minute or two before finally taking a breath and opening it.

It was one line. 'Can I see you?'

Despite everything, there was a cloudburst of hope behind my ribcage. I quickly suppressed it with the thought of the days that had passed since that evening. If he'd wanted me, I knew, he wouldn't have left it so long. I waited twenty minutes then answered: 'When?'

The response came at once. 'Tonight. I'll meet you from work.'

I felt shaky and went outside for a cigarette. It was just before four o'clock and the traffic was starting to back up at the lights, the stragglers on the school pick-up meeting the first of the afternoon rush. The emails had told me nothing. It was a slippery kind of correspondence, with no detail to mull over or interpret. There was nothing to suggest he actually wanted to see me: it was businesslike. I imagined he and Rachel had sorted things out and he wanted to make sure I wouldn't cause trouble. In the past I would have phoned Martha to ask what she thought.

Well, I could be brave, I decided. I wouldn't cry in front of him. I would give him the impression that it had been a mistake on my part, too, the result of too much to drink. He knew things had been going wrong with Lucas; I would tell him that the whole thing had been a symptom of that, nothing more. The forced courage did battle with a wave of the strongest disappointment I had ever felt.

Back inside, I went down the corridor to the lavatory and looked at myself in the mirror. That I hadn't been sleeping properly was obvious. There were grey circles under my eyes and my skin had no bloom. I wouldn't have time to go home and change, either. There was an editorial meeting at five and they always overran. I would have to do the best patch-up job I could.

For the rest of the afternoon I was tense, unable to listen properly to what anyone was saying in the meeting. The idea that I was about to talk to him was unreal. As the others packed up afterwards, I went back to the mirror, brushed my hair and put on some mascara. I stayed in the office until I was a few minutes late, then went downstairs.

He was waiting for me on the pavement, facing away across the road. I stood inside the door and watched him for a few seconds. He was wearing a dark-navy suit and stood with his hands in his pockets. Even from the rear, he looked ineffably adult. He turned round as I opened the door. My mouth went dry. His tie was off and the collar of his pale checked shirt was unbuttoned. He looked as if he'd been working hard: his eyes were tired and the stubble shadow around his chin was pronounced.

'Hello.' He didn't smile. I waited for him to move forward, perhaps give me a kiss on the cheek, but he didn't. I stood awkwardly, unsure what to do. 'Shall we walk?' he said.

We went down the High Street towards the river. The street was busy with people coming home from work, all seemingly going in the opposite direction to us. I had to weave round them to stay with him. Although I think he was trying to slow down, the extra length of his legs made it hard for me to match his pace. We didn't talk at all until we reached the bottom of the hill and had to wait at the lights for

178

the pedestrian crossing. 'I thought we could go over to Bishop's Park and walk along the river,' he said.

There was a warm breeze coming down the Thames and it played with the loose hairs around my forehead and on the nape of my neck as we crossed the bridge. I thought about standing there ten days earlier, daring the night. I felt only marginally less alone now. I had given up the idea of making conversation over the noise of the buses pulling into the stops or rushing past but the silence between us was not an easy one. I was dangerously close to tears. I realised that despite the days without him calling, part of me had been hoping that afternoon that Greg would pull me into his arms and that we would go from there.

When we reached the park we cut through the garden with its spindly rose bushes and Victorian-style streetlamps and on to the tarmac path that ran inside the railings. On our left flowed the river, strong and unchanging. The light was softening and casting a golden sheen over its breeze-dappled surface. A coxless pair went past, moving as quickly and neatly as a pond insect. 'Did you row at Cambridge?' I asked.

'No,' he said. 'I played rugby. Did you?'

'No,' I said. 'I was useless at it.'

He smiled a little but didn't say anything else. We walked on. After a minute or so I asked him how his day had been. It sounded like the desperate conversational opener it was. My head was down, my eyes watching our feet as they blurred along the tarmac. I thought about how he had held me on the terrace. How had it all disappeared?

At last he offered some conversation and told me about his latest project, a program for a record label based in Hammersmith. He asked what I was working on and I told me about an article on in-fighting at the borough council. It was like being forced to converse with a reticent stranger at a party, every line an effort.

Abruptly, still in the middle of the path, he stopped. He

took my hand and pulled me towards him, almost roughly. The suddenness of it took me by surprise. His mouth was on mine in a second but it wasn't a tentative, exploratory kiss like the first time. This one smacked of a claim on me. It was muscular and his hands were round my ears, his fingers laced into my hair. I had a lump in my throat and I felt as light-headed as if my blood-pressure had just dropped through the floor.

I pushed him off. 'You can't just . . . after everything that's happened.'

He looked at my face and saw my confusion. We were in the middle of the path and a couple on rollerblades had to separate to pass us. He either didn't notice or didn't care. I saw that he was reading me, attempting to interpret what I meant. I knew that my eyes gave away that I wanted him.

He stepped forward again and put his large hands around my face, as if it were something he wanted to keep safe. Then he leant in and slowly kissed me again. After days of self-hatred, the tenderness of it brought tears to my eyes. But it was also sexual. All the energy between us that I had felt out on the terrace was there and it glowed now like the filament in a bulb. I wanted to twine myself around him like a cat.

He pulled away. 'We'll get a taxi,' he said. He held my hand and we ran back across the grass and up the street until we reached the Fulham Palace Road. He flagged down a cab and gave his address in Shepherd's Bush. I didn't care what the driver thought of us. I wasn't thinking about anything apart from the taste of Greg's mouth and his breath in my hair and the way he was whispering into my ear, taking light nips along the edge of it. We stopped too quickly at the lights on the Hammersmith roundabout and I was thrown against him even tighter.

We arrived outside his flat and he paid the driver. I was so distracted I nearly left my bag behind. He slammed the front door shut behind us. We were in a communal hallway; there

180

was a row of pigeon holes and stairs up. 'We're on the top floor,' he said without moving. He looked at me, holding my gaze. I couldn't speak. He pushed me backwards against the wall and kissed me again. This time I felt the echo of it around my whole body. He pulled my shirt out of my skirt and ran his hands up over my torso towards my breasts, pulling down the front of my bra and trapping my nipples between his fingers. 'I want you,' he said in the base of his throat.

I nodded, glad to have the wall behind me. 'Upstairs.'

We got up to his flat. It was almost dark but he didn't turn the lights on. We went straight to his room and he took off my clothes one item at a time, dropping them on the floor, until I was naked in front of him. I heard him swallow. I reached for him and started to undo the buttons on his shirt but he stopped me. 'Not quick enough.' He pulled the shirt over his head, tore his socks off and roughly undid his trousers. Then we were on the bed and he was naked, his hand between my legs.

As we made love, I remembered what he had looked like with Rachel. It was how I had imagined it would be with him: serious. I was a prisoner under his weight: I couldn't have pushed him off if I'd wanted to. It was like a coming of age, as if I had never understood until now what my body was for. I was alive to his touch, as if there was Braille on my skin and he could read it. I surrendered myself but at the same time I gained a whole arsenal of new powers. I discovered that I could make him groan by wriggling under him. At times the expression on his face was feral, as if he were angry at what I had done to him. A strange look passed between us, something old and fierce, a look that might have passed between our ancestors. *You're mine*, Greg's eyes told me and I knew that he was seeing the same thing on my face. I felt brave, strong, as though I were tapping into a resource I'd never known I had.

181

He folded his arms around me so tightly I could hardly breathe. My face was squashed against his chest. Involuntarily I started to cry and he turned my head up so that he could see my face.

'I think it's shock,' I said.

'Shock? You mean you didn't know it was going to happen?'

How could anyone have known that something like that was going to happen? I wanted to ask. 'I hadn't heard from you,' I said instead. 'I thought you thought you'd made a mistake. And this evening, when we didn't talk . . .'

He turned on to his side, dislodging me. His voice was grave. 'I didn't call you because I thought you'd need time. You and Lucas were serious, Jo.'

Oh God, Lucas. How could I be doing this to him?

I watched the shape of Greg's mouth as he talked.

'I didn't want to storm in and force you into something if you weren't ready. I didn't know if you thought you'd made a mistake. You might have regretted it all, not wanted to see me. And even if you did, I still worried you'd think it was too soon.'

'Have you got any wine?' I said. 'I could really do with a drink.'

Without putting any clothes on, he left the room. He was entirely unselfconscious and at ease with his body. I heard his footsteps on the floor above my head and the rattle of a drawer as he looked for a corkscrew. I pulled his quilt around me. We hadn't drawn the curtain and an orange glow from the streetlight outside fell across the room and on to the bed. The room had the freedom from clutter that I associated with rooms that belonged to men but there were a good number of books on the shelves by the window. I got out of bed and went to see what he had. There were the inevitable tomes on programming and all things computer but also a wide range of non-fiction. I was impressed to see not only the obvious bestsellers but volumes on economics, international development and travel. There was a strong African flavour both to the non-fiction and also to the small collection of fiction, from Chinua Achebe, Alan Paton and Coetzee. I hopped back across the room as I heard him coming down the stairs again.

He returned and put a bottle and two glasses on the bedside table. Surreptitiously I looked at his body, the long legs, the strong thighs and buttocks, the dark hair that covered his chest.

'I felt bad,' he said. 'I felt bad about Rachel.'

The guilt came flooding back again. Rachel. I was in bed with her boyfriend. She must have slept with him here. I closed my eyes briefly to shut out the thought.

'But I also felt bad about you. I didn't want to split you and Lucas up. It wasn't until I realised that you weren't happy with him and that kiss . . . I didn't want to take advantage. It just didn't seem decent to call you straightaway.'

'I thought you didn't want me,' I said.

He put his hand behind my head, pulled me towards him and kissed me again with his strong mouth.

It was three o'clock by the time we turned off the light. Greg fell asleep just seconds before I did. It was the first time since leaving Stoneborough that I had slept easily. Whether it was the physical exhaustion or not being on my own, I wasn't sure. Certainly the gnawing loneliness of the past days had been tempered.

I woke up again at four, disorientated. It was several seconds before I remembered where I was. I didn't recognise the room immediately and, when I turned to face Greg, although I was glad it was him, the melancholy of that hour of the night got the better of me and all I could think about was that the body lying next to me wasn't Lucas's. I didn't want Lucas, I knew I didn't, and yet I missed him so much in

183

those minutes that the feeling manifested itself as a physical pain. I was moving away from him and I could never go back. It was more than the end of our relationship, it was about finishing a chapter of my life and leaving him in the past. I started to cry again, I couldn't help it. I wriggled gently across the bed so as not to disturb Greg and wept silently, trying to ease the sense of desolation that had lodged itself around my diaphragm. After five minutes or so, there was movement on the other side of the bed and I realised that I had woken him. He said nothing but stretched out his arm and pulled me back against him, where he held me tightly.

Chapter Sixteen

Although I'd hoped for a weekend with minimal time spent out of bed, my parents had telephoned and asked whether I would like to go for Sunday lunch. As I hadn't seen them for so long and I knew an olive branch when I saw one, I'd said yes. Now I was happier, it was easier to be philosophical about their reaction to the news of the break-up with Lucas. Even so, I hadn't quite forgiven them for not supporting me when I needed them. I left London just before ten o'clock on Sunday morning. Driving out on the A4, I was reminded of all the times I had taken that road to the house, using it to reach the M40. Martha and Michael had gone up there again, I knew. The pain of being excluded was as sharp as it had been the first time. I turned off and began the trawl out of south-west London through Chiswick and on to the motorway towards Southampton instead. The sky was Wedgwood blue and, although there was a slight chill in the air, I had the window open to feel it on my face.

I had spent Friday evening and all of Saturday with Greg and I had just kissed him goodbye. He had been out to buy croissants before I woke up and we had eaten them for breakfast in his sitting room. I sat cross-legged on the old blue-and-white-striped sofa in the square bay window, watching him. The sun was pouring over the roofs of the terrace opposite, casting him in a light against which I had to screw up my eyes. He was wearing dark jeans that fitted well around his hips and thighs and a faded turquoise T-shirt. His big bare feet slapped gently across the boards as he brought coffee from the kitchen. Until Wednesday I hadn't realised he wore contact lenses. This morning he was wearing his glasses, which emphasised the intelligence of his face.

When we had finished eating Greg reached across and pulled me close to him. We sat in silence for a minute or two, twining our fingers against each other's. I ran the ball of my thumb over each of his short, trimmed nails. A fine layer of dark hair covered the backs of his hands and I had to fight an urge to put his fingers in my mouth.

'Tell me about Danny,' he said.

I looked up in surprise. 'What do you want to know?'

'Why he is like he is. What's his story?'

'Well, I don't know a huge amount about his background beyond the basic facts. I've never been to his mother's house, or not inside. He doesn't talk about his family much but he can be pretty scathing about them. And he flies into a rage if anyone asks him about them.' I touched his hair and he leaned his head against my hand. 'What I do know,' I said, 'is that Danny's father is much younger than his mother. There's fifteen years between them. According to Lucas, Danny's father was a real boy about town and went out with some of the most beautiful women of the time. Then he took everyone by surprise and married this older divorcee.'

'She must have been quite something.'

'She wasn't particularly beautiful. That was one of the things that shocked people at the time: before that, he had been all about appearance. Patrick told Lucas this – he didn't especially like the people in that set but he knew them. Apparently Danny's dad was known to be quite cruel about women he didn't consider good-looking. She was forty-two or forty-three when they married.'

'So he was – what? – twenty-seven?'

'Something like that. Anyway, she was desperate for a baby and she got pregnant really quickly and everything seemed fine. But then, as soon as Danny was born, Danny's father went back to being a playboy again. And in the most public way. Lucas said he heard that it was like he deliberately set out to humiliate her.'

'Funded by her money?'

I nodded. 'The odd thing is that before they got married and even afterwards, during the pregnancy, people really did believe that he loved her. Everyone had thought originally he was after her money and of course it did turn out to be that but, if it was an act at first, he fooled everyone. Danny's mother was heartbroken.'

'She must be over seventy now, then?'

'Yes. She lives in Chelsea. I met her once. She's nice. Posh. And she and Danny's father are still married. They just live separate lives. I don't know whether he lives in London or not, even. I think he spends a lot of time in France.'

'Explains why Danny doesn't have any problems living on Lucas's money.'

'On one level. But that worries me, too, because Danny's immensely proud, as you probably realised. He always has to be better than everyone else and his job was a big part of that. The money was important but also he needs to know that he's valued higher than other people – it's where he gets his self-esteem. I don't know how he's going to get on without people telling him how brilliant he is all day.'

'I think his self-esteem is more fragile than he could bear anyone to know.'

I looked at him. His perception had surprised me several times. Since Wednesday I had learnt more about him than I had in months at the house. I was discovering new facets to him all the time; it was like being able to listen to a whole album having only previously heard tantalising snippets of individual songs. I was hungry for as much information about him as I could get, as if knowing him better could make him more mine. 'Are your parents married?' I asked.

'Yes, they're still together. They live in Australia now, just outside Melbourne. My brother emigrated and when he had children, my parents decided to move out there, too. They're close to their grandchildren and they're happy. Their house is on a cliff, looking over the sea. You'll love it.'

I got a jump of excitement in my stomach. He thought we had a future, one that reckoned in parents, and Australia.

My internal monologue faded out again as he pressed me down under him. It was a lovely form of abandonment, to concentrate on his body. But it was also the only thing that could stem my guilt about Lucas, the base flavour I could taste in everything now. Only in bed with Greg could I shake off entirely the feeling that stalked me through the course of each day, that back at Stoneborough Lucas would be paying in misery for my happiness.

I was coming into the New Forest now. Even by its own standards it looked beautiful that morning. I had once heard it described as being like a cathedral, a monument to God on earth, and there was something holy about its goodness. It was just before noon as I drove the long straight road that cleaved it in two. The trees wore their new season's leaves, bright green and highlighted by the rays of sun streaming through them. A pair of ponies cropped the soft grass by the stream at the Balmer Lodge Hotel. The sight of it all lifted my spirits. In the past few days I had begun to breathe more easily. I realised that since the beginning of the year I had felt something like constant claustrophobia, a sense of being surrounded on all sides. There was my job, the strange suffocating atmosphere at Stoneborough and my relationship with Lucas, which on some deep level I think I had always known was wrong. Now despite the hurt of my exclusion by the others, there was at least oxygen again.

By the time I reached their house, an old farm-worker's cottage on the outskirts of Lyndhurst, I was ready to see my parents. I was prepared for their disappointment about Lucas: my new secret happiness with Greg, however tentative still, was an inoculation against it.

Dad heard my car pull up and came round through the side gate from the garden to greet me. I got out of the car and locked the door. He put his arm round my shoulder and squeezed. 'Hello, my darling,' he said, kissing my cheek, his neat grey beard bristling against it. His broad face was smiling, his eyes wide as an owl's. He was in his usual weekend uniform for the spring/summer season, a pair of tired-out corduroy trousers and a short-sleeved cotton shirt with a breast pocket. 'You look well,' he said, looking me over and giving my shoulder another squeeze. 'You leave it too long between visits. We like to see you, your mother and I.'

I'd never believed the story that once one had left it one's childhood home started to get smaller. It was undeniably true, though. I had begun to notice the shrinkage when I went away to university but now, perhaps also suffering from comparison to Stoneborough, the house really did look tiny. It was hard to believe that there could be three bedrooms behind that semidetached doll's-house façade. It had been built in the thirties out of red brick and years ago my parents had put in a wisteria, which now covered the front.

'Your mother is planting out her runner beans,' Dad said. 'We'll stop her now and have some coffee.'

She was down at the far end of the thirty-foot garden, kneeling at the base of a bamboo cane and pressing earth around a seedling. She was so absorbed that she didn't hear us approaching over the grass. We gave her a slight shock and, as she looked up, I realised suddenly that she was getting older. No one thing about her had changed since Christmas, her hair was no greyer, her face no more lined, but she seemed somehow a less definite version of herself, her colours

189

infinitesimally muted. Her scent as she embraced me, how-ever, was the same as it always had been, Rive Gauche cut with the smell of the garden: rich earth and oak leaves.

After coffee Mum walked me around and showed me the new plants she was trying. She was an excellent teacher and had many educational successes, lots of whom still came to visit her when they were back in the area, but to me it seemed that she considered the garden, modest in size as it was, her greatest achievement. She took particular pride in the fact that, for most of our childhood summers, my brothers and I had eaten food she had grown. She crouched now to train a sweet pea up to the next rung on its trellis. 'I'm sorry about the other day, Jo,' she said, still concentrating on the plant. 'It was a bit insensitive of us. I think Dad and I always thought that you and Lucas would marry. It was a shock.'

'Don't worry, Mum. I was being too touchy. It just felt like the whole world was against me that day.'

'Have you heard from him?'

'No. He's furious with me.'

'But surely you haven't done anything wrong? He can't be angry if it's just that you don't think it would work between you.'

'Well, you know what it's like. People aren't exactly rational when it comes to this sort of thing,' I said, hating the lie and feeling the tide of guilt rise again.

'Hmm. Well, it's a shame but I hope you'll meet the right person soon. It can make you very happy, marriage. Your father and I have enjoyed each other's company.'

It was only very lately that my views on the subject of marriage had calmed. Until perhaps as recently as a year earlier, I reacted badly to my mother talking about it. I don't know, when I had grown up with such a good model in front of my eyes, why I had thought of it as a bourgeois trap, something that would hold me back. Mum had always said that, when I met the right person, I wouldn't be chafing to be free all the time and I could see now that perhaps she was right.

She refused my offer of help with the planting out and so I went inside to peel the vegetables for lunch. The kitchen window was open and the water drummed tunefully into the stainless-steel sink. I was glad I had come. It was good to see them both and, in an odd way, being away from Greg for the day gave me time to enjoy thinking about him.

After ten minutes or so, my father came into the kitchen and started to chop the peeled potatoes. 'Don't worry,' he said. 'I'm not going to ask about Lucas. I want to know how things are going at the office.'

'Good, actually,' I said, relieved. 'I've got something to show you.' I dried my hands and fetched my bag. In it was a piece I'd done about a local teenager who had been singled out for prosecution by a major record label for downloading music illegally. The story had been picked up by *The Times* and I'd had a call from an editor there. I'd enjoyed talking to her and at the end of the conversation she'd asked whether I would be interested in any freelance shiftwork at weekends. I'd been so excited when I hung up that I had had to go down the corridor and do a private dance in the stairwell of the fire escape. Greg had bought an especially nice bottle of wine for us to celebrate with.

Dad was delighted, too. 'Well done, Jo. That's brilliant news. Give it your all. You never know, it might be the start of something exciting.'

'She mentioned that someone on her desk was about to go on maternity leave. It might be a sort of trial.'

Lunch was late so that we could make the most of the warmth of the afternoon. We sat out at the table and read the newspapers and caught up on each other's news. Both my parents had bright A-level years and they were enjoying the teaching and expecting good results. The smell of roasting beef wound its way out of the kitchen window and made me hungry.

At four, just as we were eating, I heard my phone buzz in my handbag. I ignored it but had forgotten that, unless one picked up texts immediately, the phone would continue to pip periodically. After it did so for the third time, Dad asked why I didn't just answer it.

The message was from Greg. 'I can't wait to kiss you again,' it read. I couldn't help an enormous smile. My mother, keenly perceptive as ever, saw it.

'Oh Jo, you've met someone else.'

I couldn't deny it. It was bad enough not to have told her already. Part of me had been bursting with the news all day. I wished I could communicate to her what it felt like to go to sleep with his arms around me, although that was a conversation I could never have with my parents. I wanted to talk about it with them but I didn't want to diminish it, and I knew that they would disapprove and judge that I had traded everything with Lucas for something lesser, on foundations far less secure. Someone I had hardly known. And I could never tell them that Greg had been with Rachel.

'Does Lucas know?' she asked. 'Poor thing. So soon after Claire died, and his uncle.'

'Please don't give me a hard time. I didn't plan this.' I heard my voice rising.

'I'm surprised at you,' said Dad. 'For years you've talked about Lucas and now you've thrown him over.'

'You don't even know what's going on with Lucas at the moment,' I said. 'But you're happy to believe that the blame lies with me anyway. A lot of it does, perhaps most, but not all. So please don't lecture me without the facts.'

'Well, why don't you tell us the facts?' he asked.

I hesitated, torn between wanting to protect Lucas and wanting them to understand. 'Lucas changed,' I began. 'When Patrick died and he got that house. To start with, I thought it was OK. He said he wasn't going to let it change anything and that he would stay in his job, even though he had so much money he didn't have to. It's not just the

192

country place; there was a flat in Hampstead, too, which he's sold, and loads of art and investments and other things.'

'So what happened?'

'Well, you know he's always wanted to write?'

Dad nodded. He'd had a long conversation about that with Lucas once.

'Danny talked him into believing that he'd never be able to do it with a full-time job and so he resigned and now they're both living in the country.'

'Danny as well?' asked my mother, surprised.

'Neither of them have jobs, and Lucas wanted me to give up mine and go and live with them up there, too.' From the look on my father's face, I could see that he was beginning to understand. 'I began to lose respect for him. I need someone who is doing stuff. I'm not explaining this very well.'

'Actually I do see, Jo,' said my mother. 'It's very unstructured.'

'I need someone who's living in the real world. And then there's Danny.'

'Yes, what is Danny supposed to be doing, if Lucas is writing?' she asked.

'Working on ideas for films, he says, but really he's not doing anything. He's just taking advantage.'

'And what happened to his job? He was doing so well, wasn't he?'

'He was sacked.' I didn't tell her why.

Mum shook her head. 'Well, he won't be able to do that for long. He's thirty this year, isn't he? It's OK to drift along in your twenties but that won't look good when he's thirty-five. He's not going to be in any position to offer a girl anything, is he?'

The idea of Danny offering anyone anything, rather than taking it, made me want to laugh.

'And what about Martha? Is she seeing anyone?'

'Mum, for God's sake, it's not the only thing worth doing, you know.'

193

'What does your new man do?' said Dad quickly.

I relaxed, liking that description. 'He's a software designer.'

My parents weren't really ready to talk about Greg but I was relieved to have been able to make them understand about Lucas a little. I didn't tell them about what had happened on that final night and I was glad that I didn't have to. I was beginning to see that in a strange way I was grateful to Lucas for his violent outburst. It shared the bad behaviour a little, evened the balance sheet between us.

I stayed until the light began to fade. In the end, having been slightly apprehensive about going home, I found I was reluctant to leave. I often felt a little homesick as I drove away from my parents' house and that night the feeling was stronger than usual. It was good to have cleared the air with them. I was still faintly exasperated by my mother's seeming determination to push us all into fully paid-up adulthood but in Danny's case at least I could see what she was driving at. I wondered where he did think his life was going.

As I neared London, however, my ease of spirit began to ebb away. I was going to my house for the first time since Friday. As I parked up outside, I could see that the sitting-room lights were on. Martha was already back. I let myself in as quietly as possible and went straight to my room.

The following Thursday Greg got tickets for a new band that he thought I might like. The gig was at a small underground club just off Charing Cross Road and I took the bus up from Putney to meet him there. I'd changed into jeans and my new heels before leaving the office and as I walked down the street I became aware that I was swinging my hips with every step as if I were keeping a hula hoop going. I felt alive in a way that I didn't ever remember feeling before. Everything was suddenly so vivid: the motion of my body as I swung along the pavement, the bounce of my bag against my hip, the rise of the down on my arms against the light evening breeze, the feeling of my hair against my back where my top revealed bare skin. I could feel my breasts touching the inside of the material of it and it was like being very gently stroked. I had a new sense of physical awareness, a sudden and amazing hypersensitivity, both to my own body and to everything around me. The air smelt of city – car fumes and dust and cigarettes and the bodies of people still on the home commute – and I loved it. I smiled at a guy with thick dreadlocks smoking a rollie outside the guitar shop and he smiled back and gave a low wolf whistle as I went by. Instead of feeling embarrassed as I would have in the past, I laughed and exaggerated the swing still further. 'Hey, beautiful girl,' he called after me and although I knew it wasn't true, it felt it, just for a minute.

I could see Greg waiting for me on the corner of Manette Street, attracting surreptitious looks from the girls passing him on their way into the club, but I pretended that I hadn't noticed him. He was watching me but I wanted to savour the feeling of his eyes on me a bit longer. It was like being undressed by him: I knew he was picturing how my body looked under my clothes and I wanted him to. It was he who made me feel like this: connected. In little more than a week, he had revealed an extra dimension to the world. It was technicolour all of a sudden, after years of black and white, and the change was the more extraordinary because it came after I'd cut myself off from so much that I'd thought essential to my happiness.

Tonight the band would have only a fraction of my attention: the rest would be taken up by my senses absorbing as much of Greg as they could, the heat from his body as he stood close to me, the feel of his hand in the small of my back and slipping into the pocket of my jeans, the smell of him. My ears would be listening to the music but the rest of my body would be marking time until we got back to Shepherd's Bush and his bed again.

Chapter Seventeen

One night, more than a month later, I was woken abruptly from a deep sleep by a sound like an alarm. In my confusion it took me several seconds to understand that it was the telephone. I opened my eyes and looked at my clock: half past two. The thought of why anyone would call at that time caused me a rush of panic that left me wide awake. I got out of bed and went out on to the landing, feeling my way along the banister to the top of the stairs. The phone carried on ringing on the table in the hall below, a siren in the quiet of the night. I was amazed Martha hadn't been woken by it.

When I got downstairs I hesitated for a moment before picking up the receiver. If it was bad news – if something had happened to my parents or my brothers – I wanted a last few seconds in which I didn't know.

'Hello?'

'Jo?'

'Lucas.' I sat down on the bottom step in surprise.

There was silence for a second or two. 'Are you still there?'

'Yes,' I said. It was so good to hear his voice. 'How are you?'

'I miss you.'

I had no idea how to respond. My pleasure at hearing him started to evaporate as I realised that he was drunk. Of course he was, though. Why else would he call at that time of night?

'How about you?' he asked. 'Are you happy now? With Greg? Did you make the right decision?'

'Please don't ask that.'

'Aren't I within my rights to ask a few difficult questions? Surely you can allow me that, Joanna?' At the other end of the line there was a loud thump, and the sound of glass shattering on a stone floor. 'Fuck.'

'What's that? What's going on?'

'Nothing. Nothing. I just knocked my glass over. Forget about it.'

'Are you all right?'

'I said forget it. It doesn't matter.' I heard him swallow awkwardly and then, very faintly, the sound of a sob. 'I miss you, Jo. It hurts. It hurts so much.'

'I miss you, too.'

'Come back to me. I don't care about Greg. We can forget it, say it was all a mistake. We can start again.'

'Lucas.' I stopped. How could I tell him without hurting him more?'

'Please.'

'I can't. I'm with Greg now. I miss you as a friend.'

'A friend?' His voice rose. 'How can you say that? What we had was different, Jo. You and me – it's real.'

'You're one of my very best friends. You always will be.' I found that I was in tears now. 'But it didn't feel right, not to me.'

'What you've got with Greg can never be like what we could have, if you weren't so blind you couldn't see it. Can't you see that you're the most important thing in my life?'

I tried to speak but I couldn't find the words and the tears were coming fast. 'You're really important to me, too,' I said at last. 'But it isn't the same. I'm sorry.'

'You and he will never be happy, not properly.' His voice had turned spiteful. 'You can't see that you've got it wrong. I didn't realise how stupid you were. You're a fucking idiot,

197

Jo, as well as a stupid bitch.' Then he slammed the phone down and, as quickly and unexpectedly as he had come back into my life, he was gone.

I put my head in my hands and wept. I was just outside the door to Martha's room but I didn't care if I woke her up. I wanted someone to know now how much it was hurting me, being shunned and despised. If my friendships with them were over for ever, I needed to know. I couldn't go on in this purgatory, punished every day.

Suddenly Martha's door opened and she stood in front of me. It was the first time she'd voluntarily been in my presence since the night she'd shouted at me in the sitting room. Her stripy pyjamas glowed pale in the light through the glass panel in the front door. I looked down again, willing her not to have another go at me. Then to my complete surprise she knelt down and put her arms round me. Kindness finished me at the best of times but this, with the unexpectedness of it and my sheer gratitude, was the end. I put my arms round her, too, and cried and cried. Neither of us said anything for some time and my tears soaked through the shoulder of her pyjama jacket. Eventually I stemmed the flow a bit and pulled back.

'Come on,' she said. 'Let's go and make some tea.'

The lights in the kitchen hurt my eyes after the darkness. I sat at the table while she made the drinks. The fridge hummed into the silence. There was a cardigan on the back of one of the chairs and I put it on, cold in only the T-shirt I wore to bed.

'Forget tea, let's have hot chocolate,' she said. 'I've got marshmallows.'

One of the lovely things about Martha was her ability to inject fun into even the most unlikely situations. I felt tears come into my eyes again and tried to blink them back. I wondered why on earth she would have marshmallows and then remembered: her diet was always terrible when she was unsettled. In the weeks that we hadn't been speaking, I'd noticed that the fridge had been full of pizzas, rice pudding and bars of chocolate with little life expectancy. It was miserable.

'Come on, Jo, stop crying now. You'll be all right.' She put the mugs on the table and sat down. The marshmallows bobbed on the top, ludicrously pink and white at three in the morning. 'Was Lucas really unkind?'

'A bit. No more than I deserve.'

'Was he drunk?'

'I think so. Yes.'

She shook her head. 'I've got to tell you, he's in pieces at the moment. He's drinking so much and he gets really upset. We told him not to call you, in case he did something like this. He's OK when he's sober but when he gets pissed he gets out of control. Danny's been looking after him really well but it obviously went wrong tonight.'

'I think he hates me.'

'He doesn't. That's the problem. He needs to go through a healthy stage of hating you and then come out the other side. Things would be a lot better that way.'

I wanted to reach out and touch her hand but I couldn't. 'Thank you,' I said instead. 'For talking to me.'

She pulled an exasperated face. 'I'm not a complete cow. I couldn't lie in bed and listen to you get screamed at then cry your heart out. I had to do something.'

'Well, that's what I'm saying. Thank you.'

'You're not off the hook.' She picked up one of the marshmallows and put it in her mouth. 'I haven't forgiven you yet for what you did, although I probably will as long as you don't do anything like it again. I'm prepared to admit that whatever you've got with Greg is pretty serious. He obviously makes you happy.'

'Marth . . .'

'And anyway, I hate the way we've been living here in the

past few weeks. It's shit. I can't stand it much longer; I've been thinking about moving out.'

'So have I.' A couple of days earlier, I had been to see a room in another house. It had been nice but the thought of moving away from Martha had been so painful that I'd had to email the girl and say I'd changed my mind.

'What about Rachel?' I asked.

'What about her? I don't think she'll ever forgive you, if that's what you mean. I wouldn't even bother trying to explain or apologise – she won't hear it.'

'Have you seen her? Does she go up to the house?'

'She hasn't been up, no, but Michael and I saw her last week. She had drinks at the shop for a new designer she's launching.'

Melancholy washed over me again. In the past I would automatically have been on the guest-list for something like that. 'Did she mention me?'

'Why would she? I think she'd prefer to forget you'd ever existed.'

I took a sip of my drink to hide the fact that a new batch of tears had sprung into my eyes. I didn't want her to get impatient with me.

'I appreciate it that you haven't brought Greg here yet.'

'I wouldn't have. It didn't seem right.' I blotted my eyes on the sleeve of the cardigan.

'But if you want him to come round now, I don't mind. I do like him, as you know. This is clearly how things are going to be, so it's time for us to get used to it.'

I wished I could tell her about Greg and me. She was the one person to whom I always talked properly about my relationships. It was far too soon, though.

'Look, there's also something I want you to know,' she said. 'Something of mine.' Her voice had changed. The kind but stern tone was gone: this was the old Martha, close and confidential. Her eyes were sparkling.

'What?'

'I've started seeing someone.' She smiled, shy but proud. She folded one of her feet up under her, to cause a distraction.

'Have you? Who?'

'You've got to promise not to tell anyone.'

'Why?'

'He thinks we should keep it a secret for the moment. Just till we're sure.'

'Who? Tell me.'

She paused, about to burst the bubble of their exclusivity. 'Danny.' She laughed but a note of unease came into it as she saw my face. 'Come on. It's not that much of a surprise, is it? You know I've always liked him.'

I tried to rearrange my expression into one of neutrality. 'No. I had no idea. I mean, obviously we know he's charming. And good-looking.'

'He's gorgeous, Jo.'

'When did this happen?' Please God, I thought, not while he was seeing Michael.

'Two weeks ago. At the house, of course. Lucas got really drunk and we'd put him to bed. Michael had crashed out as usual. I don't know – we were in the drawing room pretty late and he just . . . leaned in.'

I searched my brain for what to say. I felt a strong need to tell her about Michael but I couldn't think how, without sacrificing our rapprochement. I couldn't be the one to stamp on her excitement, not now. She might never speak to me again.

'We're not doing anything wrong.' She challenged my silence. 'I know it's going to take some getting used to, given how long we've been friends, but it's fine.'

'Martha, it's not that.'

'It doesn't hurt anyone,' she said pointedly. She snatched up the empty cups. 'Can't you be happy for me? I'm getting together with someone I've always liked. I know you don't like him, for whatever ridiculous reason. You should just let it go. There are enough problems already between us all.'

'I am happy for you. I want you to be happy. Just be careful, that's all.' I decided to try and mask the message a little. 'You know he's wild.'

She smiled again. 'Part of the reason I like him.'

'Look after yourself.'

'I will but it's fine. You know, even the wild child has to settle down sometime. It'll be cool. Just don't tell anyone for now, OK?'

'Given that no one speaks to me, I think your secret is pretty safe.'

She looked at me for a moment and then we both laughed.

A fortnight later it happened again. Greg and I had been into the West End to see a film and got back to my house at about eleven. I could hear the phone ringing inside as we got out of the taxi. I fumbled for the key in my bag and pushed it into the lock. I dashed in and picked up the receiver. 'Hello?'

'Jo, it's me.'

Greg came in behind me and closed the door. He saw the look on my face.

There was silence on the phone for a second or two and then the scratch and flare of a match. I pictured Lucas turning his head to light his cigarette. 'I wanted to apologise for the last time we spoke,' he said at last.

'It doesn't matter. Let's just forget about it.'

'It does matter. I shouldn't have done it. It's no excuse but I was really drunk.'

'I know. Honestly. Forget about it.'

Greg mouthed at me, asking whether I was OK. I nodded yes and he went through to the kitchen to give me some privacy.

'It's not the only thing I feel bad about,' said Lucas. 'That last night at the house. I don't know what came over me. To grab you like that . . . When I think about it now, I just can't believe it. It was like being possessed or something, out of control.'

I remembered how he had launched at me and how frightening it was. He had looked out of control. But although I had been very frightened I knew that he had been pushed to it: it wasn't the Lucas I knew. 'It was my fault,' I said.

'No,' he said. 'It wasn't. I scared you and I am so sorry for that. I'll never forgive myself.'

Some of my unease began to dissipate. My first thought when I had picked up the phone, especially given the time, was that he had called to give me hell again.

'I've forgiven you,' I said. 'You were provoked and you didn't hurt me.'

'I am so glad about that.' Lucas paused. 'Weekends don't seem right without you. Jo, I want you to come back.'

I closed my eyes, glad he couldn't see me. 'I can't. I'm with Greg now.'

'I don't mean that. I mean, I want you to come to Stoneborough again.'

Greg padded back up the hall and crouched in front of me. 'OK?' he whispered. He stroked my hair and stepped round me to go upstairs.

'Was that him?' asked Lucas.

I considered not telling the truth but thought better of it.

'I'm lonely, Jo, for fuck's sake. I want you here again.'

'Let's give it time. I don't think any of us is ready yet.'

'I'm ready.'

'Lucas, it's too soon. Trust me. When we've all calmed down, then we'll come up to the house but not until then, OK?' I'd feared it but now it happened and there was the sound of tears on the other end of the line. 'Please don't cry,' I said.

'I can't help it. I miss you.'

The words clutched at my stomach but there was nothing I could do. There was no solution and nothing honest I could say would make any difference. I murmured platitudes as he wept. And I am ashamed to say it but as I did so I realised that I had another feeling towards him: annoyance. Greg was upstairs in my room and I wanted to be up there with him, not sitting at the bottom of the stairs again listening to Lucas cry. I wouldn't let myself hurry him or try to chivvy him off the line, though. That would have been unforgivable. Instead I waited and listened. Above me, Greg went along the landing to the bathroom and there came the buzz of his electric toothbrush. It was his way, I knew, of telling me that he was there and waiting for me, without putting pressure on me. In the end, Lucas cried himself out and hung up and I was free.

There were further calls after that and they started to become more and more frequent. I answered two of them and was rewarded once with an earful of abuse, where, raving drunk, Lucas called me a slut, and then, the following night, with tearful apologies. The night after that Martha picked up for me and told him I was out. Eventually we started taking the phone off the hook after ten o'clock and, if the mobile rang, I checked the caller display before answering. It was a horrible way to treat someone who had once been one of your closest friends but it had come to feel like the only way to deal with it. Somehow it felt kinder than listening to him and letting him say things that I knew, if he was sober, he would bitterly regret.

Chapter Eighteen

I don't know if we could have predicted what happened next. Perhaps, if we hadn't been so wrapped up in our own lives. But we weren't looking; our attention – all of ours – was elsewhere. For my part, my relationship with Greg was making it hard for me to concentrate on anything else. So much of my time was spent either with him or thinking about him. I had developed a hitherto unknown domestic urge and spent hours poring over cookbooks and plotting what I was going to make for our suppers together. I brought him small gifts – Cadbury's Creme Eggs, for example, which he loved – and slipped them into his jacket pockets for him to find later in the day. It was a very basic desire, I supposed, to want to feed the man you were falling in love with. I couldn't tell Martha for fear that she would think me hideously unreconstructed but on the other hand I thought she might understand now. Although her relationship with Danny was still covert and she had begged me not even to tell Greg, I occasionally caught her smiling vacantly out of the window or humming along to ballads on the radio. The pair of us must have been fairly stomach-turning to witness.

My happiness also seemed to be radiating, sharing its warmth with other areas of my life. The news editor at *The Times* had called and asked whether I could do a weekend, as she'd suggested she might. Although it would mean working twelve days without a break, I was thrilled. I worried Greg would be disappointed that we wouldn't be able to spend the days together but instead he told me that he had work to do as well and that we would reward ourselves for our industry with supper out, venue at his discretion.

I got an enormous kick out of walking into the offices of *The Times*. Of course, the *Gazette* was a real newspaper and the stories we reported there were news, too, but this felt like something else. Although the newsroom looked like any other slightly disorganised open-plan office I felt, finally, as if I were nearing the hub, getting close to my dream. Everything there seemed to matter. The famous staff writers whose by-lines I'd been seeing for all the years that this had been my ambition had desks there and trays with their names on. On Saturday I was shown the ropes but then I researched and wrote up a story of my own, which appeared in Monday's edition. I was outside the newsagent at the end of Greg's road as it opened and I kept my security pass in my handbag all week, getting it out surreptitiously now and again in quiet moments at the *Gazette*, to remind me.

It happened on Thursday that week. I was spending the night at Greg's and we were knotted up together on the sofa in his bay window when I heard my phone ring in my bag. 'Ignore it,' he said, sliding my bra strap off my shoulder. Eventually it stopped. 'Good.' He smiled. I touched his eyelashes with my finger and he blinked and kissed me. The phone started ringing again. 'For God's sake,' he said. 'Can't we have a bit of peace and quiet?'

Reluctantly I disentangled myself and fished in my bag. 'It's the house.'

'Don't answer it. Please, Jo.'

I put it back in my bag but I couldn't bring myself to switch it off. Three seconds later it started ringing again. 'Give it to me.' He grabbed my bag and found it. 'Jo,' he said, looking at the screen. 'It's not the house now. It's Danny's mobile.'

'What?' I could count on one hand the times Danny had ever rung me.

'You'd better answer it,' he said resignedly. He stood up and started straightening himself out, doing up the buttons I'd undone.

Angrily I answered the call. 'Danny?'

I was completely unprepared for what followed. He was hysterical, almost unable to talk. His breathing was shallow and fast; he seemed to be gasping for breath. I could make no sense at all of the stream of sound that came down the line.

'Calm down. Calm down. I can't hear you,' I said. Greg, assuming that it was Lucas, wandered into the kitchen to pour himself a glass of wine. 'Calm down, Danny. Tell me what's the matter.'

Finally he managed a complete sentence. 'Lucas has taken an overdose.'

'Jesus. Are you sure? What's happening? Where is he?'

Danny spun off into another reel of panicky rubbish.

'Is he conscious? OK, Danny – you need to get off the phone now and call an ambulance. Do you hear me? You need to call an ambulance. Of course you can. For fuck's sake, pull yourself together.'

'I can't. I can't. You need to come here. Help me. Please help me.'

'I'm coming but you need to get him to a hospital before then. I'll call an ambulance from here and I'll come as soon as I can. Until it reaches you I want you to sit with him and make sure he doesn't go to sleep. Do you understand me? We'll have to hope he's sick but if he is, I want you to make sure that he can breathe. Do not let him choke. Don't let him lie down.'

I called emergency services, then rang Danny back. The

ambulance would take some time to reach them as far out as they were. I only hoped that Lucas hung in there and that Danny was competent enough to help him if it turned critical. I wouldn't have put any money on it.

'I'll drive,' said Greg, picking up his keys. 'You can call Danny from the car.'

For the first part of the journey I felt schizophrenic. The rational part of me was talking to Danny, calming him and telling him to try getting Lucas to drink some water. The rest of my brain was running wild. I just couldn't believe that Lucas had done this. I knew he was distressed by the way things were, of course I did, but this was something else. Actually to try to kill himself. I prayed and prayed that he would be all right; I clenched my fists so hard that I cut my palms with my nails. Lucas was still conscious, Danny told me, but he had had a bottle and a half of Scotch as well as the contents of numerous packets of pills. He'd found packs and packs of painkillers in Lucas's room, the blister sheets popped, the pills gone. I tried to get him to count how many but it was beyond him. Then, about twenty minutes after I'd called it, the ambulance arrived. I heard Danny running down the stairs and opening the front door, the rush of his frightened voice, the cool control of the paramedics.

'Where are they taking him, Danny? Ask them.'

'The John Radcliffe.'

Danny was in the waiting room in Accident and Emergency when we got there. He was frantic, flitting like a panicky bird and unable to settle on the rows of vinyl chairs. He had picked up a leaflet from one of the boxes on the shelf and was tearing it into fine ribbons that fluttered behind him as he paced up and down. His trainers squeaked on the linoleum and the strip lighting made his skin an eerie green. When he saw us, he ran up the corridor to meet us, earning a disapproving look from one of the nurses. 'Thank God,' he said. 'Thank God you're here.'

'Where is he?' I asked.

'They've taken him off to get that stuff out of him. Jesus, what if I hadn't found him? He might have died.'

I didn't like to tell him that he still might, if they couldn't get rid of the aspirin and paracetamol quickly. The realisation of what he had done hit me suddenly and I sat down abruptly on one of the chairs. Greg sat down next to me and took my hand.

'I couldn't stand it if anything happened to him,' said Danny, taking a new leaflet and crushing it in his hand. 'I couldn't stand it.'

'It won't come to that, Danny,' said Greg. 'Look, come and sit down here and I'll go and get us some tea.' He went to find the machine, leaving Danny and me on our own together. There was silence for a moment or two and I watched his hands folding the paper back and forth on itself, making a concertina.

'He's the only person who has ever been there for me in my entire fucking life,' he said. 'The only person who has ever given a shit about me. The only person who has ever helped me out or wanted me around for anything other than the parties I could take them to or the people I knew or the drugs I could get them. Do you know what that's like? Do you have any concept of what that means? Do you?'

'No,' I said.

'Lucas is my family. He's my brother. You're not going to take him away from me, do you understand?'

I could see in his eyes that he blamed me but at that point he needed me enough not to be able to unleash the torrent of hatred he was damming up inside. But without saying anything he let me know that if Lucas died then he would make sure my life wasn't worth living.

He turned away and we fell silent again until Greg

reappeared carrying three plastic cups of tea in a triangle between his fingers. It was too hot and I sipped it more for something to do than because I wanted it. I was shaky and my stomach felt hollow with fear and guilt. Was this my fault? I had left Lucas for someone else, ignored his calls when he was in obvious emotional pain. I had switched my phone off when he had needed me. It seemed unbelievable now that I could have done that. What sort of person was I?

I looked round at the others in the waiting room, talking in low voices or distractedly picking up the outdated magazines and putting them down. Danny was up and pacing again.

'Come on, Danny, let's go out for a cigarette. I think we both need one,' said Greg, standing.

'I can't. What if there's news?'

'Jo will come and get us.'

Danny shot me a bitter look and then followed him. When they returned, I went out and stood on the tarmac outside the department. It was a clear night and from the hospital's vantage point on the hill I could see the lights of North Oxford sprinkled out below and their corresponding numbers in the sky above me, far enough from the city centre to be pin-point bright in the indigo sky. I smoked a cigarette, then another. Lucas, you idiot, I thought. You poor idiot. I remembered Patrick then. Of course. He had taken pills, too. I had been so caught up in our own immediate situation that I had almost forgotten about the other sources of Lucas's grief.

I went back in and we had another cup of scalding tea. At last a junior doctor came to tell us that they'd pumped Lucas's stomach and that, all being well, he would be OK, although he would have to stay in for observation. Danny put his head in his hands and stared at his shoes for at least a minute.

'I won't come in,' said Greg. 'I'll wait out here in case you need me.'

Lucas was in a bed in a side room, leaning back against a

bank of pillows as if he had lost a fight. His face and the
hands that lay palm down on the waffle blanket were blood-
less but his eyes were rimmed with red. Walking in, I felt the
awful embarrassment that I always do when faced with those
in hospital, as if their status as ill people makes them strange,
simultaneously lesser than those still walking around and at
the same time more important, the data of their bodies
monitored and analysed with a respect normally reserved
for cultic auguries.

I let Danny go to him first but it was my eyes he sought out.
'You came,' he said. His voice was as cracked as if he hadn't
spoken in years.

'Lucas.' Danny sat down on the chair by the side of the bed
and rested his forehead on the blanket. 'Promise me you will
never do that again. Do you hear me?'

'Yes.' He looked at me over Danny's head.

I approached the bed cautiously and stood at the edge of it.
He was attached to a drip and, where the line had gone into
his forearm, it had made a small bruise in vivid purple.

'Why did you do it?' said Danny. 'What was so wrong that
you couldn't talk to me about it?'

'I don't know, I can't explain.' His hand stroked the cover. 'I
felt very sad.' Tears came into his eyes and fell down his cheeks
in two straight lines. He made no move to brush them away.

'You can always talk to me. About anything. If there's
anything wrong, if I'm doing anything wrong, all you have to
do is tell me. Just never, ever do that again.'

Lucas said nothing but nodded slowly and dislodged
another pair of tears.

I still hadn't said anything. I didn't trust myself to.

A nurse came in and poured a beaker of water from a
scratched plastic jug. She put it on the table that crossed the
bed over Lucas's knees. 'Are you all right?' she asked. 'You
should try and drink as much as possible. I know it'll hurt.'
She went out again and left us to it.

211

'Danny, you look terrible,' Lucas croaked.

'You won't be winning any beauty contests either, believe me,' he said, smiling.

'Why don't you go and have a cigarette?'

He looked as if he were about to protest but he respected Lucas's request and got up. He skirted me very carefully, as if the thought of touching me even for a second was repulsive to him. As soon as he was out of the room, Lucas reached out and took hold of my arm. We looked at each other.

'Why did you do it?' I said. 'Did you mean to kill yourself? You nearly managed it.'

'I don't want to live my life like this,' he said. 'I've got no one left. I need you to be my friend again.'

'All you had to do was say. You didn't have to . . .' I looked around us.

'I did say. You didn't hear me.'

The realisation of how badly I had let him down flooded me again and brought tears into my eyes, too. Lucas pulled on my hand and made me sit on the edge of the bed. I couldn't look at his poor face. Instead, my eyes kept finding their way back to the bruise on his arm.

'I know you're going out with Greg now and that's not going to change,' he said. 'I have to accept it. Jo, you remember Elizabeth said that when Patrick and my mother split up he didn't let it spoil everything? Patrick was always friends with my parents. He could have lost them but he didn't.'

'You're not going to lose me.'

'I nearly did. I couldn't let it happen.'

'You wouldn't have lost me in the long term. It was a question of letting some time pass. Rachel won't ever talk to me again but our friendship is stronger than that. We both know it.' I felt as though I were in a film, delivering lines written for me by someone else. I wanted to mean them – I did mean them – but the pull of the old was now meeting a strong counter-force. My magnetic north had moved.

He squeezed my hand. 'The summer's coming and it's beautiful at the house. You should see it. I'm going to restart my novel and I'll need your editorial opinion.'

There was no way I could say no. I smiled as genuinely as I could and I brushed his hair back off his face. 'But let's take it gently, OK? No pressure on either side. You accept that you're stuck with me now for life?'

He tried to laugh but it hurt his throat too much. Pain shot across his face.

'Calm down,' I said. 'One step at a time. But there's something else I want you to do when you get out of here. You've got to promise me.'

'What?'

'I want you to cut down on how much you're drinking.'

He moved his eyes away so that they no longer met mine. 'I know. When I was upset, it was the only thing that made me feel any better. In the end I felt worse, but there was this golden hour where I felt OK, happy.' He looked at me again. 'Jo, you've got to help me. I don't want to be an alcoholic. I don't want to turn into my dad.'

Although he looked exhausted, Danny insisted on staying with Lucas. He'd charmed an extra blanket out of the nurse and was going to try and get a couple of hours' rest in the chair by the bed.

I saw him briefly outside before I went. Despite all the tension between us and his failure to cope with the crisis of that evening, I felt the closest to understanding him then than I had ever done. And I was moved by his dedication to Lucas; I realised its roots went far deeper than I'd ever suspected. I tried to convey some of the feeling to him as we said good-bye. 'Danny,' I said, 'you did a good job this evening, keeping him going. Talking to him . . .'

213

I trailed off as I saw his expression.

'What else was I going to do, Joanna?' he said. 'Sit there and let him die?'

'Of course not. I meant . . .'

His eyes were narrowed, the kohl rims around them especially dark against the blue. 'Nothing changes because he wants you back here. Look what you did to him.' He flicked his hand out sharply, indicating our surroundings. 'This is your fault.'

'Danny . . .'

'You can say what you like but you know it is. You did this, Joanna. Because of you, he nearly died.'

I turned and walked away. I knew he had chosen his words with the deliberate purpose of wounding me but they found their mark anyway.

He was lashing out, releasing some of his fear but he was also punishing me for having seen his weakness. I would pay for being the person he had had to call that evening. I would also pay for having been told how deeply his feelings for Lucas ran. He could no longer pretend that he was someone with no baggage, too exalted to be troubled with emotional relationships like the rest of us. I realised then that at no point that night had he called Martha.

I went to find Greg in the waiting room and we walked out into the first hour of the new morning. It was just gone five o'clock and I could see it was going to be one of those early summer days in Oxford that are almost painful in their beauty, when the leaves are fresh and every lungful of air seems to be full of the ingredients for happiness. I had seen a lot of this time in the morning when I had been a student but for much better reasons. It was hard to believe that, a decade later, we were back here and I was visiting Lucas after his attempted suicide.

We crossed the tarmac back to the car. 'He wants you to go back to the house,' said Greg, kicking a small stone and watching it skitter away.

'He says that he misses me and . . .'

'That's what this is all about. He's in love with you.'

'We were close for a long time and . . .'

'He loves you and he wants you back.'

'I honestly don't think so. It started like that but it's changed. I think I've become a sort of symbol of all the things that he's lost.' As I said it, I felt sure I was right. 'His parents and Patrick are gone for ever; I'm the one thing that he stands a chance of clawing back. It's not about me – it's about not losing anything else.'

'I'm telling you, he wants you back.' We reached the car and got in. The doors shut heavily. Greg looked at me oddly. 'I don't think you're really over him. I mean, you can't be, can you, if you're willing to go back there?'

I was incredulous. 'What? You think I still want Lucas?'

He shrugged. 'Well, don't you? I wouldn't go rushing round to spend time with Rachel. I think you're still in love with him.' He looked out of the window, avoiding eye contact. 'And if you love him, I don't know where that leaves us.'

A void opened in front of me. 'That's crazy,' I said.

'What am I supposed to think, Joanna? You're so tied up with him.'

His tone was one I'd never heard before: it was detached. It frightened me, as if the closeness I'd already come to depend on had been snatched back. 'I don't love Lucas.' I could hear the panic in my voice. 'Not romantically. The last thing I want to do is go back there now but he's made it impossible for me to say no. It's emotional blackmail,' I said. 'Please, Greg. You know it is. I'm being manipulated. I care about him and I can't leave him to waste away up there. But I want to be with you. You must see that.'

Still he said nothing. I put my hand on his arm but he ignored it.

'It's because of me that this happened,' I said.

215

He spun back to look at me; his eyes were hard. 'It isn't your fault. Don't ever let him or anyone else make you think that.'

I couldn't tell him what Danny had said. And I couldn't mention my other new reason for needing to go back: to prove to Danny that he wasn't the only one who was important to Lucas, that I was his friend, too.

'I just can't stand the thought of him still wanting you and having this hold over you. And if you keep going back, he'll never let you go properly,' he said. 'We'll never be free of this.'

'I don't know what else I can do. I'm trapped.'

There was silence for a moment or two and I thought about that. By putting me in this position, Lucas must have known that he would cause a problem in my relationship with Greg, too. The thought made me angry.

'You feel responsible for him, don't you?'

As soon as he said it, I realised he was right. I felt exactly the same about Lucas as I did about my younger brothers: if either was in trouble, I would drop everything to help. And not just because I wanted to but because I was compelled to by something completely internal, distinct from any conscious sense of duty or the expectation of others. I'd never identified the feeling before.

'You can't be Lucas's protector for ever, Joanna.'

'Not for ever. Just now, while he's still grieving. He's been hurt.'

'Yes, but that's a risk you take when you fall in love with someone. They can always leave you.'

Chapter Nineteen

The chestnut trees along the drive formed a deep green tunnel all the way from the real world to the house. Summer had arrived here while I'd been away, just as Lucas had said it had. The last of the light filtered down between the huge leaves but along the verges the darkness was creeping, turning the undergrowth into a black inscrutable mass. As I turned the car off the road from the village I had had a sense of saying goodbye to normality, a last deep breath before the underwater plunge. In the rearview the drive closed in behind me. My stomach jumped with unease at the prospect of being at Stoneborough again. Whatever it was I felt at the house had no power over me in London; I didn't want to submit myself to its hold again. I dreaded that sensation of being watched, the feeling that there was someone or something there that could see without being seen.

I wished Greg were with me. Although Lucas had said that he was welcome, he hadn't felt comfortable with the idea, not the first time I went back. He also didn't think I should have come up tonight. I had come straight from *The Times* where I was in the middle of my third weekend shift in a row. I had driven to the office so that I would be ready for a quick getaway from London when I finished. I was due back there at nine in the morning. I knew I was cutting it fine but it had been ten days since Lucas's overdose and I'd told him I

217

couldn't come the previous weekend. The hurt in his voice when I'd told him I couldn't make this one either had made me search for a way to make it possible. I had worked three weeks straight and hadn't really caught up on the night's sleep I'd missed when we were at the hospital. I'd struggled to stay awake on the motorway. It had been a warm day and the car was hot, although that wasn't the sole reason that my hands had been clammy on the wheel.

It was past nine by the time I pulled up on the gravel circle. I switched off the engine and yawned. Outside the car the air smelled different. Instead of the tang of hot streets, here there was that warm sweet fragrance peculiar to an English evening in early summer, as if the land were gently exhaling. A bat swooped and dived in the navy sky over my head before darting away. I turned to look at the house's closed face. 'I'm not afraid of you,' I said aloud but somehow the dauntlessness I had meant to project died in the air and my voice was only a thin, cowed ribbon of sound. I had a sudden intimation of the vulnerability I had felt here before and marched up the path to ring the bell, keen to be in company.

It was the familiar Lucas who opened the door, not the angry, violent one of the night we split up or the beaten, broken-hearted version from the hospital. I felt a sudden urge to rush into his arms and hold him, to fix that incarnation of him and prevent the return of either of the others. I stepped forward and he touched me lightly on the shoulder. Neither of us said anything and he took my overnight bag and put it at the bottom of the stairs. He coughed. 'Come through. Danny's found some good stuff in the cellar. We were expecting you a little earlier so he's opened it already. Hope you don't mind.'

'Of course not.'

'I'm not drinking. I'm having a total break for a couple of weeks.'

'That sounds like a good idea.'

In the kitchen Michael jumped up to greet me. It had been at least two months since I'd seen him, I realised. Danny stayed seated at the table. He didn't say hello but, when he was sure no one else was looking, raised one ironic eyebrow. Lucas got out a glass for me from the cupboard but Martha shooed him into a chair.

My arrival had interrupted her telling a story about the refuge. She recapped the beginning for me and then continued. I was grateful for the opportunity to sit quietly for a few minutes. I wondered, though, whether anyone else noticed how often her eyes flicked to Danny to gauge the effect her jokes had. She was a good raconteur and I was pleased that he responded to her. I knew it was too much to hope that things would go well between them – the secrecy that he had pressed on her told me that – but I couldn't bear for him to treat her with disdain. I wouldn't be able to keep the silence she had begged me to if he was rude or dismissive of her. I was interested to note, however, that he was also acknowledging Michael's existence again and Michael was responding. Maybe that particular wound was healing.

'We're just going to have an omelette, Jo, as it's late,' said Lucas, pouring another glass of orange juice. 'I'll start it now you're here.'

'No, you sit there, Lucas,' said Michael, getting up. 'I'll do it.'

The kitchen with its high ceiling had always been cold by this time of night but now the air coming in through the French windows was warm. I was hot even in my light summer shirt. I stifled another yawn, wondering how late it would be before I could slip away to bed. Michael was cracking the eggs into a large earthenware bowl with painstaking precision and I longed to hurry him.

After we'd eaten, Martha stood up to go to the loo and Lucas moved into her place. 'Thank you for coming,' he said quietly.

219

'You don't have to thank me, idiot,' I said. 'It's lovely to be here.'

'I've got something to show you. I know you need to get some sleep but it won't take long.'

My heart sank but I smiled. 'Of course.' I looked at my watch: it was gone eleven. 'I just need to make a quick phone call,' I said, 'then I'll be with you.'

His mouth tightened a little as he thought about who I would be calling at that time, then, with an effort, he smiled again. 'Whenever you're ready.'

The table lamps were the only source of light in the hall and the night had already claimed it for its own, its syrupy darkness swallowing the walls and the busts on their pillars, the moonlight from the dome only penetrating as far as the winding banisters above my head. I didn't want to ring Greg from there with its invisible listening ears, real or imagined, and it didn't seem right to call on the landline anyway, when Lucas would pay the bill.

There was no reception at all inside so I had to go out into the garden to use my mobile. I left the house by the side door and went carefully down the steps from the terrace to the lawn. The sky was not black but a rich purple and the moon was full, a perfect creamy disc so immediate I felt I could stand on tiptoe and touch it. The light it cast was peculiarly bright: I could see the garden distinctly. I walked round the foot of the house, not wanting to stray too far, a little afraid, despite myself, of what might lurk in the shadows further out. I walked round until I found a spot with a signal. Danny had told me in the past that it was better away from the house but standing alone in the middle of the vast expanse of lawn made me feel too exposed, as if, in a hideous battering of wings, something might swoop out of the air and take me.

I needed to hear Greg's voice and to know that the real world was still going on without me. It was kicking-out time at the pubs and the streets in Shepherd's Bush would be alive with people going either home or on elsewhere. I wished I was there, listening to the sound of it from my favourite spot on his sofa.

'Jo?' He picked up just as I thought the call would ring out. 'How is it?'

'It's fine,' I said. 'He's making a real effort. No one's mentioning the other day but they're all dashing round, treating him with kid gloves.'

'And how are you?' he asked. 'How was work today?'

'Great. Rebecca called in, too, and she mentioned that the dates for the maternity cover are fixed now and that we should talk.'

'That's fantastic. Make sure you get there OK tomorrow. I think you took a bit of a risk going up there tonight – but you know that.'

I did; we'd spoken about it at length. 'It was the only way I could keep Lucas happy,' I said again now. 'And as we discussed, it does mean I'm only away from you for one night . . .'

'I miss you. I want you back here, in my bed.' He growled, caveman-style. 'And tell Lucas that if he as much as tries to touch you, I'll take him apart.'

When I got back inside Lucas took me upstairs to Patrick's study. I was so tired it was difficult to keep my eyes open. I could have wept when he turned on the cine projector. 'Look,' he said.

It is early evening and the sun is poised above the house like a new penny. Shadows are stretching across the paving stones and playing in the gently moving leaves of the wisteria. The far end of the terrace is still in sunlight and there, lolling on large cushions and stretched out on rugs and blankets, are Patrick's friends. Bottles of red wine stand on the stones and on a wooden board there is a piece of liquefying cheese and the snub end of a baguette. Elizabeth is leaning back on a scarlet cushion displaying her body, naked apart from a pair of black knickers. Thomas Parrish has a possessive arm around her shoulders, its weight and thick black hair in marked contrast to her smooth brown skin. She is built on a different scale to him altogether: by comparison she looks like a precocious tempting child. He leans in so that his lips are against her ear and his nose is in the dark hair that falls around her shoulders. She laughs confidently, throwing her head back, and the silent noise causes Justin, Lucas's father, to look up from where he is lying. He says something that makes them both laugh again before turning back to Claire, the camera following him.

He and Claire are sharing a large striped rug. Like Elizabeth, Claire is wearing only the bottom half of a bikini, hers a swirl of yellow and green with ties at the side. Her shyness in front of the lens is evident again: she sits with her knees drawn up and her arms wrapped tightly around them. Her breasts are hidden and on her shoulders are the pale marks of a bikini top worn on an earlier day. Justin lies on his side behind her wearing shorts made of cut-off jeans. He is improbably brown and his chest is flat and muscled. He looks piratical as he runs his finger inside the elastic of her bikini bottoms, tracing the skin around her hip and the small of her back. The camera watches as Parrish passes him a joint and Justin takes a toke, causing its end to flare orange. He pulls himself up and leans round in front of Claire, who resists at first, gently smiling, but then lets him exhale the contents of his lungs into her mouth. Keeping her eyes on his, she holds it for three or four seconds and then breathes out the heavy smoke into the fading light.

On the balustrade, apart from the group, is Patrick. He is fully dressed except for shoes and looks out from the terrace over the lawn to the trees at the bottom; it is a moment or two before he turns to face the camera. He smiles at the cameraman and speaks briefly, before pulling a pack of cigarettes from his pocket, lighting one and then turning back to his view of the garden.

'Your parents look happy together,' I said, biting back a yawn.

'Yes,' said Lucas, and his voice had a smile in it. 'They do, don't they? But that's why I wanted you to see it. They're there, all three of them, even though my mother is with my father now. They're still friends.'

Despite my exhaustion, I hardly slept. The heat had risen through the house and my room on the top floor felt like a kiln. I tried leaving the curtains open to encourage in what little breeze there was but the exceptional brightness of the moon made the room too light. And as well as that – and despite my best attempts to be rational – I was afraid. I could feel the house's atmosphere, that eerie swirling in the dark places in the corners of the room and the folds of the curtains and behind the furniture. It wasn't explicit; there was no sudden breathless rush, as if the air had been sucked out to make a vacuum that dragged the walls in on me, but there was a feeling of underlying menace, a flexing of muscle. I kept my eyes pressed tightly shut all night, childishly afraid of what might be standing at the end of the bed if I were to open them.

At about three o'clock I began to panic about how little sleep I was going to get. Despite having come so close to losing Lucas and thus being especially careful of him, I admitted to myself that I resented him now. If I hadn't had to come up to the house, I wouldn't have been in this situation, I thought, as I turned over again and tried to find a cool patch on the pillow with my cheek. I was going to be shattered for the whole of the next day and I needed to be on top form. If I could do the maternity cover, then I would be

223

able to leave the *Gazette* and, even if there wasn't a permanent job after the six months, I would have real national newspaper experience on my CV.

I woke to find that I had slept through my alarm. The room was as bright as though it were midday. It was a quarter to eight and I was due at my desk in Wapping at nine. There was no way I could get there by then. There was no time to shower or do my hair. I grabbed the outfit I had laid out the night before and roughly cleaned my teeth. I was at the front door within ten minutes.

Lucas was waiting for me in the hall.

'I'm sorry,' I said, rushing past him, scrabbling in my bag for my car key. 'I can't stop and talk. I'll call you tonight, OK?'

He followed me out on to the drive, picking his way across the gravel in bare feet. He indicated that I should wind down my window. 'Will you come again?' he asked, kneeling down.

'Yes,' I said. 'Of course.'

He smiled. 'And bring Greg next time, if he will. I'll get used to it.'

I was an hour late and when I got to the desk I used, there was a Post-it note stuck to the screen of the computer: 'Rebecca rang. She was expecting you in at nine. Please call her at home immediately.'

Chapter Twenty

In the end it wasn't me who persuaded Greg to go back to the house. Although the weather had been good for a couple of weeks, the last days of June mustered all their energy and came on like a riot. London was close to unbearable. Remembering it now, I wonder whether Lucas saw his opportunity. My mobile rang on Friday evening while I was in the shower, trying to lose the dirty, used feeling of being too hot in the city. 'Could you get that, Greg?' I shouted over the drumming of the water. I came up the landing to my room just as he was finishing the call.

'It was Lucas,' said Greg, sliding the phone back on to the bedside table.

I stopped and looked at him.

'He's asking whether we want to go up. He says there's a pool in the river in the wood. They're going to swim tomorrow.'

'What?' I said. 'Are you saying you want to go there?'

'I'd like a swim. Anything to feel cool.'

'But we could swim somewhere else.'

'Jo, Lucas and I have talked, and it's OK. I don't want to be the reason why you can't be friends. That doesn't solve anything. If he's decent enough to forgive me, the least I can do is face him. I told him we'd go – if you want to, of course. And you're not working this weekend so it made sense.'

'Thank you,' I said. 'It means a lot to me.'

Greg drove us up to Stoneborough the following day. I was attempting to distract myself from my nerves by reading the paper; I'd get carsick when we finally started to move but I was safe for now. Both lanes on the Hammersmith flyover were stationary. A petrol-scented heat haze shimmered over the road ahead of us but inside the air conditioning was keeping us slightly too cool. I could feel the hairs on my arms rising. I was impressed by Greg's black Mercedes, despite myself. Like so many things about him, it seemed more adult than anything else connected with me. Even if I could have afforded one, it would never have occurred to me to buy a car like it.

The roads were busy all the way. On the section of motorway out beyond High Wycombe, the shiny roofs of the cars ahead stretched away like beads on a multicoloured necklace. The countryside was ripening. The violent yellow of the oilseed rape was gone and now the cornfields were turning the palest shade of silver gold. There was no breeze today to run through them like the touch of invisible fingers. The crop stood erect and motionless in the stifling air.

The others were in the garden when we arrived but they hung back and let Lucas come to meet us. Greg slung our bags over his shoulder and put his arm around me, protective and possessive at once. I didn't want to hug Lucas in front of Greg so I ended up giving him an awkward pat.

Lucas and Greg shook hands. 'Thanks for coming, mate,' Lucas said.

Greg nodded. 'Thanks for having us. We're looking forward to a swim. London's disgusting. You did the right thing in getting out when you could.'

'The bed's been made up in your old room, Greg,' said

226

Lucas, and I looked away quickly in case he tried to meet my eye. 'If you want to go and change into your swimming gear.'

Although we'd been together for almost three months, it still felt odd to go to what I thought of as his and Rachel's room. I would have to try not to imagine them together in that big bed, just as I had disciplined myself not to see Rachel in his flat in Shepherd's Bush. If I let myself think about it, disbelief at what I'd done to her came rushing up on me and then the awful sinking-mud of the guilt. If Greg and I were to have a future, I had to let it go.

When we came down the others were on the terrace and we set off for the river. Michael and Danny went ahead with Martha, who swung a straw bag full of towels in front of her and behind like a metronome. The boys were striding out and she put in quick extra steps now and again to keep up.

'I've been watching more of the cines, Jo,' said Lucas as we tramped across the crisping grass, the heat from the sun warming our backs. 'It's really odd watching your parents smoke grass and your mother sunbathing topless.' He gave a short laugh. 'What chance did I ever stand of rebelling?'

I thought of his law career, now abandoned.

'How's the writing going?' asked Greg.

'Good, actually. I'm feeling really positive about it.'

'And how are you feeling generally?' I said. I had debated with myself whether I ought to mention his overdose and decided yes. We shouldn't pretend it hadn't happened, however much we wanted to.

'OK. Good. I feel happier. They said I should see a counsellor but I didn't really see the need. Things are much better now.'

'Perhaps you should anyway,' I said, 'just to . . .'

'Where do we go from here, Lucas?' Martha shouted.

The others waited until we caught them up and Lucas led us into the wood. It was like entering another world. As soon as we came under the trees the light changed to an aqueous

227

green and the air felt cool and medicinal. We might have discovered an underwater kingdom or slipped back in time, maybe as far as the Middle Ages. I could see that there had once been a path but no one had walked it for a while. We followed its traces as best we could. Brambles, nature's barbed wire, covered everything. They snagged my clothes and tore at my skin as we picked our way through. Underfoot the ground was spongy with moss and the leaves of past seasons. Greg went ahead of me and held the elder branches that snapped back as soon as they were released, full of fresh sap. Thirty or so yards in, a fallen tree blocked the way. Danny and Greg vaulted over it but, doubting my athleticism, I sat down on it and swung my legs round, leaving a round patch of green dust on my backside.

'It's like something out of bloody "Sleeping Beauty",' said Martha, as she detached the prickles of a briar that clung to her T-shirt. 'How much more of this?'

'You're such a girl, Martha,' said Danny, swinging his hips from side to side in a deft slalom through the undergrowth.

She laughed. 'Wait for me then.'

'It's amazing in here.' Greg stopped me for a second and raised his head.

I looked up. The trees grew so thickly that little sun filtered through. Where it did, it pierced the canopy in sharp, bright beams, casting small pools of light on the ground around us. There was birdsong above our heads then a fluster of wings and leaves as a blackbird made a break for freedom and punctured the thick vegetation out into the clear air.

'It's great, isn't it? I used to play here all the time when I was a child,' Lucas called back to us. 'I could hide for hours – no one ever found me.'

We picked our way through for ten minutes. At last we came to a place where the trees and bushes thinned out and gave way to a flat bank of soft mossy grass. There was the river, just as Lucas had described it. As it flowed down to the clearing it was about ten feet wide and looked deep, running within the bounds that it had worn for itself, but here in front of us it swelled out in a broad bulb, as if allowing itself a moment to idle in the sun. This broad expanse, probably twenty feet long, was shallower and a paler green. The water was clear and its surface scintillated with sunlight, a watery counterpart to the bank, which was speckled by the light reaching through the leaves overhead. Where the water tapered to the edge, I could see white pebbles gleaming up and a small amount of ribbony weed, combed forward by the current like silky hair.

'Who's first in? Come on, girls.'

'After you, Danny.'

Michael had taken his trainers and socks off and was sitting on the tiny cliff at the edge of the bank, about to slip his feet into the water. 'My God, it's bitter. Are you serious about swimming?'

Lucas smiled and sat down, propping his back against the ridged trunk of a large beech tree. 'Of course. But I've done it before, so I'm not going in first.'

Martha was paddling, walking carefully up and down the edge, her feet a strange marble white under the water. 'It only feels cold because of the air temperature. It's OK once you get used to it.'

'Then put your money where your mouth is, Martha,' said Danny.

'I didn't bring a costume.' She looked at him sideways.

'I'm sure no one will mind if you go in without.'

'Funny.' She laughed, a sweet flirtatious laugh that I was amazed no one else seemed to recognise for what it was.

To our right, about twenty feet upstream, there was a splash. I turned and saw the last of the spray fall as the river reclaimed the displaced water. Under the surface a body glided by. Just when I thought that he could hold his breath no longer, he angled up and Greg's head and shoulders broke

229

the surface. He shook his head like a dog, sending droplets of water spinning in a bright circle around him. 'Come on in, the water's lovely,' he laughed.

'Is it freezing?' I shouted.

'Refreshing.' He dived back down.

'We can't let him beat us, Martha.' I started to unlace my plimsolls. 'Come on, just wear your underwear.'

I stepped into the shallows. The water was blue-cold and invigorating; it was like getting into a shot of frozen vodka. I waded a little further out. Now my body was operating in two temperature zones, my shoulders and arms warmed by the sun, the flesh below my knees beginning to go numb.

'Come on, Jo,' Greg called. All or nothing, I thought. I took another few steps and then plunged forward. The water was so cold it was painful. I swam as fast as I could over to Greg and put my arms around him in the hope of some heat.

'Brrr,' I said, teeth chattering.

'Look warm,' he whispered to me. 'Or we'll never get the others in.' He slipped out of my arms and down into the water. I felt a tug at my feet as he pulled me under. Beneath the surface, it was silent apart from the crystal sound of the river sluicing past. The current was strong; it wanted to carry me with it. I could hear my own heartbeat. I surfaced again and gasped for breath. Greg came up next to me, smiling. 'Your costume's gone completely see-through.'

Michael swam up beside us. 'My balls are like frozen peas,' he said. 'This can't be good for you.'

On the bank, there was the sound of wine being opened. Lucas poured himself a glass and downed it, thinking every-one preoccupied. I looked at Greg, who had also noticed. Martha was standing in the shallows now in a pair of raspberry-coloured lacy pants. Her body was long and lean, her hips slim enough to be boyish but with an undeniable female curve out from the waist. I saw Lucas glance up and see her. He turned away, embarrassed, but then sneaked

230

another look. 'Are you trying to upstage me, Martha?' I shouted across to her. 'What's with just the knickers?'

'I wasn't wearing a bra,' she shouted back. 'How stupid do I feel?'

'Get in quickly then.'

She took a final look at Danny and then launched herself in. She swam efficiently over to where the three of us were already treading water. 'God, it's freezing,' she said. 'I'm going to get those two in. Lucas,' she yelled.

'OK, OK.' He stood up and took off his clothes, dropping them in a pile. It was strange, seeing his body; I had come to know it well and now it was off-bounds, withdrawn from me for ever. I felt a little shock of regret. He was thinner than Greg, but for someone who never took purposeful exercise he was in surprisingly good shape. Martha wolf-whistled. 'Cut it out, Marth,' he said, but I saw him fight down a small smile. He walked upstream to the place where Greg had gone in and with a spring he left the bank and cut into the water, which closed immediately over his body. For five or six seconds he disappeared, then resurfaced downstream from us. 'Yes,' he said. 'It's just as cold as it used to be.' His head was as dark and sleek as a seal's.

Danny took some persuading. 'Honestly,' he said. 'I'm fine. I'm just the right temperature – I don't need to cool down.'

'Come on,' said Martha. 'Just swim.'

'After I've had a cigarette.'

Every second that he sat on the edge of the bank made us more determined to get him in. Eventually he ran out of stalling tactics and stripped down to his black cotton boxers. He stepped in at the edge and strode about.

'For God's sake, Danny, will you just get in?' Lucas swam closer to him.

'All right, all right, let me acclimatise.'

'Come on,' said Michael. 'I'm starting to look like a pickled walnut.'

It took Danny five minutes to get far enough in for the water to reach his thighs and lap at the bottom of his shorts. Eventually Lucas lost patience, swam up behind him and pushed him forward into deeper water. I don't know if anyone else saw it but a look of utter panic flashed across his face as he realised he was falling. There was a splash and he disappeared below the surface, face forward. The current pulled him away from us.

A moment or two passed. His head came up for a second and there was the guttural choking sound of river water swallowed the wrong way. His body bobbed up and down like a fishing float and his arms flailed in the water and the air above his head.

Martha and Michael laughed, thinking it was a joke. 'Very funny, Danny,' said Lucas, swimming back to his place midstream, but there was no answer.

'Bloody hell, Jo,' Greg said quietly. 'He really can't swim.'

He crossed the water to Danny, took his arm and lifted his mouth out of the river. Danny gasped and slipped down again. I caught sight of his face as he went under. His expression was one of terror. He thought he was going to drown. Greg bobbed down and caught him under the armpits and brought him up to the surface. He held his chin until Danny caught his breath and stopped panicking. Then he took him nearer the bank, where he could stand again. Somehow Greg made it look like they were swimming together but the others had seen Danny struggling. They looked away and tried to pretend they hadn't, as did I.

'Sorry, mate,' I heard Greg say to him. 'We should have warned you. It's bloody cold. I'm getting out. Let's have a glass of that wine.' They picked their way to the edge and climbed out. Compared to Danny, Greg's body looked rough and huge, wet Labrador to Danny's greyhound. Danny was shivering but trying to disguise his shock. 'Get some clothes on,' Greg told him, throwing him a towel.

'I'm getting chilly,' I said to the others. 'I'm getting out, too.' The air was a fresh assault and I wrapped my towel tightly around me. I realised that I had forgotten to bring my underwear so I took off my costume and pulled on my T-shirt and jeans over bare skin as inconspicuously as I could. Greg was pouring the wine that Lucas had opened. I went to sit next to him in the sun and rubbed my arms to get rid of the goosebumps.

He put his hands around my ear. 'I know you're not wearing any knickers. In a few minutes you and I are going for a walk.'

As the sun went down, we took cushions and a pile of blankets out to the terrace. Danny brought the stereo out and spent a quarter of an hour fiddling with extension leads and speakers, eventually trailing the cable across the flag-stones from the library window. It was clear from the less than usually nonchalant way he was carrying himself that he was feeling his earlier embarrassment acutely. I had wondered whether he would thank Greg for helping him so subtly but he never mentioned the incident again. Greg asked me later what sort of parents didn't teach their child to swim. It was such a simple thing; my mother had taught my brothers and me as soon as she could, in case we ever fell into water unsupervised.

The music Danny put on was wonderful. The beat was melancholic and insistent, and above it a woman's voice, clear and strong, sang snatches of Spanish that sounded like a lament. I lay on my back, watching as the sky softened in colours of mother-of-pearl, and bands of blue-black light began to rise above the wood.

Greg raised himself on his elbows. 'This is great. Who is it?'

'Friends of mine. They're not signed. They're out in Ibiza, getting exposure.'

233

I rolled on to my front and Greg rested his hand on my skin, where my T-shirt rode up in the small of my back. Lucas saw it and looked quickly away, his face unreadable. Danny was lighting candles now, shielding each little flame with a cupped hand. Night had crept around us, and the circle of light drew us into a ring. We lay facing each other, like spokes in a wheel. Only our faces and shoulders were illuminated; our bodies disappeared into the darkness. It was as though we were preparing for a seance, to contact those long dead.

Danny went inside and returned with a bottle of absinthe. Martha groaned. 'God, do we have to? Remember how sick we were last time?'

'It'll be fine. This is better quality stuff. You'll enjoy it.' He winked at her and rejoined the circle, twisting the cap off the bottle and taking a huge swig before passing it to her. Whether he was treating himself for the shock of the afternoon or trying to regain face, it was plain he was on a mission. When the bottle came round to me, I misjudged it and took a far larger mouthful than I had intended. It burned my throat like a line of flame on the way down.

Lucas had made jugs of Long Island iced tea so potent I wondered whether there was actually any Coke in them at all, and between that and the absinthe it wasn't long before everything began to lose its edge. I was grateful for it: I wanted to be drunk, to numb my unease around Lucas. I'd felt it all day but most keenly when he'd caught Greg and me coming back from our tryst in the woods. He had gone back to the house at the same time as the others and had been watching from the balustrade as Greg and I had come stumbling out of the trees together about twenty minutes later, laughing as I picked dead leaves out of my hair. I'd felt the weight of his stare even from that distance and I'd moved away from Greg at once. By the time we reached the house, Lucas had disappeared, as if I'd imagined him there.

234

Danny turned up the volume on the stereo so that the garden was suddenly full of music. It seemed to reach as far as the wood. The walls of the house bounced it back at us and it filled the sky, right up to the stars, which seemed especially bright. We got up and danced, the stones warm under our bare feet. The music was faster now but the woman's voice still reached through my chest wall to my heart. I could feel rivulets of sweat running between my breasts and Danny took off his T-shirt and danced bare-chested like a beautiful sort of savage. My feet, soft after a winter in shoes, became sore but I couldn't stop. It was as if the music and the alcohol were a sort of spell and I was safe inside it as long as I kept going. I think the others felt the same: although it was fun to dance, it also felt necessary. We paused only to drink. Lucas was in a world of his own. I could see the tip of his cigarette whirling in the darkness as he spun round and round.

I remember how still it was beyond the whirl and noise of the terrace, with the sky free of cloud and just a faint breeze that seemed to move the leaves of the trees in time with the shimmering music. I remember Lucas being exceptionally drunk, even more than the rest of us. Suddenly he darted out of the loose circle we had been in and jumped on to the narrow balustrade. The rest of us stopped dancing immediately.

'Look at this,' he said, taking three quick steps along the top. The stone wasn't wide enough for his feet side by side: he had one in front of the other, Egyptian-style.

'Lucas, for God's sake, get down.'

'Calm down, Joanna.' He took another two steps forward. He was coming up to the corner where the terrace began to run sideways along the edge of the lawn and the steps descended into the garden.

'Mate,' said Danny. 'Get down.'

'I'm going to walk along to the end. Watch this.' He cut

across the corner and walked reasonably steadily for about ten feet.

Danny marked him as he went along, but kept his distance, not wanting to provoke him into any sudden movements. Lucas's eyes were bright with the effort. 'Come down before you hurt yourself.'

'Oh ye of little faith.' He managed another stretch but the strain was beginning to show. On the last few steps, he wobbled and out his arms to balance himself. I thought of the fifteen-foot drop into the garden. Would he survive that, if he fell?

It looked like he was going to make it. About five feet from the end, he was going well and planting his feet carefully. But as he took what would have been one of his final steps, one of the top stones moved under him, the cement worn away, and his balance was lost. He spun his arms but although he tried to tip his weight towards the house so that he fell on to the terrace he went the other way instead.

We stood stock still in horror, unable to believe what had just happened. The music was still playing at top volume, the emotive voice piercing the night air. We ran to the edge and looked over. Lucas had fallen not into the garden but on to the stone steps, six or eight feet below us. He lay on his back motionless. All of a sudden, he opened his eyes. 'Ow,' he said, and laughed.

Chapter Twenty-One

The next day Lucas's bruise covered the whole of his lower back, from the cleft of his buttocks to where his ribcage came in at the front. It was a vicious purple-black. He had taken his T-shirt off and was leaning forward to let Martha apply witch hazel with a big pad of cotton wool. Its sweet smell spread quickly through the noon air. He winced, even though she was touching him as gently as possible. The area looked swollen and must have taken the full brunt of his fall. He was extremely lucky not to have damaged his back.

'You should get this looked at,' Martha told him. 'It's huge, Lucas, and you're obviously in pain.'

'It's just a bruise, Marth. I'll be OK.'

'You might have hurt your kidneys.'

'Honestly, it's fine.' He flinched again as she started on a new area.

The sun was directly overhead and nothing cast a shadow. If I had had to guess, I'd have put the temperature in the mid-eighties. I watched the ice in the water jug melting, the cubes becoming smaller and smaller until they vanished completely. A couple of cabbage white butterflies rose from the flowerbed below and danced above our heads, their wings bright against the deep blue of the sky. Among us there was the subdued atmosphere of people with churning hangovers. Greg was lying down inside, preferring the cool.

Martha finished doing Lucas's back and handed him his T-shirt. 'Put this on or you'll burn, too.' He drew himself up carefully and very slowly lifted his arms to pull it over his head. Gingerly he stood and went inside the house. Five minutes or so passed and he returned, elbowing the side door open and carrying two bottles of wine, glasses held in bunches between his fingers like inverted tulips. I couldn't believe my eyes. He sat down slowly on his cushion and took a corkscrew from his pocket. He opened the first bottle and emptied it into four of the glasses. 'Martha?' He held one out.

'I couldn't,' she said. 'I'm so dehydrated.'

'Jo? Wine?'

'Not for me.'

Danny put up his hand in a halting gesture. 'Not today, mate.'

'You've all gone soft on me. Are you really the friends I had at university?'

I looked out over the garden for a moment, knowing I was about to step into dangerous territory. 'Lucas, I thought you were taking it easy for a couple of weeks.'

There was silence for a moment or two. No one said anything.

'We got wrecked last night,' I went on. 'Why not wait till later?'

He moved the three remaining glasses of wine into a line, picked up the first, swallowed the contents, then smacked it down again. The stem snapped. He picked up the second, then the third and drank them, too. His Adam's apple plunged in his throat and he gagged. 'Because I don't want to. All right?' He got to his feet. 'Don't you think it's hard enough for me, watching you with him, knowing what you're doing, in the woods, in my house?'

I looked down.

'Just leave me alone.' He went down the steps and on to the lawn. When he was far enough away from the bottom of the terrace to be visible again, he turned to face us and flung his arms open. 'Piss off, all of you.' He walked as fast as his back would allow in the direction of the wood.

We watched him until he vanished into the trees. 'What do we do now?' I said. 'Should we go after him?'

'I think you're the wrong person to do it, either way,' said Michael.

'What if he's gone to the river and falls in?' Martha said.

'It'd take more than a bottle of wine these days,' Danny said. 'This happens a lot. He flies off the handle and disappears. He'll be back in a couple of hours, acting like nothing happened.'

'I've never seen him get angry like this. I don't like it.' Martha began to collect the pieces of broken glass.

'None of us do.' He stubbed out his cigarette.

'I think he should reconsider about the counsellor,' I said. 'It would do him good, even just to talk.'

'Lucas doesn't need a counsellor, Joanna,' said Danny, his voice full of poison. 'I'm here for him all the time and that's all he needs.'

Lucas was gone for more than two hours and, when he did return, he was not alone.

The girl was tall, almost as tall as he was. She was wearing a black bikini top and a scarlet sarong that tied tightly around her hips and ended just above her knees in a fringe of tassels. Her black hair was gathered into a ponytail that reached halfway down her back. She moved with long, confident strides, keeping pace with Lucas's quick walk, the swinging of hair and tassels lending her the lilting, easy appearance of a gently rocking boat. They disappeared from view as they came up the side and we composed ourselves casually on the rugs.

'Hi,' called Lucas from the top of the steps. They came over and stood in front of us, blocking out the sun. 'This is

239

the most amazing thing. Look who I found down by the river.' We peered up at the girl against the sun and she smiled down at us. There was something familiar about her face but none of us had met her before. When no one said anything, Lucas explained, as if it were the most obvious thing in the world. 'This is Diana.'

I had heard the name before but couldn't think where. Suddenly my mind supplied the answer: Diana, Elizabeth's daughter. That was why she looked familiar: the long dark hair, the height, the pale, full lips on the tanned face.

He introduced us, going round the circle. 'Hey,' she said. 'Would you like a drink? There's wine. Or some orange juice?'

'Juice would be great. Thank you.' Lucas went inside and she sat down, folding her slim legs to one side. The fronts of her flip-flops each bore a red fabric rose.

'I love your shoes,' I said, to break the silence. None of us had said anything but she didn't seem fazed. She was looking at us with open interest. There was something not quite English about her confidence and unmasked curiosity.

'Thanks,' she said, smiling at me. 'I bought them in Cape Town. I've just got back.'

'I was in South Africa at the end of last year,' said Greg, who had rejoined us now, looking slightly improved. 'What did you think of it?'

'I've never been anywhere like it.' She took a packet of cigarettes out of a canvas bag printed with a pattern of horses chasing each other, nose to tail. She lit up and exhaled, blinking away the smoke that got in her eyes. 'It has so much energy. And then you drive out and there's that coastline and you realise there's nothing between you and Antarctica.'

'Did you go to the parks? Just open sky and bush for miles.' Greg was getting animated. I felt a little put out that he'd never spoken to me about it like this. 'Sometimes out there, I felt like I was the first person to see it.'

Lucas returned with orange juice and a bottle of wine running with condensation.

'What are you going to do now you're back?' asked Martha.

'Well, I don't have to work just yet. Patrick left me a bit of money, as you know.' She looked at Lucas. 'So I thought I'd take time and try to find the right place to start. I want to be a photographer.'

'Right,' said Martha, her tone sounding genuine but revealing its slight edge to those of us who knew her well.

Danny waved Lucas away and poured Diana's orange juice himself. 'What I don't understand,' he said, 'is how Lucas found you in the wood.'

'I was swimming,' she said.

'It was like something out of a dream,' Lucas cut in. 'I went down to the river for a swim myself. But it was so cool underneath the trees I sat down for a bit first and fell asleep.'

None of us said anything about the way he had stormed off. It was exactly as Danny had predicted: he was acting as if nothing had happened. I could imagine him falling asleep, though; the combination of lack of sleep, the pain of the bruise and the best part of a bottle of wine would have been a knockout.

'Anyway, God knows how much later I woke up and I heard this splash. I couldn't believe it. Diana was diving off upstream – you know, Greg, where you went in yesterday. I didn't recognise her at first – it's been years since we saw each other. I really did think I was dreaming.'

'Diana and the nymphs bathing,' I said.

'It was embarrassing for both of us,' said Diana. 'I thought I was alone so I'd stripped off. Something so liberating about swimming naked.' She raised her eyebrows. It was an un-usual expression, I thought. Someone as beautiful as she was couldn't help but know it and yet this gesture made her

241

momentarily – and knowingly, it seemed – clownlike. It was so unlike her mother's self-conscious poise.

'Isn't something bad supposed to happen to people who catch Diana bathing? The virgin goddess, untouched and unseen by men?' asked Michael.

'Well, it's not ideal,' I said. 'Look what happened to Actaeon. Artemis – same goddess, different name – changed him into a stag and he was ripped to pieces by his own dogs. And when Teiresias saw Athena bathing, she blinded him. Yes, Lucas, you'd better watch it.'

'It's not all bad. He did get the gift of prophecy and immortality.'

'Yeah, and spent his whole deathless existence roaming around from city to city in beggars' rags with nobody listening to a word he said.'

'Emphasise the positive, why don't you?'

Diana laughed. 'Well, I'll do my best not to make you blind, Lucas.' She took a sip of her juice and looked at him over the edge of the glass.

'I'd appreciate it.'

'I tried to get Lucas to swim,' she said to the rest of us. 'But he wouldn't.'

Of course not, I thought. He wanted to keep his back hidden.

'You look very like your mother,' said Danny. 'Every bit as beautiful.'

'Thanks,' she said, looking a little uncomfortable. 'I never used to be able to see it myself but they say people get more and more like their parents, don't they?'

'God help us,' said Martha.

'So how long is it since you've seen each other?' asked Danny.

'Years. I was eight, I think,' said Diana.

'Childhood sweethearts – that's adorable.'

'Oh nothing like that,' said Lucas. 'We used to play together all the time but after my dad died Diana went to boarding school and we were away in the holidays a lot. We always seemed to miss each other.'

'It was a bit rude of me, wasn't it, just pitching up for a swim, having not seen you for so long. I rang the house at lunchtime and there was no answer. I thought you were probably out. Mum was sure you wouldn't mind.'

'Of course not,' said Danny. 'You should come up whenever. You should come for dinner. Bring Elizabeth; she must be back from Rome now and I promised her a lunch. We could substitute a supper here.'

She smiled softly at Lucas. 'That'd be great, and I'll ask Mum.'

'What did you think of her?' asked Greg, winding down the window to trail his hand in the car's cool slipstream. Long golden grass and cow parsley flashed past us in a lacy blur. 'She was pretty confident, wasn't she? Especially since she hadn't met any of us before. On the plus side, though, if she and Lucas become big pals again, it might take the heat off us.'

'Let's hope so,' I said. I had mixed feelings about her. There was no reason for me to dislike her, of course: she had been friendly and open. I couldn't deny, though, that I felt challenged by how quickly Greg had responded to her. The idea that he might find her attractive made me nauseous. At times I had such an appetite for him that I thought about taking bites out of him, sinking my teeth into the flesh of his upper arms or his buttocks. I didn't think I could stand it if he fancied her. A little voice spoke to me now from a dark chamber at the back of my mind: he left Rachel for you; what's to say he wouldn't leave you for someone else? I slammed the door on it quickly.

'I think Danny was pretty taken with her.' He indicated to turn right on to the main road. 'He was drooling like an old spaniel. Every bit as beautiful as your mother – I mean, honestly.'

243

I thought of Martha. She would have noticed it as well, if Greg had. And probably Michael had, too. Danny's sexual appetite was close to being out of control; at least when he'd had a job, there had been restrictions of time. With Diana not working and around in Stoneborough during the week, he could run her and Martha concurrently and probably derive huge satisfaction from the intrigue. It would be one way of redeploying his intellectual energy, currently without an outlet, as well as ensuring a double supply of ego-boosting attention. Poor Martha. My heart contracted with fear for her.

Chapter Twenty-Two

The following Thursday was her birthday. I gave her my present – a chunky red perspex bracelet and the new Gorillaz album – in the morning and Michael, Greg and I planned to take her for cocktails down by the river after work. Greg and I had arranged to meet her at home at seven-thirty but when we got there there was no sign of her. Her birthday cards were lined up on the mantelpiece though, and there were empty envelopes on the coffee table, so she must have been home to open her post.

'Martha?' I called but there was no response.

'Her bedroom door is closed,' said Greg.

Unless she was changing, Martha very rarely closed her door during the day. I went downstairs and knocked on it gently. 'Martha?' There was no response but I thought I heard a movement within so I said her name again. Again there was no answer so I opened the door a few inches and looked in.

She was sitting on the edge of her bed with her head bowed, her hair falling forward over her face. Her hands were in her lap. She looked up as I came in. 'I'm being ridiculous,' she said, sniffing and taking a tissue from the box on her bedside table to wipe her eyes. 'I'll be all right in a minute, honestly.'

Martha never cried. 'Don't be silly,' I said, going to sit next to her. 'What's the matter? You're not allowed to cry today.'

'No, it's really stupid,' she said. 'I can't believe I'm letting myself get upset about it. My mother forgot my birthday, that's all.'

I thought about the empty envelopes in the sitting room. 'Oh Marth, you know what the post is like. You'll probably get her card or parcel tomorrow. They can never get anything here on time.'

She shook her head. 'No, I called her. She forgot. She didn't even realise when I dropped hints. I told her in the end and she got defensive and said that she couldn't be expected to remember all these dates. I'm an only child, for God's sake – that's one date a year.'

I had heard of Martha's mother even before I met Martha. Patricia was one of the figureheads of seventies feminism, mentioned in the same breath as Germaine Greer, Betty Friedan and Gloria Steinem. I'd envied Martha as soon as I'd found out the connection. I'd thought it must be great to have such a firebrand as a mother, an intellectual power-house and someone who had played a major part in effecting a sea-change in attitudes to women. I soon realised that, though the idea of her was good, the reality was somewhat more difficult to live with.

I'd met her only once, at the end of the summer term in our first year at Oxford, when she was over from America paying her annual visit to her ex-husband, Martha's father, with whom she remained on friendly terms. I'd been so nervous beforehand and her appearance had done nothing to reassure me. She'd been wearing boot-cut black jeans with a tight white T-shirt under which there was clearly no bra. Her hair was coloured tomato red and she was accompanied by a miasma of spicy scent. Although she was in her late fifties, she was still somehow of the moment. The conversation that day had revolved around her and I'd felt sorry for Martha, who had been looking forward to her visit so much. She was preparing to give a paper in London on the changing role of the mother in contemporary society and she'd talked about how women had had to smother their own ambitions when they had children. 'I hope I didn't smother yours too much,' Martha had said, heavy on the irony.

'What?' Patricia had said, as if remembering with surprise that Martha was in fact her daughter. 'Well, no. Your father looked after you a lot. It wasn't too bad.'

Mostly Martha made light of it but at times like this I knew she found it hard that her mother seemed to regard mother-hood as an insidious form of bondage. 'You know,' she said, 'I don't mind at all about cards or presents. It's just, when she forgets, it makes me feel like she doesn't care.'

Greg had come in and was leaning against the windowsill, his long legs extending across the room towards us. 'Marth, you can't think like that,' he said. 'How could she not love you to bits?'

She smiled at him gratefully. 'Thanks. You know, I don't know what I'd do without my friends. Danny called earlier. Lucas is doing a dinner on Saturday night, a combined birthday supper for me with a welcome back to Diana. You two are coming, aren't you?'

With some anxiety, I waited for Greg to reply, not wanting to force his hand.

'Of course. Your birthday supper – wouldn't miss it for the world,' he said.

'And I'm not working at *The Times*.'

'Cool.' She smiled again. 'By the way, Danny says Diana has been round two or three times swimming and Lucas is writing again. Apparently he's been locked in the study for hours.'

'Sounds like she might be good for him,' I said, with a slight pang.

We didn't arrive at the house until lunchtime. On the drive was Michael's new car, a silver Audi TT. We'd heard all

247

about it at Martha's birthday drinks; he was endearingly proud and had taken the previous day off work to collect it from the garage. Martha rang on the doorbell but there was no answer. We rang again and although we could hear the chiming inside no one came.

'They'll be outside on an afternoon like this, probably on the terrace.' Greg set off round to the side of the house.

There was no one there either but the door to the flower lobby was wide open. We went in and checked the kitchen and the drawing room. The house was quieter than I could ever remember it. I stood at the bottom of the stairs and tipped my head backwards. The painted ceiling came into view. In the heat, the man on the chaise looked particularly languid. 'Hello?' I shouted up through the centre of the place. A few seconds passed and the last reverberations of my voice echoed off the walls.

'Hello?' Danny appeared at the mouth of the passageway. 'Oh, it's you.'

'Were you expecting someone else?'

'We're in the kitchen garden.' He turned and walked off. Greg rolled his eyes.

By the time we got out there, Danny had resumed what was obviously his former position on a pretty white-painted garden bench he had dragged alongside the raised bed in which Lucas and Michael were crouched. Lucas stood to greet me. 'Strawberries,' he said. 'We're going to have them for supper.' His knackered Radiohead T-shirt had two circles of sweat under the arms.

'Hey,' called out a female voice from inside the French windows.

'Diana, hello,' I said, surprised.

'I think I need a glass of water,' said Michael. He stood up and stretched, his hands in the small of his back. 'It's nearly unbearable. Look, the air's actually shimmering.'

248

'It's supposed to break today, they said on the radio. We'll eat inside this evening, just in case,' said Lucas.

Diana wandered out to us. She was wearing a white T-shirt and a skirt the colour of a piece of green glass washed up on the beach. The outfit gave her the appearance of a land-locked mermaid. 'Hi and goodbye,' she said. 'I'm going to go home now. I've got some pictures to develop and I want a shower before dinner.'

'Do you need a lift?' he asked. 'I'll take you down in the Jaguar.'

'No. I like to walk.' She leant over and gave him a kiss on the cheek. She had the kind of easy familiarity with him that I used to have. The thought made me sad. 'See you later.' She raised her hand in a goodbye to the rest of us and there was the light jangle of silver bracelets.

We waited until she'd gone. 'It must be good to see her again,' Martha said.

'Yes,' said Lucas. 'It is.'

'She's hot,' Danny said. 'Simple as that.'

Martha had cut two bowls of buttermilk roses for the table and their scent was heavy as incense. As Diana and Elizabeth arrived for dinner, Michael had been showing us his car and its thermometer had read eighty-nine degrees. If the humidity increased any further, breathing would be like inhaling soup. We had pushed up the sash windows as far as they would go but the air was dead. I felt sick with it. It was too early for the sky to be darkening, but from my seat at the table I could see a roll of black cloud mounting over the wood, like a breaker waiting to crest, the body of it becoming darker and darker as the minutes passed. The house was full of an uneasy penumbrous light, as if a giant stood over the place casting it in shadow.

Tonight Elizabeth was wearing a cream linen shift dress with a simple bronze cuff on one wrist. Despite the heat, she looked crisp enough to step on to a yacht in St Tropez at a moment's notice. 'I remember we had an incredible storm here that first summer,' she said now. 'It was almost biblical – lightning non-stop for what seemed like hours, sheets of rain. We joked about what we'd all done – whether it was divine retribution. We had visions of being swept from the house by floodwater, drowned for the sinners we no doubt were.' She laughed. 'The power was out for a couple of days. It's so far off the beaten track here that it was last to get reconnected. Patrick took charge, though, as he always did. It was actually rather fun. We were like scouts, heating up soup on a primus stove, swimming in the river instead of bathing. It was the same the time we got snowed in. He was like that, as you know, Lucas.' She smiled at him. 'He took charge and made sure everything was all right. I think that's why people were drawn to him, especially women. He made people feel safe.' I watched her happy animation as she remembered. I realised that, as she was getting to know us better, her froideur was disappearing and the real Elizabeth emerging from behind the façade. I wondered whether it was possible that she might have been shy.

'Did you ever feel jealous of the other women?' asked Danny.

Martha's eyes flicked on to him again, as they had been doing all evening.

'Danny,' I said, 'perhaps Elizabeth would prefer not to talk about it.'

He looked at me as though I were a housemaid who had spoken out of turn.

'Oh, I don't mind. It's lovely to have the opportunity to remember. I've really enjoyed talking to Danny about him over our lunches. The years I spent with Patrick were some of the happiest of my life. Of course, eventually we drifted apart; there were pressures of work and then I met Diana's father but we stayed close. I wonder, if he hadn't died . . .'

Lucas stood abruptly to clear the table. I got up to help but Diana waved me back into my seat. 'Don't worry, Jo, I've got this.' Without stacking the bowls, she took four, arranging them up her arm. 'Years of waitressing experience.' She turned lightly towards the kitchen, the material of her dress swinging around her brown calves. Whether it was consciously a dress for seduction I didn't know, but even I was finding it difficult not to look at her. Cut on the bias, it was the colour of fine dark chocolate and the fall of it around her breasts and hips was such that she looked as if she'd been dipped in it. Her hair was shining and fell over her shoulders around its narrow tied straps. It was a dress to make a man yearn to unwrap her and swallow her up. I had seen Danny watching her and Greg, too, although when he noticed that I'd seen he looked quickly away.

There was the rattle of plates from the kitchen and the sound of another bottle of wine being opened.

'Danny,' said Elizabeth confidentially, 'how is Lucas? I've been so worried.'

'He's making progress,' he said. 'I'm doing my best to look after him.'

She smiled at him gratefully, as if he were doing her a favour. There was something very old-fashioned about the way in which she made herself his subordinate. 'You know,' she said, 'sometimes you remind me of a young Patrick. You have that same sort of strength. And the way you are with Lucas is a little like the way things were between him and Justin, at least to start with. Patrick looked out for him. I suppose it was a brotherly thing but it was particularly strong between them.'

An expression of surprised pleasure passed across his face. 'It's interesting you should say that,' he said, lowering his voice. 'It's something I think about, too, sometimes. I've always tried to look out for Lucas. He's less worldly than me, less robust . . .'

I wondered whether Elizabeth would have the same opinion of him if she knew how he had fallen apart when he found Lucas that night. Now, though, she settled her eyes back on his as watchfully as a cat, and stretched her arm towards him, exposing the smooth white skin on the inside of her wrist.

'What changed?' said Michael. 'You said "at least to start with".'

'Oh well, when Justin got his role in that television series, he had his own money for the first time. Patrick didn't have to keep bailing him out any more. It changed things between them a bit, evened them up.'

Diana came through the swing door with a bowl of new potatoes and Danny quickly moved his hand away from Elizabeth's. 'Is there anything we can do, darling?' she asked.

'No, Mum, everything's fine.' She returned to the kitchen. A moment or two later there was a loud 'Christ' and the cymbal crash of a saucepan lid on the stone floor. Diana's laugh was loud and genuine and Lucas's joined it, bass to her alto.

'It's wonderful that they get on so well,' said Elizabeth, taking a cigarette from her silver case.

'Yes, absolutely.' Danny lit it for her. 'And she's so attractive. Very much her mother's daughter.'

I saw Martha look into her lap and I nudged her foot under the table so that she glanced up at me. *It'll be OK*, I tried to say wordlessly. But I didn't believe it. I only hoped that, if Danny did make a move on Diana, it wouldn't be in front of her.

The kitchen door swung open and Lucas brought in a huge serving plate bearing two chickens dressed with watercress. 'Sorry,' he said. 'I have no idea what possessed me to do a roast on a day like this.' He rolled the sleeves of his grey cotton shirt to the elbow. As he leant forward to start carving, a dark curl fell into his eyes. His hair was getting

252

very long. I couldn't think that he'd had it cut since he'd moved to the house.

'Look at the colour of that cloud,' said Greg. 'Surely it has to break soon.' I turned to the window. The sky over the wood was now the shade of Lucas's bruise and just as angry.

'I want the storm so much,' said Martha, 'just to be cool again.'

As we drank our coffee I watched the cloud move inexorably up from the wood and merge itself with the growing darkness that rose from behind the house to meet it. The light went quickly and Lucas switched on the table lamps on the sideboard and lit the candles. As he sat down again, there was a clap of thunder so loud I thought at first that the roof had fallen in. We all jumped.

'Jesus Christ,' said Martha, knocking her coffee over the white linen cloth. The stain soaked in and left a residue of grounds like silt.

There was a tremendous crack. A bolt of forked lightning tore the sky like a piece of sugar paper. The flash was so bright that for a split second the room was lighter than day. The faces round the table were illuminated, blanched, by it. Diana started counting quietly and only reached four before the thunder came again, just as loud. 'It's close,' she said. 'But it's not raining. Everything's so dry. I hope it doesn't start a fire.' We got up and stood at the open windows to watch. Greg was behind me and put his arms round my shoulders. There was another bolt of lightning and, as it jagged down, the whole front lawn and the drive were revealed in an eerie electric light. The thunder followed almost at once, as loud as the sound of a steel-hulled liner running aground.

'Who pissed off Zeus?' said Martha.

Into the silence that followed came a quiet pattering outside on the path, like the slow introduction to a song, the beat growing more persistent. Spots the size of two-pence pieces started to freckle the flagstones. 'At last,' said Diana. She turned round excitedly, her eyes full of a new idea. 'I'm going outside to get cool – who's coming?'

Before anyone could say anything, she was gone and we heard the front door opening. There were quick, light footsteps on the stones and she appeared in front of the window, lit only by the glow from the lamps inside. 'The rain's warm,' she said. She threw her arms up as if waiting for something to come out of the sky and embrace her. Her dress was already soaked through and it clung to her gleaming skin.

'Diana, be careful. It's dangerous. You'll get struck,' shouted Elizabeth.

'No, I won't. It'll get the house first.' She pushed her hair off her face. 'Put some music on, Lucas.'

Danny was already by the stereo. He checked the CD and slid the drawer back into the machine. After a second or two the air was filled with the sound of his friend's track with its sample of the keening, sensual Spanish lament.

'Louder,' Diana called to him.

From the window we watched her as she started to move. If it had been anyone else, it would have looked ridiculous. Her dress, now black with water, stuck to the curves of her waist and hips, and her long hair snaked down her back. She closed her eyes against the rain and turned her face up towards it. She seemed natural in an elemental sense. Another flash of lightning lit up the sky. She looked, I thought, like a maenad, transported by something powerful and invisible. There was nothing virginal about the way she moved: the sensuality of it was darker and more knowing, a homage not to her namesake, the maiden goddess, but amoral Dionysus. We stood motionless, watching.

'This is ridiculous,' said Elizabeth. 'She'll be killed.' She turned away from the window and went to the table for her wine glass.

It wasn't until he appeared in the garden that I realised that

254

Lucas had gone. Laughing, he slid his hand around Diana's waist and picked up her rhythm, moving his body with hers. Soon his shirt was soaking, too, the fabric darkening in patches until all of it was gunmetal. His hair formed dark ringlets.

'Come on, then.' Greg took Martha and me by the hand and pulled us outside.

'I don't want to,' I shouted but he didn't listen, choosing not to or unable to hear me over the pounding of the rain and the thunder and the beat of the music. Michael came to the front doorstep and kicked off his shoes. We joined Diana and Lucas and we danced as a group. I was self-conscious at first but with each crack and roar from the sky I felt less and less myself, more a tiny piece of something bigger than me and out of my control and understanding.

Lucas danced closer and said something that I couldn't hear.

'What?' The sky was electrified by another bolt of lightning.

He was forced to move away as Greg danced over and wrapped his arms aggressively around me. He kissed me hard, the rain channelling over the contours of our one joined face.

'Where's Danny?' said Martha, turning round. There was an explosion of simultaneous lightning and thunder and she stopped dancing and stood perfectly still. We followed her gaze.

Inside the house, framed in silhouette by the light in the room behind them, Danny and Elizabeth were kissing, their bodies tight together and oblivious to the storm.

We had stood in the rain staring until eventually Greg spoke and we followed him inside. In the hallway we looked at each other blankly. The dining-room door was open and we kept away from it as if it harboured contagion. The storm was still overhead and the lightning played through the ring of small windows below the dome like a strobe or the lights of an ambulance, illuminating the painting with electric blue. The flickering effect brought the tableau alive: the characters seemed to be moving, each flash catching them differently, showing now the man on the couch, now the dark-haired woman at his feet, now the golden Ganymede proffering his *krater* with terrible animation.

Water dripped off us and pooled around our feet. I looked at Martha. She was trembling, subtly enough for it to be the start of a chill from her wet clothes but recognisable to me as the first sign of distress. She was biting her lower lip and her eyes were wide, as if she feared that closing them would encourage the tears she knew were on their way.

'Let's not get cold,' said Greg. 'Let's get upstairs and get changed.'

'If Lucas can lend you a T-shirt, I've got a spare pair of jeans you can have, Diana,' I said. 'They'll do for now, until you get back to the village.'

She came up to our room and I found them for her. I realised that, of all of us, she was the least shocked. In fact, she seemed hardly even surprised. The wild self-abandonment of her dancing had been replaced by a strange resignation. 'Are you OK?' I asked her.

'Yes, I'm used to it. She's been doing this since I was a child.' She hesitated, uncertain, it seemed, whether or not she should say more. 'It's because she's the last of the great romantics. She's like a teenager – she thinks that finding someone who loves her will answer every question and solve every problem. She thinks every new affair is "the one" and she's heartbroken every time it goes wrong.'

When I'd got dry, I went to Martha's room. She hadn't showered or changed out of her wet things but was lying face down on the bed. The sheets around her were damp with rainwater. I said her name quietly but she didn't respond so I put my hand on the back of her head and smoothed the tangle of her sodden hair.

'I'm an idiot,' she said, her voice muffled by the pillow. 'Go on, tell me you told me so.'

'I wouldn't.'

On the bedside table I saw the birthday present he had given her, an old leather-bound copy of *Middlemarch*, which he knew was her favourite. I had been impressed by that.

'I believed him,' she said. 'And I fell for the oldest line of all, that we only had to be quiet about it in the beginning, until we were sure. But I was sure straightaway. I let myself really care about him. I'm so fucking dumb.'

'It isn't your fault,' I said. 'He isn't like normal people. He doesn't have a conscience. He really doesn't care how his behaviour affects others. Oh Martha, it's hard now but you'll be glad in the long run, I promise. I want you to fall in love with someone who deserves you. He's not good enough to polish your shoes. Imagine if he did this later, if you'd got married and had children.' I thought how unlikely it was that he would ever do those things. 'He'd give you the biggest run-around. He'd make you so unhappy.'

'I've never felt like that about anyone. He made me feel as if the risks were worth taking. He makes everything feel . . . exciting. Jo, I can't bear the thought that I won't ever wake up with him again.'

I thought of telling her about Michael. I wanted her to know that she wasn't the only person to have fallen for Danny's peacock-tail seduction. I also wanted to shock her, to decimate her image of him so that she could never be persuaded of his goodness again, even if he used the full extent of his charm on her. It was the thought of the impact the news might have on her friendship with Michael that stopped me; of us all, she was probably closest to him and I was loath to let Danny ruin that, too.

She turned over at last and looked at me. Her eyes were

swollen and her cheeks as flushed as though she had just stepped out of a scalding bath. 'You haven't told anyone about this, have you?' She pulled her knees up and hugged them to her chest. 'I couldn't stand it if everyone knew how stupid I'd been.'

The atmosphere among us was subdued for the rest of that evening. Martha stayed upstairs and Greg, Michael and I helped Lucas and Diana wash up. Then we poured large brandies and sat in the kitchen. The centre of the storm had moved off a little and was now rumbling in the distance, over the Chilterns. It was still raining, though, and we left the French windows open and listened to the strangely soothing sound of it, like blank radio interference after a disturbing broadcast. Danny and Elizabeth had gone. We didn't need to check to know it: the air in the house was different, as if its particles had changed their charge.

Later, when we were in bed, I turned over in my head the question of whether I should tell Greg about Martha. I felt as though I was boiling with secrets and I wanted to discuss them with him, partly to ease the pressure but also to rid myself of the feeling that I was being dishonest with him. If our relationship was going to work, I couldn't keep things from him. But I didn't know whether it was more disloyal to Martha to discuss it with him or to Greg not to. Then I thought about how he had been the night Lucas was taken to hospital: I was sure I could trust him. 'Can I tell you something?' I said, making the decision.

'Of course. What is it?' He sat up and puffed up his pillow.

'Martha's been having a fling with Danny.'

He stopped. 'My God. What, you mean tonight, when . . . ?' He shook his head, disbelieving. 'Shit. Poor Marth.'

'I know.'

'But I thought she knew better about him. Surely she wouldn't touch him?'

'Apparently she's liked him for years. It speaks volumes that she never told me.'

'God, he's a bastard. How could he do that to her? She's such a sweetheart.'

It was a relief to talk to him about it and to have someone to share my indignation that I decided to tell him everything. His expression when I told him about Michael as well was sheer incredulity. 'So he's been sleeping with both of them and no one knows? Shit. And neither of them knows about the other?'

'No. And now it looks like he's starting something with Elizabeth.'

By morning the weather system had shifted to the east and we turned on the news and watched pictures of it wreaking havoc in East Anglia, causing rivers to break their banks and sweeping cars into ditches.

'Our beautiful British summer,' said Lucas, getting up to switch off the set.

Danny wasn't anywhere to be seen and so we assumed that he'd spent the night at Elizabeth's house in the village. It struck me as important that we took Martha back to London before he reappeared. I wanted to remove her from a situation where she might have to face him and be hurt further, either by his blithe indifference or by some turkey-cock display of his new conquest. I spun a flimsy line about having a lot of stuff to do for the *Gazette* – an excuse utterly transparent to anyone who had ever heard me talk about the place – and we left.

Chapter Twenty-Three

I was very happy when *The Times* called and asked whether I would like to work the following weekend. After the disaster of my being so late, I had been worried that I had blown it, especially when they hadn't needed me since. I hadn't wanted to give much detail that morning about why it had been so necessary to go to the country – it hadn't seemed right to talk about Lucas's fragility to someone who'd never met him – but I had managed, I thought, to convey how important it had been. I had apologised profusely and promised that it wouldn't happen again.

The piece I was working on now was about a change in the legislation for funding of British-made films and I was making good progress. Looking around the newsroom I was filled with the knowledge that I'd made the right decision about my career: there wasn't anything I would rather be doing than this. It was exhilarating to realise it and I was smiling as I flicked back through my notes. I was also looking forward to an uninterrupted evening on my own with Greg. It seemed like some time since we'd had a weekend to ourselves.

Martha and Michael had stayed in London, too. Poor Martha had been in a terrible state the previous evening, when normally we would have been driving up to Stoneborough. I could see that she longed to be at the house just to be near Danny and yet was terrified at the same time of seeing him again in case she betrayed how much she had cared for him and laid herself open to his terrible scorn. Needless to say, he hadn't called. Michael was going to a drinks party thrown by one of his colleagues and he'd asked Martha to go with him. She'd been reluctant but I'd told her she should, rather than spend the evening at home feeling melancholy.

On the desk beside me, my telephone rang. I answered it, assuming it would be one of the people I wanted to interview and for whom I'd left messages.

It was Lucas. 'I need to talk to you,' he said.

'I'm at work,' I said, dropping my voice and looking over the top of the partition to see if there was anyone in the vicinity who could hear me. 'How did you get this number?'

'Your mobile's off so I called your house. Martha told me where you were so I just rang the switchboard.'

'Look, Lucas, I really don't mean to be rude but I have to get this piece done. I'm on trial here – I shouldn't be getting personal calls. Can't I ring you later?'

'It's important,' he said. 'And you'll be with Greg later so we won't be able to talk privately. I won't take up much of your time.'

My heart sank. I needed to concentrate on what I was doing and I really couldn't let myself be plunged into another Stoneborough mini-drama. And yet I remembered what had happened the last time I hadn't taken his calls. I knew I wouldn't forgive myself if it happened again. 'Go on then,' I said. 'But make it snappy or you'll get me into trouble.'

He hesitated for a second. 'OK. To cut to the chase, Jo, I think I'm falling in love with Diana.'

My immediate reaction was shock. I'd had no idea that that was going to happen. Then an unexpected and wild jealousy surged through me. 'Have you slept together?' I said without thinking, as if he was cheating on me and I had every right to know. I glanced up quickly to check no one was looking at me; I wasn't sure how loud my voice had been. I had known, of course, that Lucas would meet someone else one day but I hadn't expected it to happen so soon. It was a blow to have been replaced with such ease.

He seemed unfazed by my question. 'Last night. Diana cooked and we had supper outside on the lawn.' He paused, as if torn between wanting to keep the memory private and the need to share his excitement. 'It was really late – probably about two – and everything was so still, absolutely silent. It was like being the last people left in the world. We'd talked about everything: my parents, Patrick, Elizabeth, what it was like being round that group when we were children. It's strange, Jo. In a way I feel as if I've been waiting for her to come back all my life.'

'Lucas . . .' I could see Rebecca approaching, back from buying lunch at the canteen. Her desk was two along from mine. She'd be able to hear every word I said but there was no way I could end the call now.

'And it helps, having her here now when you're off in London. And because she was there when we were children, she understands.'

I couldn't tell whether or not the barb was intentional so said nothing.

'I feel like life is starting up again. It's so weird: the last time Diana and I were together was in that wood and we found each other there again, twenty years later.'

He was waiting for me to speak now. Rebecca sat down and moved her mouse to clear the screensaver. It was unfortunate that she was in the office; she'd only come in to finish off a piece she hadn't managed to complete the previous day.

Lucas continued, provoked by my silence to greater emphasis. 'Jo, when she kissed me, it was like falling in love and everything making sense. I never thought I would say this but you were right to break it off. I think it's the real thing this time.'

'That's wonderful,' I said as quietly as possible while still being audible to him. 'I'm happy for you.' Say it like you mean it, Joanna, I thought to myself, glad that he couldn't see me. I looked up just in time to catch Rebecca's questioning eye. I made an apologetic face.

Finally, after assurances that I would call him at some later point over the weekend, he rang off. The call left me unsettled. On the one hand, the news could be seen as a relief. Perhaps if he was going to be with Diana now, the baton of responsibility for him could be passed on. It might also mean a let-up in the pressure of his scrutiny of me. But despite those things, I felt a backwash of desolation. His finding someone else was another station along the road away from our shared history, a further erosion of the bond between us. I was also hurt by the message lying like a reef beneath the surface of his words: he had wanted to tell me how out of the picture I was. I told myself off. Why shouldn't he want to gloat a little about his new relationship? I had no right to feel slighted. And he and Diana had experienced something that gave them a tighter bond than most people ever had. Perhaps she really did understand him in a way that an outsider could never do.

Rebecca stayed until the end of the day and, after I'd filed my piece and begun to pack up my things, she asked if she could have a quiet word. She indicated a desk in the corner, away from the others. Even before she began, the way she composed her face told me the news wasn't good.

'I'm so sorry, Joanna,' she said. 'I like you and I think you'll be a good journalist but I just get the impression that you have too many commitments elsewhere. We need someone who can focus on what needs to be done here. I've been

263

trialling someone else as well and I'm afraid that I've decided to give the maternity-cover job to him.'

On the tube back from Wapping to Shepherd's Bush I sat in a state of unblinking disbelief. It was only when I reached Greg's flat that the reality of it hit me and the tears came. And the thing was, she was right: I was overcommitted. How could I give anything else my full attention when there was so much going on between us all and when I was responsible for Lucas's fragile emotional wellbeing? Although I knew it was partly my fault for not telling him straight off that I would call him later, my mental picture of him was now crystallising. Lucas was becoming a burden and, though I hated myself for the cruelty, I couldn't help it. Because of him, I had wasted the biggest opportunity I'd ever had.

Chapter Twenty-Four

The following weekend, Greg decided we should go camping at the beach. I was initially resistant but gave in under the pressure of his kindness. The sea, he said, was his prescription for all woes, personal and professional. He had been so understanding that week that I couldn't refuse and anyway he'd assured me that a night under canvas with him would be an entirely different proposition from the camping I'd done with my parents.

We left London late on Saturday morning. I watched him as he drove. He was wearing a yellow T-shirt that fitted snugly across his chest and a pair of knackered blue jeans that emphasised the length of his thighs with their curving muscle. I wanted to reach across and squeeze one, to feel its mix of softness and resistance. He had been for a run before breakfast and returned breathing fast, his navy running shirt clinging to his back with sweat. He gave off a primal fitness, a readiness for anything.

The countryside spread out on either side of us now, voluptuous and green again. The roads were all familiar but I didn't say anything. We stopped at the beach at Lepe, near Beaulieu, about five miles from my parents' house. I had been there hundreds of times before; it was where my parents used to take me and my brothers to swim. For me, the place had as many layers of memories as there were colours to suck through on one of the giant gobstoppers Dad used to buy for us at the shop set back from the front. As a small child I had been a regular, spending my pocket money on ice cream, wincing across the shingle on bare feet to get back to my mother again. I remembered feeling proud that, compared to the children on holiday from places like Birmingham and London, I was a local. I had thought them very citified. In the sixth form, it became a different sort of destination. My friends and I used to come down to drink cider and smoke cigarettes, either on our own or with guys from the college in Brockenhurst. We would lie on the beach and talk about what we were going to do with our lives. I could recall describing my big dream of being a journalist on a national paper and my determination that it would happen. In my teenage arrogance I had talked about how people who didn't achieve what they set out to had only themselves to blame for letting other things distract them. My ambition had burned like a coal then and I couldn't see how I would become one of those who didn't make it.

Greg must have seen the look on my face for he leaned across and stroked my hair. 'Come on, try not to think about it.'

We left the car in the top field and sat on the silky grass that covered the cliff. It tickled my legs where my shorts exposed them. Glad that I had thought to put my bikini on at home, I took off my shirt and let the sun get hot on my shoulders. I felt the tension in them relax a little. The heat was rising from the Solent and the shape of the Isle of Wight was imprecise against the deep blue of the sky. It seemed to rise out of the water like the spine of some enormous wallowing sea creature, perhaps a dinosaur like the ones that used to roam there. 'You know that I know this place, don't you?' I said.

'Yes,' he said. 'I wanted to come here with you. I've been here on my own before and you grew up near here and I wanted to tie the two together. I suppose it's a way of making you part of my experiences and me part of yours.'

'You're gate-crashing my past.'

He turned on his side and smiled. 'Do you mind?'

'No.' I kissed him.

We went down to the shore to swim. Afterwards we sat a little way up the shingle and dried off, watching the water drop away until the tide was fully out and a curvaceous landscape of mud, driftwood and debris was revealed. When we returned to the car, the families on the beach were beginning to pack up and go. Next to us was a Volvo whose back seat was thronged with kids. The mother of at least some of them was kneeling at the open door trying to brush the sand off a small pair of wriggling feet and to wedge them into a pair of jelly shoes. In the past few weeks I had been turning the thought of children over in my mind. Something was changing. I no longer had an immediate anti-reaction to the idea. In fact, I liked the image I had formulated of Greg and me with a child. Also, although I could barely admit it even to myself, I found something sexy about the idea of being pregnant with his child. That came as a complete shock, after years of considering the desire to have children a form of biological career-wrecking ambush on women.

We carried the tent to where the beach rounded the lip of Southampton Water and pitched it on an area of grass sheltered by gorse bushes from the slight breeze. As the power went out of the sun and the shadow of the pine trees began to lengthen, Greg collected driftwood and lit a fire. We sat by it and watched the yachts coming up with the making tide. His prescription had been the right one. There was something about the sea, its simultaneous power to adapt and complete immutability, its unfaltering rhythm, that stemmed the flow of anger and regret that had engulfed me. Being with him relaxed me as well. He had the ability to

267

live in the moment and when I was with him it became easier for me, too.

After dark we watched the lights of the big ships passing in and out of Southampton, speculating on their destinations, cargo ships to Australia and the Far East, passenger ferries to France and the Channel Islands. I turned on to my back to look at the stars. They were one of the things I missed most about living in London, where it was easy to forget that there was a natural universe and we were part of it. I had the smell of wood smoke in my hair. Greg shifted closer to me and put his arms around my shoulder. 'Let's bring our children here,' he said.

Chapter Twenty-Five

It was almost a fortnight before Lucas called to apologise. It must have been Martha who told him what had happened. I hadn't trusted myself to in case I lost my temper. By the time he rang, though, my feelings about it, initially so raw, had hardened into a sort of resigned acceptance and I could at least think about it without the primal scream of frustration that had ripped through me at first. The disappointment, however, had not diminished; on the contrary, it seemed to be growing stronger from day to day. More than anything, my job at the *Gazette* now seemed entirely futile. What was the point of working there if it wasn't a stepping-stone to something better? I no longer felt I was serving an apprentice-ship but instead saw that, unless something dramatic happened, I was there for the long haul, condemned to a future of parochial stories in a run-down office with no chance of a salary that matched those of my peers. The prize had been snatched away and what I was left with was something even tawdrier than I had allowed myself to acknowledge.

I also worried about how it would change Greg's percep-tion of me. While I had the shot at a job on a national, I felt that I could hold my own with a boyfriend who was doing as well as he was. Now that I had been relegated to the *Gazette* again, I couldn't shake the feeling that anyone meeting us as a couple would think I was riding on his coat-tails. Nothing he

Haldimand County Public Library
JARVIS BRANCH

had said had even suggested he thought this but my own pride made me keenly aware of it.

'Jo, I am so, so sorry,' Lucas said now. 'I really didn't realise how serious it was. You should have said.'

'I did try.' It occurred to me that, having not worked for months, he had ceased to understand what it was like, that there were obligations and one's personal life couldn't come first.

'I don't know what I can do to make it up to you.'

I didn't say anything.

'Are you coming up this weekend? Please come. I'll cook something amazing. Anything you want.' He sounded desperate but I found I didn't care.

'You don't have to do that,' I said. I had made a decision. I would go up to the house that weekend and I would talk to him properly. I needed to find a way to resolve the situation. I couldn't go on like this, living my life on a piece of elastic that he had only to tug on to drag me back away from the future and into that bizarre stasis that I had started to dread.

Diana was making a stew for supper when we arrived. She was wearing tight jeans with a rainbow-striped belt and her hair was tied in an artfully effortless-looking knot at the back of her head. She kissed me hello and then returned to stir the huge pot on the stove-top. Lucas wandered up behind her and slid his hands round her hips as she faced the cooker. Even with bare feet she was almost the same height as he was, three or four inches taller than me. She took the cigarette from his lips, had a drag and put it back with a smile. She was imbued with a sultry sexiness that I willed Greg not to see. Lucas caught me watching and smiled. I looked away quickly.

But I couldn't help watching them that evening. They had become very close very fast. The emotional intimacy had been there to start with, of course, in dormant form, but they seemed to have slipped together physically so comfortably, like a hand into a pocket. Lucas had the ease of long familiarity around her and I saw that he knew it and was enjoying the effect it had on me.

We sat at the kitchen table to eat. The double doors were open and the candles that Diana had lit had attracted a couple of moths, which she cupped in her hands and took out into the garden again. 'I hate it when they do that,' she said. 'I can't stand the idea of their wings being burnt.'

Later in the evening I left the room to go and fetch more cigarettes from the car and I met Lucas in the corridor on my way back. 'OK?' I asked, from habit.

'I'm so happy, Jo,' he replied.

Despite everything, even my anger about the job, I was jealous. It wasn't that I wanted him: the idea of being with anyone other than Greg was unthinkable now. It was the pain of being replaced, of feeling the framework that had been around me through university and my twenties crumbling away still further.

As soon as we got up to our room that night I pressed Greg against the wall and kissed him, undoing the top buttons of his shirt and running my hand over his coarse chest hair. I tugged at the buckle on his belt with one hand, pulling my own T-shirt over my head with the other. 'What's up with you?' he said into my hair.

'Do you love me?' I pulled his shirt out and pushed the two remaining buttons through, missing his lips in my hurry to kiss him again. He held me away from him by the shoulders, forcing me to stop and look at his face. My eyes were on his mouth, in particular on the full lower lip that I found so compulsive.

'Let me show you,' he said. He lifted me up and dropped me gently backwards on to the bed.

One thing that often struck me about the house was how much more we were governed by the weather there. In the city, weather influenced the view from the office window. At Stoneborough, rain changed everything.

The sound of it against the glass the next morning, even though it was as light as if the wisteria were rustling against the pane, told me that the plan to spend the day outside was off. By mid-morning it had grown in conviction. As we drank coffee in the kitchen the rain was hitting the ground with such force that it drilled pockmarks into the soil of the raised beds. 'Weather like this either makes me all pent-up and full of energy or so idle I can hardly move,' Diana said, watching it.

'Which is it today?' asked Lucas.

'Idle,' she said. 'Let's not do anything. Let's get some DVDs out and watch them in those big leather chairs in Patrick's study.'

Greg wanted a bath so I offered to go into Oxford to pick up the DVDs, glad to have the time alone to order my thoughts. Before I went, though, there was something I wanted to check. Making sure there was no one else around, I slipped into the library and closed the door behind me. The atmosphere in there was muted, not hostile but not friendly either. I had the paranoid sense now that the house was conserving its energy, biding its time. Moving one of the ladders along, I scanned the shelf until I found what I was looking for: the George Eliot novels. Sure enough, *Middlemarch* was missing, the other volumes pushed together to hide its absence. Bloody Danny: he couldn't even buy her a book.

It was strange to drive Greg's car, like borrowing someone else's shoes and feeling the shape of their feet rather than one's own. I wasn't familiar with automatics so I took the country route into town, approaching it from Boar's Hill and parking there for a few minutes to look at the view. It was the postcard angle on the city, just its sand-coloured spires, framed by a rich canvas of green, a rural idyll with a cosmopolitan centre. Today it was hunkered down under the low wet sky. I still hadn't worked out how I was going to raise with Lucas the fact that I couldn't keep coming to Stoneborough all the time. I thought again about what I had said to Greg in the car-park at the hospital, that it wasn't that Lucas wanted me any more, just that I was a symbol of the old order, which he clung to for stability. I understood that need and I also felt the pain of moving on but it had to be done. Perhaps now he had Diana he would feel he was at the beginning of a new chapter. And anyway, I reminded myself, I wasn't severing the link between us.

On the return journey, I turned the radio off to listen to the swish of the tyres along the wet road and the beat of the windscreen wipers. The rain had set in for the day. The clouds had lowered and compacted, as if someone had smoothed a dove-grey blanket across the sky and tucked it in at the horizon. The drive was like a rain forest, the huge leaves of the chestnuts emerald green and dripping, the potholes filled with water the colour of cold coffee. Even the house itself looked changed. The stone of the façade was dark. I tucked the DVDs under my jacket and made a dash for the front door. I got soaked nonetheless.

In the end, we didn't put the films on until late afternoon. Though it wasn't yet six o'clock, the rain was falling so heavily that it was bringing night in early. The sky was shading to indigo and it looked less like August than one of those days in October before the hour goes forward. Up in the study Diana wandered around, looking at things. 'I love this room. Patrick had such a good eye for design.' She ran her finger along the top of the bureau, drawing a line in the dust. 'You ought to ask the cleaner to do in here next week. And it's about time you went through some of this, Lucas.' She indicated the piles of paperwork that hadn't been

273

touched in all the time we'd been coming to the house. 'I'll help you.'

Lost in Translation was Greg's choice and that went on first. We were about halfway through when the door cranked open and we were dragged back into real life by the sight of Danny, dripping wet and exultant. He shook his hair, sending water spinning around him. 'Here you all are,' he said. 'I wondered where everyone had disappeared to. You shouldn't leave the front door open like that. Anyone could walk in.'

Lucas stood up. 'I haven't seen you in days. Where have you been?'

'You never write, you never call . . . You're like a Jewish mother, mate.'

'I was worried about you, believe it or not.'

'Sorry, Lucas.' His voice was sincere. 'I was in London trying to get some stuff together for this film I'm thinking about.' That was news. As far as I'd known, Danny had hardly given work a second thought since he'd moved to Stoneborough.

'Were you with my mother?' asked Diana.

'Yes.'

In the silence Lucas turned slightly to touch her shoulder. Danny waved a hand at the screen. 'Good film. Though I suppose it helps if you're Francis Ford Coppola's daughter.'

'She's a good director, Coppola or not,' said Lucas.

'Admit it, Lucas. Family talks.' Danny shifted his weight on to the other foot. 'Listen, mate, could I have a quick word?'

'Sure.'

'In private?'

Lucas sighed. 'OK, but it'll have to be quick. We're in the middle of this.' He followed Danny out and their footsteps retreated down the landing.

After five minutes Lucas still hadn't returned so I went

downstairs to make a pot of tea. As I approached the kitchen, I could hear that he had obviously had the same idea. There was the sound of the kettle nearing the boil and also voices. Something about the tone of Lucas's made me stop. I drew back into the shadow at the mouth of the passage to the flower lobby to listen.

'I can't understand why you need more,' he was saying.

'It's what it costs to live these days – things are expensive.'

'But I gave you a thousand pounds last week.'

'I know but I've been in London. It's not country prices there. And I want to be able to take Elizabeth out. I can't let her buy everything for me as if I were some sort of gigolo.'

'You've got your cards. I cleared those for you.'

'I don't want to run them up again. I know how stupid that was. You see, I do listen to you sometimes.'

Lucas sighed. 'Look, OK then, but I won't be able to get it for you until tomorrow.'

'Thanks, mate, it's appreciated. I don't know what I'd do without you. You're the only person I can rely on.' There was the shuffle of feet and a gentle thump, and I imagined Danny patting Lucas heavily on the back. 'By the way,' he said, 'how are things going with Diana?'

'It's early days,' said Lucas.

'She's a great girl. You should hold on to her.'

It was very hard to sit through the remainder of the film. I had known Lucas was supporting Danny, he had been open about that from the start, but I had had no idea about the scale of it. A thousand pounds a week – it was hardly credible. I'd never spent that amount – I'd never had it. And Danny didn't even have to cover rent or other domestic bills: those were all found. It certainly explained why his wardrobe hadn't seemed to suffer in the months we'd been coming to the house and how there had been a steady stream of new shoes, new jeans, new T-shirts. But I had heard exactly how he had played Lucas: it was cynical and masterly.

As soon as I could, I took Greg aside and we went to our room.

'Are you going to say something?' he asked. 'The credit-card bills were thirty thousand pounds.'

'I don't know. How can I? I can't tell him that I was listening in the corridor and anyway, it's not my business. It's his money – he can do what he likes with it.' I walked to the window and looked out. The garden had disappeared into the darkness but the rain was still beating across the pane.

'Are you going to talk to him about easing up on the amount we come here?' he said.

I turned round again, surprised. It was such a sensitive issue between us, one which, apart from my being apologetic and his being decent, we never discussed. I had told him about my decision to talk to Lucas. I wanted to show him I was ready to move on and concentrate on our relationship and I had seen that it had made him happy.

Nevertheless I hesitated now. It was infuriating but just when I had screwed up all my anger about the job and my need to loose myself from the Gordian knot into which I was tied at the house, Danny's touching Lucas for money had prompted me to feel protective of him again. I looked at Greg, who had arranged his face into a neutral expression. 'Yes,' I said. 'I am going to talk to him. Tonight.'

I found Lucas in the library after supper. He had drawn the long tapestry curtains and the thorough darkness gave the room a winter feel. All that was missing was a fire in the grate like the one we had had on the night in January when he and I got together. He had ensconced himself in one of the armchairs and was reading, a large glass of whisky on the side table at his right hand. His hair was falling forward over his eyes and he seemed thoroughly engrossed. I watched him for a second or two, remembering all the other times I had seen him like that at university, at our parents' houses, on holidays, in our various flats in London.

'Lucas,' I said, shutting the door gently behind me.

He looked up and smiled as he saw me.

'Can we talk?' I asked.

'Of course. Come and sit down.' He pulled the other armchair over so that it was close to his. 'Do you want a drink?'

He poured me a whisky and I took a sip of it for fortification.

'What do you want to talk about?' he asked, when he was back in his chair. His face was full of anticipation but not, I thought, of anything that he didn't want to hear, which surprised me.

'This is very hard,' I stalled.

'Out with it.' He smiled.

'Lucas, I'm struggling to keep things under control. I feel like I haven't got enough time. There are things I need to get on with now. I'm thirty soon and I haven't got any kind of job that I'm proud of. I'm not doing myself justice.'

He said nothing.

'It's not that I don't enjoy coming here . . .' I broke off. 'I just need to start devoting time to other things.'

The look on his face was no longer one of happy expectation. 'So what are you saying? You want to stop coming?'

'No. Of course not. I want to see you, of course I do. It's just that I can't keep coming every weekend, or even every other weekend.'

His expression was stony and he turned away from me to add another inch of whisky to his glass.

I don't know what it was that compelled me to go on and broach the other subject. Perhaps it was my old inability not to talk into an uncomfortable silence. Perhaps it was simple, purely motivated concern, a need to tell him that I was

277

worried on his behalf and still cared deeply about the things that affected him, even as I took a step away from him. Perhaps, though, it was another example of that old impulse of mine to compete with Danny, always to be a better friend than him to Lucas. Perhaps then, when I had seemed to be putting distance between Lucas and myself, I also wanted him to question Danny's status in his life, too.

'Lucas, are things OK with Danny?'

'Why do you ask?'

'No real reason.' The desire to discuss it was gone at once, vanquished by the weight of his tone.

'There must be some reason.'

'I don't know. He's difficult sometimes.'

'It's only you who thinks that.' His voice was rising now and he swigged his drink away in one angry mouthful. 'For some reason you have a problem with him and none of the rest of us understand it. I mean, what is it about him that gets under your skin so much, Joanna? Is it that I'm so close to him? Come on, if we're being honest tonight.' He stared, daring me.

'I don't trust him.'

Lucas snorted. 'Why? What has he ever done?'

I couldn't tell him that under his nose Danny had been sleeping with both Michael and Martha. I couldn't tell him about the threats he'd made to me. Who would he believe, Danny with his silver tongue, or me with my known pre-judice against him? I was determined to say something with some substance, though. I couldn't bear him to think that I was motivated by petty jealousy. 'I'm worried that he's using you.'

It was the worst thing I could possibly have said. I realised it as soon as the words left my mouth.

Lucas reared from his chair. His whole body showed his anger, hands in fists and teeth clenched so tightly I thought he might crack them. His face was black. If I'd been a man, I'm sure he would have hit me. I shrank back and he towered over me, looming into my personal space.

'I can't fucking believe you, Joanna. I can't believe you can sit there in my chair drinking my whisky and say that about Danny, the most loyal of all my friends – since school, since before I even met you. Why do you do this? Why do you insist on this over and over and over again? You're wrong. He's my best friend, far better than you ever were. You've never been loyal to me like he has.'

'That's not true.'

'Yes,' he said. 'It is. Why? Are you going to tell me how loyal you are? So loyal you cheated on me?'

I stood up, feeling the floor tilt beneath me. I knew I had to get out of that room. The air was thick and inert; Lucas's fury seemed to be burning off the oxygen. He didn't move and I had to angle my body awkwardly to get past him. I caught the faintest trace of Patrick's old aftershave in the air and the stronger aroma of the whisky on his breath. As calmly as possible, I walked away and pulled the door closed behind me. Then I ran up the stairs.

Greg was working but he put his laptop aside as soon as he saw me.

'I can't do this any more,' I said. 'I'm tired of the control and watching every word I say. I'm tired of being the villain and having my sin thrown in my face. I'm suffocating.'

He put his arms round me and held me but my lungs were so tight I had to stand away from him. It was as if the house had siphoned off all its air. Once I'd started to cough, I couldn't stop. I cursed Lucas for this, for reducing me to a struggling mess of anger, frustration and guilt.

My instinct was to go outside and fill my lungs with gallon after gallon of air that had never come under the shifting taint of the house. I wanted to drive away and never return, rub at the map until it developed a hole where Stoneborough lay, making it untraceable for ever. But Lucas was

279

downstairs and he seemed to me then like the embodiment of the spirit of the place, keeping me there, trapped upstairs. I pushed up the sash window and breathed in as much as my feeble pulmonary system would allow, as if the house were on fire behind me and I was fighting for any air that wasn't permeated with acrid, stinking smoke. I sucked at my inhaler until I shook.

'We'll go first thing in the morning,' he said.

By the time I was calmer, it was late enough to sleep. While Greg was in the bathroom, I lay alone in our bed. I turned on to my side and pulled my knees up towards my chest. At any other time I would have felt comforted in that childish position but now I felt oddly exposed. The room, for all its elegance, had the warmth and comfort of a cell. The bed stretched for feet on either side of me, and the expensive cotton sheets felt starched and cold. The ceiling was impossibly high above my head. As I looked at it, it seemed to get further away still, as if retreating into the ether and refusing to protect me.

And then I felt the boom of blood through my ears and the house's secret pulse. Tonight it was full of gleeful victory; it was whispering about me, laughing at me. The sound now was like the skittering of a million insects, their shiny chitin shells clicking and rustling as they swarmed over one another in a shimmering tide of tiny bodies. I put my hands over my ears to block it but then it became internal, as if whatever it was had moved inside my head and was nestling into the soft tissue of my brain like a parasite. But again, its presence seemed outside me, all around me. I didn't dare open my eyes.

As Greg's footsteps came along the corridor, the jeering began to fade, the pulsing beat to quieten. When he opened the door I was sitting up, looking as calm as I could. I didn't want him to see me like that, almost paralysed by a fear that became absurd as soon as there was someone else in the room. Even to me, it seemed like the behaviour of someone not very far from madness.

He turned out the light and slid into bed behind me, pulling me back against him so that we made spoons. Over my shoulder, his breath smelled of mint. I could feel the warmth of his thighs behind mine and the hair on his chest tickling my back. My pulse began to slow. I reached for his hand and put mine inside it. 'I promise,' I said, 'that when we leave this place things will be normal.'

Sleep came quickly for him but it eluded me yet again. I had feared the return of the terrible pulsing but it wasn't that that kept me awake. Downstairs Lucas was drunk. The sound of his voice reached up through the house like a cold hand. My parents hadn't argued much when I was a child but on the few occasions they had I remembered feeling like this as I lay in my bed, remote from it and unable to catch the words, my heart clutching with fear that what was going on between them would spin out of control and change my world.

Finally he stood in the hall and shouted. I hadn't heard him so drunk since the night we split up; his voice swooped and then soared again, filling the centre of the house. I heard my name and Greg's and angry imprecations. Suddenly, just as I thought I couldn't bear it any longer, it stopped and there were racking sobs. Then, gentle, there was Diana's voice as she led him away.

We woke to a wide bright sky. The rain had cried itself out and the asthmatic tension that had bound the house had relaxed a little, although I could still feel it, pulling at the edges of my lungs with the power of an unhappy memory.

When I slept on an argument I often woke to find that the vehement convictions of the night before had evaporated like pure spirit. Today my determination to leave was as strong as it had been when I eventually slept. We packed as soon as we woke.

Downstairs there was no sign of Lucas or Diana but the kitchen doors were open into the garden. We walked out and followed their voices through the wrought-iron gate into the orchard beyond. There was the low hum of insects in the espalier trees along the back wall and the warm breeze was freighted with the scent of ripening pears. It was too benevolent a day.

From the gate, only their legs were visible; their upper bodies were concealed by the rustling foliage of the lower branches. On the ground were large bowls from the kitchen, some already filled with huge green apples. The sun hadn't yet burnt off the rain and the bottoms of my jeans were quickly soaked by the ankle-length grass. They both saw us approaching, I knew it, but only Diana acknowledged us.

'Hi,' she said. 'These are ripe. We can have an apple pie this afternoon.'

Her tone seemed innocent of any knowledge of an argument. I wondered whether it was her policy for peace-making, just to pretend that nothing had happened.

'Lucas,' I said. 'We're going to go now.'

A long moment passed before he answered. At last he stepped back and faced me. As he moved he brushed a low branch and dislodged a shower of rainwater, which fell into the long grass. His hangover was clearly giving him hell: he looked as if he might have to turn away and throw up at any moment. His skin had a clammy pallor at odds with the beauty of the morning.

'I'm going to have a party,' he said suddenly.

'A dinner party?' said Diana brightly.

'A proper party. For my thirtieth. The second Saturday of September. I'll have it here and I'll invite everyone. Everyone we've lost touch with this year. Friends, friends of friends, their friends. An enormous party. We'll have a marquee on the lawn, dinner and dancing. It's relatively short notice but we'll manage. I'll throw money at it.' He reached into his

282

pocket and took out his cigarettes. He lit one, turning his head away.

He looked at me intently, all his focus on selling me the idea. 'In a way it'll be our party, not just mine. A celebration of our time here. It'll probably be one of the last decent weeks of weather. You haven't had any holiday, have you? Come up for a couple of days beforehand. We'll go out on a high.'

Our friendship, our years of shared history and everything it had meant to both of us hung like his smoke in the air between us. Allow me this, he seemed to say, and after that you're free to go. Let us mark the end of our decade.

'OK,' I said.

Chapter Twenty-Six

We had agreed to go up to Stoneborough two days before the party itself, to help Lucas and Diana prepare. Before we went, Greg and I spent a quiet evening in London. We had supper at a noodle bar in Notting Hill Gate and then walked back down Holland Park to Shepherd's Bush. We opened the window in the bedroom to let in the night breeze with its whisper of autumn and I stayed awake long after his breathing had slowed, listening to the city cooling around us, the clacking of the last tubes through Goldhawk Road station and the Australian voices loud after an evening at the Walkabout on the Green. Normally in London I didn't need Greg to be awake with me like I did in the country; when he was asleep here I just missed him, as if he had been taken somewhere I couldn't contact him. That night, though, I wanted to wrap his body around me and use his lovely solidity as a shield against the new and pervasive sense of foreboding that had been rising around me like a mist that the sun wouldn't burn off.

It was more than a month since I'd seen Lucas and the time only exacerbated my nervousness at seeing him. We procrastinated and delayed so much that it was five o'clock by the time we reached the house the next day. The garden was saturated with the warm yellow light of late afternoon. Everyone was outside and Diana and Michael were playing badminton on the lawn over an old-fashioned string net. Holes in the mesh and a definite sag in the middle bore witness to its long exile in the barn. A cloud of midges hung in the air on Michael's side and his slight form ducked around it as he played. I stood for a minute watching the shuttlecock with its retro crown of feathers beat its way back and forth over the net, lulled by the regular sound of the rubber tip against the taut strings of the rackets.

They finished the game and came up the stone steps to the terrace. 'Hello, sweetheart,' said Michael, pecking me on the cheek. The touch of his skin was hot and damp and its usual tired grey had been vanquished. Sometimes even the thought of a few days off was enough.

Lucas handed me a glass of Pimm's swimming with fruit. He was acutely aware of the unspoken contract between us, it was clear. I could feel it in the distance that he kept, the way he was treating me like a guest again. Three days, I had thought, when he came to meet us at the car with a polite smile, just three days. 'How many people are coming?' I asked now, as he turned back and poured himself a refill.

'Just under a hundred and fifty in total.'

'That's a big party,' said Martha, looking up from her book.

'Yeah, I'm pleased,' he said, fishing an unwieldy slice of orange from his glass and tossing it into the flowerbed below. 'I was worried that no one would bother but it seems everyone's been dying to get up here to see the place.'

'What do you want us to do to help?'

'Actually, Diana and I have done a lot of it. It's largely scene-setting now.'

'We're going to have lots of candles in the garden and sprays of fairy lights woven into the creeper up here.' Diana indicated with her hand. 'We're going for Greek bacchanal meets Roman banquet.'

Michael was moving his thumb over the buttons of his mobile with a practised speed. In return it gave a defiant beep.

He tried again and had the same response. 'Can I use the landline?' he asked. 'I always forget the reception's so unreliable out here.' He got up and tucked the phone into his pocket.

'Danny's been helpful, too,' said Lucas, avoiding my eye.

Diana laughed. 'Not in practical terms.'

'Well, no, but you remember the CD we had on that night on the terrace? Those DJs who are friends of his? He's got them to do the party, after the jazz group.'

'I think I saw them mentioned in *Time Out*,' said Greg. 'Didn't they do a set at Elysium recently?'

I drained my glass and moved down on to the cushions next to him. I slipped my feet out of my sandals, pressing them on to the flagstones to feel the warmth baked in by the sun. When everyone stopped talking, the silence in the garden was so absolute it seemed to have depth. Looking out over it, I saw a scene that might have been the same for a hundred years. Generations had been seeded, grown and fallen here but it was unchanged. In a sudden access of understanding I saw that we were completely incidental. The house owned and governed this garden and it would continue, regardless of us. In that second, I pulled my feet off the stone and shoved them back into my shoes. I had – fleetingly – the sense that the warmth I felt there was the heat of a body, evidence of the house's beating heart.

The next day Greg drove into town with Lucas and Michael to choose the wine. While they were gone Diana, Martha and I carried blankets down on to the lawn and stretched out to sunbathe. I spread the news review section of the paper in front of me and embarked on a piece about US foreign policy. In minutes, however, the sun had sapped me of all resolve and I lay with my head on my forearm, the sun heavy on my back, the nape of my neck damp.

'This is probably the last bit of sunbathing weather this year,' said Martha.

'I love autumn, though.' Diana rubbed tanning oil on to her calves. The muscles there were defined, slightly too much to fit the ideal. 'I get that feeling of anticipation about it. All the good things are in autumn – Halloween, bonfire night, then Christmas. It's like a time to get on with things after the holidays, life starting up again.'

'What are you going to do?' I asked. 'Isn't it difficult to be a professional photographer, even if you're good?'

She sat up and took a pack of cigarettes from her bag. She lit one and I watched the wraith of smoke rise until it disappeared against a sky the colour of a drop of ink in water. 'A small gallery in London wants to show four of my pictures. It's been on the cards for a bit. I won a competition while I was doing my MA and got to know the guy who owns it.'

'That's great,' I said. 'Congratulations.'

'Thanks.' She took a long drag and exhaled slowly. 'He also put me in touch with another photographer who exhibits there, a really good one actually, and he's offered me a job as his assistant, which gives me a way to earn some money and learn at the same time.' She turned to face me. 'It will mean moving to London.'

'Is that a problem?' said Martha, not understanding.

'From my point of view, no. I want to. But it means leaving Lucas.'

'Oh.'

'Yeah.' She flicked the ash from her cigarette into the grass. 'I have to do it. It's too good an opportunity.' There was anxiety in her eyes. 'I'm torn because I want to be with him but then, he has to know that I can't live here in a bubble. I have to be part of the real world.'

She leant forward and undid the clasp on her bikini before pulling the neck strap over her head. 'Do you mind? While the boys aren't here? It's odd, it doesn't bother me to be topless in front of them but sometimes I think they get embarrassed.' She lay down and settled her shoulders against the blanket. I glanced at her from behind my sunglasses. There was nothing self-conscious about her. She looked as natural a part of the scene as the grass, the trees and the sky. Feeling prudish I undid my top, too, and stretched out next to her, hoping, although there was no one to see, that I looked more confident than I felt.

'Are things going well otherwise?' I said. I launched the words up into the air. I couldn't have said them if we'd been face to face: her relationship with Lucas was none of my business and I had no right to ask. Somehow, though, I felt strangely responsible for both of them, Lucas for the old reasons but Diana, too. Knowing Lucas's volatility made me want to open a channel for her to talk if she needed to.

'I love him,' she replied, frank and unembarrassed. 'I did when we were children, too. We were so close and he wasn't like the other boys I knew. He was kind. I suppose he was sensitive, even then. I want to look after him now. He's had a tough time. He needs someone to love him and get him better again.'

I said nothing, unsure whether she counted me among the reasons for his tough time.

'He told me that he's talked to you about his drinking,' she went on. 'He worries that he's like his father, doesn't he? I try to tell him he's not. I mean, I know he's drinking way too much and he has to stop but his dad was in a different league. He was a complete slave to alcohol, Jo; even when I was six or seven I could see that. And maybe that would happen to Lucas if he carried on but I won't let it.'

'You'll be good for him,' I said.

She turned on her side and looked at me over the top of her sunglasses. 'I hope so. I hope he lets me. He's still very caught up in other things. Sometimes he's so distant that I can't get near him.'

*　　*　　*

288

Greg and I drove into town on our own the next day, to give ourselves a break. We went for coffee at Georgina's, the tiny café tucked under the glass-panelled roof of the Covered Market. The students wouldn't be back until the end of the month so we had a table to ourselves. The speckled bowls of rice and pasta salad behind the glass counter and the scent of toasted bagels took me back to the afternoons in our final year when Lucas, Martha and I came here for tea, on breaks from the lower reading rooms of the Bodleian. Rachel, doing English, worked on the floor above us and was more conscientious. Occasionally, though, she would join us and the four of us would find a space together on one of the long pine tables. It was strange to find it exactly the same, the old carpet as dangerously wrinkled as ever and the newspapers in their position on the low bench at the top of the stairs. The same film posters covered the ceiling and they were playing *Parklife* by Blur, an album that had been released while we were students. It was as if my old life were continuing and I had somehow slipped into a different existence, from which I might look over and see my younger self drinking a mug of tea and moaning about how much work there was to do before the exams. Now, though, I was sitting with Rachel's ex-boyfriend and she and I didn't speak any more. I felt the familiar guilty black tug at the bottom of my stomach.

'I wonder if Lucas invited Rachel to the party,' I said.

Greg clicked the catch on his watch open and shut. 'He did. She said no. I asked him yesterday.'

'You didn't tell me that.'

'Sorry.' He added sugar to his coffee and stirred it without meeting my eye.

I expected him to go on but he didn't. A sudden anxiety gripped me. 'Do you still love her?' I blurted out.

'Of course not. How can you ask me that?' He looked flabbergasted. 'But I do like her and I regret that she had to be hurt for us to get together. That's all. God, Jo, how can you even think . . . when you and me are like this?'

'Sorry, sorry, I . . . That was ridiculous. Sorry.' I pretended to rummage in my handbag, mortified to have doubted him. A few moments passed in which he contemplated the scars in the table's wooden surface and I feigned a fascination in the posters on the ceiling above us.

'What did you want to do in town?' I said, as Damon Albarn started in on the chorus of 'Girls and Boys'.

'A couple of things. I thought we should get Lucas a present,' he said.

'What do you buy the man who has everything?'

'Lucas doesn't have everything, though, does he? He's not a consumer, not like Danny. He buys books and CDs but it was Danny who bought the TV. He doesn't have many clothes, either. He spends all his money on food and drink and entertaining. This party alone must be costing thousands.'

'That's what matters to Lucas, having friends around him,' I said.

'I had one idea,' he said. He opened his bag and found the book he was reading, *The Count of Monte Cristo*. He was a big reader of classics. I wondered what the Count had to do with Lucas's present. Greg flipped through the pages until they fell open and he took out a photograph that he handed to me.

When I saw what it was, I was taken by genuine surprise. The picture showed us all in the drawing room at Stoneborough that first evening, New Year's Eve. We were dancing. Danny was with Rachel, his hands on the waist of her punky silver dress. She looked exhilarated, beaming with what was unmistakably a look of love at the photographer. I realised with another lurch of my stomach who it must have been. Martha, Michael and I were in a loose circle, as if around an imaginary handbag. We had drunk quite a bit by

290

that stage. Martha's cheeks were rosy and my hair had abandoned any pretence of a style. Michael was cutting a particularly interesting move involving the drawing of his fingers across his eyes. Behind us was the room itself, so impressive to me then, so familiar now. The fire was burning and the low lamps cast their pools of golden light over the rich reds and greens of the traditional furnishings. Lucas was sitting the dance out. He watched from the chesterfield with an amused expression. When I saw photographs like this, I understood the wisdom of his no-dancing policy.

'I thought we could have it blown up and framed for him,' said Greg. 'What do you think?'

I looked back at it. The nostalgia was so strong it was painful. 'He'll love it.'

We finished our coffee and went down the steep stairs into the market. Again, nothing seemed to have changed. The flowers massed in buckets outside the florist's on the corner could have been the same ones we came to buy for each other after exams and the air still carried the iron tang of the carcasses hanging up outside the butcher's, a bloody top note against the anonymous vegetable smell of the place. Although the market was small, it was still possible to get confused in the net of its aisles. Greg led me out towards the High Street and then, to my surprise, ushered me into the expensive dress shop there.

'What are we doing here?' I asked.

'We've come to choose something for the party,' he smiled. 'I want you to have a dress you like, not some old thing you feel you have to wear because it's what you've already got.'

'I can't do that. Not in here. I haven't got enough money, Greg.' I looked around at the few rails and their outfits that cost the equivalent of half my rent for the month. I felt a surge of longing accompanied by a sense of the impossibility of ever owning anything like these dresses with their diaphanous layers and bursts of beads and sequins. I thought of

Rachel again. This was the sort of place she shopped. I wondered whether she had ever brought Greg here but quickly fought the thought away. I had to learn not to resent the past.

Back in London Greg had sat on the end of my bed watching while I tried on my two evening dresses. Both were veterans and I wasn't enthuasiastic about either. I had a red velvet one that was a good eight or nine years old and reminded me of a university ball when I'd drunk so much that I'd ended up passing out on one of the benches. It was well cut, though, and good quality, which weighed in its favour against the other, a cheap black number that gave me a décolletage like the mid-Atlantic rift. I'd been wearing that one when I asked for his opinion.

'Well, it's certainly a showcase for your assets,' he'd said, suppressing a grin.

'You're not helping. What about the red one?'

'Bring the black.' He saw my face and held his hand out. 'Come here.' He pulled me close to him and buried his face in my cantilevered bosom. His hair tickled my chin. 'I think you'll look gorgeous.' I'd felt his hands starting to slide up the outside of my thighs, inside the dress, and he'd looked up at me with that particular light in his eyes that I had come to recognise well.

'Greg, we can't. We're supposed to be at the house. We'll be late.'

'Stuff them,' he'd said and hooked his thumbs into the sides of my knickers on his hands' downward journey.

'You're thinking about what I'm thinking about, aren't you?' he asked now, with a knowing smile. 'Perhaps, if you're quick enough about choosing something, we could try that again before lunch.'

'I can't afford to get anything here.'

'Jo, are you being deliberately obtuse? I want to buy you a dress.'

'No. No way. I can't. I'm not that sort of girl. I don't feel comfortable with it.'

'It's got nothing to do with being that sort of girl. Think of it from my point of view. I want to buy you a present and you're not letting me. Now get on with it. You're wasting time.'

The marquee had arrived by the time we got back. As we parked on the front drive, the men from the hire company were carrying the enormous canvas round to the lawn from their van. We said a quick hello and then sneaked inside and upstairs to our room before anyone saw us.

When we came back down Diana was at the kitchen table making the place cards for dinner. On her left was a stack of plain cream cards and on her right a much smaller pile of the ones she'd already written. I picked one up. It was beautifully done, her black ink calligraphy confident and professional. 'Robert Clifford,' I read. 'There's a name I haven't heard for a long time. He was a friend of Lucas's from school.'

'I hadn't realised how many people had accepted until I started this,' said Diana, crossing a name off the list and taking a fresh card.

'How can I help?'

'The marquee guys could probably do with a cup of tea. Would you mind?'

I made up a tray and took it outside. They'd rolled the canvas over the frame and all it needed now was to be pegged down. I went inside. The sun filtering through the thick material was muted, casting the interior in a strange sort of half-light. It was the largest marquee they had, Lucas had told me, and it did feel huge. I imagined what it would be like by the following evening, the tables laid and the band playing, and got a rush of excitement. I liked big parties, ones so huge they became almost impersonal and where, beyond a certain point in the evening, one could wander

293

among the other guests with hardly an interruption. That was my plan, to keep a low profile and enjoy it as if I were anyone else, just let the time pass until it was all over.

After lunch Diana was going to walk Greg and Michael round the garden, to explain how she wanted the Roman candles laid out. 'Lucas, why don't you and Jo do the seating plan?' she'd said on her way out, giving him a handwritten list of all those who had accepted. 'It's no good my doing it. I don't know the politics.' She'd left us alone in the kitchen and we'd hesitated. I was touched by her action. It was obvious that she'd meant it as an opportunity for us to talk.

'We'll go up to the study for some peace and quiet,' said Lucas. I followed him upstairs, past all the boxes, which now filled the back of the house. The caterers had delivered their equipment in advance and the passageway was lined with crates of glassware and dinner services. Cases and cases of wine were stacked in the flower lobby. There were stands for the flowers that we were going to do the next day and also two kegs of beer.

In the study he flipped down the lid of the desk and laid out the plan, fifteen tables of ten. We sat side by side, careful not to let our arms touch, respectful of each other's calls on the placement. We began to fill in names, avoiding putting together groups of people who knew each other too well or not at all, and any potentially acrimonious exes. I realised that it had been more than a year since I'd seen or spoken to a lot of the people on the list and that we must be completely out of touch with their news. 'You've invited Paul,' I said. 'I haven't seen him for ages. I didn't even know he was back from Hong Kong.'

'He's just back. He rang me the other day. I thought you'd like to see him.'

'Definitely. God, do you remember the time he had that party at his parents' house, while they were away?'

'When he and Martha wanted a bonfire but the weather

had been so dry and it ended up burning half their lawn?'
Lucas grinned.

'And everyone was running in and out of the kitchen with
bowls of water, like something from *The Sorcerer's Appren-
tice*. That was funny.'

'Terrifying until it went out, though.' He laughed.

'Yes, although it would have been worse if we'd been
sober. We would have realised how close we were to setting
the actual house on fire.' I wrote Paul's name down and
turned back to the list.

'I've invited Marianne, too,' he said. 'We've got to be
really careful not to put her anywhere near Roger.'

'I thought that was a bit better now.'

He shook his head. 'No, she'll never forgive him. It was her
sister, though.'

We looked at each other. There was a dancing light in
Lucas's eyes and his amusement was as infectious as ever. He
raised his eyebrows and I couldn't stop myself from laughing.
'Don't,' I said. 'It's too mean of us.'

'Sorry. I don't know why that cracks me up so much. I
think it's just because it's like something out of *Dear Deirdre*.
"My boyfriend ran off with my sister."'

The laughing dispelled much of the tension in the air and
we both relaxed. I turned my attention back to the plan.
After a quarter of an hour or so, I moved my chair back and
looked round the room. 'It's tidier in here,' I said.

'We had a clean-up, sorted out some of the paperwork. It's
a bit less chaotic.' He got up and went to the window. Taking
me by complete surprise, he put his fingers in his mouth and
wolf-whistled loudly. 'Looks great from this angle,' he
shouted. I heard Diana laugh.

'Tomorrow should be good,' he said, sitting down at the
desk again. 'Thank you again for coming – it means a lot to
me, as you know. It's going to be an end and a beginning.
The beginning of my new life, getting going on my book

properly, but also a kind of goodbye to Patrick. A send-off and a thank you. I've got something to show you.' He pulled open one of the drawers and removed a roll of paper about a metre long that he spread out on the desk, carefully weighting down the corners with books from the stack on the floor. 'Do you recognise it?'

I stared at it. 'It's the picture on the ceiling.' I leant in to get a better look. It was all there, the design for the painting that filled the dome in the main hall. It was a charcoal sketch, smudged but instantly recognisable. There were all the characters, the huge man lolling on his chaise longue with the women at his hands and his feet, the beautiful Ganymede with his drinking bowl, the huddle of men behind and the children in the foreground. The trailing vines, too, were sketched in. 'It's amazing,' I said. Even on such a small scale, the grandeur of the finished painting was visible.

'But look,' said Lucas, running his finger down the edge of the paper to the bottom right-hand corner. 'Look at this. PCH. Patrick Charles Heathfield.' He took another roll of paper from the drawer. 'There's more. Detailed sketches.' He laid three smaller pieces of paper out on the desk. There they were, ink studies of the faces of the women and of the illustration of the hares and deer chasing each other in perpetuity around the edge of the golden drinking bowl. The lines were fine and clear, the ink more of a match for time than the charcoal.

'What does it mean? Patrick painted the ceiling?' I said. 'Did you know?'

'Never.' He smiled and shook his head.

'Why not? That's mad. If he did, why didn't he tell you?'

'I don't know why no one ever told me but I'm almost one hundred per cent sure it was him. Take another look at the women.'

I recognised them from the films more than anything. The finished painting looked so like a classical scene in the

Renaissance style that it had never occurred to me to try to ascribe the women real human identities, but on the sketches, at close range, there could be no doubt about who they were. Claire and Elizabeth, in their twenties, stared up at me from their two dimensions. I grabbed Lucas's arm. 'It's your mother. And Elizabeth.'

'Have a guess who the children are, then,' he said.

'My God, Lucas, you're in a painting.' I laughed. 'And Patrick was a painter, a really, really good one.'

Lucas was laughing, too, clearly pleased by my reaction to the news. 'I knew you'd like it. Only you and I and Diana know at the moment. It's incredible, isn't it? I'm seeing a Patrick I never knew.'

I stood up and walked out on to the landing. Exactly like the first time I ever saw the picture, light was streaming in through the windows at the base of the dome, flooding the space above. The light was softer now, though, than the intense winter light of that first morning. It offered a kinder view of the painting. Tipping my head back to look at it properly, I realised I was looking at a family portrait. Now I knew what I did, the two children were clearly a male and a female. I turned to Lucas beside me. 'So who's the man on the couch?'

'I think it's Patrick, don't you?' he said.

We went back into the study. I still couldn't quite believe it. If Patrick had painted the ceiling, and it did seem he had, why didn't anyone know about it? Lucas explained that he had come for the Christmas holidays once and found the painting under way. 'The scheme of it was sketched out on the plaster,' he said, 'and the part with the wine bowl was painted in. Patrick told me that the artist had gone to see his family in America for Christmas and wouldn't be back until I'd gone to school. At Easter that year we went to Italy on one of Patrick's educational tours – makes sense now, Italy, given the style of it – and when I came back for the summer holiday, it was finished and the alleged artist was gone.'

'He must have worked like a demon to do it in less than a year,' I said.

'He was like that,' Lucas replied. 'No half measures – ever.'

'So why the hell didn't anyone know he did it?'

He turned up his palms and shrugged. His face was lit by his smile and I couldn't take my eyes off him. At first, I couldn't understand what it was about his expression that was so arresting and then I realised: I was looking at the old Lucas, the one I hadn't seen for months. He was still there; beneath everything that had happened during the year – the difficulties between us and his drinking – the old, kind Lucas was still there. The thought made my heart happy. Perhaps, even after everything, with some more time that Lucas would become the dominant one.

He turned to the projector. 'There's something else I want to show you,' he said, picking out a cassette. 'It was the last one in the box.' He snapped on the machine and the familiar round-cornered square of light filled the wall above the fireplace. The iron rings clattered along the rails as he pulled the curtains and plunged the room into darkness.

The camera is outside the study. It is a secret eye. The hand that holds it is steady for the most part but now and then a tremor moves the lens and it catches the edge of the door in close-up, the glossy white paint, the familiar knot in the wood at eye-level.

Inside the room are two Elizabeths. One is a silhouette in front of the window, her face in shadow, the sun falling through her thick black hair from behind, turning it blue. The other sits at a table in the evening, a white silk dress fitting closely around her shoulders and her breasts. One hand cups her jaw, the other holds a cigarette between the middle and index fingers, the touch so light it seems she might drop it at any time, just let it fall without noticing.

The second Elizabeth looks like a Helen of Troy. The artist has captured the haematite sheen of her hair, the nacre skin. She is a woman whose beauty might lead a man to lose himself.

The first runs her fingers over the surface of her alter-ego, feeling where the paint is thick and textured, where its smoothness lets her lines flow. She lingers in front of the easel, enchanted.

She turns and, in the fear of discovery, the lens ducks, shows the doorjamb. A few seconds pass in examination of the landing's pale-green carpet until, reassured that its presence is undetected, the camera resumes its position in the crook of the open door.

Elizabeth is looking at some paintings that have been leant up against the wall, their blind sides showing. She goes through the canvases quickly, as though leafing through an outsize book, scanning each one before flicking it back to rest against her left hand. She finds the one she is looking for and slides it out of the stack on the edge of its temporary wooden frame, pulling it into the centre of the room.

She rests it against the wall and, before she stands in front of it, the camera shows us the picture. It is unmistakably Lucas's mother, Claire, a portrait of her painted in the library downstairs, that serious head still with its youthful beauty, the shine about her we'd seen in the cine with Justin, despite her awkwardness. From the style, it is clear that the same artist painted this picture.

Elizabeth walks to the table in the corner of the room and picks up a Stanley knife. She finds her place in front of the picture again, positioning her feet like a ballet dancer. Even when she thinks herself unseen, she plays to an audience. Her thumb rubs slowly up and down the knife's grey granulated handle. Stepping up to the picture, she incises a line across Lucas's mother's throat with a surgical cleanness. So alive is the picture that it is a surprise that no quick line of scarlet

299

*springs up as the knife passes. She steps back, considers
her work, then throws herself at the painting, all self-
consciousness gone. She stabs at it, her hair flying, the muscle
standing out in the arm that plunges the knife into the sturdy
canvas again and again and again.*

I stared at Lucas, aghast. 'What . . . ?'

'I don't know,' he said. 'When the party's over, I'm going
to find out.'

'When did you find it?'

'Last week. As I said, this was the last.'

'Why would she . . . ?'

'I've no idea. I just don't know.' He sat down on the arm of
the chair next to mine.

Perhaps it was because we'd been laughing earlier that I
was comfortable enough to take his hand like I used to and
rub my thumb against his fingers in our old gesture of
comfort. There was a moment when we looked at each other
in the semi-darkness, the world shut out along with the light
by the thick curtains. I heard Diana's high laugh as if it were
coming to us through a great depth of water. 'I'm sure it
won't be anything, Lucas. It'll be OK.'

'I hope so. I don't know what to think. But thank you.' He
leaned in and gave me a gentle kiss on the cheek.

Greg and I cooked supper and the six of us ate at the kitchen
table. The room was hot from the oven and I opened the
French windows to let in some fresh air.

'Well, this is it,' said Diana, spooning carrots on to her
plate. 'This time tomorrow, we'll be invaded.'

There were footsteps in the hall and Danny appeared in the
doorway. 'Bloody hell, what's going on here?' he said. 'Are
you getting ready for a party or a siege?' He had clearly spent
much of the week in the garden: his arms, where the cap
sleeves of his T-shirt ended, were the colour of toffee. I

glanced at Martha, who was looking at her hands. 'So, are you looking forward to it?' he asked Lucas.

'Yes, of course. It should be good.'

'I've got a surprise for you, too. That's all I came to say, really, that your present's just arrived and I'll bring it with me tomorrow. It's really special. In fact, I bet it'll be the best birthday present you've ever had.' He seemed very pleased with it, whatever it was.

Lucas feigned polite enthusiasm but I could see why he wouldn't be much thrilled by the idea. Danny would have put it on a credit card, I thought, so Lucas would end up paying for it anyway.

Chapter Twenty-Seven

At eight, just as the guests were beginning to arrive, the wood began to whisper. A sudden breeze toyed with the canopy, chasing the leaves this way and that, and raising a susurrus that could be heard as far back as the house. The few scraps of cloud that had protected the garden from the vault of the night sky were driven away, leaving the stars to prickle there coldly. The avenue of Roman candles that led round from the drive to the lawn started to spit and flicker, the flames blown out of shape, and the clusters of tea-lights here and there on walls and steps and along the windowsills sputtered and went out.

Lucas had opened a bottle of champagne at seven and I took my glass up to drink while I got ready. I had been trying to stay calm all afternoon but with little success. I was sick with nerves. I had woken that morning with a low-level thrum already established in my ears. The house was preparing itself, I could feel it. The atmosphere had been muted in the early part of the day, as if only warming up, but it was intensifying now. I kept with the others, not wanting to be alone, especially in the hall, where the beat was strongest. I had been taking long routes through the garden all day to avoid having to cross it on my own.

I showered and took my new dress out of its protective cover. It was ruby red, modest at the front but cut deeply enough at the back to hang in two low swags at the base of my spine. I had laid out my necklace on the dressing table earlier and picked it up now but found my hands were shaking too much to do up the tiny clasp.

'Here,' said Greg. 'Let me do that.'

I stood still while his fingers moved gently on the back of my neck. 'I hate seeing you like this,' he said.

'I'm sorry. I am trying not to worry.'

'It'll be all right. We'll have fun tonight and after that things will be easier.'

'I don't know,' I said. 'Something doesn't feel right. I'm worried about Martha being near Danny after a few drinks or Danny taking exception to Michael's new boyfriend. Something, probably something really minor, just blowing up out of all proportion.'

'It's good news about Michael's new man, though, isn't it?' he said, changing the conversation. 'That's a positive thing. Come on, admit it, worry-wart.'

After two days of Michael being incessantly on the landline or struggling to get enough reception to send a text, Lucas had asked whom he was trying to contact with such urgency. We'd expected work, a deal he was trying to play down so as not to let it dominate his few days off, but instead he'd smiled rather shyly and said that he was seeing someone new, someone he'd met at the party to which he'd taken Martha. Lucas had demanded to know why he hadn't said something earlier and had issued a late invitation. As the only people who knew about the history between Danny and Michael, only Greg and I had seen the potential for trouble.

I moved over to the window and saw the first guests arriving. Though I had mixed feelings for the place I resisted the idea of strangers flooding Stoneborough, puncturing the invisible shield between the house and the world outside. Although it had often seemed barely to tolerate us, so much had happened here, and that made it our place. On the other hand, perhaps fresh blood was what it needed, an influx of new people to stir the stale, overbreathed air between us, the complicated tangle of emotion and history that we had worked up over the past nine months.

It was a couple I didn't recognise. The woman wore a dress in kingfisher blue and she shielded the front of her hair from the breeze with a hand by her forehead. They hugged Lucas and chatted to him for a few minutes before another pair appeared. Then they drifted away and walked about the garden admiring Diana's stage-setting for the evening. From this vantage point Lucas looked high and happy.

A couple of women from the catering company were now going around wind-proofing the tea-lights by putting them in glasses, and the Roman candles created avenues and focal points here and there around the lawn, by the white wooden bench and near some late-blooming roses in the border. There was a long table laid out with ranks of glasses for champagne and two of the dinner-suited bartenders standing by, ready to mix cocktails to order. Up on the terrace tiny fairy lights were woven among the leaves of the creeper just as Diana had described.

While Greg did his tie in the mirror, I sat on the low chair and watched as the lawn began to fill with people. Even from a distance I could read the sense of occasion in their bearing. They held themselves straight, addressing each other in formal silence on the other side of the glass, like film extras providing a quiet but bustling backdrop. There were dresses in every colour, as if an upmarket florist's had been raided for its rose reds and pinks, irises and magnolias and lilacs and deep evergreens. The skirts fluttered like the wings of exotic birds. It was an old-fashioned scene; the wind might have been blowing not across Oxfordshire but Long Island Sound and Jay Gatsby might have stepped away just a moment before.

I stood up and smoothed my own skirt down with damp palms.

'Ready?' he asked, holding out his hand.

I had forgotten that Greg didn't know many of my other friends. The seven of us had grown so intertwined in the house it seemed amazing that those outside the Stoneborough circle hadn't even met him. 'Do you feel like a debutante at your coming-out party?' I asked, as we went down the side steps on to the lawn.

'More like a semi-domesticated animal being reintroduced to the wild. I like this dress.' He slid a finger down my lower spine and under the back of the dress into the cleft of my buttocks.

'You're not at all domesticated,' I said, pushing his hand away before anyone could see and instead slipping mine into his pocket with its cool silk lining.

The dark was thickening around us, the cerulean sky deepening to black. There was a string quartet playing and the wind snatched at the music, making the notes burgeon and shrink. In my ears they jarred with the house's own pulse, which I realised with horror had carried outside its walls for the first time. Its relentless beat was infecting the garden now.

I thought of *The Bacchae*, Lucas's and my favourite of the Greek tragedies, and how at the beginning the messenger describes the women of Thebes running wild on the mountain to the inspired Phrygian rhythms of Dionysus himself, that cruel, amoral god come to avenge himself on the city that wouldn't acknowledge him. We had once seen the play in an antique amphitheatre in Greece at nightfall and I had understood how those women had lost themselves in the ecstatic rhythm of his dance. The beat was intoxicating, like a drug, both then and now here tonight. Though it had always frightened me before, out in the garden it was less civilised and calculated, more natural; there was something seductive about it, as if it wanted me to stop fighting and give in at last. Even as I thought about it, its tempo was increasing and yet instead of feeling dizzy or nauseous as I did inside the house, I was starting to feel persuaded by it. I knew I had to fight it bitterly, like someone slipping into unconsciousness has to resist sleep.

'Hello, lovebirds.' Danny was crossing the grass towards us, leading Elizabeth gently by the hand, as if she were a shy child. I had never seen two people more ready for their close-up. Danny's dinner suit was immaculate – it looked brand new – and so it had fallen to his hair to carry the burden of his rumpled rock-god image for the night. It stuck up obligingly in just the right all-wrong way. Elizabeth looked so young I wondered for a moment if it could really be her. Her dress was a dove-grey silk cut low at the neckline and worn with a Nehru jacket in a pewter shade. Her hair, dark as balsamic vinegar, was down on her shoulders and parted on the side. It gave her a strangely gamine look. I watched her face for a moment as she told Greg how handsome he looked, trying to identify there some trace of the hatred I had seen in her younger self on the film Lucas had shown me. It had been the sort of hatred I imagined must leave a mark on a person, perceptible to someone who knew about it, if not immediately to everyone. She was serene, however; there was nothing in her eyes or the set of her mouth even to suggest that she was capable of such emotion. In fact, if anything, I saw signs of the softness I now knew she had but had never expected when I first met her.

'Is something wrong?' she asked.

I realised I had been staring. 'No. You look lovely.'

'Thank you. I like your dress, too. Can I see the back?'

I turned to show her and while she was distracted Greg took Danny's arm and said quietly, 'Take it easy this evening.'

306

Danny laughed and began to walk away. 'Come on, Liz,' he said. 'I want to show you off.'

Before throwing ourselves into the thick of it, we took fresh glasses of champagne and tried the dim sum that the waitresses were circulating. It was a shock to realise how much had happened in the nine months that we had been so absorbed by our life at the house, as if everyone else had moved on while our backs had been turned. A guy that Lucas and I had got to know at university had accepted a job in Australia and was due to leave in a fortnight's time, probably for ever. Sarah and Graham, two of Lucas's fellow law trainees, had married. 'We were lying in bed one Saturday and suddenly it seemed like the right thing to do. We got dressed and went and booked the registry office straight-away,' she explained, holding out her hand and showing me a wedding ring. 'Shortest engagement ever.'

'And honestly not a way of getting out of buying two rings,' said Graham, resting his head against hers. I laughed, knowing that I was supposed to. I felt disconnected. Things that would once have been big news to me felt distant and irrelevant, like celebrity gossip. I was nervous of introducing Greg to people who knew Rachel, sure that she would have told them the story. Although I doubted anyone would come out and say anything, I dreaded seeing judgement in their eyes. In fact, no one spoke to me about her at all and somehow that felt even worse, as though what I had done was so bad that it couldn't even be acknowledged.

In the end it was quite by accident that I overheard someone talking about her. I was waiting at the cocktail table, behind a girl who had been in our year at Oxford but whom Lucas had always liked more than I had. She was talking to a man I didn't know, maybe her boyfriend. 'You know I was telling you the other day about that friend of mine? The one who'd set up a boutique in Richmond that was doing really well?' she said in a voice both irritating for its interrogative tone and rather louder than one I would have chosen to discuss someone known to a lot of the people at the party. 'I've just heard that she won an award for hottest independent fashion retailer. I can't remember whether it was *Vogue* or *Harper's*. Apparently she's thinking of setting up a shop in New York now, showcasing new British designers.'

The man she was with nodded distractedly, evidently more interested in the progress of his drink, but I felt as if I had suddenly been plunged into icy water. It wasn't that I wasn't pleased for Rachel: she deserved to do well. It was a combination of two realisations. The first was that the others must have known and didn't tell me. The other was the undeniable fact that Rachel was a success. The award was one thing but the thought of the New York project caused me a physical pang. In my wilder fantasies about my career, I had dreamed of being poached from a high-profile feature-writing gig on a paper in London to go and work in Manhattan. I was so far from that it felt almost hubristic ever to have entertained the thought. And yet for Rachel, it was a possibility, it seemed, and in the near future. To my horror, I felt tears pricking at the back of my eyes and I relinquished my place in the crush for cocktails and found a clear bit of lawn where I could wander undisturbed in the shadows for a minute or two.

When I had regained my composure I rejoined the throng. Lucas was more extrovert than I had ever seen him. Talking to whole groups of people, laughing, embracing new arrivals, making sure everyone had a drink, he was the epicentre of the party in a way he normally resisted. At one point in the evening, I looked over at him and he reminded me of his father on the cine, golden somehow, the camera's cool focus. On the other hand, it was the first time I really believed in him as the owner of Stoneborough, Patrick's rightful heir. He fitted the house now. Although he had encouraged us to think of it as ours, tonight it was his. His dinner suit was one of his uncle's, too. There was something a little retro about the cut of it, difficult to put a finger on. Maybe the slight nip in at the waist or the almost imperceptible flare of the trousers. It had been too good to leave in the cupboard, certainly.

Martha was like a humming-bird. I saw her here and there speaking to people, never staying long with one group but moving on quickly, as if she were looking for someone. She was drinking fast and I thought that when I had a chance I would tell her to be careful. I didn't want her to lose control tonight. Diana noticed it, too, and asked me if she was OK. I said yes, as far as I knew.

Michael brought his new boyfriend over to meet us. He was a tall, slim man with black-rimmed glasses and cropped hair that was receding slightly at the temples. The crinkles at the corners of his eyes gave him a permanent smile. 'This is Richard,' said Michael proudly. 'Jo and Greg, very good friends of mine.' Immediately, cutting through the crowd like a shark in a swimming area, Danny appeared at my elbow.

'You must be the new boyfriend,' he said, shaking Richard's hand and holding it a moment or two longer than necessary. 'Do look after Michael. He and I are very, very close.'

Michael looked horrified but Richard didn't miss a beat. 'I'm sorry, you didn't tell me your name.'

Danny gave it, a small furrow appearing between his eyebrows.

Richard looked upwards with a puzzled expression, as if searching his mental archives.

'Michael and I were an item at the beginning of the year,' Danny prompted. I felt my eyes widen. I had never heard him even hint at it before.

Richard shook his head, as if mystified. 'Sorry. I'm surprised I haven't heard of you.'

Danny's face was a mask of barely suppressed fury. He

said something about leaving Elizabeth on her own and was gone. Michael laughed and squeezed Richard's arm. 'Thank you.'

Richard smiled at him. 'Well, you can't go round being intimidated by Hoxton poppets like that.' He took Michael's empty glass and replaced it with a full one from a passing tray. I hoped that Danny wouldn't feel the need to retaliate.

The gong was struck for dinner. The big round noise of it filled the garden, its reverberations bouncing off the wall of the house, which loomed over us, above the side of the terrace. There was a surge into the marquee and a bottleneck formed while the guests looked at the board to find their places. I hung back, finishing my drink. The silence of a Stoneborough night had been thoroughly routed. The conversation of a hundred and fifty people melted into one sound like the rumble of industrial machinery, the occasional voice or laugh making itself heard above it. The air was thick with perfume and smoke.

Diana's design for the decoration of the marquee was inspired. That afternoon we had dressed the tables and the shoulder-height candle-stands with the greenery that we had cut in the wood. There were candles everywhere, making the entire interior a play of light and flickering shadow. Thick church candles were clustered along the tables at the sides and each of the dining tables themselves had a clutch of them, too, offering their own flattering but untrustworthy light. We had woven ivy around them and snaked it out towards the place settings over the heavy white damask tablecloths. Tall dishes spilled grapes from Patrick's vines, opulent and purple, the tendrils curling around the leaves we had cut with them. The arrangements of ivy and laurel looked so natural it was like the wood had seeded itself here of its own accord during the afternoon and was now growing with some crazy fervour, as if it wanted to claim the place back for the wild.

310

Diana and I had been into town again to look for other items to suggest the theme and had found wooden pan pipes in Oxfam. These were scattered here and there on the tables and woven in among the greenery. She had also borrowed a papier-mâché goat mask from a friend who worked in costume at the theatre and it now peered out from the tallest arrangement, at eye-level with the guests filing in to find their places, its mad stare oddly suggestive. The candlelight glanced off the cutlery and the glasses and the jewellery of the women as they moved around to find their places, weaving an enchantment that was now more than the sum of its parts, the living breathing soul of the party.

Greg and I were at the same table at dinner but he was on the other side of the round, too far away to speak to. On my right was a man whom I'd met several times before although I couldn't remember where. It was too rude to ask. He droned on about his job and I was grateful: it saved me having to talk. Whenever I took a sip of my wine, he topped up the glass. A layer of insulation laid itself between me and the world, leaving me inside with the drumbeat it seemed only I could hear. I shut out the crowd and focused on the sound of it and it soothed me. If I gave myself over to it, even temporarily, it had a strange kind of beauty, an intricate and lovely logic. The sounds of so many people having dinner – laughter, cutlery against plates, the chinking of wine glasses – receded. I could lose myself in alcohol tonight, I thought, drown everything in glass after glass of red wine. I wanted to be oblivious and to an extent I was, to the food, the conversation. The only external thing of which I was really aware was the positioning of the members of our group. Even though my own seat faced away from the body of the room, I could feel where the others were as sharply as if a map of them had been branded into my back.

Greg came to talk to me after the pudding dishes had been cleared, crouching down next to my chair. 'You OK?' he

311

asked. 'You're drinking a lot. You need to stay *compos mentis*, in case anything does kick off. Come and get some fresh air.' I pushed my chair back and we wove our way out between the tables. The waitresses were offering coffee and cigars, and people had relaxed and were leaning back in their seats or swapping places to talk to other friends. The sound of their voices, punctuated with raucous laughter, was now approaching a roar.

Even though the entrance to the marquee was open, it was noticeably colder outside. I felt the goose pimples rise on my arms and rubbed at them. The wind, gaining strength all the time, lifted my hair and blew it around my face. It was gusting around the marquee, causing the sides to billow and shake like slack sails. We went up the steps to the terrace and sat down among the huge sheepskins and terracotta oil lamps that Diana had planned as a chill-out area for later. The air seemed purer away from the marquee and I was grateful for it. Greg pulled me towards him and brought me inside his jacket. We were silent for a minute or two.

'I've been thinking,' he said. 'What are your thoughts on moving in together?'

'Really?'

The light from the lamp played over his face, casting one side into darkness and illuminating the other, showing me one serious eye. 'I don't want only to see you at weekends and now and then in the week. I want to be with you properly, Jo. Share your life and have you around to share mine.'

'That sounds very adult,' I said, laughing a little.

'We are adults,' he said.

I knew that, of course, and yet in another way I think I hadn't really known it until then. I saw suddenly that I had been stuck in my previous stage of development, like a butterfly too long in its chrysalis form. I hadn't made any effort to move on while it was still possible to drift along without real commitments, in stasis. And this past year had been part of that, an excuse to drift a little longer and to imagine that we were a group apart from ordinary life, at least while we were at the house. I was ready to leave the group behind now. I was hungry for normal life. Normal adult life.

'We don't have to if you don't want to,' he said.

I smiled. 'I do want to. Very much.'

He kissed me gently. 'I love you.'

From the tent there was the sound of a fork ringing against a glass and the growl of conversation slowly began to subside. I didn't want to go back inside. It felt like a retrograde step now, when there was suddenly a huge new vista spread out in front of us. I wanted to stay where I was inside Greg's jacket, the noise from the party like the music played over the credits at the end of a film, a reminder of what has happened but also the end of it. Reluctantly, though, we got up and went slowly down the steps. The edges were now demarcated with candles but it was a long way down for anyone who lost his footing in the dark. Greg went first, holding his hand out behind him so I could follow. I remembered the night Lucas had fallen.

Rather than create a disturbance by pushing back to our table, we stood at the back of the marquee to hear Lucas speak. He was already on his feet, holding his glass. Someone at a table near us wolf-whistled. It was a strange feeling to look at him, the focus of the room. Being the host endowed him with a sort of celebrity status. Here, again, was the Lucas that I had loved: a little diffident, generous, intelligent, handsome in an understated way. But that fond nostalgia was cut through with a red streak of nameless fear, like a ribbon of blood in water.

He took a sip of wine and began. 'First, thank you all for coming tonight.'

'The pleasure's mine,' said someone loudly, causing a laugh.

313

Lucas smiled. 'It means a lot to me to see everyone here, enjoying this house. As I'm sure most of you know, last year I lost both my mother and an uncle to whom I was very close. That's my excuse for dropping off the face of the earth for so long. My uncle – Patrick – left me this place and whenever I look around here I am reminded of him. He was hugely important to me when I was growing up and I miss him every day. I know that he would be happy if he could see Stoneborough tonight.' He took another sip of wine. 'The main thing this past year has made me realise is how important your friends are. You know who you are.' He raised his glass. 'Thank you – I'll never forget it.'

My eyes flicked over to Danny's table. I wanted to read his expression, to see his face as he congratulated himself on being one of Lucas's true friends. He wasn't there. I scanned the room quickly but couldn't find him. As I turned back, however, I caught Lucas's eye and he smiled.

He cleared his throat, as if preparing to deliver bad news. 'You may also know that tomorrow is my thirtieth birthday.' There was an ironic cheer. 'In ordinary circumstances this would have been a dire prospect but, at the risk of being sickmaking, I'm going to say that circumstances haven't been ordinary since I met Diana again. Diana was a childhood friend of mine, and if I haven't already introduced you to her tonight, I will. She's the most beautiful, talented and sexy woman I know.' He looked at me again and this time it felt like a challenge. He was staring quite openly; it must have been obvious to other people. What the hell was he trying to do? To break the contact, I looked instead at Diana. She was sitting next to him, driving the tine of a fork through the linen of her napkin, eyes down and acutely embarrassed at being the object of so much attention. 'I'd like to be with her for the rest of my life,' Lucas went on. Diana stopped puncturing the cloth and reached up to put her hand on his arm, making him bend down to catch the words that she murmured.

314

'Apparently I've got to shut up now – I'm being embarrassing.' He laughed. 'Anyway, a toast. To my mother and to Patrick and to Diana.'

After the speech, we went to find Martha. We found her talking to Michael and Richard, with whom she seemed to have formed an instant rapport as she sometimes did with people. She was laughing as we joined them. 'Richard's trying to set me up with a friend of his,' she explained.

'Have you met him? Is he nice?'

'Yes, at the party where they met.' She waved a hand at Michael. 'I'm trying to tell Richard I'm not interested in a relationship at the moment.'

'And I'm trying to tell her that's rubbish,' he said. 'And John's gorgeous.'

When the jazz started, we all danced. The music was excellent. All three members of the band looked retirement age and the navy blazers they were hotly stuffed into wouldn't have been out of place at an old servicemen's reunion but the music they played was jaunty and golden. The notes ran out and pushed themselves forward, eager to beguile and seduce, then took a step back, played it cool. The dance floor was soon packed. It was now very hot inside the marquee and after the first number Greg took off his jacket and slung it over the back of a nearby chair. I took my inhaler from the pocket and had two surreptitious puffs. The tension, the heat and the density of the smoke were all affecting my lungs. The formal face of the evening was now beginning to slip. People were considerably less composed than they had been three hours previously. The rivers of champagne, wine and cocktails were doing their work. I was surrounded by big leering eyes, hungry to consume every sensation the evening had to offer, the drink, the food, the music, the female flesh exposed by all the expensive dresses. The image, a sort of hideous carnival of desire, made me sick and claustrophobic. The girl dancing next to me gave up trying to salvage her chignon and let her hair fall over her shoulders with abandonment, making me think again of those bacchant women on their mountainside, shaking off the restraints of their normal lives. The hands of the man she was with ran all over her, not caring who saw.

I lasted two more songs then had to stop because of my breathlessness. I threaded my way out towards the exit and emerged gratefully into the fresh air. I stood quietly, drawing lungfuls of it and savouring the feel of the cold wind on my face and bare arms.

'Jo.' Suddenly Diana appeared in front of me. She had the look of a ship's figurehead, shoulders left bare by her dress, the wind blowing her hair back from her face as if she were breasting the waves. 'Have you seen Lucas?'

Perhaps it was my conscience that made the pulse quicken in my temples, perhaps it was some sixth sense of intensification, a subconscious realisation that the evening was narrowing.

'Are you looking for me, Diana?' Lucas emerged from the marquee. Greg and Elizabeth were just behind him.

'Danny asked me to find you. He says your present is ready.' She tried to keep her shawl under control as the wind threatened to whip it away.

Lucas looked annoyed. 'Couldn't it have waited until tomorrow?' He raised his voice to make himself heard and the words billowed around us.

'He says you'll want to see it.'

'What?' He leaned in to hear her.

'I said, he says you'll want to see it.'

'I don't know what he's got you,' said Elizabeth. 'He wouldn't even tell me.'

'Come on, then. Quickly.'

For reasons that neither Greg nor I could explain later, we followed them inside. When the front door shut behind us, it was like entering a different world again, the party disappearing as if it were only a dream, the sombre silence of the hall becoming reality. The place was in darkness except for the light from the two lamps on the low chest. The ceiling was hidden but I had the sense that the people up there were craning down to see what was going on. I could almost hear the creak of the couch as Patrick leaned forward. He was waiting.

Behind us the drawing-room door opened and Danny appeared. He was flushed. 'Lucas,' he said. 'Are you ready?'

I turned to look at Lucas but he was staring in the direction of the drawing room. His face was ashen. I turned again. Nothing could have prepared me for what I saw. Standing behind Danny was a man.

'Justin,' said Elizabeth.

'Lucas,' said Diana. 'Your father.'

Chapter Twenty-Eight

The man who stood behind Danny was like a shade from the underworld, incorporeal as a sheet of smoke. I might have been able to put my hand straight through him. He looked as lost as if he had abnegated his free will and been blown in by the wind. He was sun-bleached, like a photograph of himself left on a windowsill for a whole summer and faded to a uniform overexposed yellow, only the outlines of his original image still visible. This man was Justin, I could see that, but it was not the Justin that I had seen on the cine films. That golden quality was long gone, hardly even a memory any more. His hair, thin and lifeless, was a dull yellow, no hint of gold or bronze in it. His skin was the same: there was no warmth in its grey tone. It was as if his body knew that it had to grow something to contain the organs within and had come up with this approximation of skin, a pallid sickly covering.

Only one part of his body had colour and that was his eyes, wide open, full of fear and wonderment and unconcealed hunger. They were a startling colour, a burnt-out paraffin blue surely not achievable organically except through some prolonged health crisis. And then I knew I had seen them before. I had seen them in the pub the second evening we had ever spent at Stoneborough, the night Lucas had cooked and we had kissed on the terrace. He had been waiting all the time.

318

'Lucas?' Danny's voice broke into the silence.

I followed his stare. Lucas was trapped in a bubble of shock so profound that he could not move. It was as if he were suspended in time, waiting for someone to move the clock on to the next second and let him come to life again. His eyes were on his father, unblinking, perhaps not seeing at all. His mouth was slightly open but he didn't seem to be breathing.

Suddenly he dropped to his knees and rolled his body forward, his arms folded over his head. There was an animal sound of the nearest thing to pure grief I ever want to hear. His whole body was in that cry, as if every cell was screaming out in primal pain. The noise of it filled the hall and echoed in the ceiling above us, returning again and again in waves.

'What have you done, Danny?' Diana's voice reached me now in the inner space in my head where the echo of Lucas's cry and the house's accelerating drumbeat met in an eerie throbbing music. She had turned to him, fierce as a lioness. Justin shrank back, as if behind a shield.

Danny was staring at Lucas, who was now beginning to shake as though with hypothermia. He looked up at Diana and I saw that in his eyes there was a sort of disbelieving shock. 'I didn't know,' he said. 'I didn't know that . . .'

'Take Justin in there,' she said, her voice cold. 'Go and sit down.'

Elizabeth was seized by indecision. She looked at Danny and then at Lucas, then back at Danny. 'And you, Mum,' said Diana, more gently. 'Go and sit down.'

We knelt on either side of Lucas. Diana put her arm across his back and started to murmur to him, words I could hardly hear but a rhythm that was soothing, almost a croon. She rocked with him, her body absorbing the violent shaking of his. At last he broke and began to cry with heaving sobs. Diana looked at me over his back. Her eyes were full of the same fear I knew mine would show her. That huge echoing

319

cavern of a room served only to highlight how vulnerable he was and how powerless we were to help him.

After a couple of minutes he became calmer and Greg lifted him to his feet, supporting him with an arm under his. It was clear that his legs had no rigidity. Greg took out a packet of cigarettes, lit one and put it between Lucas's trembling fingers.

'It's him,' Lucas said on a juddering out-breath. 'It's really him.'

Greg walked him into the drawing room. Justin was sitting on one of the chesterfields, right on the edge, as if he knew he shouldn't be there and was ready to spring up as soon as anyone caught him. His face had caught some colour: there was a feverish flush in his cheeks below those ravenous blue eyes. I found I couldn't look at him directly; the sense of need he emanated was too intense. Danny was standing in front of the unlit hearth and he turned quickly as he saw us. The fingers of his left hand were working away at the cuff link on his other sleeve, turning the silver disc round and round. Elizabeth still didn't know where to look; her eyes flicked between him and Justin as though she was charged with keeping them both under close guard.

Diana sat Lucas down on the other chesterfield and took his hand. Greg and I stayed back. I wasn't sure whether we were part of his support or an intrusion but I was rooted there.

'You . . . What are you doing here?'

His father's mouth opened but the words didn't come. 'Lucas,' he said finally, his voice as cracked as if he hadn't spoken in all the time he'd been away.

'We thought you were dead.'

Justin hid his face in his hands. I saw how thin his shoulders were and how fine the covering of hair across his pale scalp.

'How could you do it to us? To Mum, for God's sake?'

'You don't understand,' came a voice through the hands at last.

'How could I? How could anyone understand what you did?'

Seconds passed and then Justin raised his head and blotted his eyes on his sleeve. He cleared his throat richly and shakily reached for his cigarettes. After several failed attempts, his lighter yielded a flame and he gulped at the cigarette, as if using the inhalations to suppress the sobbing still in his throat. With the palm of his free hand, he smoothed his hair across the top of his head over and over again, as a mother might do to a small child in distress. 'I never wanted to leave,' he said. 'You have to believe me.'

'Why? Why do I have to believe anything you say? You've been gone for twenty years. Twenty years.'

'It was the most painful thing I ever did.'

'Please, just don't.' Lucas put up his hands, as if protecting himself from the words. 'Don't tell me that.'

'Just let me . . .'

'If it was so painful to you, why did you do it? Why?'

'Because I had to.'

Lucas snorted. 'Because you ran that man over? You're a coward. You should have stayed and faced it. Were you afraid of prison? Was that it?' His voice was full of scorn. 'You deserved it. You should have gone to prison just for the pain you caused Mum. You let her believe you were dead. How could you do that to her?'

'I did it because I loved her.'

Lucas gave a cry of anguish and started up from his seat. Diana pulled him back down.

'Lucas, listen,' she said.

'Then make him tell me why, for fuck's sake. Make him tell me why he left a man to die in the ditch like road-kill. Tell me why I've grown up knowing I'm the son of a man who

321

could do that.' His skin had a morgue pallor; I thought he might throw up.

'Please . . .' said Justin.

'Lucas,' said Diana again. 'Let him speak.'

'You don't understand, Lucas,' cried Justin in frustration. 'It wasn't me.'

'For God's sake!'

'It wasn't just me that day. Patrick was there, too.'

There was silence in the room. In that moment, the ground beneath us seemed to shift, moving the house on its foundations and rendering the whole edifice unsound. My skin went cold, as if the fingers of the wind had reached inside and touched my bare arms and the back of my neck.

'You're lying,' said Lucas at last, his voice quiet as a prayer.

'No.' Justin lowered his eyes.

'Tell me. Tell me how.'

'Some of what you know is true. I was drinking at the house and I took the car out. I was going too fast, probably on the wrong side of the road, I'm not sure.'

Lucas said nothing. His eyes were trained on Justin's face.

'I can still hear the sound of him hitting the windscreen. It happened so quickly but the noise . . . it was so loud. Like a thump but soft and . . . wet. And then he went over the roof. Oh God.'

He looked as though he was going to break down but he swallowed hard and steadied himself. Lucas waited while he lit another cigarette, saying nothing.

'I managed to stop the car and I went back to look for him. At first I couldn't see him. It was summertime – you know that – and there was so much stuff everywhere, long grass and cow parsley and just . . . green. Then I realised he'd gone into the ditch. Lucas, he wasn't moving. His trousers were torn and there was bone sticking out through the material on one leg. It was all jagged and bloody – like meat. I was sick in the grass. He wasn't moving. There was blood coming from his eye.'

None of us said anything. I looked at Lucas. His face wore the expression of someone who knew that his world was about to change for ever.

'I was desperate. I drove back to the house to find Patrick. I relied on him, even then. We all did. He knew how to handle things. He was walking down the drive and when I told him what had happened, he made me get out of the driving seat and he got in and took us back there. He parked down in the field, where we wouldn't be seen from the road. I couldn't stop crying. He slapped me, I think. He went to look, then he got back in the car.'

'Then what happened?'

'He said I had killed him. He was dead.'

Justin looked at Lucas imploringly and I was struck by how ugly he was, how unappealing his desperate need made him and how the bones of his face, visible under the skin, seemed a reminder of his mortality, hard to look at. 'He said it was time for a few home truths. I was a parasite. He said that I was destroying Claire and you with my drinking; I was dragging you down, draining the life out of you both. Now I had killed someone. He said if I was caught I'd go to prison and he didn't give a damn if I burned in hell but it would finish Claire and he couldn't let that happen.'

He took another drag on his cigarette but it was smoked down to the filter and it burnt him. He ground it out in the ashtray with a trembling hand. His fingers were yellow with nicotine.

'He said the only way I could make things better was to go. If I did, he would help me. When the police came, which they would, he would tell them he hadn't seen me. I had to disappear without a trace. He said I had to lie low for a few days and then call him at the gallery. He would arrange money for me in an account under a different name. I wasn't

323

to touch my own bank account or ever try to contact any of you again. Everyone would assume I was dead and eventually stop looking for me.' There were tears in his eyes now, washing that intense blue even brighter. 'After all, as he said, everyone knew I was a fuck-up. No one would struggle to believe I'd killed myself or drunk myself into oblivion.'

Lucas's head was bowed and I could see the pressure of Diana's grip on his hand. 'And if you didn't go along with it?' he said.

'How could I stay? He was right – I was pulling your mother apart. She was struggling so hard and I was destroying everything. As fast as she earned money, I was spending it. I went on benders, didn't come home. I was ill a lot of the time. It was terrible for a child to be around that. I had to go, to give you both a chance. Lucas, imagine if your mother had had to watch me go to prison. I couldn't have let her tie her life to me.'

Lucas still didn't look up. The tremor in his shoulders was visible even from where I was standing.

'But there was another reason. Patrick told me that if I ever contacted you or your mother again, he would lead the police straight to me, wherever I was hiding.'

I didn't have to look at Justin to know he was telling the truth. None of us could doubt it. It was in his voice, a sincerity as clear as harp notes.

'It all happened so quickly. One minute I was here and the next I was on a train, being taken away from you both, and I was never going to see you again.' He was weeping openly now and making no effort to hide it. 'He drove the car out of the field and left it at the side of the road. He took my wallet and he left it inside, with the keys. No one could know he'd seen me. I had to hide in the field round the corner while he went back to the house to get his car and then he took me to the station.'

'No one came,' said Diana. 'While the car was there. While you were hiding.'

'It was Sunday afternoon and it was just a stretch of lane. And it was twenty years ago. Even now, when there are cars everywhere, there's not much through traffic in Stoneborough.' His shoulders dropped in despair. 'Do you know how much I wish someone had come? If I'd known then what I know now.'

'He wasn't dead, was he?' said Diana. Her voice was sympathetic.

He turned his eyes to her. 'No. He wasn't.'

'Other walkers came along with a dog and it found him. He was still alive and they called an ambulance,' said Diana. 'He didn't die until later that night, in hospital. They think he would have survived if he'd been brought in straightaway.'

'Yes. Yes. But it was hours later by the time he was found. He'd lost too much blood. I never knew.'

'But Patrick knew,' said Lucas. 'He wasn't drunk. He knew to feel for a pulse. He lied to you and then left that man to die.'

'Yes.'

Lucas put his hands over his face and then ran them up, knotting his fingers into his hair.

'For twenty years, I believed a lie. I'd been so drunk and frightened that I hadn't been able to tell for myself. I trusted Patrick. I believed what he told me. I never would have left that man there if I knew there was a chance he'd survive.'

Lucas began to weep again, the same racking sobs that had shaken his body in the hall. Danny went to him and put a hand on his shoulder and I watched as Lucas reached up and took it, gripping on to him as if he were a raft. Danny's own face was blank with shock.

'I just don't understand why,' said Lucas eventually.

'Because he loved your mother. No, it was more than that. It was a kind of madness. He was obsessed with her. Completely obsessed. He wanted to . . . possess her. She was the only thing he couldn't persuade or buy or charm.

325

That just made him want her even more. He thought if I was gone he'd get her.'

I thought of Patrick and Claire on the first cines we'd seen. The way Patrick had looked at her as he'd stroked back her hair. Μήδεν άγάν, I thought. *Nothing in excess.*

'He was with Mum before you were, wasn't he?'

'Did she tell you that?'

'No. It doesn't matter how I know. Tell me how it happened.'

'Before I met her I'd been away filming. Patrick and I weren't close but we stayed in touch for our parents' sake. They hated the idea of us not getting on. Even before Claire, Patrick thought I was some sort of threat. God knows why. He beat me in everything. He was cleverer, more successful, richer – everything. Even as kids, he was Oxbridge material and I scraped along two years behind him. There was this rubbish about me being better-looking than him but that's crap.'

I thought of how he looked on the films and knew that the sort of beauty he'd had then was something that couldn't be dismissed. It was a form of power, however much he was denying it now, a currency, just like talent or wealth.

'Anyway, we hadn't seen each other for months so I came up here for a weekend and I met Claire. I loved her, Lucas, from the first moment I saw her. It was the real thing. The only person I ever came close to loving as much was you.

'And the real miracle was that she felt the same. Somehow she could see that I was something apart from this supposed beauty' – he spat the word out – 'which was all anyone else ever cared about. She knew me. What your mother and I felt for each other was mutual, right from the start. We made each other so happy. And it made me happy that I could make her happy, this incredible woman . . . it was like realising why I was put on the earth.' He smiled for the first time as he remembered, going back to the memory as if to a dog-eared favourite photograph.

'So she left him.'

'Yes. We were as honest and gentle about it as we possibly could have been but he went nearly insane with jealousy. In London he used to come round to Claire's flat at three o'clock in the morning, crying and shouting and pressing on the bell. If we didn't answer, he just carried on. The neighbours called the police a couple of times. He refused to sell a picture to a director who gave me a job. He even threatened to kill himself. It was a very difficult time. For a while I thought it wasn't going to be possible for us to have any sort of relationship with him at all.'

Again I thought of the cines, the scene on the terrace with the picnic on that summer's afternoon. Justin's hands on Claire, his fingers sliding around the edge of her bikini while Patrick sat stonily on the balustrade, fully dressed despite the heat. I had thought her uneasiness was shyness of the camera but I saw now that she had been thinking of Patrick's hurt and didn't want him to see them.

'Then something changed,' said Justin. 'I think he realised that if he carried on the way he had been he would lose her completely, even as a friend. He didn't give a toss about me. I think he might have killed me if he thought he could get away with it. He hated me for taking her – God, he hated me. It finished any chance of our ever having a proper relationship. We were civil to each other for her sake, but that was it.'

'Why did you still come here?'

'For her. She liked the people who came here, the artists. They had become her friends. And she liked him. She told me that she had mistaken friendship for attraction. She said once that Patrick was the man she had thought she loved before she discovered what love really meant.'

Greg took my hand and squeezed it.

'I was always a drinker, even then. A bit more than

everyone else but it was still fine, under control. But then I couldn't get work. You were growing up and I wasn't earning enough to keep the three of us. That TV drama I'd done just before I met your mother was a big hit. I thought I was made, and I did get work for a few years but then it all just evaporated. Claire was doing her best with the money from her books but it wasn't enough. She would have liked another baby but we couldn't afford it. I was a failure. Not enough of a man to keep my wife and child. Patrick was always offering handouts but I wouldn't take them. How could I? He would have owned us.' His face had taken on its pinched look again as he remembered. 'And as well as that, I had the feeling all the time that he was waiting. Watching me and waiting for me to screw up. And I did, didn't I? I played right into his hands. Oh Lucas, if I could do anything to turn back the clock I would. Anything.'

'Where did you go? Afterwards?'

'Morocco. I knew the police would be looking for me so I needed to go abroad, somewhere where I could be anony-mous. I've been living there under a different name. I drank for the best part of sixteen years, trying to obliterate it all. The guilt of thinking I'd killed someone. I wouldn't wish it on my worst enemy. The pain of not being with you and your mother any more. It tore me apart. I didn't know there was pain like that in the world.'

'You don't drink any more?'

'No. One day I woke up and I was in hospital; I'd been found unconscious in the street, half dead. They cleaned me up and wouldn't let me go. I haven't had a drink since, not one.' There was pride in his voice. 'I thought about you and your mother all the time. I've got all her books. They were the only thing that gave me a connection to you. They were so sad. I felt she was writing to me, to let me know she still thought about me.'

'She never stopped loving you. She loved you till the day she died.'

Justin began to weep again. I had never seen anyone so broken.

'Didn't she look for me?'

'Patrick insisted on doing it for her. For years he made this big show of trying to find out what had happened. He told Mum that he'd tried private detectives and everything. He made out he'd spent a fortune.'

'And she believed that? She didn't look for me herself?'

'After you left, she had a breakdown. She wasn't able to.' Justin closed his eyes.

'She wouldn't let Patrick give up, though. Eventually he told her it was destructive. He tried to have you declared dead but she wouldn't let him. In the end he told her you had to be dead, because if you'd been alive, you would have come back to her.'

Justin gave a horrible cry and put his hands over his ears. 'It makes me sick to think of it. Sick. I had nightmares where he tried to get her back. He was all over her. I saw him trying to pretend he was your father.'

'So why did you wait so long to come back? Why only now?'

'I came back last year, after she died. I saw her obituary in the paper, Lucas. Patrick didn't even tell me she was ill. The woman I loved died and I read about it in the paper, thousands of miles away. After that, I knew I had to come back, to ask him to let me have another chance with you, to get to know you at least, before it was too late. I didn't come back before because I thought he would hand me over to the police, but after Claire died I didn't care – she was gone and nothing I did could hurt her any more. But it all went wrong. Patrick was terrified to see me. It was like he'd seen a ghost. He was so frightened, Lucas, I could smell it on him. All those years of blackmail. That man left for dead. He told me that he would think about the best way for me to meet you, to sort it out, and that I should come back the next day and we'd talk. When I came back, he was dead, full of pills and booze, slumped in a chair upstairs. He was a coward, too.'

Lucas was staring. 'You were here then? I found the body. You saw it before me.'

'Yes, but when I found it, I ran. Back to Marrakesh. Think about it: the long-lost brother returns and the next day Patrick's dead. What does that look like to you, when the last thing the police knew they were looking for me for a hit-and-run? I'm a weak man, Lucas. That must be pretty clear.'

'It doesn't explain why you're back now.'

'I came back in January. I think your friend there recognises me.' Justin pointed at me and Lucas turned his head quickly.

'New Year's Day,' I said. 'You were in the pub. I hadn't seen a picture of you before and when I did I didn't make the connection. You look so different.'

He nodded, acknowledging it. 'I went there to see if I could find out anything about you, Lucas. It was incredible to see your friends, talking about you. Grown-ups. The last time I saw you, you were ten years old. It was amazing. You were there, so close.'

'And you didn't think to come up to the house and find me?'

Justin nodded slowly. 'Yes, I did think about it. For days. But I couldn't. I wasn't ready. I was afraid that you would reject me. I needed to be ready, to know what to say. I went back again, while I thought about what to do.'

'So how did Danny find you?'

'I came back again a week ago. I'd had time to think and I knew I had to make contact with you. I was still scared as hell but I had to do it. I went to the pub again, to see if I could find anything out, ask the locals, and I met Danny there.'

There was a silence. Justin's anticipation was almost palpable. He was waiting for Lucas's response as if waiting for his sentence to be handed down.

330

'He ruined your life,' said Elizabeth. We all turned to look at her. She had sat down suddenly on the low Victorian chair by the wall.

'Yes,' he said. 'And he ruined yours, too, didn't he? You've never been able to move on, not really. I couldn't believe it when Danny told me you were still here.'

'I loved him.' There was a note of disbelief in her voice.

'But he never loved you.'

Her public face, usually arranged so carefully, was gone. It was horrible to witness the unprotected person underneath. 'That's not true,' she said weakly.

'It is, Elizabeth. Can't you let it go, even now, when you know what he did? And think about what he did to you. He used you.'

'No.'

'Yes. He did. He used you to make Claire jealous. To pretend to her that he was happy without her and that she hadn't been everything to him. You wanted him, too, of course. Beneath all that *image*, you were as vulnerable as anyone else. You looked at Patrick and you saw someone who would protect you. Nothing's changed, has it?' he said and his eyes found Danny. 'You're still looking for someone to look after you. The man who'll make everything all right. I think you've been looking for Patrick – or what you thought he was – all your life.'

'Stop it,' said Lucas. 'This is cruel.'

'No, Lucas,' she said. 'He's right. Patrick did use me. He took me on because I looked like her, I know that. Sometimes he could make it work. Sometimes it was like he had convinced himself that he was with her. He could be loving but then he went cold. Can you imagine what that's like? To know the man you love is only with you because you remind him of someone else?'

'You tried to make it work, though, didn't you? You tried everything. Running round trying to help people like she did, modelling for him, copying her. It was sad.'

331

'It was your fault. If you'd been more of a man, it would never have happened,' she hissed back at him. 'Patrick wouldn't have thought he could get her back. He would have given up. But all the time she was with you he thought he could get her back. You were right before. He did know you'd screw up sooner or later.'

'At least Claire loved me. What we had was real, not some piece of artifice and pretence. You tried every trick in the book, didn't you, stroking his ego, flaunting your body at him. Jesus, the way you used to sunbathe. There wasn't a man within fifty miles without a hard-on apart from the one you wanted.'

'Get out,' said Lucas, getting to his feet. 'Both of you. I can't listen to this.'

'Lucas, I'm sorry.' Elizabeth was on her feet.

'Please. Just go.'

I thought she would protest but she didn't. Instead she drew her shoulders back and walked out of the room with as much dignity as she could muster. She had to pass Greg and me, and I saw that she was pale. The youthfulness she had had earlier in the evening was gone; for the first time in the months I had known her she looked her age.

'And you, Justin. Go now, please. I need to be on my own. I need to think.'

'Lucas.' Justin turned to him, his starving eyes full of fear. 'Son . . .'

'No.'

I saw that Justin had hoped that Lucas would pull him into his arms, give him some sign that he was forgiven. The rejection was written on his body, in the fall of his shoulders and the bowing of his head. As he passed us, I swear the air grew momentarily colder, the way it is supposed to when there is a ghost in the room.

When they were gone, Lucas slumped back on to the chesterfield. None of us said anything. While Justin had been telling his story, I hadn't heard the wind but now it filled the silence, throwing itself against the house as if it wanted to blow it down. I could feel it buffeting the walls. A fresh gust brought us the sound of a woman's shrill laughter. The party. It was still going on. It seemed incredible, impossible. I wished now for a second that it might be swept clean away by the wind, taken up as if by a tornado and thrown down somewhere else, leaving Lucas in peace to forget that it had ever happened. But it carried on, the music and the shouting and the laughter now all clearly audible in the larger silence that threatened to swallow us.

'I need to be alone,' he said eventually. 'Jo, Greg, could you go now?'

'Take care of yourself, Lucas,' said Greg, nodding at Diana.

I went forward and put my hand on his shoulder. I felt him flinch and my mind emptied of anything to say. This was so far beyond my experience, his position so alien to me that it was frightening. I felt pity for him but also fear, both for him and of him. Greg took my hand and led me away.

Out in the hall, I raised my eyes to look at them, the audience above our heads. I was half afraid that they might have sprung to life now. At first, they were hidden by the gloom that filled the centre of the building but, as we climbed the stairs, the light from the cloudless night outside flooded the bowl of the ceiling and let me see them. Tonight at last I knew for certain what I was looking at. It was the scene of Patrick's victory, his triumph over them all.

Now that I knew, it was so obvious: Claire humbled at his feet, adoring him in paint when she wouldn't in life but also revered herself in the purity that marked her out from Elizabeth, who stooped to kiss Patrick's hand, her sexuality a weapon but the only one she had. In the background was the Ganymede figure with his drinking bowl. I saw now that it must be Justin, relegated behind the imperial couch, a

333

servant, his golden beauty reduced to proffering his bowl with desperate need. How had I missed it?

And there, in the centre of it all was Patrick, victor, master of all he surveyed, the king of his castle, the subduer of his enemies. The man who had, in full knowledge, left another man to die. In that shifting, mobile face, I now saw evil. And I understood finally that while we were in his house we were in its thrall. Stoneborough was soaked with it. It lingered here now, even after his death, the malign spirit of the house that had goaded me and taunted me, its true nature hidden from me until tonight.

As we threw our things into the suitcases, the tempo of the beat in my ears increased again. It was drumming so fast and so loud now I was frightened it would drive me mad. It was as if I were running, pursued, and could hear my own heart screaming with panic, two hundred beats a minute. I followed Greg closely on our way downstairs, not wanting to be left alone even for a second. This time I kept my head down, terrified to meet those eyes again. I could feel the weight of them on my back, laughing at me, scorning my naivety.

Outside, it was like the climax of a terrible rite. The DJs were on now and the electronic beats and awful lamenting lyrics sounded like music written to announce the Furies, arriving to seek vengeance for old wrongs. There were people everywhere, reeling drunk, laughing like hideous caricatures of themselves. I kept my eyes on the ground as much as possible as we negotiated our way through to the walled garden to reach the back of the house where our car was parked for the night. There was a couple near the gate, he burying his face in her neck while his hips ground her body against the wall, one of her legs raised, her dress riding up round her waist. The woman's face was a mask of agonised pleasure.

We got into the car and Greg started the engine. We moved out of the yard and on to the long straight stretch back into the village, the headlights making a tunnel of light under the horse chestnuts, whose great leaves had begun to crisp. I clutched my inhaler between short breathless gasps. Greg looked over at me in concern. With only the puttering of the engine as we negotiated the potholes, the sound of the leaves being beaten this way and that by the wind filled the car. They too wanted us out. The whispering, swirling noise urged us down the drive and away from Stoneborough. *Go, go.* The presence of the house pushed at our backs, its beat loud in my ears. I kept my eyes trained forward. Though it was ludicrous, I had the idea that if I looked in the rearview mirror I would witness a hideous *danse macabre* on the track behind us, faceless people risen from the dead and moving their worm-eaten bodies to the music of Lucas's party, led in the dance by Patrick.

Chapter Twenty-Nine

When I try now to think back to the week after that party, I find I have almost no recollection of it. It is as if all my mental energy then was concentrated on attempting to assimilate what had happened, leaving nothing left over for the laying down of memory. What I have instead is a sort of impression of that time, one that is physical rather than mental. It manifests itself as a creeping feeling, a coldness over my skin and the contraction of my stomach muscles. It is like the nameless fear that comes at four o'clock in the morning, in the blackest minutes, when it seems the sun might never rise again.

When I have made myself analyse it, I find it has at least three separate strands. One of these, and in many ways the most straightforward, was the sheer difficulty of grasping the fact of Justin's return, his resurrection. The jaundiced, sickly picture of him haunted me. He seemed to me then – and still does – like a warning, a salutary example like the ones found in old-fashioned books written to scare moral lessons into children. Or perhaps he is more like a character from Greek mythology. There was something Promethean about him, certainly. I have always thought that that punishment was one of the most horrible in all the Greek legends, the relentlessness of that one act of theft being repaid with an eternity of pain born anew every day.

Thinking about Patrick was far worse. I tried in vain to find a way to reconcile this new version of him with the man I had known. It was like listening to two different pieces of music playing simultaneously in one room. I couldn't conceive of how a person could live with the sort of secret that he had had for all those years, could conduct the business of a life – earning a living, sleeping, eating – while at the base of it all was the knowledge that he had blackmailed his own brother and then abandoned a man, a man completely innocent of any involvement, to die like an animal at the side of the road. How had he been able to be close to his brother's wife and child – to hold them the very afternoon of the accident, as Lucas had told me that he had?

The only thing that I found in common between the two Patricks was scale. The Patrick I knew had been epic, an Atlas of a man who seemed to carry the world so lightly, so able to deal with the magnitude of it, to be a key figure in many lives, even in mine. The second Patrick had also been mighty, mighty enough to have carried a secret that would have crushed others under its weight and never to have shown the strain. It was a terrifying power and to think about it too hard was to look into places darker than I had ever wanted to see.

Patrick had cast his shadow over our world and now I wanted to run from under it. I wanted to be free of that miasma, the sickening fallout of what he had done, raining down on everything that he had touched and polluting it even now, after twenty years and his death. I wanted to be free of the knowledge that I had liked him and admired him. I had held him up as an idol, the urbane, artistic exemplar of everything I aspired to be and now I wanted to forget that he had ever existed.

The major element of my impression of that time, however, was fear for Lucas. I knew he would be tormented by the knowledge of what Patrick had done, his surrogate father, the man who had made himself indispensable to Claire and worked himself into the substance of their lives like a death-watch beetle. And at the very time he was most vulnerable, he was also presented with his father and his broken, starving need.

I had expected him to be in touch, to want to talk, but there was nothing, no communication at all. I couldn't decide whether to ring him. On the one hand, I felt compelled to, both by my anxiety and by a pressing sense of duty, but on the other, his silence seemed to indicate that he wanted to be left alone, to be given space to try to come to terms with what had happened. I thought of ringing Diana as a way of getting news while also keeping my distance. I realised, however, that I didn't have her mobile number; she had never needed to give it to me. I tried ringing directory enquiries for Elizabeth's cottage in the village but she wasn't listed.

It is a terrible thing to admit but as that week began to slip into the next, I was glad that the silence continued. I would have been ashamed to tell anyone, even Greg, how much I wanted the responsibility for Lucas to be lifted from my shoulders, the long task finally to finish. I wanted to move on into the world whose threshold was now under my feet, the one Greg had opened up. But I also wanted to put as much distance as possible between us and Stoneborough. Despite everything that had happened, the dread I felt at the thought of the place still seemed potent, not a memory attached to a situation now resolved. I couldn't shake the feeling that the house still had business with us.

Danny was the person it would have been possible to contact. I brought up his number several times but when I saw his name displayed on the screen I couldn't call it. I just couldn't bring myself to talk to him. Although I knew that Justin would have found his way to Lucas sooner or later, I held Danny entirely responsible for the high theatre of his appearance at the party, the hideous finale. It fitted Danny's conception of how life should be, a series of intense experiences to be milked for sensation then forgotten, but this latest piece of puppet-mastery was hard to forgive. The alarm I had seen in his eyes when Lucas saw his father for the first time told me that he'd had no idea of what Justin would tell Lucas but he hadn't even seemed to have anticipated the profound effect Justin's reappearance itself would have. His presentation of Justin as a birthday gift was almost psychopathic in its complete failure to understand its potential impact. This time he had miscalculated wildly in the pursuit of his desire to be the person who made the difference in Lucas's life.

It was nearly three weeks before Lucas called. I was at Greg's flat getting ready to go to bed when my mobile rang. As soon as he spoke, I could tell he was drunk. 'Jo?' he said, his voice thick.

'Lucas.' I didn't know what to say.

He was trying unsuccessfully to suppress tears. 'Sorry, sorry.'

'Don't worry,' I said.

'I don't know if I can forgive him, Jo.' He sobbed and tried to swallow the sound of it. 'I'm trying but in a lot of ways I hate him. When he went, I used to pray he'd come back. I used to make bargains with God – if I get the best mark in the exam, Dad won't be dead. If I can make Mum happy, he'll come back.' He choked. 'And now he's here, I wish he'd stayed lost. He's pathetic. But none of that is anything compared to Patrick. Jesus – for twenty years I let him be a sort of dad to me. It's fucking sick. What kind of evil bastard was he? And we let him into our lives. With our arms wide open.'

He was raging and although I tried, there was nothing I could do to calm him. Eventually he started sobbing so hard he couldn't speak at all and he hung up without saying goodbye.

I heard nothing the next day so after work I called the house. Diana answered on the third ring. She sounded flustered. It was early evening, maybe half-past seven, but she told me that Lucas was asleep and she hadn't wanted the sound of the telephone to wake him.

'He's finding it difficult,' she told me, when I asked. 'He's started seeing his father a bit but it's going to take a lot to build up trust between them again. I just hope he can keep it together. Danny's spending a lot of time with him; he's cut right back on the amount he sees my mother. I think he's trying to be especially supportive, to make up for bringing Justin here like that.'

She sounded tired and I asked if she was all right.

'I'm fine,' she said, then hesitated. 'Actually, Jo, it's hard. Lucas is drinking and he's quite bad-tempered. I'm trying not to make a big thing of it because I know he has so much else going on but it isn't easy. He's got terrible insomnia, too – that's why he's in bed now. He can't seem to sleep at night. He says that he lies awake and all he can think about is how he's surrounded by everything that's happened and it's choking him. He said he feels like it's sucking the air out of his lungs.'

I could imagine it. Even the thought of the house now induced in me a wave of that claustrophobic feeling, the sickness and shortness of breath. The hideous drumming of the night of the party that hadn't faded until we were out of the village. I never wanted to experience it again. I thought of Patrick's terrible triumphant eyes looking down on everything that happened within those walls.

'He's got to sell the house,' I said. 'He's got to sell it and get out. He shouldn't be there any more.'

'He won't hear of it. I suggested it and he got angry with

me. He thinks he's tied here, that there's some bond between him and the house. And he's watching the films constantly. I think he associates them and the house with that time – when it all started to go wrong.'

After that first time, Lucas called me often, almost always late at night and always drunk. The conversations varied. Sometimes he was angry and he railed against Patrick and his father with a corrosive bitterness. Sometimes he was in the grip of a deep depression and spoke of how he was unpicking his memories of Patrick now and sewing them up again with different thread. I answered every time or, if I'd been unable to for some reason, I rang him back as soon as I could. The calls made me hollow with sadness, partly because of my powerlessness to help him. Time seemed only to be making the situation harder for him, as the weeks passed and there was no sudden *deus ex machina* to give an alternative version of the story, one in which Patrick and his father were redeemed. All there was was the dull realisation that these were the facts that he would have to live with for the rest of his life.

There were times, too, when he would go on long melancholic rambles through our past. It was as if he had a rosary between his fingers and all our memories were beads on it. He would ask me whether I remembered the time we went skinny-dipping in November or the dinner we'd co-hosted in London that had started on a Friday and finished on Sunday night. It wasn't just the drunken escapades or the running jokes or the episodes of bad behaviour to which he went back. Often the times he remembered were the quiet ones, the hours in the university library burning the midnight oil before finals or lying on the grass among the remnants of a picnic in the University Parks afterwards, the times when we'd been so close, in such harmony that we had hardly needed to talk at all.

*   *   *

In a polarisation that seemed especially cruel, my relationship with Greg was making me intensely happy. I could swing from an extreme of helpless anxiety about Lucas to the sort of euphoria that made me grin at strangers in the street. It was a sort of energy that I could tap into at any time just by thinking about him. In fact I wonder whether, if it hadn't been for that potent source of joy, I would have been able to listen for so long without being slowly eaten away by Lucas's misery.

Something else that made me happy was that Martha, too, seemed to be enjoying life again. Despite her initial protestations that she wasn't interested, Michael and Richard had set her up with Richard's friend John. Her affair with Danny had made her cautious but it was obvious that she was starting to fall in love with John, and he with her. The first time she invited him round for supper I had seen how he watched her as she laughed and moved about the kitchen. He was a banker but about as far removed from the straight, conventional stereotype as it was possible to imagine. His face moved with a kindly mischief that matched hers.

As the year drew to a close Greg and I spent our Saturdays visiting estate agents and looking round houses. Eventually, after seeing countless shabby places, we found a flat that occupied the top two floors of a tall house in Kilburn. Once we'd put in our offer, things happened quickly and by the middle of December we were able to move in.

'Isn't it a bit adult?' Greg teased, after we went to sign the contracts. 'Buying a place with me?' It hadn't even occurred to me. The only part of the process that had caused me the faintest touch of anything apart from excitement was how much larger his contribution to the down-payment had been. The savings I had been able to make from my salary at the *Gazette* over the years were negligible: the sum I had put in was less than a tenth of the whole.

Even though we weren't going to spend Christmas there, I put up some holly and hung a big sprig of mistletoe from the light fitting by the front door. Whichever one of us was home from work first that week would race to the door as soon as we heard the other's key and wait, poised, under it. It was often a while before we were in a position to start cooking supper. We made love all over the flat, in amongst all the stuff we hadn't yet unpacked, the bags and boxes that carried the things we brought from our separate lives to the one we were building together.

Chapter Thirty

Greg and I spent Christmas with my family. I was touched by how keen he was to make a good impression on them all but he needn't have worried. My parents took to him immediately and both my brothers thought he was great, especially Ant, with whom he spoke for hours about artificial intelligence, the subject of his doctorate. In fact, the visit went so well that we ended up staying an extra two days. We went for long walks out on the common, where the sky was a searing blue and the frost seemed not only to cover the gorse and the crisp grass but to permeate the air, which tasted fresh on the tongue and full of the promise of a new year.

At the end of the first week in January, the weather changed and a thick layer of cloud swallowed London. The sky turned sullen and the cold was no longer refreshing but malicious: it scoured one's face as soon as one stepped out of doors. The forecasts promised the same for the rest of the week and then a further drop in temperature, after which the periodic biting sleet would be followed by a heavy snowfall across the country. I was looking forward to that, to the transformation, however momentary, of a grey London with a Christmas hangover into a picturesque, old-fashioned winter scene.

The flat was beginning to take shape. We spent the Saturday of that week unpacking the last boxes and making a list of the things that neither of us owned. I'd lived with Martha for so long that it was a shock to discover that what was hers hadn't been mine. I particularly missed her yellow toaster. On Sunday we caught the tube into town, planning to find a warm pub afterwards to compensate for the nightmare of shopping at sale time. We were struggling down the Tottenham Court Road with our haul – the toaster, a wok and three saucepans – when my mobile started ringing. Greg took the things I'd been carrying while I looked for it in my handbag. It was a number I didn't know and it was a second or two before I recognised Diana's voice.

'I'm sorry for calling you like this,' she said. 'I got your number from Lucas's phone.' The wind wherever she was made a tearing sound as it reached me.

'Is everything OK?'

'Are you in London? Would you mind if I came and met you?'

We found a pub not far from the British Museum and texted Diana with the details. We were only a few streets away from Lucas's old flat; I wondered who had it now. My memories of it were so vivid that they might have been made only the previous day but again, the time we'd spent together there seemed to belong to a different life. It was hard to believe that Lucas had moved out less than a year previously.

Diana took half an hour to reach us. I saw the two men at the table next to us look up as she appeared in the doorway and scanned the room to find us. She was wearing tight-fitting jeans with boots and a black leather jacket over a cream polo-neck. Her long hair was tied back in a ponytail. We stood to greet her and Greg went to buy her a drink. At close range, she looked far more tired than her initial impression had suggested.

'I'm sorry to foist myself on you like this,' she said, looking in her large leather shoulder bag for her cigarettes. 'I needed to see you.'

'Is Lucas in town, too?'

'No. He's in the country.' She flicked the lighter and the small flame showed me the circles under her eyes. 'I'm staying at my mother's place. She's got a flat in Notting Hill.' She crossed her legs and I registered a pang of envy at the long, slim legs in their expensive denim.

'Are you working here now?' I was surprised Lucas hadn't told me.

'Since three weeks before Christmas. I couldn't put it off any longer. I'd tried to wait until the New Year so that I could have a bit more uninterrupted time with Lucas but Trevor's old assistant had to leave and he'd been really patient already, for a number of reasons.' She looked up gratefully as Greg returned with her wine. 'So I've been commuting, or sort of. I've been here in the week, sleeping over at Mum's flat, and then back at Stoneborough for weekends and a night in the week, too, if I could.' She fixed her gaze on her glass. 'Look, what I wanted to tell you is that Lucas and I aren't together any more. I thought you should know.'

A wave of fear swept over me. 'What happened?' I asked.

She looked up and her face was empty. 'I loved him – I still do. But I can't stay now.' She hesitated again. 'I feel so disloyal even telling you this. But if anyone's going to under-stand, it's you, Jo. You know how much he was drinking – even before his father came back. He's on the edge. But I never thought that he would get violent.'

'Violent?' said Greg.

'Last night I told him that I needed a more permanent base in London and that I was going to rent a place of my own here, instead of using Mum's all the time. He went crazy. He was shouting all these horrible things at me. In the end I made a run for it but he came after me and caught me by the neck of my T-shirt. I couldn't breathe. I was struggling and he picked up a bottle from the table and pressed it against my

346

cheek. He was staring at me like a madman, saying that he was going to smash it in my face. I kept eye contact with him, hoping that he would come round and realise what he was doing. He did in the end, but it was the worst minute of my life. I really thought he was going to do it. Then he started crying and crunched up in a ball on the floor and I went.'

My guilt was instant. If I hadn't kept Lucas's near-attack on me a secret, maybe it would have saved the same thing happening to her. She looked so wretched now I wanted to put my arms around her but her self-containment held me off.

'It must be the drink, mustn't it?' she said, her eyes imploring me. 'Obviously none of us can even start to imagine what he's gone through in the past eighteen months and he's finding it so hard with Justin, but I don't think that's the real Lucas. I won't believe it.'

'Why do you think he reacted like that?' asked Greg.

'He thinks everyone leaves him,' she said. 'I knew it would be hard to come here and work. I couldn't even mention it without him losing his temper. I caught him with my mobile once. I thought he was going through my messages and that was bad enough but it turned out he was looking for Trevor's number. A couple of days afterwards I got a call from him asking me to change my mind. Lucas had told him I didn't want the job after all.' She pulled a face. 'You can imagine the argument we had.'

'He was scared of losing you,' said Greg.

She lit another cigarette, a slight tremor in her hands. 'I don't know. I mean, we'd become close friends again. But I don't think things were right between us. I don't think he likes me as much as he wants everyone to believe.'

I said nothing but there was an uneasy stirring in my stomach.

'I don't think he's over you, Jo.'

'It's old history,' I said.

347

'Yes, and on one level I think he knows that, too. Don't take this the wrong way but I think he's in love with the idea of you, not the reality. He's romanticised you and your time together and woven it all into this great *thing* that nothing else can ever rival. Sometimes I even wonder whether Danny suggested he go out with me just to try and make you jealous.'

I frowned. 'No, Lucas wouldn't. Why do you think that?'

'It's nothing concrete. I don't know. Just, you remember how Danny always went on about how great I was, when I first met you all? I thought he was going to come on to me, maybe, but then I noticed he didn't do it when Lucas wasn't there. It was like he was trying to advertise me or something. If he and I were ever in a room on our own, he dropped it completely.' She shook her head. 'I don't know, perhaps that's just in my mind because of the way Patrick used my mother.'

'I'm sure Lucas wouldn't do that,' said Greg, reaching over for her hand. 'Look at the way he reacted when you tried to go.'

'Thanks.' She smiled weakly. 'I just feel really lost. I love him and I want to help him but I can't stay now, can I, after last night? I was so frightened. And even if I did stay, I can't help him.' A fierce light came into her eyes. 'I'd do it, if I thought it would make any difference. But even if last night hadn't happened, I can't get near him. You know Lucas is giving Danny a lot of money? And Danny's dropped my mother.'

'Has he?' Lucas hadn't told me that, either.

'He just went cold. It started after the party, when he wanted to spend more time with Lucas, and now he doesn't bother to see her at all. She's so upset about it, poor Mum. And he's like a sort of force field; I can't get close to Lucas because Danny's repelling me all the time.' She looked up. 'He hates you, doesn't he?'

348

I grinned. 'Yes, he does.'

'It's because Lucas loves you and there's nothing he can do about it.'

'Although he likes everyone to think that he doesn't give a toss about anything,' I said, 'it isn't true. The money's part of it; Danny must loathe having to rely on him. But it's not the main reason. He loves Lucas and he hates himself for it because it makes him weak.'

'It has to be wrong to leave them there together when Lucas is like this.'

'Diana, if he has threatened you, you can't go back.' Greg's voice was firm. 'He and Danny will have to sort themselves out, however long it takes.'

Chapter Thirty-One

Lucas's attack on Diana put me in a dilemma. I knew how terrifying it was to be the focus of his anger and of course I could never excuse what he'd done. Nonetheless, that it had happened told me that he must be in a very poor emotional state: he would never behave like that unless under extreme duress. I agreed with Greg that I should telephone him. I rang for the first time the following evening, both on the landline and his mobile, but neither was answered. I left messages, too, but got no response.

It was three days before he called me back and, when he did, it was gone eleven and I could hear the drink in his voice again. He wasn't angry: the tone of his voice was new. He sounded worn out now, and desperate. I tried to talk to him about Diana but he was moving the conversation in a different direction. He seemed to be edging around some-thing, leading me up to it, then backing away as if he'd changed his mind. If I hadn't known better, I would have questioned whether he was on drugs, his thought seemed so fractured. Eventually I asked him outright whether there was something he wanted to talk about. He ignored me at first and started asking questions about me: how my job was, the new flat. Then suddenly the dam seemed to give way. 'I don't know who I can trust any more,' he said, and his voice was rushed and paranoid. 'Can I trust you?'

'What's happened?'

'I found something out.'

'What, Lucas?' I asked.

'Everything's fucked up. It's so fucked up.' His voice was getting louder, as if he couldn't express how he felt except in volume.

'Tell me. I might be able to help.' I tried to sound calm but my heart was beginning to beat faster.

'I can't. I can't.'

'Lucas, anything – and I do mean anything – you tell me stays secret. Whatever it is. If you need to talk to someone, you can talk to me.'

'Promise me.'

'I promise,' I said.

He still havered. I heard him open his mouth as if to speak and then bite back the words again, as though they had tried to escape him and he had caught them at the last possible moment.

'Anything, Lucas.'

Then he spat it at me, as if he couldn't bear to have it in his mouth a second longer. 'My father killed him.'

Now I really began to worry about his mental state. We had all heard what Justin had said about that day and it had been obvious that he was telling the truth. Clearly Lucas was very confused.

'Don't you understand, Joanna?' he said, frustrated at my lack of response. 'He killed Patrick.'

'Lucas, Patrick committed suicide,' I said.

'Stop talking to me like I'm mad,' he shouted at me. 'I'm not mad. I'm telling you, my father killed Patrick. He made it look like suicide. The night he came back, he had a gun. He sat upstairs with Patrick and watched while he swallowed the pills. He made him do it. He said unless he did it, he'd shoot him.'

I closed my eyes, his words beginning to make horrible sense. 'How do you know this?' I said at last.

'My father told me.'

'Where is he now?'

'Gone.'

'Why did he tell you, Lucas?'

'We've been trying to get to know each other, you know that. Patrick was all we talked about – he was our common enemy. He was about all we had in common, actually.' He laughed bitterly and the sound of it brought the hairs up on my arms. 'And then yesterday he told me. Like he was proud of it. He thought I'd congratulate him. I told you – it's fucked up. When he found out about Mum, he went back to Morocco to think about what he was going to do. He wasn't working out a way to see me at all. He was making a plan. Then he came here and did it. He murdered him. My uncle left some poor bastard to die and my dad's a murderer. Jesus Christ.'

'Do you know where he's gone?' I said, concentrating on facts to try and still the ground, which was again shifting beneath me.

There was a long pause before he spoke again. I realised that he was crying. 'No, and I don't want to know. He's gone and that's it. I never want to see him again. I might have hated Patrick when I found out what he did but now I hate them both. What Patrick did was . . . but killing him . . .'

'Are you going to tell anyone? The police?'

'No. It's time to bury it. Forget my whole sick family. Forget they ever existed. I just want it all to be over.' His voice changed again, the paranoia returning. 'You're not going to tell anyone, are you? You promised.'

'No, I'm not going to tell anyone. What happens is entirely up to you.'

'Nothing's going to happen. It's finished.'

I didn't sleep that night. What he had told me about his father was shocking, of course, but I had developed a sort of

352

immunity when it came to stories about his family, as if I had been exposed to so many that I'd built up a natural internal defence. If I'd heard the same about anyone else's father, it would have been overwhelming but the Heathfields had lost their power to horrify me now. The real shock had been Lucas, his disturbance, the paranoia that seemed to verge on the pathological. He needed help but I couldn't work out how I could give it to him. He was like an animal so badly beaten that it had lost the ability to let people show it kindness.

Chapter Thirty-Two

A week later, Greg and I went out to dinner with one of his colleagues and his wife. In the taxi back I burrowed against him for the warmth. Although the snow still hadn't arrived, the forecast said it was imminent: the temperature outside had dropped below freezing and the streets were almost deserted. The driver put the heater on and it blew hot air at our feet. I was mildly drunk and Greg laughed at me as he pulled me inside his coat and we kissed. He was leaving in the morning to spend the rest of the week working onsite with a client, a light-engineering firm outside Birmingham. We hadn't spent a night apart since we moved into our flat and neither of us was looking forward to it, even though he would only be gone for three days. I wanted to wind myself around him like ivy now so that he couldn't go.

When we reached home, there was a figure standing on the pavement. I watched him as Greg paid the fare. The street was badly lit and I couldn't make out his face. He was wearing a heavy coat that hung from his shoulders as if from a wire hanger that couldn't cope with the weight of it. A knitted hat was pulled down close to his eyes. He was agitated, walking in small circles, shooting glances at our cab as if he were waiting for us.

The driver noticed him, too. 'That your house? Sure you want to get out?' he asked. 'I'll take you round the block, if you like, see if he disappears.'

'Thanks,' said Greg. 'I think we'll all right.' He hopped out of the cab and I got out behind him, a little afraid even though he was with me. As we got closer the figure stopped pacing and stood still. 'Hello, Lucas,' I heard Greg say.

Upstairs Lucas sat in the middle of our sofa. The coat was like a shell, such an integral part of him that neither of us tried to get him to take it off. He seemed so fragile I worried that without it he would disintegrate, just crumble into bits. He kept the hat on, too, and underneath it, his eyes were wide. I was reminded of his father on the night that he turned up at the house: he had that same febrile look. It was hard to calculate how much weight he had lost. He had been lighter than usual for the past year but now his body seemed to have changed completely. He was properly thin, the sort of thinness that comes only as a result of neglect. His skin had always been soft and smooth but now it looked papery and there were several nicks along his jaw, the result of the poor shave that he'd had about three days previously.

'Can I get you anything?' asked Greg.

'Could I have a cup of tea?'

I went into the kitchen and put the kettle on. I was glad that I had told Greg the truth about Patrick's death. It was a secret that I hadn't been able to keep from him. He wouldn't let Lucas suspect that he knew. While the water boiled I stood at the window. It looked out on to the silent street and the tree whose bare branches reached back towards the house as if to touch it with entreating fingers. The street seemed to be waiting for something, perhaps the snow.

When I gave Lucas his tea, he slopped half of it on to the carpet. He seemed hardly to notice. There was a slight tremor in his lovely artistic hands as they cradled the mug and his nails were bitten down to their quicks. I felt a sudden urge to put my arms around him and tell him that everything was going to be all right.

He must have felt me looking at him because he glanced up and gave me an uneven smile. 'I'm sorry,' he said. 'For turning up like this. I had to see you.'

'That's OK,' said Greg. 'It's no problem.'

'I needed to apologise.'

'For what?'

'Being such a nightmare. For all this shit about my family.'

'Lucas, it was beyond your control. It was between Patrick and your father. You're not to blame,' I said.

He let his gaze drift around the room, taking in the new rug that my parents had given us for Christmas and the lamp that had been by the bed in Greg's old flat, now promoted. Seeing the place through his eyes, I saw that it must look settled. We had an orchid on the mantelpiece – that had been Martha's housewarming present – and photographs on the side table, including one of Greg and me that my brother had taken at my parents' house. I had seen Lucas notice it earlier. I knew he would recognise the background.

He seemed to come out of his reverie and his eyes met mine again. 'I also wanted to tell you that things are going to change. I'm sorry for making things difficult between us. And I see what you mean now: I shouldn't live at Stoneborough all the time. You're right: I can't go on like this, cut off from real life. Can I smoke?'

I passed him an ashtray and he lit a cigarette and drew on it avidly. 'I don't want to be like my dad,' he said. 'I don't want to drink and drink until I lose everything that matters to me. I came very close to that.' He looked at me again and I had to look away.

'But that's not all. I see what you mean about Danny now. All this time you've been warning me about him and I wouldn't listen. You were right, Jo.'

It seemed too much to hope for that now, when I had almost despaired, Lucas should finally see. 'What changed?' I asked. I could feel my heart lifting in my chest.

'He has. I don't know why. You know he's split up with Elizabeth?'

I nodded, although I didn't tell him how. I didn't want to raise the subject of Diana now, when it seemed we were about to broach the topic that had been verboten for so long.

'He flies off the handle. This morning I refused to give him money and he went into a rage. I've never seen him like that. It was frightening. He's always been mercurial, I know. But I never thought it would be directed at me.'

'What did he do? Did he hurt you?'

He looked at me solemnly. 'No. Not this time. But he's asking for more and more money. I don't know what he's spending it on. It's not Elizabeth any more so what is it? Maybe it's drugs – maybe that's why he's so irrational. To be honest, I'm scared. I feel like I can't say no to him in case . . .'

'In case what?'

He shook his head. 'I don't know. Maybe I'm overreacting. I just thought I should tell someone, that's all.' He stood up suddenly. 'I should go. It's time for me to stop keeping you up all night with my problems.' He grinned apologetically.

'It's late. Why don't you stay? Look, I'm working in Birmingham tomorrow. I'm aiming to be there by ten. I could take you back to Stoneborough first thing,' said Greg.

Lucas looked at him, seeming to weigh it up in his mind. For a moment I thought he was going to agree.

'Go on,' I said. 'Stay. I'll bunk off work tomorrow and we can spend the day together. I'd like that.'

'No. I should go back tonight. And I've got the car here anyway.'

'Don't drive now,' I said. 'You look exhausted.'

'I'm fine. I haven't been drinking.'

He was at the door. 'I'll see myself out,' he said.

'Lucas . . .'

'Yes?'

'Wait a minute. Come here.' I went towards him and put my arms round him. Despite his thinness, he pulled me against him with surprising strength. My nose was against the shoulder of his coat. He smelt clean, the smell of his soap powder as familiar to me as my own scent. I returned the pressure of the hug and found I didn't want to let him go. 'I'm so glad things are beginning to straighten themselves out,' I said. 'It's really good to see you a bit happier.'

'I am happier,' he said. 'And thank you.'

'There's nothing to thank me for.' I raised my face and looked at him. His large eyes were fixed on mine. 'You know that you mean the world to me.'

'I don't know what I'd do without you,' he said, smiling.

'Good to see you, Lucas, and look after yourself.' Greg shook his hand as we moved apart. 'We'll see you soon.'

Lucas turned to go and then paused to look back at us again. His face was like a pale moon across which a shadow was slowly moving. He nodded goodbye and then he was gone. I heard his footsteps drumming on the three flights of stairs down and then the slam of the front door, softened by distance. I pushed up the sash window and called goodbye to him again but I was too high and the breeze took my voice before it could reach him. He crossed the street to the Jaguar, which I hadn't seen earlier, got in and pulled away. I watched until his tail lights disappeared around the corner.

Chapter Thirty-Three

Greg left at just after seven, before the sun had even begun to rise. I went down to the car to wave him off. Ice was shining along the street. No one had taken the spot that the Jaguar had occupied the previous evening, I saw: the marks of Lucas's tyres were still distinct.

'Get inside, Jo – you'll freeze,' Greg said, pulling me in for another kiss.

'I can't. I've got to make sure you're mine before you go. I can't have one of those Birmingham girls stealing you.'

He laughed and kissed me again. 'I think you're safe.'

He got into the car at last, promising to text to let me know he had arrived safely. I waved from the doorstep until he rounded the corner then ran back upstairs for a shower. My own schedule for the morning was busy. I had an interview to do with the headmistress of a large state senior school in Putney. It was also deadline day, which meant I would have to write up the piece in the space of two hours.

As I might have predicted, the interview overran. The headmistress hadn't been as stern as she'd sounded when I called; in fact, she'd been rather talkative and it was half-past twelve by the time I was able to make my way back to the office. The wind blowing down Putney High Street was excoriating and even without it, the air itself was so cold that I felt as though it were freezing my face on to my skull;

my forehead and cheekbones began to ache. The sky was a mousy, insipid yellow and even as I walked, the first flakes of the long-promised snow began to sift down around me. With the wind, a heavy snowfall would cause drifts in the country, even if it didn't have the opportunity to settle in town. I hoped Greg had got to the Midlands before it started.

I'd had my phone off all morning and when I got to my desk I switched it on to see if he'd sent a text. There wasn't one but there were seven missed calls. They couldn't have been from the office: my arrival had been greeted with the usual indifference. Please God, I thought, let him not have had an accident. My heart in my mouth, I scrolled through the menu until it showed me the numbers. There was only one: Lucas's mobile.

I rang it and while I listened to the tone I thought how worried he had been about Danny. He didn't pick up and I was diverted to his answer service. I tried the landline instead but it rang for a long time before the automated voice told me that there was no one available to take my call. I rang the mobile again and this time left a message, asking him to get in touch as soon as he could. I began to dial Martha's number then remembered that she was away in Paris, a surprise that John had arranged.

Outside the snow was beginning to fall with intent. The flakes were larger and moved past the window with a hypnotic regularity. I thought about Greg again. Usually I tried not to call him at work but I was sure that no one would mind him being interrupted briefly today, given the weather. I called his mobile and was surprised when it rang but he didn't answer. Normally if he was in a meeting and couldn't be disturbed he switched his phone off. If it was on, he almost invariably answered. I left him a message asking him just to let me know that he was OK and then tried Lucas again. Nothing. My unease ratcheted up another level. I went outside for a cigarette while I thought about what to do. I had to smoke quickly: my hands were red with cold after a minute. In my pocket my mobile vibrated as a message arrived. It was from Lucas. Two words: 'I'm sorry.'

My heart started to hammer. What did he mean? I wanted to talk to Greg. I tried his mobile fruitlessly one more time and then made a decision.

Back at my computer I brought up Google and typed in the name of the company in Birmingham. It was a family firm, I knew, dynamic but still small. They would know where he was on the premises and put me through to him. I would apologise later for interrupting if it turned out to be nothing.

The receptionist's voice had the musical cadence of the Black Country. Embarrassed at sounding like the over-worried girlfriend that I was, I explained that I was trying to get hold of him. 'Greg Sorrell?' she said. 'Will you hold on a minute, please?' I heard her put the receiver on her desk and get up. Somewhere in the background her voice mingled with a deeper male one in low conversation.

'Hello?' she said, picking back up again. 'I've just asked our MD, who he was supposed to be meeting today. I'm afraid he hasn't arrived.'

I told Stephen I wasn't feeling well and left the office as quickly as possible, not even bothering to turn off my computer. I couldn't have cared less about the deadline. He could sack me if he wanted to. My heart was pounding as I ran to the tube and it didn't slow down in the three-quarters of an hour it took me to get back to Kilburn. The trains were running even more haphazardly than usual, the snow affecting the track where it lay overground at the ends of the lines. I stood the whole way, as if somehow that might make the journey quicker.

The car was parked ten minutes' walk away from the station and I was still wearing the heels that I'd put on for the meeting. Although the snow wasn't yet thick on the ground, enough had fallen to cover the pavement and, where other feet had pressed it down, it was slippery as soap. Several times I felt myself about to fall and readjusted only at the last minute. When I finally reached the car, I found there wasn't enough petrol in it to get me all the way to the house. I would have to stop at a garage. And I still hadn't heard from Greg. My mind was presenting me with images of his car upturned on an icy carriageway or tangled beyond recognition in a terrible wreck. They made me sick to my stomach.

Though it was still only mid-afternoon, the traffic wasn't light and it took twenty minutes just to get on to the North Circular. The snow was falling fast and the wipers kept up a steady beat as they cleared the windscreen again and again. To anyone else on the road, my driving must have looked dangerously erratic. I was accelerating too quickly, then having to stop sharp almost at once to avoid hitting the car in front. I would have given anything then to have been able to teleport myself to the house or even to have had an easier journey out of town. It wasn't until I reached the M40 that there was any clear road ahead of me at all. I put my foot to the floor and pushed the poor car as hard as I could. I didn't doubt that something had happened at Stoneborough, but what? Had Lucas finally made a stand against Danny? Had Danny retaliated? I knew that, if he had, he would have had no qualms about applying pressure exactly where it would hurt Lucas most. If Danny had threatened to leave, I feared Lucas would have broken down; he wasn't mentally strong enough any more. I felt my pulse accelerate.

As the snow brought the night in early and the light began to fade, the temperature dropped further still. I took my hands off the wheel for a second or two to rub them together, hoping to get the blood flowing into my fingertips again. Out towards High Wycombe, where the land fell away from the road into fields and smallholdings, everything was the same white. Under any other circumstances I would have thought it beautiful. There were gritters out but, while I was grateful for the parts of the carriageway that they had already done, they were like pack animals, slow-moving and happily oblivious to my desperate need to get through the bottlenecks of traffic they caused, especially where the road narrowed to two lanes.

As soon as I left the motorway after the cut through the Chilterns, the roads grew more hazardous still. No gritters had been through the web of lanes that led to the house. The car slid often but I couldn't make myself slow down any more. When I reached Stoneborough village, it was like a fantasy of English winter. The thatched cottages were covered with a layer of snow that looked like icing on gingerbread. On the ground it had hardly been disturbed at all. Mine was perhaps the third car that had been through since it started. The pond was iced over and the reeds around it offered a stiff resistance to the wind.

There were no lights on at the cottage that I now knew to be Elizabeth's; it looked closed up, as if she had gone away. I drove on, and after a few minutes I reached the bottom of the track up to the house. The wood on my left was already a mass of impenetrable darkness and the drive itself was visible only as far as the arc of my headlights. I had the feeling that I was not at the start of a road but on the edge of a hole that, if I chose to venture further, would take me deep underground. Shaking my shoulders to rid myself of the feeling, I turned the car slowly, feeling the wheels slide sideways. The snow in front of me, although not so deep as where the ground was unsheltered, was crisp and virgin. The pounding in my ears started immediately, quickly falling into a rhythm with the beat of the wipers. I realised that the night of the party had enabled it to widen its reach beyond the house permanently. Above me the trees were bare of leaves just like the first time we'd come here, when I'd thought of an enchanted wood that would ensnare all who ventured in.

My chest eased with relief as I turned on to the gravel and saw Greg's car. I said a silent prayer of thanks. He'd been able to get here quicker than me, of course. And he would be there to help me with whatever waited inside.

The front door was wide open.

There were no lights on. The house stared blindly into the dying afternoon. I got out of the car and felt my feet sink into the snow. I stumbled up the path, slipping in my heels. Fear made me hesitate a second on the doorstep but I went in, feeling the tempo of the beat in my ears accelerate again. I flung open the drawing-room door, hoping that I would find them around the fire, not having noticed that the light had gone, but there was no one there. The room looked like a squat. There were glasses and bottles everywhere, and plates bearing the remnants of meals long ago digested. The ashtrays were full to overflowing. Newspapers and food wrappers littered the carpet. I went over to the fireplace. It was cold.

The light had gone almost completely in the hall and, as I crossed it, something crunched under my feet. I stopped still at once. The floor was covered with a rough powder, like coarse sand. There were also large chunks of whatever it was, lumps and uneven cubes of the stuff. Turning on the lamp, I saw traces of colour amongst it, rich reds and pomegranate pink and gold and a Mediterranean sky-blue. It was plaster and I knew where it came from.

The painting – that magnificent, horrible work of art – was ruined. There were craters in it, huge areas gone, like a patch of no man's land above my head. It had been shot at, it must have been. It was too high to get at any other way, impossible to throw paint over or spray from a can. The faces of both Patrick and Justin had been obliterated, blown away. I stepped out from under it, as if away from the scene of a crime.

In the kitchen every surface was covered with unwashed pans and crockery and empty bottles. The kettle was cold when I pressed my fingers against it. A thin film of dust had settled over everything and there was a rich stink of rotting food. The cleaner couldn't have been for weeks. I ran back down the passage into the hall. 'Lucas!' I screamed through the heart of the house. 'Greg!' The beating in my ears intensified and I made myself look up again. Even now, damaged as his physical presence was, I could still feel his power. Patrick. The place was tense with excitement, as if he couldn't wait for me to discover the latest move in his game. 'What have you done?' I asked him out loud. 'What have you done?'

I searched each room in turn, running from one to the next, throwing doors open, leaving the lights on behind me, partly in haste, partly for comfort and their protection against the shadows. All the bedrooms were empty.

I hesitated again before going up the second flight of stairs to the gallery landing. There was my first bedroom at the house, Lucas's room, the studio.

There was nothing in mine. The sheets on the bed were pulled as tight as ever, not a wrinkle on them. I took a deep breath and pushed open the door to Lucas's room. The air smelt stale. Again there were dirty plates and two whisky bottles by the bed, empty. On the bedside table, the glass broken, was the photo of us all that Greg and I had given him on the night of the party. The duvet had slipped on to the floor. My heart was pounding so hard now that the blood was booming in my ears.

The door of the study was closed. It was the last room. If they weren't in the house, where would they be? It was too cold to be outside. Had something happened that meant they had had to leave? But Greg's car was still on the drive.

I opened the door.

They weren't there. A glance in the half-light showed the chairs, the roll-top desk but no Lucas, no Greg, no Danny.

And then I saw it, at first just a shape on the carpet, a formless mass in the gloom. In a horrible dawning, I realised it was a body, a man's body in a heavy outdoor coat.

I crossed the room and sank to my knees beside him. I put my hand on his face and tried to turn it up towards me. It was Greg.

I must have given a small cry because he made a low sound in his throat. 'Jo,' he said and I wanted to weep with gratitude.

'What's happened? What's happened to you?'

He attempted to move his body towards me but couldn't. He took a sharp in-breath and even in the near-darkness I saw the bolt of pain that went across his face.

'What happened?'

'I've been shot. I can't move.'

'Shot?'

'My hip. I don't know, I can't tell. It's broken, shattered. Jo, I think I've lost a lot of blood.'

It was then I realised that my knees were wet. I put my hands down on the carpet next to me and it was sodden, the pile of it spongy and cold. I gave another cry but this time not from shock but fear. I moved my hand down to where his coat lay over his thigh and very gently lifted it. The material was soaked.

He swallowed and I saw that he was trying not to show me how much pain he was in, not to frighten me. 'Call an ambulance,' he said. 'Call an ambulance and then go and find Lucas.'

'I can't. I can't leave you.'

'Call an ambulance and find Lucas. Please, Jo.' He tried to move and caused himself another spasm of pain. 'Please. He's a danger to himself.'

'Will you be . . . ?' I couldn't finish the question.

'Please. He'd never hurt you.'

My eyes were accustomed to the lack of light and now I could see his, the pupils as large as they could be, full of suppressed fear and pleading with me to do as he asked. I stood up and felt the damp as my knees left the carpet. I held down a sob so as not to panic him. As I turned back, my eyes moved over the window. One of the panes was broken and icy air was rushing through it. And then I saw them, the footprints in the snow, only just visible, leading to the wood.

My mobile had no signal so I had to use the landline downstairs. I called an ambulance in a state of unreality, everything seeming to float around me, the calm voice at the other end of the line, the furniture, the floor. The operator confirmed that an ambulance would be sent at once but the snow was making the roads very difficult to pass, especially as far out as we were. I begged her to do everything she could, hoping against hope that there was something.

I don't remember leaving the house or how I got down the terrace steps. What I will never forget is how long it took to cross the lawn, which seemed to stretch even as I ran, following the traces of Lucas's weaving footsteps, in time to the beat in my ears. The snow whipped into my face and the air took my breath away but my inhaler was in the car. I tried to think about what I might find in the wood. For a second I wondered whether Danny would be with him then realised there was only one set of prints. Was it Lucas who had the gun? Was that what Greg had meant about him not hurting me? I was afraid for myself then, for just a moment. I had never told Greg about Lucas's attack on me; he was wrong to think he would never hurt me. If he was wild with grief, he didn't have control.

But these thoughts were crowded out of my head by images of Greg in pain, lying alone on the top floor, still bleeding. I realised I hadn't even switched on the light: he was there in darkness, on his own in that terrible house. When I reached the edge of the wood, a violent spasm went across my stomach. Vomit rose in my throat and I was sick until there was nothing left to come up. I dry-heaved then, feeling the muscle contracting. Fear swept over me again and the fresh sweat on my forehead seemed suddenly to freeze but I knew I had to go in.

I stumbled over and over again as I picked my way through the undergrowth. I took off my shoes and ran in my stockinged feet, hardly feeling the brambles and fallen branches as they cut me. Although it had been dark in the house, outside it was still dusk and the bare branches overhead allowed the little light there was to reach down to ground-level. The branches clattered in the wind but the sound was only background noise to the pulse of the place, the pounding of my heart and my laboured breathing.

Just before I reached the clearing I stopped. If Lucas was going to be anywhere, he would be here. I stumbled forward and quickly scanned round. I couldn't see him. 'Lucas!' I startled a rook. It flew out in front of me with a great beating of wings. I screamed at the shock of it.

The river slipped darkly past, its surface broken by the wind, black as the Styx. I stepped towards it. At the edges, where the water pooled, there was ice.

Then I saw him. Caught in a bank of reeds a couple of metres away, face down, with ice in his hair.

As I ran back my mind separated itself from my body and I could observe myself from the outside. I was on automatic pilot, running, stumbling blindly, falling in the snow. I had dropped my shoes somewhere in the wood and I could hardly feel my feet now. My hands were numb, too, from the freezing water. I had tried to pull Lucas on to the bank but he was waterlogged and too heavy. I had had no choice but to leave him where he was. At least I hadn't been able to see his face, reproaching me for leaving him there in the clearing as the night shut down around him.

I wasn't sure how long I had been gone from Greg; perhaps

twenty minutes, perhaps longer. It seemed like hours. The house loomed in front of me, light now spilling from almost every window. It looked like an ocean-going liner alone on an empty sea. I didn't want to think what the atmosphere inside would be. I imagined laughter echoing around the hall, high and shrieking like the call of carrion eaters. A celebration, like Lucas's party but in negative, with Patrick and the house marking their victory over him, their enemy's son brought down at last.

There was no ambulance waiting on the drive, no safe blue light to herald the intervention of the real world into this waking nightmare.

The front door was still open. I ran in and across the hall to the bottom of the stairs. Numb as my feet were, I could feel the rubble of the ceiling under them and I skidded on it, sending it spinning across the floor. It was as cold inside as out; any heat there may have been had fled through the door's yawning maw.

When I reached the study I turned on the light. Greg was in the same position but what I hadn't seen in the gloom before was the carpet. Spreading out from the lower part of his body was a bloodstain about a foot and a half across. Even from the door I could see that the carpet was not merely covered but soaked with it. I closed my eyes to help suppress the gasp that rose in my throat.

I knelt beside him again. His eyes were closed and he hadn't moved in response to my return. A terrible fear gripped me. I put my hand on his shoulder and softly called his name.

His eyelids flickered and then opened. A small smile came to his lips. 'Hello,' he said.

'I called the ambulance. It's coming.'

He moved his head slightly. 'Lucas.'

I hesitated. The words seemed too monumental to speak normally. 'Lucas is dead.' Finally the tears started, flooding

369

down my cheeks, the heat of them magnified by the coldness of my skin. The pressure was building in my chest. I wanted to howl with the misery of it, Lucas's body in that black, icy water and Greg here, bleeding and bleeding, barely even conscious any more.

His eyes were closed again and I couldn't tell whether it was because he was struggling to take in the news or because he was slipping back. I took the hand that wasn't trapped under his body. It was cold as a stone. How long had he been lying here before I came, the air rushing in through the broken window? His coat was some protection but not nearly enough. I saw that he was shivering. 'You're so cold, darling,' I said. 'I need to get you warm again.'

'Don't go now,' he said, his eyes opening wide again.

'I'll only be a second.' I bent down so that my face was next to his on the carpet and kissed him very gently. His lips, too, were freezing. I stood up and ran to the front of the house, praying that, although I hadn't heard it, the ambulance would be pulling up, help coming. The drive was empty except for our cars, even now being covered by the snow. The wind was making a drift over the front-wheel arch of Greg's, swallowing it.

The sheets on my old bed wouldn't be enough to keep him warm; I ran down the landing to Lucas's room, gathered up his duvet and ran back as fast as I could. I dragged over one of the armchairs and sat down on the carpet in front of it. I couldn't move him for fear of causing him more pain or making the bleeding worse but I lifted his head so that it rested on my thighs and so that I could see his beautiful face. The move, although very slight, caused pain to rip through him and he took a ragged in-breath. 'You're OK,' I said. 'You're OK now.'

'The ambulance?'

'It's coming, sweetheart. It's coming.' I smoothed the hair back from his head and the stroking seemed to soothe him.

He closed his eyes. 'Don't go to sleep, Greg. I need you to talk to me. Don't leave me here on my own in the dark. You need to keep me company until the ambulance comes.'

'I'm not sleeping,' he said, the sound low in his throat. I could feel the effort it was taking for him to talk.

'Tell me what happened. I need to know.'

'Lucas rang me. As I was coming up the motorway. He was crying.' He coughed and winced again. 'He said Danny was going mad and I had to come here. I nearly didn't but he sounded so scared, Jo.'

'When I got here, I heard shouting, terrible shouting, so I ran up here as fast as I could. Danny had a gun.'

'Danny? He was here?'

'Yes.' With huge effort he lifted his arm and reached for my hand. Usually it was my hands that needed warming; over the last couple of months I had made a nuisance of myself sliding them under his jumper and warming them on his skin. He'd pretended to hate it and we'd had play fights that almost always ended in bed. I squeezed his fingers now and rubbed them with mine, trying to keep the circulation going in them.

'I thought Danny was threatening Lucas. I tried talking to him but he handed the gun to Lucas.'

'What?'

'It was a set-up, Jo. They got me here so that Lucas could kill me.' His eyes looked up at me, wide and full of anguish. I wondered whether the excessive blood loss was making him delusional.

'I don't understand.'

'Danny wanted Lucas to kill me. He was talking to him all the time, trying to poison him. He said that I had stolen you and that the only way for him to get you back was to kill me. While I was alive, you would never go back to him.'

'And Lucas was listening to him? He did this?'

371

'He was lost. You shouldn't blame him for what he did. He'd been pushed too far. Danny was inside his head.'

'Lucas shot you.'

'But he lost his nerve. Danny was goading and goading. In the end, Lucas pulled the trigger. But he didn't aim for my chest. At first I didn't feel anything. I fell over. I know it's pretty bad. Will you look?'

Without changing position, I reached out my free hand and gently folded back the duvet and then the material of the coat where the wound was. I felt my gorge rising. All of his right hip and the top part of his leg was a mass of blood and torn flesh, the fabric of the suit I had watched him put on earlier that day now mingled with scraps of his skin and muscle and clots of congealing blood. My tears started flowing again.

'How do I look?' he asked. 'Do you still fancy me?'

'I will always fancy you. I love you. I love you so much.'

'I love you,' he said. 'Don't forget. Ever.'

'I won't be able to forget. You'll be around to show me.'

'Do you think the ambulance is coming, Jo?' he said, closing his eyes again.

'Greg, don't sleep. You need to tell me what happened next. Come on.' I shook his shoulder a little and felt guilty as the movement travelled down his body and hurt him. His eyes opened again. 'What happened, after Lucas shot you?'

He looked dazed for a moment, as if I were speaking to him from a place very far away. Then he seemed to focus again. 'He turned on Danny. Like he'd suddenly woken up and realised. Danny didn't give up, though. He went on and on. He said we'd been sleeping together behind Lucas's back for months. I'd made him look like a fool and he should be a man and finish the job.'

'But why?'

'Because he wanted Lucas. He needed him. He wanted you out of the picture. While you and Lucas were still friends,

372

Lucas wouldn't be his. If Lucas killed me, your friendship would be over for ever.' He tried to move, to make himself more comfortable, but the pain was too great.

The words swam in my head and wouldn't settle. And yet it made awful sense.

'But Lucas couldn't shoot me again. He was crying and sobbing, saying sorry over and over again. And Danny was going on and on and on. But then he said to him, "What's the matter, Lucas? Why can't you kill him? He stole Joanna, just like Patrick stole your mother. Aren't you your father's son?"'

'Oh God.'

'Lucas lost it. He turned the gun on Danny. He told him to get out of the house and never come back. If he did, he would shoot him. He meant it. Danny ran, Jo.' The effort of talking had tired him and he closed his eyes again. 'Lucas said sorry,' said Greg so quietly that I had to bend my ear closer to hear him. 'He said sorry.'

My tears were dripping off my face and on to his but they didn't make him open his eyes now or reach up to sweep them away or touch me. His features were settling. 'Greg. Greg. Wake up.'

'Can you hear the ambulance, Jo?' he asked. 'Can you hear it?'

For a mad, wonderful moment, I thought that he had heard it and I strained my ears for the sounds of a vehicle, for a motor or doors slamming or quick feet on the staircase. There was nothing. Nothing at all. And then I realised that something had changed. The wind had dropped almost to nothing and besides that the beating in my head, the horrible pounding rhythm that had accompanied me so often at the house, had ceased. There was complete quiet. The drums in my ears had fallen silent at last. Their absence was so profound it was almost a sound in itself. Even at the very beginning of our year, the house had seemed fraught, at times so overwrought that it had been almost impossible to breathe the air. And as I had come to know it, I had understood that that atmosphere was malicious, intending harm and revelling in every hurt that it brewed within its walls. Now it felt only empty.

As the silence wove around us, I thought about who I could call and I realised I was alone. The group was finished for ever. That many-headed entity that had absorbed us, protected us, entertained us, made us feel a part of something larger than ourselves, and finally threatened to destroy us, was slain. Martha was away. Rachel, of course, was lost to me for ever. Michael, too, had barely been in contact since the party, his time swallowed by long hours at the bank and his relationship. Danny was gone; I hoped I never found out where. And Lucas was dead.

I looked down at Greg as he lay in my arms. It was just us now. In the harsh light from the bulb overhead, his skin was pale and, when I touched my fingers against his cheek, it was too cold. I reached round for a cushion from the chair and, lifting his head as gently as possible, I put the pillow beneath it and moved my legs away so that I could stand. The discomfort registered on his face but he said nothing. Careful not to put any pressure on his wound, I tucked the duvet in around him, moving his arms so that they were covered. I drew the curtains and switched on the desk lamp; its mellow light made the room feel warmer immediately. The fireplace had been used over the winter: there was ash in the grate and a small amount of coal and kindling in the scuttle. Using the poker, I swept back the ashes and set a fire. It took at once and the sound was like another life in the room, a positive presence. It would be enough to last us, I hoped, until the ambulance finally got through.

Acknowledgements

I am grateful to a number of people for their help and encouragement.

I would like to thank Joachim Jessen and Cordelia Borchardt in Germany, my first agent and editor, without whose faith and enthusiasm this book might not have seen the light of day.

The vision, effort and kindness of the Bloomsbury team go beyond all possible expectation. In particular, I would like to thank my editor, Katie Bond, for putting so much of her enormous talent behind this book. Thank you also to Jenny Parrott, to Mary Tomlinson, for spotless copy-editing, and to Trâm-Anh Doan and Anna Robinson.

My agent, Laura Longrigg at MBA, is an invaluable source of editorial wisdom and support.

In America I am grateful for the input and guidance of Susanna Porter at Random House and also to Jillian Quint.

Huge thanks go to my early readers, especially to Elizabeth Wright, Caroline Bland and Jan Michael, and to Anne Church Bigelow, Katy Darby, John Marzillier and Jenny Stanton. I would also like to say thank you to one of my very earliest readers, Ann Fox, a great inspiration.

Last but very far from least, I would like to thank my parents and my sisters, Polly and Sophie, whose encouragement and belief have always been constant, and appreciated.

A NOTE ON THE AUTHOR

Lucie Whitehouse was born in Warwickshire in 1975, read Classics at Oxford University and now lives in London. This is her first novel.

A NOTE ON THE TYPE

The text of this book is set in Linotype Sabon, named after the type founder, Jacques Sabon. It was designed by Jan Tschichold and jointly developed by Linotype, Monotype and Stempel, in response to a need for a typeface to be available in identical form for mechanical hot metal composition and hand composition using foundry type.

Tschichold based his design for Sabon roman on a font engraved by Garamond, and Sabon italic on a font by Granjon. It was first used in 1966 and has proved an enduring modern classic.

Haldimand County Public Library
JARVIS BRANCH
Haldimand County Public Library

3 3990 00370 2944

THE HOUSE AT MIDNIGHT

MAY 2 3 2008

JUN 0 3 2008

JUN 2 1 2008

JUL 2 5 2008

OCT 2 4 2008

JAN 0 2 2009

MAR 0 2012

JUN 1 2 2013

JUN 1 3 2013

OCT 0 9 2014

DISCARDED

MAY - - 2008